M000208257

A FERAL CHORUS

MATTHEW J. WHITE

 Helvellyn Press

First published in the United States of America and Great Britain in 2023 by Helvellyn Press, Houston, Texas

Copyright © 2023 Matthew J. White

All rights reserved. No part of this book may be reproduced in any form or by any electronic or mechanical means, including information storage and retrieval systems, without permission in writing from the publisher, except by reviewers, who may quote brief passages in a review.

The moral right of the author has been asserted.

This is a work of fiction. Names, characters, businesses, places, events, locales, and incidents are either the products of the author's imagination or used in a fictitious manner. Except in the case of historical fact, any resemblance to actual persons, living or dead, or actual events is purely coincidental.

Hardcover ISBN: 978-1-7391031-0-1
Paperback ISBN: 978-1-7391031-3-2
eBook ISBN: 978-1-7391031-2-5

Library of Congress Control Number: 2023935269

Helvellyn Press
helvellynpress.com

A

FERAL

CHORUS

It is a most mortifying reflection for a man to consider what he has done, compared to what he might have done.
—Samuel Johnson

Chapter One

A YEAR SINCE MY RETURN TO HOUSTON, and here I was, still chaperoning eager suburbanites around ten acres of floodlit concrete. My latest pair had been wandering up and down the rows of Chevy Tahoes for the better part of two hours. Dale Massey returned to a High Country in Satin Steel Metallic for what had to be the fifth time. The beefy property appraiser squatted down next to the three-ton SUV and muttered an approval in the direction of the chrome-trimmed running boards. He was attempting to talk his cheerful wife, Mallory, into this top-of-the-line model on the basis of the more powerful engine and air-ride suspension, but I could tell she judged these upgrades frivolous—pointless male vanity—and the Premier in Empire Beige to be the more responsible choice. She took him aside, pressed a manicured hand into the small of his expansive back, and breathed words of prudence upward toward one of his formidable ears.

Big Dale pressed his case with appreciably less restraint.

"Honey, this one's got the adaptive shocks. You don't want the kids bouncing around like they're on a mechanical bull, do you? You know how sick Randy gets in the back of

5

the Durango." He turned to me. "What do you think, Guy?"

I shot Dale an agnostic smile. Was he serious? What did he expect me to say? "Yep, that's the one, buddy. Screw the Premier, it's air-ride all the way. Go big or go home!"

Forget that. Not happening. If I were to endorse Dale's plan to add two hundred dollars to the Masseys' monthly nut on the pretense of easing little Randy's gastrointestinal discomforts, jaunty Mallory was liable to turn sour and march him right back out to their old Dodge, no matter its worn ball joints and oxidized clear coat.

My phone vibrated in my pocket. Unlike Dean Peas, I don't take calls when I'm working a sale, but spousal friction warrants exception. Mallory had seen through Dale's brazen attempt to capitalize on poor Randy's sensitive plumbing. Her accommodating smile had been replaced by the somber countenance of female reproach. Dale had much work to do if he wanted to enjoy the extra low-end grunt of that big 6.2-liter V8, so I excused myself and strolled behind a row of highly incentivized Malibus to take the call.

It was Aunt Imogen. Uncle Harry had been due home by six thirty. It was now eight, and there was no sign of him, and he wasn't answering his phone. She had called building security; nobody picked up. She was worried, his memory problems and all. Could I swing by the office and check on him?

I told the couple I had to run.

"Really sorry, something's come up. Ask Krystal at reception to page Jake Hodges. He'll take care of you. You can't go wrong with either of these beauts."

I wasn't exaggerating there. Hodges was a solid guy. He'd get the deal done at a fair price and without all the hemming and hawing and pointless padding back and forth of Dean Peas. Not only would Peas jerk them around on the price, he'd inflate the deal with hefty charges for paint sealant and the Concierge Service Plan—flagrant banditry, nothing more than a thin coat of spray-on wax and a free ride home in whatever demo happened to be lurking around the service department that day. Peas's bumbling mendacity was legendary. He'd present the paperwork with his hairy hand over the extras. If the customer noticed the ruse, he'd play dumb and try to salvage the deal by throwing in a few embossed key chains or other inane dross. The only reason Peas had the job was because he was the son-in-law of the owner, Beau Holloway. I figured it would be better for business if Holloway cut Peas a check every month and told him to stay home, pick up the slack around the house, take the load off Holloway's daughter. Either that or move him over to used cars, where people at least expected devious tricks such as the hairy hand.

I jumped on the freeway and headed north, back into Houston proper. Dusk had melted into night, the week into the weekend. A wall of taillights winked scarlet shades of red as the sea of disaffected motorists jostled for position on the coarse cement. An absurd jalopy entered the freeway at the next on-ramp. It hurtled to the outside lane and cut off several vehicles in the process. A chorus of wild honking ensued. The jalopy man stuck his arm out the window and waved. His limp gesture was a shameful display, the same "I'm sorry but not really" arm waggle offered up by seniors jumping the line in a crowded pharmacy.

Who were all these slapdash drivers in their steel cages, and where were they going? The great mystery of Eisenhower's blanket arterials! Rush hour was over, but it still took me twenty-five minutes to make it back into town, even with one bout of aggressive tailgating. I'd attempted to ride dirty bumpers all the way up 59, but Dad's ivory '68

Alfa Romeo GTV spat out a refrain of mechanical objections every time I hit the gas pedal. The old Italian 2+2 had been running rough lately, the valves chattering away, some unidentifiable vibrations evident at full throttle.

I exited the freeway onto Shepherd, crossed Westheimer at speed, and almost rearranged a mass of bike riders frolicking in the middle of the road. It was one of those organized deals the cops turned a blind eye to. Hipsters dawdled across the intersection, a mess of glow sticks and streamers and silly outfits, thinking themselves great transgressives. I waited out the entitled mob with my palm clamped on the horn, then proceeded to Harry's building and turned into the semicircular drive. I pulled up to the entrance, parked under the awning, and jumped out. As I shut my door, I heard a squeaky voice behind me.

"Sir, hey, sir, you can't park your vehicle there. You're going to have to move it to the designated parking area."

I turned to face the squeaking and saw a security guard I didn't recognize. He was a squat fellow in a dull white shirt and loose-fitting trousers. The shirt had ornamental strips of black fabric attached to the shoulders in the fashion of decorated admirals and municipal bus drivers. The insignia on the cloth was a muddle of gold chevrons and stars reminiscent of the flag of some war-torn banana republic. The hyperbolic ensemble wasn't projecting an air of law and order so much as one of corrupt bureaucracy.

"Look, I'll be right back," I said. "I just need to run upstairs for a second." I moved toward the entrance, my access card in hand, a remnant from the days when I'd worked for Harry, before I quit law school.

"Sir, did you hear me? This location is for pickups and drop-offs only."

He pointed to a sign, "Pickup and Drop-off Only," his

face deforming into a smug wince.

"Yeah, yeah, I heard you. What's your name?"

"Clay Busby. Clay Busby Jr." He grabbed his pants by the belt loops and tugged from side to side in a futile attempt to corkscrew them back up his lumbersome trunk. I interpreted this rodeo-clown pants fiddling and his pained frown as signs he was ready and willing to die on this hill of arbitrary arrangement.

"Clay, look, I admit your position, while a tad literal, has some merit, but I don't have time to argue." I started for the entrance again and waved back at him. "Follow me. We need to check on my uncle. He's not answering his phone."

He mumbled on a bit, his little pink hands miming complaints. He declared my defiant ingress was likely to cause a wave of rampant lawlessness. The debunked broken-window theory! When it became apparent I wasn't going to bend to his disproven postulates, he relented. I ran up the whitewashed stairwell to the third floor and the offices of Harry Fentress & Associates. Clay Jr. followed, puffing up a storm behind me.

I unlocked the door and pushed it inward. The bottom caught on the fleecy burnt-orange carpet, which was disintegrating like rural asphalt. Years ago, Harry had sued the manufacturer, Eternal Life Carpets, for deceptive trade practices on the basis that its carpet didn't last a year, let alone eternity. He'd discovered most Eternal Life customers were no more satisfied than he was, and a class-action lawsuit ensued with Harry at the helm.

Eternal Life claimed in its defense that the company name was merely creative marketing, a harmless reference to the deep and profound Christian faith of its founder, Delbert Mixon. The jury, which Harry made sure to stack with born-again believers, didn't appreciate Mixon's exploitation of the good Lord's name for carpet revenues and took less than two hours to deliver a punishing verdict against the company. Eternal Life went belly-up soon thereafter, so all Harry ended up with was a truckload of the crummy carpet in an array of out-of-fashion pile lengths and distasteful colors. He stored this unfortunate surplus in a barn on his ranch in Waller County, forty-five miles northwest of town. After the office carpet wore through, which took about six months, his ranch hand, Rogelio, replaced it with a fresh roll from the barn. Rogelio was a pretty good carpet man despite his lack of experience. He managed to get it tucked into the corners pretty good, his only letdown some slight buckling around the door thresholds.

I called out Harry's name as we hustled past empty offices, relics of bygone days when the firm was thriving. His corner suite was at the end of a long hallway, past a large green artificial ficus, which the building's plant lady, Imelda, tended with care. She emptied gallons of water into its pot with regularity and even said a few kind words to it now and then. She was a sweet, grandmotherly soul, and the fake tree bore no deleterious effects, so nobody had the heart to tell her she was wasting her time.

Harry's door was open and his lights were on. I rushed in, and there he was, slumped forward, harsh fluorescent beams reflecting off his liver-spotted crown. I lifted him off the mahogany desk and pried his bony fingers loose from a crystal lowball with nothing but watery brown dregs at the bottom. He was cold to the touch, and I couldn't locate a pulse.

I stood there and fixated on my favorite uncle's timeworn chassis. Acute incredulity faded into a melancholy ache. Meanwhile, Clay Jr., who was over by Harry's fish tank, had devolved into a fleshy sac of hysteria. He yelled out a mess of desperate suggestions. Did I know CPR? Surely the office had a first-aid kit somewhere, stuffed with potent smelling salts we could waft under Harry's hairy nostrils? How was I with the maneuvers of Dr. Hasselhoff?

"It's Heimlich," I said as I returned Harry's comb-over to the position of maximum concealment.

Clay Jr. ignored me and continued to panic. "We've got to kick-start his ticker!" he blurted out, pointing to the center of Harry's lifeless body. He said what we needed was a fat hypodermic full of adrenaline we could plunge into Harry's sternum. He'd seen it in a documentary about some rock band, and he claimed it worked, at least to some passable degree. The lead singer had been able to record up a storm of new hair metal in no time, although he now suffered bouts of paralysis in his lower extremities. Clay said this side effect was unfortunate, the charismatic exuberance of the headbanger's performance neutered by his post-resuscitation rigidity.

"He used to run around, doing his thing, boogieing down, but now he kinda stays put in the center of the stage, by his microphone. But at least he isn't worm food, I guess."

I told Clay I was not familiar with the catalog of Moist Ruin and had no opinion on the trade-offs faced by its now-immobile front man. Undeterred, he babbled on. The fish soon tired of Clay's nonsense too. They moved, in formation, to the far side of the tank and hid behind a large coral-covered rock. I drew the line when he pulled out his phone to search for the coordinates of the nearest emergency defibrillator.

"Will you calm down," I told Clay, who had taken to shifting from foot to foot with the lethargic energy of a pet rabbit. "Trust me, he's gone, and wiring him up like a dead battery isn't going to bring him back."

11

I walked over to the credenza and picked up a bottle of single malt. I poured Clay two fingers and told him to call 911 and wait by the front door to let the medics in. After he left, I poured four fingers for myself and finished it off in two substantial swigs, savoring the caustic burn as the alcohol slipped downward. Fortified by the heady uprush, I grabbed Harry's phone and made the call. Imogen picked up on the first ring.

The ambulance arrived in twenty minutes. The EMTs performed a battery of pointless procedures based solely on liability concerns. They yelled medical terms at each other like two soap-opera surgeons in cutthroat competition for a promotion to prime time. When they were done covering their asses, they strapped Harry to an aluminum gurney with scissor legs. They torqued him down and wheeled him out while Clay Jr. shouted clearances like he was Ishmael helping Captain Ahab moor the *Pequod* in stormy waters.

"You've got twelve inches on your starboard side and about eight on your port," he bleated. The medics must not have been familiar with nautical orientations, because they bounced Harry off one wall, then the other, before finally pitching him into the elevator.

I sat in Harry's office and finished off the last of the whiskey. By the time I made it home, it was approaching midnight. My wife, Whitney, was already asleep. When I'd called to give her the bad news about Harry, she hadn't answered. She'd been working long hours recently, so I decided not to wake her.

I climbed into bed and stared at the ceiling fan as it rotated above us. The housing oscillated benignly, the dusty blades in a state of unbalance. A few months ago, Whit had told me she'd read about a woman from Cincinnati who'd been struck with total amnesia after a wonky fan careened off her bedroom ceiling and crashed down onto her skull, causing damage to her frontal lobe. In that fateful moment, the woman lost all memory of the first twenty-eight years of her life. Overnight, her husband became a handsy suitor, and her kids had to demonstrate the versatility of peanut butter. Whit had noticed our fan wobbling and demanded I do something about it. I told her they were minor vibrations, no cause for concern. One morning, after about the tenth time she brought up the fan tragedy, I probed deeper.

"How did it fall off the ceiling?" I asked her. "Did the bracket break, or was it not mounted to the cross member properly?"

"I don't know, Guy," she said, and turned her back on me to attend to her herbal tea. "It was in some magazine at the dentist's office."

"I bet it was a mounting issue. The installer probably missed the stud."

"I have no idea. Just fix it, please, before it kills us both in our sleep."

I'd never met Sharon Carmichael, DDS, but I surmised from Whitney's unhealthy paranoia that she favored periodicals that played up the probability of mechanical catastrophe, not to mention the likelihood of debilitating injury—a dangerous combination, like mixing fertilizer with diesel fuel. But, I admit, I had no other reason to doubt the amnesiac's sad story. Regardless, the fix was simple. All it would take was a trip to the hardware store for a few of those stick-on rubber weights. That and a bit of trial and error to get the balance right. A tedious job, granted, but no more than an hour or so from start to finish. Yet months had passed and I still hadn't gotten around to it.

My procrastination annoyed Whitney no end. A few days ago, after we got into bed, she accused me of grave lapses.

"You're like some college kid, whiling your way down the Guadalupe in an inner tube," she said as she eyed the fan. "Can you please tell me when you're going to grow up and start taking things seriously?" I'd pointed out it was a silly analogy given she knew I had a mild butyl allergy.

I turned over and attempted to go to sleep. As I lay there on the expensive memory-foam mattress, ensconced in the high-thread-count sheets, I tried to take my mind off Harry's untimely passing by considering the flow of the esteemed rivers of the Hill Country. I was rusty on Central Texas's riparian geography, so when I was done with the Guadalupe, my mind went blank. After a bout of deep concentration, the Frio and the Medina materialized, albeit in a rather vague manner. I considered their hazy effluences for a good fifteen minutes before I succumbed to the hypnotic spin of the jittery blades as they cut through the thick summer air.

Chapter Two

HARRY'S FUNERAL WAS SET FOR SUNDOWN a week from Saturday. His last will and testament entreated Imogen to "ensure I am interred on my ranch in the manner I entered this world so the honest Texas soil may caress my bare skin and take me back whence I came." Imogen decided to interpret this testamentary mandate loosely, so while he would be laid to rest in a shady corner of his beloved homestead, the au naturel business was shelved. Instead, she secured a rough-hewn post-oak casket with brass handles that everyone agreed Harry would have sanctioned being it had been fashioned by a local craftsman known for his sturdy tables.

Per Harry's instructions, Imogen commissioned a commodious grave of legal depth pursuant to the dictates of section 714 of the Health and Safety Code. And she appointed six men from among Harry's closest friends and family to schlep him into position during the service. The funeral people had put the hard sell on her to spring for the Soft-Glide lowering system—an intricate apparatus of gears and pulleys—but she believed Harry would have frowned on a mechanized descent.

Harry had directed that the service be kept simple—an

intimate ceremony with no grandiloquent pomp about Jehovah's ceaseless jamboree. And being a man who'd had little time for the dictatorial nature of organized religion, his will forbade the presence of a pulpiteer-for-hire, who would surely have delivered a dreary requiem about a life well lived of which he knew nothing of substance.

Late afternoon on Saturday, a steady stream of mourners set out for the grave site, which was a quarter mile from the main house, in the shade of a couple of mature magnolias. Beyond, in a flat pasture, a herd of sinewy heifers roamed between barbed wire, oblivious to the solemn occasion about to take place on their doorstep.

The coffin was parked on a bier of Rogelio's design—an improvised frame of lumber he'd cobbled together, in situ, after Stevie Hooper had taken exception to our original plan. Stevie and his brother Frank had delivered Harry from cold storage earlier in the day. They rolled up in an F-150, and we all stood there, confused. Where was the hearse? Who were these scruffy subcontractors?

Stevie was clad in a soiled T-shirt and frayed jean shorts. His ball cap squatted low on his straggly hair. Frank was a glum-looking man with a coarse, unkempt beard that appeared to grow in real time.

"Where y'all want him?" Stevie said as he opened the mottled tailgate.

Our plan was to place the coffin on a beach towel with "Sun and Fun, South Padre Island" printed on it in loopy cursive. The towel wasn't optimal, but a dearth of suitable fabrics forced our hand. And we all agreed the royal shade of blue and quality Egyptian cotton offset the tacky writing, most of which would be covered by the coffin anyway.

"Over there, on that towel," I said.

Stevie looked over at the towel, then back at us. "No,

no, y'all can't do that." He gestured with his ashy cigarette and shook his head.

"Why not?" I turned to the others. They all shrugged, equally confused.

"Nah, won't work."

Nobody spoke up, so I said, "Yeah, okay, but why, what's the—"

"Y'all wanna be fumbling about, trying to get that coffin off the ground with all these folk around?" Stevie motioned to a cluster of unoccupied folding chairs. "That'd be a train wreck. Wouldn't make y'all look good, running around, squatting down, your tails in the air."

Stevie had a point. This was supposed to be a funeral, not some ass-jouncing aerobics extravaganza. He continued, "Plus puttin' a man down there on the dirt before he's buried, that's disrespectful. Don't matter what kinda life he lived, a man deserves better than that."

Nobody piped up to defend our group consensus from the Hooper onslaught. I didn't care for Stevie. He reminded me of a bad-tempered baby carping about a dirty diaper, his bilious complaints filling the air with a fetid menace. I was about to set him straight, but Harry's cousin, a professorial man named Jim, spoke up first.

"He wouldn't be on the ground, he'd be on the towel, so technically—"

Stevie cut him off. "Man's splittin' hairs. Look, y'all can have any kind of funeral y'all want out here, I'm just the hired help." He raised his arms as if under arrest, at which point a fat glob of ash fell from his cigarette and landed in Frank's beard. We all waited for the inevitable brush fire, but surprisingly, the ash disappeared into the thick briar patch without incident. Satisfied they'd put us in our places, they turned back to the truck and unlashed the coffin from

17

the bed.

We all looked at each other. What now? Stevie's practical admonitions held merit, but no man of reputable character enjoys bending to the will of well-groomed tyrants, let alone the decrees of this frowzy pair. Thankfully, Rogelio had overheard the commotion and arrived back on the scene with a wheelbarrow full of four-by-fours and a circular saw. In no time, we had Harry sitting proud.

The funeral was a casual affair. About fifty of us were arranged in a semicircle, shifting around on the slippery plastic chairs, hunting for purchase. An iconic image in her flowing lace and black boots, Imogen stood and turned to face the audience of close friends and family. Her silver hair shimmied like an aspen in the gentle breeze, except for when a few powerful gusts blew it around her head, obscuring her face and forcing her to pause to brush back the unruly intrusion.

Imogen's tribute was unscripted and impassioned. The words of love and respect gushed out in fits and spurts, emotion spewing forth like crude from a leaky well. As a coda to her eulogy, she read passages from a couple of Harry's favorite books. We were treated to a selection of impenetrable truths from Cormac McCarthy about man's enduring struggle to make sense of a cruel universe, followed by a few rather more optimistic sentiments from the prolific chronicler of flatland destiny Louis L'Amour. The adults in the audience fidgeted in their chairs as they tried in vain to reconcile the dissonant orthodoxies. One little girl began to cry during the passage from *Blood Meridian*, which I blamed on McCarthy until I looked over and saw that her brother was refusing to share his Hot Tamales with her.

Imogen closed her notebook and asked if anyone else

wanted to speak, maybe share a memory or story about Harry. After my mother paid tribute to her older brother and Harry's daughter, Tanya, broke down in the middle of a sugary poem, a pear-shaped guy stood and said he'd always laughed when Harry referred to America's Team as the Arkansas Cowboys after Jerry Jones took over and trampled his Razorback trotters all over the operation.

Next, an older gentleman dressed in a seersucker suit wrestled himself to his feet. I recognized him to be the renowned lawyer Preston Rusk. He recited the legendary yarn about the trial of former Harris County commissioner Bobby Blanchard on a charge of public urination. Harry had been a senior associate when Rusk selected him to sit second chair at the defense table.

Rusk claimed the prosecution's sole evidence against Blanchard had been the eyewitness testimony of a cop who had not seen the act in question but claimed the puddle at the corner of Walker and Milam was definitely urine because it "steamed like a fresh cow patty." Harry had cooked up an impromptu courtroom demonstration with dry ice and a thermos of coffee to prove it was just as likely to have been the remnants of a hot beverage.

Rusk was relishing the spotlight. "When Harry pours that coffee onto the ice, it steams like crazy. The prosecutor jumps around and objects all over the place, and the gallery, which is packed on account of Blanchard's prominent governmental position, is all atwitter. The prosecutor calls for a mistrial, which the judge denies, and although he admonishes the jury to disregard Harry's unauthorized demonstration, the damage to the state's supposedly airtight case is done. The jury comes back with a unanimous not-guilty verdict, didn't take them more than fifteen minutes. Blanchard was ecstatic, but the case didn't do his reputation much good. He was voted out in the next election by a landslide. The one thing I did learn from that trial was Harry would've made one hell of a chemist."

All the young boys in attendance snickered and snorted at Rusk's forbidden fruits. The little girls weren't as impressed. They frowned at the boys and wrinkled their little button noses in disgust. Everyone else roared with appreciation. The audacity of the old boy! The delivery!

What bad luck to follow this crowd-pleaser, a classic tale of universal necessity and the scientific method. I mumbled a few things about how much my uncle had done for me over the years: the clerking job at his firm and the other wheel-greasing, mentoring, and whatnot. I didn't mention I'd dropped out of law school at the end of my second year and now worked at Beau Holloway Chevrolet. I wasn't ashamed of my close association with GM's most frugal brand, but a few bored children had started to circle Harry's box like a kettle of hungry vultures, so I decided it best to move things along.

After a couple more people offered remembrances, Imogen nodded, and the six of us charged with lowering Harry into his grave stood and approached the casket. We slid three thick nylon straps under the coffin, choked down, and pulled hard. When Harry was a couple of feet off the ground, we walked him into position over his hole. Being unfamiliar with the coffin-handling proficiency of these men, I'd hoped for a practice run with a few timbers of roughly equivalent weight or a roll or two of the shoddy carpet. But Harry's poker buddy Emory was late, so all we'd had time for was a quick run-through, which consisted of nothing more than standing around, backs bent, while we moved our hands up and down in a listless fashion— embarrassing mimicry we ended almost immediately.

On the count of three, we began to feed out length while the levelheaded Jim repeated "Steeaaady" over and over. We fed and fed, but Harry never hit bottom. I looked down and realized I was about out of strap. I yelled to the others to stop. We peered down around the sides of the casket. One thing was for sure—this was no shallow grave, some half-hearted strip-mining of the topsoil born of commercial considerations. No sir! Rogelio had gone to town with the Bobcat and dug the old *consejero*, his beloved counselor, a tomb fit for a family of ancient Coptics.

There was a hushed consultation. Should we take a chance and drop Harry from this indeterminable height? Were we two feet from bottom? Or four? Possibly more? The group was split down the middle. It was me and Jim and Harry's brother-in-law Roy Nettle on one side. We pointed out to Emory and the other two on the "in favor of dropping" side that if their riverboat gambling didn't pan out, they'd be the ones climbing down into the pit to sort Harry out. Needless to say, we reached a quick consensus, raised Harry up, and deposited him back onto Rogelio's handiwork.

I hurried over to Imogen and whispered in her ear. She thought for a second, then summoned her grandson Luke, Tanya's boy.

"One minute, everyone," she said as Luke trotted over. "I bet Harry hasn't even noticed this brief delay. I'm sure he's already moved on, found his next big case, or at least a bottle of scotch."

The crowd let out a nervous chuckle in recognition of the tense situation diffused by folksy humor. Imogen continued, "Don't worry, Luke'll be back in a jiffy. He runs cross-country for the varsity track team."

We all watched the lanky boy run off in the direction

of a large barn. Moments later, young Luke exited the barn and sprinted back with perfect runner form, a coil of rope under his arm. Luke basked in the glory of his adolescent fitness as he galloped toward us, probably hoping his heroic strides would translate into female attention at the post-service barbecue. He jogged up, handed us the rope, and sat back down next to his mother, who, much to his annoyance, proceeded to pick pieces of hay off the back of his baggy suit.

We eyeballed the rope and gave it a few sharp tugs. A series of communal nods and low-register grunts evidenced the consensus that the fibers appeared to be of acceptable tensile strength for the job at hand. Before we could locate something to cut it with, a rawboned man in starched jeans and a leather waistcoat walked up with a giant knife. The serrated blade was at least eight inches long, and the compass embedded in the handle gleamed in the afternoon sun as the man waved the knife around. I sensed from his eager hauteur he'd been waiting a good portion of his adult life for the moment he could whip out this monstrosity and offer primeval assistance to a helpless assembly.

Glory at hand, the man asked us for our desired lengths. After rough measurements were provided, he looped the rope over the blade and embarked on the first cut. It took forever. The robust twine resisted the man's furious motions, the menacing knife exposed as a fraud, some ludicrous ego-boosting appurtenance. After what seemed like an eternity, the man finished the final cut and slunk away, rubbing his forearms and retiring to his seat in embarrassment.

Once Harry was successfully positioned for the after-life, Imogen approached the hole. The other mourners formed a crooked line behind her. Each person, in turn, threw a handful of coarse, heavy soil onto the lid of the coffin. The fistfuls of the earthen gumbo registered contact with plangent splats. One little boy of about three, who had on a sky-blue T-shirt, striped shorts, and bright orange Crocs, kept scampering back for more dirt. After about ten trips to the dirt pile, his mother bent down and scooped him up. She cradled her mutinous trophy salmon in both arms while he tried his best to wriggle free from her tight grasp.

Whitney declined to participate in the dirt ritual on account of her new manicure, so I stood in line on my own. When my turn came, I approached the grave and threw a handful of wet mud onto Harry's box. The lid was pretty much covered by then, which I surmised to be a good sign. I wasn't sure what the point of the dirt ritual was, but whatever the purpose, I deemed Harry's friends and family to have shown up on game day.

After everyone else who was so inclined had taken a turn with the dirt, a ruddy-faced man began to blare out a tune on the bagpipes, another of Harry's testatorial commandments. Harry had taken great pride in the fact that he was one-eighth Scottish, the descendant of a clan that landed in South Carolina in the 1760s. The McEvers were of hardy stock, but a summer of sweltering palmetto heat was all it took for them to ditch their oppressive Highland togs and proceed to intermarry with other, more appropriately clad settlers.

The pipe man wore heavy tartan and knee-high socks, honoring his forebearers while making no concession to the weather. He clasped the bladder under his arm and kneaded the hairy pigskin while he worked his fingers up and down the protruding tube.

The little salmon boy had been freed from his mother's

arms. He danced up a storm at the feet of the piper, kicking up a cloud of dust with his fluorescent footwear. A wispy blond girl in a flowery dress sprang up to accompany the boy. She put her hands on her waist and whipped her skinny legs up, down, and around in what looked to be a homage to a long-forgotten Gypsy dance. The piper stared straight ahead with the blank expression of a weary beefeater, not letting on how he felt about his earnest accompaniment. The rest of us stood in silence, enjoying the performance of the odd trio while the last few bars of "Going Home" trailed off, the resonant hum of the Gaelic reeds melting into the heat of the languid afternoon.

Chapter Three

HARRY WAS GONE, HIS LAST WISHES carried out, more or less. The next week, Imogen asked me to do her a favor. Would I hold things together at the firm, temporarily, maybe prepare an assessment of the pending cases so she could decide what to do from there?

"Don't you go sugarcoating things, you hear, Guy?" she told me. "I know Harry should've retired several years ago, but what could I do? The law was his first love. I wasn't going to be the one to take it away from him. He'd have never forgiven me, the stubborn old mule."

Harry's sudden passing had surprised everyone because he'd been in great physical shape for a man of sixty-seven. He had walked eighteen holes a week, cut brush on his ranch, and even did some sort of senescent yoga. Imogen had cooked up the yoga routine, an inventive fusion of Eastern disciplines and Native American techniques she found on the web page of a woman from Taos named Anastasia Gifford. I'd never heard that the great people of the plains had been partial to stretching their hamstrings before buffalo hunts, but Imogen claimed the Gifford lady had done her homework.

In recent years, Harry's memory had been the pressing concern. I'd heard numerous stories about the lapses. He forgot to feed his fish, which split a peaceful community of aquarium dwellers into camps of ravenous cannibals and petrified prey, the tank a Colosseum of piscine horror. One tiger-striped angelfish of previously sunny demeanor turned combative and disposed of three yellow-tailed mollies within a week before Harry's secretary, Janice, discovered the carnage and deposited the offender in a nearby storm drain.

Harry's lack of command of the firm's docket had been even more concerning. He forgot hearings and showed up, uninvited, to others, covering up each embarrassment with a cheerful wave and humorous bon mot. He couldn't keep facts straight, which led him to sign up weak cases and turn down lucrative ones. Generous settlement offers were rejected with harsh words and lousy ones accepted with enthusiasm. I'd swung by the office one day to take him to lunch and heard him cackling, "Shove it, you fossilized prick," into his phone, which was disturbing not because Harry was a stranger to coarse language, but because he had just turned down Louie Grasso's offer of $75,000 on a case that wasn't worth half that much.

I called the dealership to change my schedule. Until things were straight, I'd work all day at the firm and nights at the lot. Whitney wouldn't be pleased about my diminished commission checks, but then again, Whitney wasn't pleased with much of anything when it came to my professional endeavors.

Krystal answered and paged the sales manager, Dave Trout. He picked up after five minutes of earsplitting Celine Dion and her legendary five-octave resound.

"Did Hodges close the deal with the Masseys?" I asked

Trout.

"Who?"

"The Masseys. Dale. Stout fellow. Chirpy wife. Tahoe."

"Oh, them. Hodges? No, Dean was working that one."

"You're kidding. I told them to find Hodges. How did Peas get ahold of them?"

"I dunno. Seemed like it was going pretty well. Dean looked to have them all sewn up. He and the husband were carrying on like old friends. The guy really appreciated the coffee mugs."

"So he closed them?"

"Ah, no, well, not yet. The wife said she needed time to think it over. Said they'd get back with us."

Mallory! It was just like dull-witted Dean Peas to misread the familial power structure. Mallory, the mercurial matron. The grande dame of the House of Massey. She was the key to that high-margin Tahoe deal. Forget sturdy Dale and his winsome fantasies.

I felt sorry for Trout, so I didn't push my grievances against Peas. I knew he wanted to get rid of that dead weight as much as anybody, but he was a man whose authority had been neutered by the age-old scourge of nepotism—the way of ancient clans to which we are still beholden to this very day.

"Just do your best to keep Peas and his swag bag away from my customers, will you?" I told Trout. He ignored me and began to grumble about my shift changes, annoyed he'd have to redo the schedule. He prepared it by hand each month, a prolonged session of analog masochism, taking an entire morning to squeeze our names into the slit-sized boxes on the schedule sheet.

Next, I called a meeting of the firm's personnel. That didn't take long because the head count had dwindled to

27

two by the time of Harry's death. Janice Munger, Harry's long-suffering secretary, was a nervous, high-strung lady of indeterminable age, beaten down by years of serving as a bulwark against bad-tempered insurance lawyers and imperious court staff. Harry's paralegal, Barb Coates, was a strapping, jovial brunette with a gravelly laugh and the cropped brown hair of a *Mayflower* pilgrim. Harry had hired Barb after Monty Short stole Reese Walters away earlier in the year. Short offered Reese a dollar more an hour and seventy-five-minute lunch breaks. When that didn't work, he threw in additional enticements, such as a space heater and a fancy coffee machine. The coffee machine was enough to tip the scales in Short's favor because Harry was not about to unload his double-burner Bunn setup for a contraption that took "those damn fiddly pods," as he'd put it.

We went into the conference room and sat around the glossy oak table. The two women sized me up. Janice peered out through round pink glasses of the sort favored by daytime talk-show hosts. Barb looked on with expectant amusement, as if she were about to witness the virgin performance of a child conjurer.

What to say to put these ladies at ease? I mumbled a few words about Harry and his legacy, how it was our duty to help sort out where things stood, not only for Imogen but for the clients too. I tried to read my audience. What were their reactions to my solemn old saws? Were my words hitting home, my sincerity palpable? I was not to be blessed with useful feedback, because Janice inexplicably snapped. Fat tears began to streak down her ruby cheeks. She'd held it together through the funeral, but now raw sorrow, a torrent of unpasteurized grief, spewed out at an alarming velocity.

What a frightening, mysterious outpouring! Incontinent emotion of the type usually reserved for kidnapped children and sudden insolvency. Defenseless, I froze. I inventoried my knowledge of Janice and realized it was shockingly light. It came, almost exclusively, from the array of framed photos that encircled her LaserJet printer. I scoured my mind for her desktop memories. She had a daughter who used to be a twirler at a high school named Jarvis, which had an unidentifiable bird of prey as its mascot. The Jarvis Eagles? The Jarvis Falcons? Who knew? The embossed bird head on the girl's sequined outfit certainly didn't give it away. Other photos established that the girl was now up at TCU, studying something or other, still launching her chrome rods high into the air.

What else? Cruise ships, a whole armada of them, surrounding her printer like it was Cuba during Kennedy's high-stakes blockade. Of course, how could I have forgotten that Janice had embarked on many cruises to sun-soaked Caribbean isles, and that she favored the British protectorates? She had also padded down the cobbled streets of many European capitals in the western part of the Schengen Area, but I had seen no evidence she'd ventured behind the erstwhile iron curtain into Slavic territories.

"I'm sorry, I just . . . I mean, it's all such a shock," said Janice. "I checked on him before I left, and he looked fine, told me to enjoy my weekend. I never thought that'd be the last time I ever saw him. Just like what happened with Jerry."

I sat uncomfortably rigid, petrified like a lump of fossilized amber. Thankfully, Barb stood and grabbed some tissues off the sideboard. She went over, rubbed Janice's shoulder, and handed her the flowery box. They were the kind with the lotion built in, so Janice could cry a river without having to worry about a red nose or chapped skin, or so the Kleenex people claimed in their earnest commercials.

Janice took a handful, wiped away the errant tears, and told us a good part of her life story.

"I worked for Harry for ages. I was only twenty-eight when Jerry died. I couldn't believe he was gone. Our daughter, Bethany, was only two."

She told us her husband, Jerry Munger, had been a utility lineman until he died in an unfortunate accident that OSHA refused to investigate, the federal letter nothing more than two sentences of bureaucratic buck passing. Everyone assumed Jerry's death was caused by a high-voltage mishap, but surprisingly, it had nothing to do with the restless flow of electrons. He was up a forty-foot pole replacing a faulty fuse cutout (or so I surmised from Janice's rather vague rendition of Jerry's tragic demise) when he somehow lost his footing, slipped back down the creosoted shaft, crashed into the ground, and broke his neck.

The investigators from the electric company were stumped. Jerry Munger, of all people? The man was a legend on southern pine. He'd even won a silver medal in the 1988 Texas Pole Climbing Championship in Lufkin. The only person to best his time to the top of the 120-foot competition log was a stringy forester from Nacogdoches. The Nacogdochan had perfected the bowlegged shimmy of an agile primate, so there was no shame in Jerry's second place, Janice told us with a widow's pride.

The medical examiner hedged his bets, as small-town pathologists are wont to do. His report detailed numerous puncture wounds and lesions on Jerry's face and neck, but how did they get there? The examiner concluded some force of nature had set on poor Jerry Munger with a primordial fury. But what? A swarm of angry African bees? A demented squirrel juiced up on the electromagnetic flux? A territorial screech owl protecting her downy young? Everybody had an opinion, but no consensus was ever reached.

"I somehow found my way to Harry," said Janice. "I think a coworker of Jerry's recommended him. He took the case, god bless him."

God bless him was right. From what I'd just heard, to say liability had been weak would be a gross understatement. How could the electric company be held responsible for the vicissitudes of Mother Nature in all her capricious glory? But Harry, being Harry, managed to wrangle a decent settlement out of the stingy company.

"He got me enough to pay off the mortgage and set up a college fund for Bethany," said Janice. "She's up at TCU studying finance and twirling for the marching band."

A hint of satisfaction crept into the corners of Janice's mouth. This was deep pride, delight in her offspring, a river with many tributaries given Bethany's baton work for the Horned Frogs and her promising future in pecuniary dealings.

Janice continued, "Harry could see with Jerry gone, I needed to go back to work, so he offered me a job as a file clerk. Part-time, flexible hours. The man's a saint. I showed up on the first day and I couldn't believe it, there's three of us in that small file room. All widows." She chuckled through a sob. "We used to fight over every scrap of paper that came in there. One thing I'll tell you, those files were immaculate."

Janice went on and on. We got Dickensian-length descriptions of her years with the firm and a healthy dose of Bethany's halftime glories and struggles with young love. After she finished, she apologized but said she was in no state to work right now, it was all too raw. She had decided to take an extended vacation to Branson, Missouri, to relax and take in some homespun schmaltz. She was particularly excited about a family of god-fearing fiddlers called the Pattersons, who had garnered a 4.7-star rating on a prominent travel website, the reviewers lauding their dexterous fingers and pious banter.

I took this news with a mixture of trepidation and relief. I had just lost 50 percent of my workforce in fifteen minutes, not a good measure by any fancy HR metric. I had, however, retained the half that hadn't broken down in a fit of convulsive misery.

Janice told us more about her Branson plans. Barb and I listened with the synthetic enthusiasm of hostages forced to break bread with their captor. She said she'd planned to take in the performance of a group of skilled acrobats from Beijing until she read the more recent reviews. Apparently, due to a visa snafu, the gravity-defying troupe from the Hebei province had been replaced by a gang of lead-booted American imposters. Their bumbling attempts at aerial majesty more closely resembled something out of a grade-school talent show, or so a woman named Patsy F. from Decatur, Illinois, had written in her review entitled "Buyer Beware!!!"

"Can you believe it?" said Janice. "How could they go and switch the performers out like that?"

We strained to read the review on her phone. I noted Pasty F. did say in the latter part of her assessment that the concession staff was friendly and the popcorn was well buttered. I said these mitigating factors might have been enough for a more charitable critic to lift their review out of one-star territory. Barb agreed, but Janice said she trusted Pasty F.—she'd had boots on the ground, so it made sense to trust her approach to the weighting.

The theater manager wasn't taking the likes of Patsy F. lying down. He'd posted a response to her review: "sorry you dont enjoy show patsy f but we cannot be blame for conduct of immigration services, we recruit AMAZING USA ACROBATS from county fairs and circus schools in all 48 states including dominican republic, so sad people like you do not know talent and hard work of fellow citizens, have a blessed day!"

Janice left us in a flurry of sadness and anticipation, Harry dead and buried but the wonders of southern Missouri mere days away. Barb and I decided to use the rest of the afternoon to sort Harry's active cases into three piles. In all honesty, it was Barb who came up with the pile idea.

The first pile would be dedicated to the problem cases—the ones Harry had taken as a favor or as a result of his impaired cognition. These were cases with questionable liability, paltry damages, or judgment-proof defendants. The second would consist of decent cases that needed time and money to be invested, and the third would comprise mature cases nearing trial or settlement.

The first case exiled to pile number one was Shane Burt's masterpiece of human stupidity. Burt, evidently no candidate for Mensa, or even community college for that matter, had gotten stuck in a disused phone box for the better part of twenty-four hours. The red box was of authentic British origin, one of several dotting the ritzy Upper Kirby district of Houston, installed in an attempt to bestow what the district's marketing people described as a regal authenticity upon the commercial endeavors of the local merchants.

The facts were murky, but the gist was that in a fit of drunken bravado, Burt had somehow pried open the door of the box. Whatever happened after that, the end result was indisputable—he ended up locked inside.

The commuters who zipped by the next morning must

have assumed Burt's frantic flailings were exhortations to take advantage of generous discounts on quality merchandise, because they responded to his furious waves with appreciative nods while not slowing down in the least. It wasn't until midevening that he was able to flag down a passing jogger, who called 911. Thirty minutes later, the fire department arrived and used the Jaws of Life to cut Burt free, much to the chagrin of the executive director of the management district, who claimed she could have been on the scene in ten minutes with the key if someone had bothered to notify her. Now she was stuck with a mangled hunk of British miscellanea, sans a door. Her concerns were myriad, ranging from disease-ridden pigeons to soporific hobos. Not exactly what the local merchants had in mind when the project was given the go-ahead by unanimous vote.

Harry had filed suit based upon some creative theories of attractive nuisance and false imprisonment, seeking $100,000 in damages for Shane Burt's mental anguish. He played up Burt's humiliation at the hands of the throngs of morning commuters and the ignominy of being dubbed the "Human Goldfish" by the *Bayou City Beacon*, a local weekly. The district's attorney offered $5,000—nuisance value. He'd asserted Burt should be happy his client wasn't counterclaiming for the damage to the box, which had been imported from across the Atlantic at no small cost.

I scanned the case notes. Harry must have experienced a moment of lucidity, because the last entry read, "Recommended to Burt we counter with $15,000, then settle in the $7,500 to $10,000 range. Stubborn bastard wants to hold out for $35,000, the payoff on his bass boat." I threw the file down on the table in disgust and scribbled out a reminder to take Shane Burt and his fishing dreams to the woodshed.

We kept at it for the next couple of hours. By then, the pile of rejects was shoulder high and listed like a Delhi high-rise. It contained cases with all manner of dubious claims and eggshell plaintiffs. Barb summarized the cases, and I assigned them to the appropriate pile.

"Woman bitten by her neighbor's ocelot in a trailer park in Alvin, loses left arm below the elbow."

"Shit pile."

"Man drinks large bottle of hot sauce on a dare, ends up with colitis, among other intestinal ailments. Claim is failure to warn."

"Shit pile."

"Worker in warehouse demoted from forklift driver to latrine duty. Claiming intentional infliction of emotional distress."

"Shit pile."

And so it went. Barb retrieved a thin file from one of the cabinets and scanned the factual summary.

"What about this one?" She handed me the file for the matter of *Irving Timms v. the Hungry Roadrunner Cantina.*

The Hungry Roadrunner was a new joint with a festive south-of-the-border theme. Opening night had been going swell according to the summary. I imagined the place packed with people drinking salty bottom-shelf margaritas and munching on tacos filled with unidentifiable fish. Not my scene, to be honest, but a picture of pleasant conviviality for some, I suppose. Next thing you know, the colorful wicker chairs started to implode, spindly wooden legs flying around the restaurant like bowling pins.

Irv Timms was one of the victims of the budget seating. No small man, he went to the ground hard. He suffered crippling gluteal contusions and a fractured tailbone. Ten months later, he was still hobbling about with a walker, his dutiful wife trailing behind, inflatable donut in hand.

That very night, before anyone had the opportunity to inspect the chairs, the Roadrunner people went to work. The busboys were sent out with the company credit card and returned with boxes of zinc-plated L-brackets and thick coach screws. They worked through the night to reinforce each and every chair. Now, even on Cinco de Mayo, drunk revelers with no knowledge of the heroic exploits of Ignacio Zaragoza and his small band of patriots would be able to dance all over them without fear of serious injury.

Harry had sued, alleging negligence, but the restaurant's insurance company was trying to shift the blame to Timms and his ample rump.

"Sounds like a decent case," said Barb. "He has, what, thirty thousand dollars in medical bills? And they fixed the chairs the same evening. Why would they do that unless there was something wrong with them?"

"Subsequent remedial measures," I said.

"Yeah, so?"

"Inadmissible."

"Why?"

"Torts 101. The theory is, when people screw up, we want them to correct the situation, make things right as soon as possible. Nobody would fix anything if it could be held against them later."

Barb nodded. She said she felt sorry for Irv Timms, an innocent victim of shoddy craftsmanship and the dictates of public policy. I shrugged and climbed onto the conference table. Barb handed me the Timms file, and I placed it atop the shit pile. The tower teetered in response to the imposition. Thankfully, after a couple of worrying sways, it steadied itself. Not wanting to tempt fate by burdening the imposing stack further, we called it a day.

Chapter Four

THE NEXT COUPLE OF WEEKS WENT BY in a blur. I was running on empty, rushing back and forth between Harry's office and the dealership. I managed to salvage the Tahoe deal. Big Dale came back in with his tail between his legs. He brought along little Randy, a serious, skinny boy with spiky blond hair and no obvious signs of digestive ailments. The mismatched pair looked like a slapstick duo from the silent film era as they strolled across the concrete toward me. The kid made a beeline for the Corvettes, striding with purpose, his mind full of childhood dreams. He considered the row of low-slung sports cars, pulled out his phone, and began to snap away with the prolific diligence of a claims adjuster.

Dean Peas stared at the boy from inside the showroom, his square head pressed to the glass. I guessed he was trying to figure out if the diminutive figure was a prospect. Even at that distance, it should have been easy to tell the difference between a child and, say, a jockey or small gymnast, but little Randy's professional insurance demeanor had thrown Dean Peas for a loop. I tried to draw Peas out of the show-room by telepathic force. I needed a good laugh, and what could be funnier than the look on dumb Dean's face when he realized his mark's gangly legs wouldn't come within two feet of the pedals?

I shook my head at Peas and his false hope and turned back to Dale. He wouldn't look me in the eye. We went to my cubicle, and I presented him with the paperwork for the Premier, the High Country now nothing but a distant fantasy. He scribbled his signature with the indifference of a parolee signing for paltry belongings after serving a long sentence. We were soon joined by Randy, who perused the documents with great focus and pointed out a few blanks Dale had forgotten to initial.

When we were done, Dale declined my offer to walk him through the interior features, grabbed the keys, and ushered Randy out the door. This was no sweat off my back, but I guessed Dale was going to struggle with some of the finer features, such as the lumbar adjustment and the rear fog lights. Maybe he was counting on Randy to come to the rescue if he suffered lower-back discomfort on the way home? Made sense. My gut told me that if we were still in the golden age of the VCR, Dale would have no choice but to rely on Randy to do his weekly programming.

It was a slow night. I idled in my cubicle and contemplated incongruities. How was it that Randy and Dale were such polar opposites? Was the kid adopted? My mind ran free with the possibilities. Had baby Randy been abandoned in a rat-infested alley by sunken-cheeked heroin addicts? Or freed from some bleak Russian orphanage in the dead of a subzero winter? Possibly rescued from the padlocked outhouse of sadistic foster parents who'd somehow slipped through the vetting process? But then I remembered Mallory. She and Randy shared the same slender build and subtle acuity, which cut against my tragic speculation.

Maybe there were a few skeins of Mallory's DNA in the mix, just none of Dale's? That made the most sense. While I hate to stereotype, there was something about Dale's ready capitulation and flaccid handshake that made me suspect nature had lost patience with that anemic offshoot of the Massey family tree.

The next day, I was back at Harry's office. Barb had embarked on the mammoth task of auditing Harry's books.

"Look at this." She handed me an open file. The case was against the City of Houston. Harry had represented a man by the name of Willis Delaney. Delaney used to own a dilapidated apartment complex in a rapidly gentrifying area east of downtown. Before the events that led to the lawsuit, the city had been on Delaney's back for years, claiming the place was a run-down eyesore, not to mention a magnet for cut-rate prostitution and drug dealing.

Delaney's lawyer at the onset of the dispute, a man by the name of Thaddeus Blow, had responded with a slew of letters, impenetrable screeds written in the language of the historians of antiquity. Blow countered that the Dynasty Terrace catered to a misunderstood, entrepreneurial clientele. Delaney's tenants were the righteous heirs to the time-honored tradition of feudal bartering, driven by the perverted forces of modern, highly regulated capitalism to avail themselves of more creative means of mercantile exchange.

"So?" I asked.

"Keep reading," said Barb.

I went back to the file. The city ultimately tired of Blow's highfalutin tosh. It decided to invoke its omnipotent powers under the state's eminent domain statutes and seize the complex. Once Delaney was paid off on the cheap, it planned to turn the thriving black-market bazaar into a pile of smoky rubble, then replace the ruin with a park.

Delaney, representing himself by then, continued the furious letter-writing campaign. These aggrieved tomes were, sadly, full of constitutional misreadings. I wasn't surprised. Everyone's a scholar of our great organizational charter these days. You can't walk a block without hearing some layman's turgid gibberish about this amendment or the other, but they'd all stare at you slack-jawed if you asked them to explain the incorporation doctrine or quizzed them on the specifics of *Berman v. Parker*.

Why did Harry take this case? He was no fan of men like Willis Delaney, bottom-feeders who gorged themselves on a buffet of human misfortune. But throw in a city bent on imperial overreach and a healthy 35 percent contingency fee?

Barb piped up. "See these emails? A park? Yeah, right. The city planned to hold on to the property for a few years, then flip it to a developer for a hefty profit."

Frightened Harry would expose its underhanded scheming to a hungry press, the city rolled over and agreed to pay Delaney an extra $500,000 if he signed a robust confidentiality agreement. Delaney netted about $300,000, and Harry took in roughly $200,000 for his fee and expenses.

"Vintage Harry," I said. "There aren't too many lawyers around that can scare the city out of half a million dollars."

"But here's the thing," said Barb. "I can't find any evidence we received the funds. Based on the settlement documents, the check should've cleared months ago. I've gone through both bank accounts and nothing. So I called the attorney for the city, and she emailed me this."

Barb thrust a piece of paper in my direction. It was a canceled check. A logo dominated the top-left corner of the instrument. The circular motif featured a steam engine with smoke billowing out of a diamond-shaped chimney. Below the iron horse, an antiquated plow sat, unmanned, in a patch of dirt. The fourth-largest city in America, and this was our sacred seal—a Monopoly token and an agricultural implement of an eighteenth-century smallholder?

"What's with the logo?" I asked Barb. "Is this check genuine?"

She told me it was indeed authentic, but she agreed with my assessment of the unfortunate iconography. I went back to the check. The amount was correct—$500,000. It was made payable to both Willis Delaney and Harry Fentress, a customary practice that required both the client and their lawyer to sign prior to deposit.

Barb flipped the check over and pointed to the endorsement box. "Take a look at the signatures."

I picked up the check. Delaney's signature was penned in the puffy scrawl of a bombastic narcissist. Harry's name was signed in the same ornate style.

"Jesus. Are you telling me a man known for warehousing budget streetwalkers in a run-down tenement is walking around town with two hundred grand of Harry's money?"

Barb tapped a finger on the forged signature. "*I'm* not telling you anything."

I called Imogen and relayed the news about the misappropriated fee.

"You must be kidding me," she said. "How could someone take advantage of poor Harry like that? It's despicable. What's the world coming to?"

"Don't worry. We'll get to the bottom of it."

"Listen, Guy, I've been thinking about something, and this discovery of yours, well, it makes me more sure of it."

"Actually, it was Barb who—"

41

"How would you feel about going back to law school, finishing up your last couple of semesters, then taking over the firm for good? What's a year in the grand scheme of things?"

Not more career talk, my least favorite of digressions. I told her I wasn't sure. A lot could happen in a year. I hunted for excuses, finding utility in a couple of my many aborted college majors. Did she know Tolstoy knocked out the first draft of *War and Peace* in twelve months? And what about 69 AD, when the bloodthirsty Romans went through three emperors?

Imogen discounted my historical excuses. She brushed off the productivity of the old Russian master as the extraordinary output of a compulsive personality and attributed the Roman turnover to anger-management issues. Having dispatched my arguments, she proposed a generous arrangement.

"We'll split the fees from the existing cases, including Mr. Delaney's case. I'll leave my portion in the firm until you've passed the bar and are up on your feet."

It had been a long time since I'd quit law school and moved back to Beaumont to help Mom pick up the pieces after Dad died. It took two years to straighten out the Straight Arrow Auto Emporium. We wound the business down, a process that took forever because the inventory had gone stale while Dad was ill. We found a tenant for the premises and sold the remaining cars off, one by one, until there was nothing left but old clunkers. We gave the clunkers to our mechanic, Alphonso, and his cousin, a sleepy, small-eared man named Ruiz. They rounded up two amigos, roped the last eight vehicles together in pairs, and rolled out onto the interstate, a little lemon train destined for Mexico, or possibly frontiers beyond.

I'd only been back in Houston a year and was making decent money. But was I going to sell Chevys for the rest of my life, lining the pockets of Beau Holloway and his listless family? I pictured myself twenty years from now. At best, I'd be in Dave Trout's shoes, forced to spend a good part of my day in service of the corporate hierarchy, hounding underperforming dolts like Dean Peas and scribbling out shift changes for ungrateful employees while I battled to ensure my handwriting didn't violate the boundaries of the inadequately sized boxes.

I told Imogen first things first. I'd do my best to recover the money from Delaney. And while I appreciated her generous proposal, I needed time to think it over.

"Well, whatever you decide, if you get Harry's money back from this Delaney character, we're splitting it," said Imogen. "All the work you're putting in at the firm. I don't know what I'd do without you."

I hung up, reclined in Harry's chair, and propped my feet up on his desk. I studied the fish, or what remained of them. They floated around, same as usual, not seeming to miss Harry in the least. I walked over to the tank and tapped on the glass. They scattered, infantry under mortar attack, darts of bright color shooting off in all directions. Oops. I'd forgotten about the refractory effect of liquid, a phenomenon that causes sound to travel with greater intensity through water. I offered them a meek apology and sat back down, hoping I hadn't damaged sensitive membranes. I picked up the Delaney file and leafed through it again, the fish still hiding somewhere in the murky recesses of their glass lockup.

Chapter Five

I NEEDED TO TRACK DOWN WILLIS DELANEY, and fast. He was liable to be spreading Harry's money around like a lottery winner with nagging insecurities. Willis Delaney. I repeated the unsavory moniker and fanned out the contents of his file on Harry's desk. I envied our colonial forebears and their debtors' prisons and sturdy stocks. Tell me Delaney, how long would you last with a smattering of the local citizenry, chosen for their aim, meting out doses of painful shame with every rotten tomato? Delaney, a man who probably couldn't even name one Supreme Court justice, oblivious to the fact that all that stood between him and vegetable retribution was what some argued was an overly broad reading of the Eighth Amendment.

I dialed Delaney's landline. No longer in service. I scanned his client information sheet again. The space for his cell phone number was empty. His emergency contact was a man by the name of Alton Dugas. Emergency contact? What was Harry running, a daycare? I guessed this was one of Janice's ideas—overcaution born from the memory of great loss. Still, her nod to the protocols of junior sports leagues had produced a promising lead, so who was I to judge? I dialed the Dugas number and a woman answered.

"AD Towing," she said in a raspy voice.

"AD?" I said.

"Yeah, that's right, you want a gold star or something?"

"AD as in 'Alton Dugas'?"

"That's what you say."

"Excuse me?"

"Why can't it just be AD as in AD? Why's everything got to mean something these days?"

"You mean AD as in 'anno Domini'?"

"Huh? Who?"

"The year of the Lord," I said in a misguided attempt to explain the Latin.

"Yeah, that's it, wise guy, and I'm the Virgin Mary. Look here, Jesus, you need a tow? 'Cause I'm about to go on break." She pronounced Jesus "Hey Zeus" for some unknown reason.

"No, I'm actually looking for Alton Dugas."

The woman cleared her throat with a sandpaper cough. Her long pause led me to believe the majority of people who called for Dugas were not bearing news of impending knighthood or other ennoblements.

"I ain't saying I know nobody named that, but if I did, he definitely ain't here now. If you wanna leave a message and someone with that name happens to come by, I'll try to pass it along, but I ain't makin' any promises."

The woman was toying with me, her salty jibing probably armor to shroud self-perceived deficiencies, possibly a lifetime of cruel disappointments. Fine then. I parried her obfuscation with a little misdirection of my own. I apologized for the Latin, but I told her she needed to understand that in my profession the language of ancient Italy was our stock-in-trade. I explained I was an attorney handling the estate of a long-lost relative of Mr. Dugas's. He had a large slice of the inheritance coming his way. It was imperative he call me ASAP so he could get in on it before the other heirs claimed his share.

She wanted to know how much Dugas was set to receive, and I played up the amount. I told her it was a substantial sum, enough that he wouldn't think twice about giving her a healthy raise and a nice Christmas bonus. And I was sure he'd throw in a few other perks, such as a frozen turkey on Thanksgiving and an elaborate fireworks display on the Fourth of July.

At first, she scoffed at my suggestions, especially the fireworks—something about a nasty mishap when Dugas was a small boy that had resulted in a missing thumb. But the more I talked, the more she warmed to my trickle-down ideas. I stoked the fire. I added that, in my business, I'd seen the most miserly of men renounce their tightfisted ways and become patriots of great generosity after they'd received such large, unexpected sums.

She became more and more excited. She named a wish list of items that would make her wrecker job easier. I reaffirmed that Dugas would surely spring for each and every one with philanthropic delight. A new mouse for her computer? Of course, how about a wireless one without the annoying cord, such expense a mere triviality to the newly flush Dugas? What about the potholes in the parking lot, a couple knee-deep and possibly filled with crawfish, something she had come to suspect when she spied a roving band of neighborhood boys rooting around in them after one particularly heavy rainfall? Why, definitely, those would be filled in short order, and I wouldn't be surprised if the entire lot received a nice thick coat of asphalt, the cost mere peanuts to a man of her boss's soon-to-be means.

"And why let the mudbugs go to waste? I bet Mr. Dugas will be more than happy to spring for a large net and a big stainless steel pot, and you guys can have a crawfish boil right there on the fresh tarmac!" I said all this in jest, hoping to win the woman over with a little down-home humor. But she ignored the irony and jumped right on the idea of parking-lot crawfish, denigrating Dugas for his obliviousness to company morale.

I hurried to thank the sour woman for agreeing to pass along my message and hung up. Barb walked in holding a stack of papers.

"I came up with an address for Delaney." She handed me a copy of a property tax statement.

This was progress. All we had on Delaney at present was the address of the Dynasty Terrace's management office, a single-story structure the city had turned into rubble months ago.

I scanned the statement. Delaney resided in Cedar Grove Forest, a redundantly named neighborhood in the northwest part of the city. Barb had printed out some information from the local homeowners' association website. Apparently, the development was founded in the sixties on the site of an old German dairy farm. Before the Prussian incursion, Native Americans from unidentified tribes roamed the area, hunting wild boar with sharp tusks and fishing for carp on the grassy banks of White Oak Bayou.

After the Germans tired of early mornings finessing warm teats, they sold the farmland to a developer. The area soon became a bastion for members of the middle class who sought what the website described, rather rosily, as "bucolic tranquility away from the hustle and bustle of city life." The crowning achievement, according to the text, came in the seventies when an old airfield in the middle of the development was transformed into a twenty-seven-hole golf course. During that era, the lots were ample and the handicaps low, or so the website claimed under the heading "The Golden Age of Cedar Grove Forest."

Why hadn't I heard of this sylvan paradise within the city's metes and bounds? I was about to ask Barb when she shoved a copy of newspaper article from 1994 under my nose. The headline proclaimed, "Crime Wave Shocks Once Idyllic Suburb." It was a rise-and-fall piece. The reporter chalked up the neighborhood's woes to its annexation by the city following the oil crash of the mideighties. Apparently, by the date of the piece, serious crime had become rampant and the golf course was suffering from grave neglect.

These regrettable circumstances had combined to the detriment of the local golfers. Opportunistic miscreants took to hiding behind overgrown bushes surrounding the greens. While unsuspecting golfers were lining up their putts, the thieves would sprint to the unoccupied golf carts, jump in, and tear off with full sets of clubs (minus the putters, obviously). One hostile-sounding duffer was quoted as saying he'd invested in a new driver not to gain any length on his tee shots—which were plenty long, thank you very much—but because the club had a large titanium head that would allow him to crack the skulls of any suspicious characters who manifested designs on his precious sticks.

"So much for the golden era," I said. "I guess future generations won't be reading about it in their history textbooks."

"Did you see the photo?" She pointed to a grainy image of a robust man in a short-sleeve shirt dominated by a smattering of uprooted sago palms. His nylon pants rode high around his swollen midsection, and his mesh cap was perched on a thick helmet of straight, shaggy hair. He looked like a junior-high football coach coming off a losing campaign, a surly frown dominating his paunchy face. The caption read, "Local resident Willis Delaney has decided to take matters into his own hands due to the recent criminal activity in Cedar Grove Forest."

"I don't think anybody's going to ask him to play Santa at the neighborhood Christmas party," said Barb. "Here's the house, nothing to write home about either."

She pointed out Delaney's abode on a map. It backed onto what she told me was now the eighth hole of a Frisbee golf course. The real golf course had closed a few years ago, but strips of the former fairways had been shorn away for the Frisbee people. Most of the rest of it was an overgrown mess of scrubby weeds.

I scanned a couple of the more recent newspaper articles. The residents of Cedar Grove Forest never tired of bitching about something or other, and the local press was only too happy to waste ink on them. The final piece reported that residents had begun to moan about the ragged fairways, which they claimed were a haven for snakes and other unspecified varmints. They demanded one taxpayer-subsidized plan after another to drive off the pestilence. First, they wanted regular mowing, and when that wasn't done with sufficient frequency to deter the vermin, there was a push from a group of the more cavalier residents for industrial pesticides and seasonal hunting with small-caliber arms. It was pointed out that if the culling scheme was approved, out of an abundance of caution, everyone wishing to avail themselves of the old cart paths to exercise during winter would have to wear bright orange flak jackets and undergo four hours of outdoor-awareness training.

The chairman of the residents' association, a retired

army captain who wore an eye patch and sped around on a hopped-up mobility scooter, volunteered to run the program. An evidently charitable neighbor, he asked for nothing more than a few basic amenities: a flare gun, a megaphone, and a portable toilet, his bladder likely past its sell-by date. The proposal was debated, ad nauseam, by the local authorities. Ultimately, it was rejected by a vote of 18–0 at the end of a particularly heated council meeting. While a majority of the local residents were only too happy to sanction the killing fields, the city had no interest in shouldering the liability for a pilot program that involved poorly defined boundaries and live ammunition.

Chapter Six

ARMED WITH AN ADDRESS, I SET OUT for Delaney's stomping grounds. After about twenty minutes, I exited the freeway and proceeded through the shady streets, admiring the expansive crowns of the mature trees. The houses, however, were a less laudable feature of the area. The styles were all over the place, almost as though the entire neighborhood had been designed by one of those drug-addled street artists paid by the sketch to do mean-spirited caricatures of groggy tourists. I passed squat ranch houses parked next to faux Georgians, and brutalist brick boxes with slits for windows opposite Swiss ski chalets with pitched roofs and triangular eaves.

What would the Germans make of what had become of their lush pastureland? Would they look past the architectural shortcomings with a Teutonic benevolence, chalk up the aesthetic atrocities to the inevitable march of time with a bout of hearty beer-garden backslapping? A student of history, I was considering less congenial feedback when I arrived at my destination.

Delaney's house was a one-story construction of tan brick with modest rectangular windows covered by mesh bug screens. I took a minute to assess the property for evidence of newly embraced immoderation but came up empty—there were no fancy cars in the driveway, and I spotted nothing else that manifested spendthrift tendencies. Quite the opposite, the place was run-down and in need of significant maintenance. Weathered paint was peeling from the woodwork, and the roof was covered with a slew of dead pine needles that had fallen from three thick conifers that towered over the house.

I walked up the driveway, to the front porch, and rang the bell. It lit up with a half-hearted glow, so I banged on the door a few times for good measure. After about thirty seconds, it cracked open, a security chain taut across the gap. A pair of wrinkled, suspicious raccoon eyes peered out at me.

"Mrs. Delaney?" I asked. I had no idea if Delaney was married, but this woman looked to be of a generation that frowned on unwedded cohabitation, so I decided I'd go that route first.

"Who? What do you want? I already have a yardman, and my subscriptions are up to date."

"I'm looking for a Mr. Delaney."

"I'm not interested. I'm on a fixed income."

"I just need to have a few words with—"

"I had my gutters cleaned last month, thank you very much."

"Yes, ma'am, understood. Although you're going to need to take care of those pine needles on your roof pretty soon. I'm surprised your gutter people didn't mention them, but that's not why—"

"My religious house is in good order, if you must know."

So it went. She had no use for encyclopedias, and her

freezer was already stocked with prime grade-A cuts. Her granddaughter Ellie was a top seller in her Brownie troop, so she had at least a year's supply of Do-si-dos stacked up in her cupboards. She had asked Ellie for a volume discount, but the savvy little scout girl played hardball with her old granny, and now she had no room left in her pantry for her fiber supplements. I sensed she was proud of little Ellie's business acumen but also a tad resentful of the bulk trans- action, the asymmetrical bargaining power and all.

"Good to hear, but do you know a man by the name of Willis Delaney?"

"Willis, you say?"

"Yes, I need to speak to him. I'm from a law firm. We represented him in a lawsuit. There are important matters about his settlement I need to discuss with him."

"You know Mr. Willis?"

"Mr. Willis? No, I don't know Mr. Willis. Are you sure you don't mean Mr. Delaney? I'm looking for Willis Delaney." I shoved one of Harry's letters through the gap in the hope her eyesight was better than her hearing.

"Hmm. Oh, I see, yes, Will-isss Dee-lane-eey. So you're with Mr. Willis. Why didn't you say so? Well, it took you long enough! I've been calling and calling. Anyway, you'd better come in. The sink is over there, and when you're done with that, I'll show you the bathroom."

She unlatched the door and beckoned me in. She was a tiny woman with crowlike features and jet-black hair. I guessed she was in her early seventies, possibly even older. She had on a colorful muumuu and turquoise flip-flops, and her face was spackled with various shades of thick pastel- hued makeup. I followed her and her island attire through the foyer and into a wood-paneled living room stuffed full of oversized brown furniture. On a glass coffee table sat a hardcover book on the wonders of Boca Raton and a tall stack of Frisbees in an array of colors.

The lady started to rant about the house and its failings. She claimed the roof leaked in heavy rain, and the toilets routinely blocked up, and those were the least of her problems. Shirtless Frisbee men were always overshooting the fairway and playing out of her back garden, oblivious to the out-of-bounds markers. She said she didn't mind a bit of "beefcake," even at her age, but these men had hairy chests and saggy pectorals and threw beer cans into her flower beds.

As we approached the kitchen, something crashed into the sliding glass doors with a loud thwack. The woman shook her head and sighed. She padded over to the doors, slid them open, and went out onto the brick porch. She returned a moment later with a blue Frisbee, which she added to the top of her already-substantial Frisbee pile. Before I was able to make heads or tails of this Frisbee business, she walked into the kitchen and pointed at the sink.

"Every time I use the disposal, water dribbles out from under the cabinet. Disgusting, dirty water! Mr. Willis said he'd fix it, but has he? No he hasn't! Every time I peel a few potatoes, the next thing I know, I've got this horrible potato slush all over the floor. I knew I'd be in for trouble with that man. He didn't even have the decency to show up for the closing. How can you work for a person like that?"

I suggested that consummating real estate transactions by power of attorney was perfectly legal under the Texas property statutes and no cause for unwarranted suspicion. But she just droned on about Delaney's lies, which were many and mostly unforgivable. He'd promised repairs and never performed them. He'd given her a written warranty; some good that did her now that his phone had been disconnected. He'd told her she would have marvelous lakefront views when the city converted the old golf course into a series of reservoirs, but she'd subsequently learned the plan was only to reserve a small portion of the green space for stormwater runoff, so the Frisbee hordes that invaded her garden and threw trash in her azaleas weren't going anywhere any time soon.

As if on cue, a man appeared in her yard. He was a young, broad fellow with a midsection padded with a healthy band of puppy weight. A pair of large bags were strapped over his shoulders. He deposited the bags onto the grass and proceeded to search around.

"Are you going to give him back his Frisbee?" I asked the woman.

She played dumb and gave me a Southern-lady-in-distress routine. "Why, whatever do you mean?" she said in a histrionic voice, hand on brow as if about to pass out.

"His Frisbee." I pointed to the coffee table.

"Those? No no, my dear, those are mine. I couldn't possibly part with them."

The man was getting flustered. His fruitless search had turned up nothing but an old golf ball and a dirty sock. He spotted us, walked over, and tapped on the glass. The woman gave me a stern "Don't meddle in my business" look, shuffled over to the doors, and slid one open.

"Yes, can I help you?"

"Sorry to bother you, but have you seen a blue disc?" The guy pulled a Frisbee out of one of his bags. "Like this?"

"No, we haven't seen anything of the sort, have we?" She looked in my direction as if to include me in her duplicity.

The man noticed the stack on the coffee table. "Uh, I think that's mine, on top of that pile."

"You're mistaken," said the lady. "Those belong to me."

"Huh, what?" The guy was clearly not used to this level of blatant prevarication.

"See, young man, when you sling items onto private property, the owner is entitled to confiscate them, and the owner in this instance happens to be little old me."

I wasn't sure about the legal underpinning of her finders-keepers proposition. But, god knows, I wasn't about to open a mediation.

In the face of this intractable callousness, the man fell on his sword. He told us his name was Daniel, but his friends called him Boone. He was new to the course. The eighth was a tough hole—a dogleg left, and the lady's house was on the bend, which made it easy to end up in her yard if the proper amount of fade wasn't applied. His friend Jeff, a local resident, had invited him to play a round. Did she know Jeff? He had two children and a friendly cocker spaniel that walked with a limp.

The lady had no interest in either Jeff or his progeny, although she did inquire about the origin of the spaniel limp. Boone explained it was congenital. I thought that reflected well on Jeff because he must have known about the condition when he acquired the dog, but the woman didn't credit Boone with any of his friend's empathy. She just stood there, arms crossed, scowling away.

The man unzipped his other bag and pulled out two cans of beer from a local microbrewery. He offered them to us with a nod. I reached for one of the beers, but the lady slapped my hand away.

"What are you doing? He's working!"

"Sorry, I thought . . . can I just say, I know that disc looks like a toy, but it's actually quite expensive. I'm married and we just had our first kid, so money is pretty tight."

I judged Boone a pleasant enough sort. I pictured him relaxing around a picnic table with his buddies, drinking their craft beers and swapping stories of burgeoning fatherhood. I imagined they were the type of guys who carried their offspring around in those strap-on marsupial pouches and at least attempted, on rare occasion, to change a diaper—well-meaning men but men nonetheless.

I decided enough was enough. I told the lady I wasn't fixing anything until she returned Boone's Frisbee. If she enjoyed vegetable sludge dripping on her slippers while she did the dishes, well, that was her call. My ultimatum did the trick. She walked over to the stack, retrieved the precious aerofoil, and handed it to Boone with another loud sigh. He bolted off like a captive freed from a makeshift dungeon after a childhood of suffering.

I tried to straighten the woman out on my identity.

"I don't work for Delaney, you know."

"Who?"

"Delaney. Willis Delaney. Mr. Willis. I am not under his employ."

"What, so you're some sort of contractor? I don't care as long as you fix the disposal and the other stuff."

"No, I used to be in law school. I should be a lawyer by now. I won't bore you with the details."

"Why would Mr. Willis send his lawyer to fix my sink? Are you the fellow who drew up that wretched power of attorney?"

I gave up. I had no tools but figured I would see what I could do. I opened the cabinet below the sink. A disgusting mess of food cud slopped out onto the linoleum. I bent down and saw that the drain hose had popped off the disposal flange. The lady didn't have a screwdriver, so I used a butter knife to tighten the clamp as best I could.

I eased into the role of competent handyman. Helpful advice was dispensed in a serious tone. "It should hold for a while. Go easy on it. Use lots of water when it's running. And no eggshells."

"You think I don't know how to use a disposal?" she said, and hustled me on to the next job while asking questions about Delaney. Was Mr. Willis a good man, deep down? Did Mr. Willis live up to his word? Mr. Willis this and Mr. Willis that. When I didn't respond in the affirmative, she beat herself up. She was dumb. She always trusted men like Mr. Willis and they always let her down. He was just like her third ex-husband, who'd left her for a saucy dental hygienist named Betty Chambliss. He ran off to the Delray Vista Village retirement community with this Chambliss tart, but not before he'd pocketed their emergency fund and defaulted on his alimony payments.

She pointed to a smoke detector high on the wall in the foyer. She claimed it beeped at odd times and attracted lizards. I figured I'd do this one last job, then make a run for it. I retrieved a stepladder from the garage and proceeded to change the batteries. Once she had me up in the air, she posed random questions without explaining the reasons for her curiosity.

"You from Colorado?"

"No, why do you ask?"

"Dunno. You sound like you might be from up that way, that's all . . . You like corn bread?"

"Yeah, it's pretty tasty as long as it's served with some-thing. Why?"

"No reason . . . How much do you reckon cab fare is from here to the airport?"

"About forty dollars. Why, you planning a trip?"

"No, no, goodness, at my age?"

After I plunged the toilet, I made for the front door. Before I could squeeze out, she handed me a stack of perforated pages torn out of a notebook.

"You tell Mr. Willis he needs to take care of these items pronto," she said.

I handed her back the top sheet because I suspected it to be her weekly shopping list. I promised to deliver the rest of grievance-laden pages to the elusive Mr. Willis as soon as I caught up to him.

I didn't make it back to the office until late afternoon. So Delaney had moved, but where to? Since I'd wasted precious time with all the pro bono home repairs, I decided to enlist professional help. I picked up the phone and called Harry's private investigator and all-round fixer, Angus Manning, an ex-navy SEAL who'd seen classified action in the Persian Gulf during Desert Storm.

An hour later, Manning emailed back. Delaney was in Florida. He'd bought a thirty-seven-foot Sky Bridge from a dealer in Tampa and was running fishing charters out of neighboring Clearwater. I opened the attachment. Sure enough, there was the paper trail, plain as day: boat title, slip lease, fishing permits, the works.

I perused Manning's information. Delaney must have set up his new charter business before he skipped town, because the documents contained his old Cedar Forest Grove address. I clicked on the link in Manning's email for Delaney's charter operation. It sent me to a third-party booking website. The particulars on Delaney's boat, the *Buzzard of the Brine*, consisted of nothing more than a couple of low-resolution photos of the vessel and a generic description of the available outings. I scrolled down hoping to find a way to contact Delaney. Nothing.

I sat there and stewed at the thought of the detestable

slumlord daring to abscond with Harry's money. Delaney's recent flight to the Sunshine State had bought him time, granted, but it was only a momentary reprieve. I emailed Manning back and asked him to book a flight to Florida. My mood immediately improved when I pictured Manning clambering aboard Delaney's ill-gotten vessel, barking out orders and demands while dunking the whimpering embezzler's fat head in a foot of filthy bilge water.

Chapter Seven

WHEN I ARRIVED HOME THAT EVENING, Whit wasn't there. A note on the kitchen counter read, "Gone to the launch event at the Bismarck Hotel. Leftovers in the fridge." She'd mentioned this function a few weeks ago—a Dupont Homes bash to promote a new development called the Lakes at Catalina—but between all the hours at the dealership and Harry's office, I'd forgotten about it. Since we hadn't seen much of each other the past few weeks, I decided to surprise her.

I drove downtown and parked on the street to avoid the valet parkers and their suspect custodianship. I snaked through the lobby of the hotel and took the staircase to the mezzanine, where the main ballroom was located. The event was in full swing. It was a walk-around affair with a chamber of commerce vibe. Boorish real estate agents were sniffing out free drinks like a herd of truffle swine. A crew of servers hastened around the room with trays of generic finger foods. They smiled, lips pursed, while they thrust their platters at the real estate people as if on a commission-based compensation structure. A few cub reporters from the lifestyle press stalked the room in search of anything remotely cogent to print, but they were being thwarted by the agents, who swarmed around the open bar with the frenzied purpose of five-year-old soccer players chasing halftime snacks.

At the rear of the room, a podium was positioned in the middle of a dais. Behind it, a projection screen hung down from the ceiling. In front of the stage, large poster boards with digital visualizations of the new development flanked the perimeter of the remaining space. The houses depicted on the posters resembled miniature Roman palazzos, and the lakes appeared to contain water fresh from the ice melt of the Dolomites. Fountains disgorged sparkling jets of crystalline liquid high into the azure sky while families of diverse ethnicity lolled about on the grassy shores. There was no doubt savvy creative types had taken much license when preparing these renderings. From what Whitney had told me, the area would bear scant resemblance to the picturesque, low-density vistas of the South Tyrol given Dupont Homes, a quantity-over-quality outfit, planned to pack in over a thousand cement-board boxes on the hundred and fifty acres of scrubland it had acquired on the southern outskirts of neighboring Fort Bend County.

I was scanning the room for Whit when a disheveled man with fine, tufty blond hair approached me holding two wineglasses, both full to the brim. His sparse follicles were blowing around in the jet stream of the air-conditioning like strands of wheat on an exposed rise.

"Howdy, name's Cecil. Cecil Pickett. MaXXLot Realty. Two X's, one L, all caps. XXL, as in big, you know, big-time. What do you think?"

"Catchy, you come up with it yourself?" I asked, guessing the mouthful to be an amateur's attempt at sloganeering.

"Huh? No, not that. I mean this." He motioned to one of the renderings.

"I like the fountains," I said. "Water's nice. Hope they can pull it off. They're going to need an industrial filtering system to keep it that clear though."

"You're telling me. I thought they'd skip the ponds after what happened at the last development."

"What happened?"

He moved closer. "You didn't hear?"

"No, must not have."

"Biiiig problems, my friend." He signaled to a girl dispensing miniature empanadas from a silver tray.

"Really? I heard they sold out pretty quick, especially the pond-view lots."

The empanada girl walked over. Cecil wrested the well-stocked tray from her hands and shooed her off with a backhanded wave. He deposited his wineglasses on the tray and proceeded to gobble up the tiny Mexican pastries, washing them down with extravagant swigs of cheap Shiraz.

"Don't tell anyone you heard it from me, but they had real problems with the water over there at . . . oh, what is it called?"

"Lago Imperial?" I knew the name because Whit had worked on the PR for that development. She had told me about a thin layer of algae that clogged up the fountains, but she made it sound like a minor problem.

"Yep, that's it. The environmental people were called in and everything. They threatened to close the whole place down."

"No kidding."

"Yeah, yeah, see, the plumbing contractor, he saved fifty grand by running a backup sewer line directly into the largest pond. Turned the swans shit-brown and killed all the bass. A good portion of the local kids got nasty rashes. One even got a bad case of E. coli. The boy had to have two feet of his lower intestines removed. There was a big lawsuit, and it comes out the Duponts were the ones who ordered the plumber to cut corners. The son, what's his name, the guy with the hair?"

"Ronnie?"

"Yeah, that's him. He was the one who made the sewer call. The only reason the parents settled for peanuts was because the kid admitted he'd downed a pound of ground beef the week before he got sick. Apparently, the boy's a real carnivore. Loves steak tartare."

"You don't say."

"Personally, it'd been my kid, I'd have promised him a trough full of raw meat if he kept his little trap shut."

Cecil cackled and punched my shoulder while he contemplated a comfortable retirement funded by the suffering of his offspring. He turned to his left and flagged down a waiter toting a platter of mini crab cakes. He snatched the tray from the man and tipped the crab cakes onto his empanadas. Once this blunt consolidation was complete, he scooped up his spoils, one after the other, flipping them into his cavernous mouth from an unreasonable distance with the entitled insouciance of a lazy emperor.

"Makes no difference to me if they put the Salton Sea in the middle of the damn place as long as I get my commissions before the shit hits the fan." He wiped his greasy fingers on his pants leg. "Never eat before one of these things," he advised, and belted down another quart of Shiraz.

By then, the staff and their savories were granting Cecil a wide berth. They tacked around him like he was a muddy shoal in shallow water. Whenever one of them got within thirty feet of us, he waved and yelled, "Hey, you, I know you see me over here."

All of a sudden, Cecil froze and fixed on something across the room. "Man, get a load of that. That's some primo tail over there. I wonder which one of those guys is hitting that?"

I looked over my shoulder to locate the primo tail. In the distance, with her back to us, was Whitney. She was talking to a guy I knew to be Ronnie Dupont and somebody else I didn't recognize.

My wife's honor besmirched by a debased clown who'd named his business after a fat man's sweat barrier. I deemed Cecil to have crossed the line by any relevant measure of decorum, so I decided to take some license with his profession.

"I'm surprised you people are here tonight," I said.

"Huh? Why?"

"You haven't heard?"

"Heard what?"

I shook my head. "The Supreme Court? The *Meeks* case? The opinion just dropped."

He shot me a puzzled look.

"The CPP—the Comprehensive Property Portal," I said, referring to the real estate industry's unholy cartel.

"Yeah, yeah. What about it?"

"Violates the Sherman Act. Nine–zero decision. Unanimous, which rarely happens these days, what with the partisan divide and all. Anyway, they decided it's an unlawful monopoly. Restraint of trade. You guys have to open the whole thing up. Beginning next week, anyone over sixteen who hasn't committed grand larceny gets unlimited access to the entire system. The experts are saying commissions will go down the drain, what with all the high school kids and their social media closing deals during recess. They guess you agents will be working for nothing but tips pretty soon."

"What? Are you serious? Jesus, man, this is terrible. Teenagers? Tips? Those goddamn communists! Is nothing sacred?"

I pointed out that the tsunami of adolescent competition about to come his way was actually the opposite of what Marx had in mind, but he chose to discount what he called my "socialist mumbo jumbo." I told him I wasn't surprised by his reaction. Everybody in America's a charter member of the Milton Friedman Fan Club when there's plenty of water in their moat.

"Friedman?" said Cecil. "The bleeding heart from the *New York Times*? What's he got to do with anything?"

"Forget Friedman," I said. "You remember what happened to the air traffic controllers? They used to drive Lincolns and vacation in Hawaii. That was before Reagan put his boot on their windpipes. Now they're lucky to be able to afford lease payments on a Ford Focus and a weekend in Niagara Falls." I was enjoying myself to a criminal degree.

Cecil brushed off my aeronautical analogy with a few loud snorts. He picked up his second glass of wine and drained it in one monstrous gulp, as if trying to inoculate himself against my bad news. He handed me his ravaged tray and pulled out his phone. He pecked at the screen with his greasy fingers, but he didn't have any reception.

"My god," bellowed Cecil. "The CPP? Surely it can't be over?" He strode off and tapped person after person on the shoulder to spread the bad news. Had they heard? No? Well, rumor was that Meeks and his lawyers had ruined it for everyone! The room came alive with a contagious agitation. People began to mill about, some heading for the exit in pursuit of a phone signal.

I stood there and took in the tableau of frenzied agents with slight unease. I had underestimated the brokers' attachment to their precious barrier to entry and fomented borderline panic. A man in extremely tight trousers and patent leather shoes sought reassurance from his burly companion, but the big fellow just put his hands in his pockets and shrugged. A well-dressed elderly gentleman in a fedora stumbled around the room, breathing through his mouth and cursing his fancy new cell phone. Several dazed women mistook me for a busboy and handed me their empty lipstick-stained glasses on their way out the door. A group of belligerent men had overwhelmed the helpless bartender and were removing bottles of wine from behind the makeshift bar. They elbowed each other to get at the lone corkscrew as if it were a T-shirt shot into the bleachers by a cheerleader toting one of those pneumatic air cannons.

I spotted Cecil across the room. He looked to have caught on to my ruse about Meeks and his top-notch legal representation. An angry posse of five had been assembled, with Cecil at the helm. They were pointing furiously in my direction. A misplaced urge, the madness of crowds. Their anger should have been directed inward, but they were blind to their avarice, reactionaries with no inclination to question the foul protectionism of their profession.

I didn't think it prudent to take a chance with these men who, mere minutes ago, had been forced to contemplate midlife career changes and indignant wives. So I headed in the opposite direction, into the thick of the crowd. I edged into the dense gel of land agents with the cautious reluctance of an explorer forced to wade into quicksand. I jostled my way through and emerged from the scrum not far from where Whitney stood.

Whit was giving Dupont a pep talk. He stared back at her, mouth open, brow furrowed. After each of her admonitions, he nodded and ran a chunky hand through his thick black hair. When she finished with him, she reached over and brushed a piece of lint off the wide lapel of his double-breasted suit. She hadn't seen me pop out of the crowd, so when I said her name, she turned around in confusion.

"Oh, hi. Why are you here? Is everything okay?"

"Yeah, everything's fine. I thought I'd surprise you."

"Oh. Okay. Well, I guess you succeeded."

Ronnie Dupont interrupted our awkward exchange.

"Hey, pal. Ronnie Dupont. How are you?" He thrust a large mitt at me.

I shook his hand. "Guy, the other half."

"Half of what?"

"Her." I nodded in the direction of my wife.

"Her? Huh. Oh, okay, so you're Guy the husband. Guy the guy!" He chuckled as if he'd stumbled upon some great irony.

"That's me."

"Sorry you haven't seen much of your wife the past few weeks, I've been working her pretty hard lately," he said, referring to Whit like she was a pit pony.

"No worries, I've been busy myself. Impressive renderings, by the way." For the record, I was being overly generous to the shameless puffery.

"Thanks. We wanted to tie the project to our European heritage."

His seamy familiarity with Whit was bad enough. Now this smug continental posturing. I indulged my less generous impulses.

"Isn't Dupont, with a capital D and without a space, the Acadian spelling?"

"Acadian?"

"Yeah, you know. The dispossessed Canadians. The Cajuns."

"Cajun? No, definitely not."

"I'm sure it is," I said. "That streamlined spelling reeks of immigrant practicality."

"Immigrants? What? No, sorry, buddy, you're way off. Our ancestors are from the East Coast."

"Everyone's an immigrant unless they got here via the Bering Strait."

"Huh?"

"I'm merely saying, how would one know, for sure?"

"My dad hired a team of genealogists, a firm from Salt Lake City, and I can assure you our lineage runs in a straight line from the great state of Delaware."

"Dupont is too common a name to nail down with any precision."

"I'm not sure I care for what you're implying, buddy."

"The name isn't unusual. The Gauls slapped it on anyone who lived within ten miles of a bridge."

He changed the subject. He questioned me about my employment. He asked if I was still flogging old beaters or whether I'd reenrolled in the paralegal academy. Before I could correct him, Whitney jumped in.

"What's going on? Where has everyone gone?"

"Not sure," I lied. "I think they're just anxious to see the presentation. They're a restless bunch. Plus they've had a few drinks."

"Well, we've got to get this show on the road," she said, and strode up the steps, onto the stage.

Whitney called the room to order, and what remained

of the crowd turned in her direction. Behind her, the projection screen sprang to life with an image of Ronnie Dupont and his father, Wayne. The pair stood shoulder to shoulder, their arms spread wide in a smarmy fashion. They gazed down on a little Photoshopped hamlet, which glowed with an artificial, almost biblical, luminosity. The devout theme continued at the bottom of the slide, where "The Lakes at Catalina—Welcome Home, Weary Renter" was scrawled in the gold script of suburban jewelers and high-end strip clubs.

Whitney had her "welcome home" spiel down. The Lakes at Catalina would be an affordable haven for first-time home buyers, and retirees with depleted IRAs, although Whit described them as "seniors possessed of sensible modesty." The houses would have concrete driveways and cozy attics stuffed with layer upon layer of thick insulation. Amenities would include a park with a playground, a community center with a pool, a dog park, pickleball courts, and an outdoor chess set.

The marketing plan was a single-pronged attack like the Germans at Antwerp. A blitz of billboards would be installed in strategic locations throughout the city. The double-breasted Duponts would leer down upon passing vehicles with their gluttonous, preacher-of-the-prosperity-gospel stares, beckoning motorists to visit the pastures of Catalina, where, in the treeless, flood-prone basin, they would find a frugal solace, albeit in exchange for inflated insurance premiums and brutal commutes.

By any measure of roadside promotion, this billboard intrusion would be an assault on all who took to the local byways for business or pleasure, not to mention a broadside at the legacy of Lady Bird Johnson and her lifelong campaign against highway blight. On top of that, the whole "piggybacking on the New Testament" vibe was a stretch given there was no credible evidence that Jesus, an unrepentant couch crasher, was ever possessed of a freehold interest. How long would it be before the Duponts appropriated the Lord's likeness itself in service of their mercenary aims? What was next, billboards starring Jesus, in his golden years, clad in a golf visor and a pair of hemp sandals, making sharp pivots on a pickleball court while his gray-flecked locks flopped about the collar of his embroidered tunic?

Whitney introduced Dupont and beckoned him onto the stage. She said he was the corporate director of something or other. He galloped up and bear-hugged her with the seedy enthusiasm of a drunk uncle at a high school graduation. It didn't help that Cecil was over in the corner yelling words of lecherous approval.

Whit finally wriggled free, and Dupont turned to face the audience. He spread his arms out in an impressively faithful imitation of his billboard persona, then started in on his well-rehearsed routine, reading from a piece of yellow paper he held out in front of him, elbows locked like a town crier.

The man standing next to me was lapping up the Dupont shtick. His hairless coconut was slick like a bowling lane, and he wore a skintight T-shirt that strained around the tops of his massive arms. A snake was coiled around his bicep, the tail disappearing under one of his tiny sleeves. The inker had done a crappy job on the scale pattern, so I was unable to identify the species of the snake. Whenever Dupont finished a sentence, the guy yelled out words of approval and encouragement.

"The park will have eight grills and two smokers," declared Ronnie.

"Hell yeah! Ron-nie, Ron-nie."

"The playground will have monkey bars with cushy foam mats underneath."

"True dat!"

"The pool will be cooled to ninety-five degrees all summer long."

"Go, RD, tell 'em, bruh!"

"The interfaith chapel at the community center will have oak pews and crimson seat cushions."

"Amen, Brother Dupont!"

"The outdoor chess set will have pieces the size of little people."

Somebody from the audience yelled, "Little people?"

"Yeah, bruh," roared the snake man. "You heard the man. Midgets! Giddyup and ride 'em, little cowboy!"

The snake man turned in my direction and stared as if to exhort me to get in on his shout-outs. I broke the awkward silence by asking him about his tattoo.

"What type of snake is that?"

"Diamondback."

"Did it hurt?"

"Nah. I was pretty high at the time."

"Had it long?"

"A few years. Got it after my dad died. He got bit by a rattlesnake."

"He died from a snakebite? Jesus. I mean, sorry."

"No, no, heart attack. The snake reminds me of him, that's all."

"How do you know Ronnie?"

"Don't remember, man. Think we were out one night and ended up partying together. The man's an animal. The three B's, you feel me?"

"B's?"

"Yeah, man, c'mon, bruh. Bottle service, blow, and biaatches!"

"Really? That Ronnie?" I turned my attention back to Dupont, who was droning on about the weekly one-bin recycling service. "He seems pretty tame."

"Naw, man, Ronnie D? Shit. That boy can ball. Damn straight."

"No kidding."

"Don't believe me? Check this out." He pulled out his phone, opened up YouTube, and clicked on a channel named Ronnie Rides Raw. He scrolled down a long list of Ronnie videos. I caught a few titles: "Ronnie Fellates a Magnum of Cristal," "Ronnie Moons the Cops," and "Ronnie Steers with His Feet."

He found the video he was looking for, posted by someone with the username "SlamDiggedy555." It was a compilation entitled "Ronnie Rides Raw—Greatest Hits." He selected it, and highlights came hard and fast, jarring bolts of tumult erupting on the rectangular screen. They each featured Ronnie in a different vehicular predicament. Ronnie jumping a median, his undercarriage alight with sparks as if atop a river of molten lava. Ronnie sideswiping a guardrail, then attempting an epic 360, his left arm out the window like a rodeo cowboy's. Ronnie asleep at the wheel of a Lambo, his head resting gently on a deflated airbag, the car impaled on a convenience store bollard. These scenes were interspersed with late-night news clips of dour reporters trying their best to unpack the carnage. Toward the end of the video, Ronnie's face was digitally stamped on the closing frames with a loud clank, his thick bread jowls and custard hair encircled by the words "Ronnie Rides Raw" in an angular font bringing to mind heavy metal album covers. There was a sad allure to the Rides Raw production, a sort of bacchanalian desperation permeating the Dupont mayhem that almost made me feel sorry for him.

"How's he not locked up, you know, three strikes and all?" I asked the guy.

"Pops is loaded. And straight connected. Got a team of top-notch lawyers, O. J. style. They ship Ronnie off to rehab for a few months, he comes back good as new. Takes it easy for a while, the records get expunged, then the old Ronnie's back, ridin' raw in no time!" The guy proceeded to preen like a flashy boxer, shuffling his feet in tiny bursts while doing a little dance with his elbows.

Dupont had started on about the plans for an eatery called the Catalina Chophouse. He hit his stride, intoning like a cross between Tony Robbins and a tenor with a nasty head cold. According to Dupont, the Chophouse would feature juicy slabs of prime beef, dry-aged for weeks in some sort of high-tech meat vault. He overplayed the dry-aging, losing the audience with talk of enzymes and aerobic bacteria. He tried to recover by touting the seafood entrées, some of which he claimed would be fished out of the pond in front of the restaurant. Half the audience clapped, the other half groaned, knowledge of Lago Imperial's sewer crime likely the reason for the disparate reactions.

Dupont went on and on about the Chophouse, calling it the "jewel in the Catalina crown." He said not only would the meat be tender and delicious, but every agent who sold a house in the development would get a lifetime membership in something called the Catalina Chophouse Club, or 3C Club for short. Dupont gave scant details, but I guessed it would involve some sort of flimsy membership card and hole-punch tallying system.

"All fine until you're one circle away from a bone-in rib eye and you forget to remove your wallet before washing your pants," I told Ronnie's friend.

The snake man glared at me like I'd just checked out his pecker from a neighboring urinal. He called me a "hater," a facile, much-favored trope of the zeitgeist. He was too psyched about meat for rational evaluation, and I knew this because he had taken to chanting "Meat! Meat! Meat!" After he snapped out of his meat trance, he told me he had to run because he was late for a blind date with a girl named Britnee. He made a point of telling me Britnee was spelled with two e's. I wished him good luck with this Britnee woman and her nonconformist spelling. He tried to get my phone number so we could engage in our own session of epic debauchery, but I lied and told him I was a newly converted Jehovah's Witness, and a night of the three B's sounded like it might fall under the prohibition against pagan celebration.

"Suit yourself, bruh," said the man. He turned and strode out of the ballroom, a fist raised in the air, yelling, "Here I come, lovely Britnee with the double e's."

Chapter Eight

WHITNEY SHOUTED FIRE IN THE CROWDED THEATER of our marriage three days before Angus Manning was set to fly to Florida to track down Willis Delaney and confront him about the money. I came home from the dealership one evening, opened the door, and there she was, crowding me, a look of determination on her face.

"Let's go out on the porch and talk," she said.

The last time she'd cornered me like this was to detail the specifics of a high-speed rear-end collision she'd described as a "small love tap." I grabbed a beer from the fridge, and we went out back. I considered the cost of replacement body panels while I wrestled the unwieldy Adirondack chairs into a position appropriate for serious conversation. I'd hauled the two totemic slabs of softwood back from an "Amish" furniture store up in Spring, a suburb north of town. My preference had been for a smaller, more portable option, but Whit had dismissed my practical concerns with a sharp wave and a shrill, conspiratorial laugh in the direction of Levi the salesman, a wily young Anabaptist, or so he appeared. I had my doubts about the authenticity of the enterprise on account of the shabbiness of the product—pine and nails instead of teak and screws?—but when I questioned the guy about the location and size of this supposed community of righteous woodworkers, Whit interrupted me.

"Guy, leave this nice young man alone," she said, her tone playful yet thick with instruction. Reason hopeless, I dropped my line of inquiry, at which point a triumphant smirk crept across Levi's dull mug, his path to a sale now as open as that of a halfback running a wheel route into busted coverage. Despite not being able to pin down the slippery puritan, it did nothing to shake my belief that when business hours were over, he'd ride a salesman's high out of the shop, speed home in a late-model automobile, shed his drab garb, and tune in to secular programming on a high-definition flat-screen.

The stifling August night enveloped us in its clammy breath. The mosquitoes were out and attacked in endless, seemingly coordinated waves. I doused my exposed skin with toxic levels of DEET and tried to figure out if the globs of mud stuck to the eaves were termite tunnels or merely the start of a hornets' nest.

I was in the middle of this entomological puzzling when she laid it on me. She told me she had thought long and hard about things, and it would be best, for both of us, if we engaged in something she described as a "trial separation."

"A what?"

"A trial separation."

"No, I heard you. It's just . . . what are you talking about? Where did this come from? You can't be serious."

"I've been thinking about it for a while now."

"You have? Since when? Well, there's no such thing under Texas law. You're either married or divorced."

"Guy, I don't care about the law. I'm saying we need to spend time apart. I need to figure some things out."

After I recovered enough to construct a cogent sentence, I questioned her about the source of her discontent. She answered with a detailed assessment of my career progress or, in her estimation, lack thereof.

"I thought we'd have built something by now, be established, own our own place, but you're still selling cars, and we're still renting *this*." She gestured to our modest but adequate Victorian-style shotgun. "And what you're doing over at Harry's firm, that whole thing makes me nervous. You're not a lawyer, you know. You're not even in law school anymore. Fat lot of good all that tuition money turned out to be."

"My class credits are still valid. They're like casino chips."

"What?"

"They have no expiration date, and competing establishments will take them as tender."

"Listen to me. We've hit a rut. I think it would do both of us good to spend some time apart."

I was blindsided and threw words around with the abandon of a drunk trying to convince a cop not to haul him to jail for DUI. I explained ruts. Something about how you don't hit a rut, you drive into it, or you possibly make your own if you're mired in soft ground and are careless with the gas pedal.

"Forget ruts. The point is you're stuck. You're thirty next year and you still can't commit to anything. I should have known when I met you. Six years of college! Six majors!"

"So? Aristotle didn't quit the Academy at twenty-two to get some boring day job. He stayed another fifteen years."

She was unmoved by the great polymath's extended

study amongst the olives. "So now you're Aristotle?" She listed my majors as though reading from a rap sheet. "General studies, regular history, military history—"

"Switching majors was a small part of it. I've told you a hundred times, it was soccer. Seven days a week. Carnegie had nothing on Coach Bostic."

"—literature, economics. How many's that? I think I'm missing one."

"Business. Marketing, to be specific. But only for a month, until I realized it was nothing but soul-corrupting sortilege."

"And don't even get me started on that semester you took off to play poker."

"That was before we met. Dare I remind you my winnings paid for our honeymoon? Puerto Vallarta's not the French Riviera, I admit, but if I'd had more time to work out my—"

"The other night, I heard what you did. You ruined the entire event. Half the people left before the presentation started. And the wine bill was triple what we budgeted."

"You weren't there. That Cecil guy said terrible things. And a case like *Meeks* isn't much of a stretch. I give it less than five years before they're all working at a car wash."

"Who? What? Ugh, it doesn't matter, forget it."

"Well, what is it then? Is there someone else?"

"Seriously? No, of course not. I can't believe you'd ask me that."

I noticed a pair of hornets appear around the mud humps above our heads and made a mental note to chip off the foundations of their compact earthen abode before their indefatigable labor built it into a full-sized base from which to launch hostilities against us. Anyone who's wondered how assiduous toil built the great pyramids or the hotels of Las Vegas should watch these alien creatures chew their lair into existence over the course of a few weeks. A broom handle would do the trick if I climbed up on the porch railing. Or I could try to spray it off with a hose, a cleaner and safer option assuming the water pressure was adequate.

Whitney had gone quiet. She gazed off into the distance with the plaintive visage of a newly widowed prairie woman. I couldn't quibble with her assessment from the standpoint of where things stood at that moment, so like a politician up for reelection in a recessionary cycle, I focused on the future. I told her once I recovered the money from Delaney, I'd see about going back and finishing my final year of law school. If that all worked out, I'd take the bar, then decide what to do—maybe practice law, maybe do something else. After we were set up, she could quit Dupont Homes to focus on her interior design.

"Hell, if you want, we'll move back to Beaumont and you can take some graduate classes at Lamar, become a Cardinal." I told her I was sure the ladies of Southeast Texas would kill to have the services of a designer with her refined taste. Admittedly, this was a fair amount of speculation considering I'm no great connoisseur of quality interior finishes.

She listened with her arms crossed in a stoic position of resistance, her only movements to swat insects away from her petite ears.

"Guy, you're not hearing me. Beaumont? I'm not going back there. Why would that help anything? It's you, me, us, everything's off."

"Babe, I admit, I've been a tad lackadaisical these past few years. I've gotten off course. But things are going to change. Just give me a few months to prove it to you. Once I get the Delaney money back, we'll have a hundred grand in the bank."

"Wait, what? You didn't tell me your share was going to be a hundred thousand dollars!"

"I didn't want to get your hopes up."

Whit leaned back and focused on me with an uncomfortable intensity. When she finally spoke, I sensed a weakened resolve.

"You should've . . . I don't know, Guy. Why couldn't you . . . All this time and now . . ."

Discerning an opportunity, I jumped in, entreating her to reconsider. I sensed real deliberation in her eyes, but when she next spoke, her words belied any sort of internal conflict.

"Guy, please don't. It's not just about money. It's about more than that. I was really young when we met, just a kid back then. Now I'm older, and I don't know, I feel different about a lot of things. Something is buzzing around inside of me, and I can't quiet it down. Every time I try, it comes back, like, more intense. I even went to the doctor a few weeks ago to make sure it wasn't serious, you know, like cancer."

She held her hand to her chest in what I guessed was an attempt to show me the general location of the buzzing. She said she'd had a chest X-ray, an MRI, and a few other more invasive tests, which, thank goodness, all came back clean. She was a bit of a hypochondriac, but even for her, this comprehensive battery was over the top.

We argued for a while about the separation business. I needed more firepower, so I referenced a few texts in relation to my arduous journey these past few years: Job's arbitrary torture, Homer's great saga, and a few other works of extended suffering, mainly Russian. But she just sat there and waited me out, impervious to the classic tales of pointless affliction. I begged her not to make any rash decisions, but she ignored my desperate pleas.

"I'm spending the rest of the week at Brie's place," she said, laying out the first step of her well-thought-out plan. "She's got a futon in her spare room."

"I wouldn't recommend that," I said.

"Recommend what?"

"Sleeping on a futon. The Japanese are a space-constrained people, and even they only resort to using them in emergencies. They are not built with American frames or constitutions in mind."

"What are you saying, Guy? I'm going to break the thing?"

"Not at all. I'm merely pointing out the mattress will be cheap and thin. It won't provide sufficient support for your spine. You'll end up back at that chiropractor again."

"Don't make this any harder than it already is. I'll be gone for a week. Please find a new place by then."

We went back inside, and she retrieved a sheet of red stickers onto which she'd written my first and last names in block capitals. My last name? Really? Wasn't that a bit over the top? She ignored me and began to walk around the house, stopping on occasion to slap stickers on my meager possessions with the annoyed impatience of a sheriff executing a writ of foreclosure. She told me I was required to remove the tagged items, posthaste, along with my clothes and books. Everything else was required to stay put.

After she left for Brie's, I grabbed another beer and went back out onto the porch. I tried to look on the bright side. There wasn't one. The only remotely positive development was I wouldn't have to spend the next couple of weeks dealing with body shop estimates and parts shortages. But after no more than ten seconds, the insurance panacea wore off, and I fell back into a deep funk.

My neighbors a few houses down were spit roasting a goat, the succulent smell of cabrito wafting over the fence. I was tempted to join them. I had an open invitation. *"Ven cuando quieras!"* Come over whenever, they'd told me a few months ago. I was hosing down the driveway when the family began to set up in the alley for their daughter Consuela's quinceañera, the sacred Latin rite of womanhood. The next thing I knew, I was chugging ice-cold Modelos and spinning little señoritas around, admiring their colorful dresses as they shot across the alley like wayward tumbleweeds. I even gave the old padre, Emilio, a few twirls and a kiss on his hairy cheek. When, after at least a six-pack, I dug into my wallet and mistook a fifty-dollar bill for a five, placing it in Consuela's rusty quinceañera bucket to much enthusiasm from the crowd, my lifetime invitation to all future Suarez family functions was sealed.

Part of me wanted to join my friends for a night of cold cervezas and stringy goat flesh, but I decided I'd just bring the whole gathering down with my self-indulgent melancholy. After I finished my beer, I went inside and grabbed a broom. I climbed onto the railing and made a feeble attempt to dislodge the mud nest, but I missed and took a big chip of paint off the wood instead. Before I had time to reflect on my incompetence, I was beset on all sides by angry insects bent on defending their partially constructed homestead. I fended off the attack as best I could in my sad, slightly buzzed state but soon took a direct hit on the neck from one daring kamikaze. At that point, thinking the night couldn't possibly get any worse, I went inside, grabbed a bag of peas from the freezer, placed it on the throbbing wound, and went to bed.

Chapter Nine

MY DIRE MARITAL SITUATION NECESSITATED a change of plans. What if Manning wasn't able to "talk" sense into Delaney? Then I'd be back to square one with no good news to report to Whitney. No, the only prudent course of action was to hit Delaney with a lawsuit to straitjacket his burgeoning charter operation and force him to come to terms. I called Preston Rusk, and he agreed to sign his name to the petition and attend the perfunctory court hearing to obtain a temporary restraining order.

Next, I booked a flight to Florida and purchased a pair of all-day excursions on Delaney's boat. Meanwhile, Barb arranged for a licensed process server to accompany me on my Delaney outing. My plan was simple. Instead of Manning, I would be the one to confront Delaney. On the deck of his new boat, Delaney would run straight into the long arm of Texas law. That is, assuming I remembered to take my seasickness pills. Otherwise, I'd be bent over the gunwale all morning, donating my breakfast to the unfathomable depths.

Next up, the fact that I was now officially homeless. I suppose "officially" wasn't the right word since it was unlikely I'd be woken up at a bus stop by a census worker, but it felt official nonetheless. The first night of my exile, I slept on the love seat in Harry's office. I had to dangle my legs off the end, over a big padded bolster, and woke up with excruciating pain in my anterior ligaments. The second night I tried an air mattress on the break room floor, but I was awoken around midnight by a cleaner, working the night shift, jamming an orbital floor buffer into my rib cage. On the morning after night three, when Barb found me sacked out in the corner of the reception area with a large bag of Styrofoam coffee cups under my head, I realized I had no choice but to rent an apartment.

I wanted something short-term. Nothing fancy. Three months was about what I needed to get things in order, give or take. I called around to a few modest buildings, but none offered terms of less than six months. One lady even got all up in my business.

"Three months?" she asked.

"Yep."

"Why three months?"

"That's kind of personal."

"Come on, sugar. I'm not the IRS."

"All right, fine. My wife wants a trial separation."

"Separation? What'd you do?"

"Not sure, exactly. My career's a bit off track. And she got upset about a little trouble I caused at one of her events. I made up a court case—*Meeks*—but I only started that rumor because some real estate clown named Cecil commented on her rear end."

"What? You gonna sit back and let this real estate man steal your girl?"

"No, no, that's not what's happening."

"Move you right out so she can move Mr. Cecil Meeks

right in?"

"Cecil Meeks? There's no Cecil Meeks. He's not moving anywhere."

"Let this Meeks cat paw your precious wife at his prime properties?"

"There are no properties. They will be no pawing."

"Sugar, you're in serious denial. Look, we don't do three-month leases. Best advice I can give you is to fight for your woman. Show this Cecil Meeks you mean business."

She hung up. I half-wished Cecil Meeks existed. Then at least I'd have a flesh-and-blood opponent to spar with. As it stood, I was up against veiled discontent, the source no easier to pinpoint than a carbon monoxide leak in a dark basement.

Barb overheard my frustrated murmurings and told me I was aiming too low. If I wanted a short-term deal, I needed to try a more upscale place that catered to a corporate clientele. So I swung by an apartment building not far from the office, an eight-story edifice with a lifeless façade of tan stucco. It had a made-up name, a corporate portmanteau—AmeniLuxe or some equally objectionable asininity.

The girl who showed me around the AmeniLuxe was named Liz Pendergrass. She was a fit, twenty-something go-getter with straight, shoulder-length black hair and a pair of ebony-framed glasses perched on her angular nose. Her shiny silk shirt was tucked into a tight pencil skirt, and she strode around with purpose in three-inch tan heels.

Liz Pendergrass had a businesslike demeanor to go with her businesslike ensemble. I imagined her that morning, parked in front of a mirror, applying her intricate eyeliner and dialing in her rental routine for maximum severity. I hadn't been there a minute before she started to work me over.

"You know it's a lessor's market, right?"

"What do you mean by that, exactly?" I asked.

"At present, demand far exceeds the available units."

"Oh, so you don't have anything available?"

"Yes, of course we do, but I'm just letting you know in case you're thinking I'll offer you a deal."

"So there aren't any deals available?"

She moved her head from side to side as if to seek support from a sympathetic audience. "I didn't say that."

She grilled me at length before she would even agree to give me a tour of the place. How did my credit report look? Did I have a criminal record? And not just felonies, what about Class A misdemeanors and deferred adjudications? Did I own any large animals or noisy birds?

"Large animals?"

"Correct. The checklist used to say 'large dogs,' but we like to cover our bases."

I was confused. "So you're concerned about someone trying to move in, I don't know, an alpaca?"

"A what?"

"Furry thing, long neck. Basically a blunt-nosed llama."

"You never know."

"Really? Where would it live? In a pen in the parking garage? And where would it eat, out there, by your sign?" I pointed at an expanse of lawn bordering the street that, while lush, didn't appear sufficient to nourish a highland grazer in perpetuity, although, I admit, I'm no expert on Peru's source for its world-famous blankets.

"I've seen stranger things," said Liz Pendergrass, affirming her belief that all was possible when it came to the AmeniLuxe and the animal kingdom.

She kept on with her checklist. Was I partial to heavy footwear? Did I have allergies or epileptic conditions? How was my hearing?

"What do those things have to do with anything?" I asked her.

"Which ones?"

"Well, how about epilepsy?"

"It's on the checklist."

"What about allergies?"

"How would you like to hear your neighbor sneezing through the walls?"

"So the walls are thin?"

"I didn't say that."

She didn't say this, she didn't say that. Liz Pendergrass was beyond cagey.

"What about my hearing? What's that about?"

"How is it?"

"I'm not sure you're allowed to ask that."

"Why not?"

"Heard of the ADA?"

"The what?"

"The Americans with Disabilities Act?"

"Are you disabled?"

"No, but you're not allowed to ask these medical questions, it's against federal law."

"Well, they're on the checklist, so . . ."

The sacrosanct checklist! Carved in slate tablets and lowered to earth by some pedantic deity. Kafka was digging his way out of a loamy grave at that very moment to sneak a peek at the damn thing.

After an additional ten minutes of pointed interrogation and note-taking in the margins of the checklist, Liz deemed me worthy to tour the property and view a couple of available units, although from the severe expression on her face, I'd barely made the cut.

Liz said we would start off with the gym. I told her not to bother because I wasn't a big fan of wanton grunting or the smell of other people's sweat. She brushed off my objections with a sharp "It's protocol." While we walked, she reeled off the names and specs of the fitness machines like a robot technician inventorying spare parts.

Liz beckoned me through a glass door and said, "Please excuse the mess."

I walked into the gym and Liz followed. Several pitted foam tiles from the false ceiling sat in a pile by a row of elliptical machines. A man was on a stepladder, rooting around in the cavity above. Another guy stood below, peering up into the hole. The man on the ladder was a captive audience, and his partner was taking full advantage.

"For months, the doctors thought it was heart related. I had every test under the sun. Wired me up with electrodes, made me run on one of those." He pointed to a fancy treadmill the ladder man had no way to see. "Can you believe? I'd never even heard of a rotator cuff. The doctor asked me about my hobbies. Said this type of thing is common among softball pitchers and kite people. You know, gusts of wind catching them unawares."

The ladder man was nothing to us but a pair of blue Dickies and steel-toed work boots. After a brief pause, the torsoless specter spoke, his voice muffled by the thick insulation lining the space above.

"'Member I told you about Darryl, Sue Ann's boy? Same thing. He was roping a steer up on the ranch in San Saba, and the damn animal near ripped his arm clean off. He still ain't right, but that may be on account of the shingles."

The man on the ground saw us approaching. He became self-conscious about his idle chatter, mumbled under his breath, and walked out the door, leaving the other man high and dry in the rafters. When the ladder man didn't get a response to the story of rodeo Darryl's sorry predicament, he yelled, "Robby, hey, Robby, you there, bud?"

We ignored the man and tiptoed around his ladder to conceal our presence. Liz led me through an automatic sliding door that opened onto a rectangular courtyard. A swimming pool was down at one end, surrounded by slatted chaises and stunted trees lodged in large terra cotta pots. Poolside, an old lady with a square trunk encased in a flowery one-piece bathing suit was rubbing sunscreen into the leathery back of a bald man of similar age, presumably her husband, but who could be sure? For all I knew, they'd bumped into each other at a breakfast buffet, and this was where fate had deposited them.

The sunscreen bottle must have been almost empty because it took several violent squeezes by the woman's wrinkly talons to impel even a modicum of the SPF 10 to splatter out onto the man's grainy husk.

"Don't forget my neck, and get it in the creases real good," he barked at her.

Liz Pendergrass seemed flustered by this scene of geriatric lubrication. She went into a long dissertation about the demographics of the tenants. She claimed the average age was late thirties. Suspecting a skewed distribution, I asked a few follow-up questions. When I inquired about the median age, she lowered her head and scrutinized me over the rim of her glasses like I was engaged in corporate espionage. After a few seconds of this uncomfortable reproach, she hustled me away from the pool to a large metal door.

Next up was the underground parking garage, a vast, winding concrete bunker where I guessed most of the assaults and other serious crimes took place. An impressive array of halogens lined the walls, but they were nothing but security theater given the slew of dark alcoves impervious to the high-lumen beams. I asked Liz about the incident statistics for the bloc: burglaries, car thefts, aggravated batteries, and other common malfeasances. She was evasive, claiming the numbers were nothing abnormal for a property the size of the AmeniLuxe. When I asked her about the pepper spray attached to her key chain, she claimed it was for personal use, something about half-marathons and small dogs with pointy teeth.

We pressed on, up to the third floor, where we padded down an endless hallway to a one-bedroom. Liz said it had fresh carpet and new appliances. She opened the door, and I was hit with an artificial yet not altogether unpleasing aroma of synthetic fibers. Unfortunately, the place itself was tiny, closer to the size of a walk-in closet in a McMansion than a habitation that had passed muster with the city's commercial building department.

"It will look bigger with furniture," Liz advised, reading my mind.

"What's going on with all this?" I motioned to the loose wires hanging out of the ceiling.

"We're installing new light fixtures."

"What happened to the old ones?"

"Oh, you know." She pivoted in her heels and pointed out the window at my "stunning view," which was nothing more than a messy weave of tree branches and leaves.

Liz was being evasive again, but I wasn't going to complain, the fresh illumination and all. I told her I was ready to do a deal, assuming her terms were reasonable and the paperwork didn't contain overly broad indemnification clauses. We headed back to the leasing office, where she played hardball.

"I can't do any deals on three-month leases," she said. I monitored her closely for signs of weakness. No luck, Liz Pendergrass was giving nothing away. I sensed some subconscious faculty had laid bare my brink-of-divorce desperation and imbued her with the confidence to press her advantage. Having no other options, I agreed to her terms and wrote a check for the security deposit and the first month's rent.

I borrowed a Silverado from the dealership and moved in the next day. Warren in parts was a stand-up guy. He let the salesmen take the truck home, no questions asked, as long as we brought it back with a full tank of gas. After I hauled in my boxes, I drove to a sporting goods store and bought a fold-up camping chair. Next, I swung by a grocery store and gave a bored guy in the dairy department twenty dollars for a few empty milk crates. He was suspicious at first but relaxed when he realized I wasn't some tweaker out to plunder his spray-cream inventory.

According to Liz, the place was approaching full occupancy, but I had yet to cross paths with anyone except the octogenarian tanners. I navigated the vast complex, crates in hand, scanning my keycard three times on the way to my floor. Checkpoints at every turn, it felt like visiting a retirement home—the wing where they keep the combative element locked down and sedated to assuage the unease of the masses.

I arranged my newly acquired items as if settling in for a weekend of outdoor leisure. I unfolded the camping chair, balanced my laptop on top of the milk crates, and tested my new entertainment setup. The haphazard amalgamation of plastic rods and rough bolts of green nylon fabric creaked ominously under my weight, but it held up and was, dare I say, serviceably comfortable.

I got up and hiked the window open. I peered out, and my eyes struggled to adjust. A row of modest timber-sided houses sat several stories below, their bantam backyards lit up like prison quadrangles by the building's megawatt security lights. I noticed a man standing in one of the back-yards. Clad in nothing but gray nylon shorts and flip-flops, he hovered over a black kettle grill, a pair of tongs in hand. Four large steaks sizzled away on the grill. I recognized the healthy cuts, even at my considerable distance, to be T-bones. He was flipping the meat every ten seconds or so, pausing between each flip to inspect the slab of protein flopping about in his tongs. The flipping was excessive, definitely no way to get a good char.

"Hey there," I yelled.

The man searched around, trying to locate the voice.

"Up here." I waved.

He finally spotted me. "'Sup, bro," he shouted, in a tone that made me think he wasn't thrilled to make my acquaintance.

I debated whether to give the man my opinion on his grilling technique, maybe offer a few helpful pointers. I decided against it given male sensitivities to advice on crude arts. If the man wanted to flip his T-bones, let him flip his T-bones. Instead, I yelled that I was his new neighbor, and it was nice to meet him. I realized I was stretching the definition of "neighbor," but I couldn't think of another word to describe our adjacency. Should I wrap a beer in a towel and throw it down to him in a gesture of goodwill? Probably not. I exhausted my reserve of small talk at the same time the man's steaks were done. I wished him happy eating, closed the window, pumped up my air mattress, and called it a night.

Chapter Ten

THE FOLLOWING WEDNESDAY, A CAB PULLED UP to the AmeniLuxe to take me to the airport for my flight to Tampa. I opened the door of the sedan, threw my suitcase and backpack onto the backseat, and hopped in. The driver was supine shouldered and simian hairy. He wore a neon-green fleece vest over a pink Hawaiian shirt in a rather garish attempt at climatic hedging. After mumbling a curt greeting, he tucked into a box of sausage kolaches that sat open on the passenger seat.

I'd hoped for a quiet ride because of my aversion to conversing with strangers without seeing their lips move, but the driver had other ideas. After a couple of blocks and a few askance glances in his rearview mirror, the man began to yap away. He told me how much he hated driving to the "little airport," the flat-rate fare wholly inadequate for his trouble. He described the route as a "goddamn nightmare," what with the clogged freeways and having to navigate through what he claimed were "some of the shittiest neighborhoods in the city."

"We should get combat pay for going anywhere south of 610," he said, and honked at an old lady in a Lexus who

94

was attempting to merge into our lane.

I held my breath in anticipation of the next outburst, but thankfully, the driver went quiet when I didn't second his grievances. He resumed downing kolaches, each one disappearing in no more than two bites, and tuned the cab's radio to a talk show, murmuring approvals when a caller described the ills that had befallen the country since Nixon abandoned the gold standard.

We neared the airport, and I thought I was in the clear. But when we stopped at a red light, the driver piped up again.

"See that?" He gestured out the window.

"What?"

"Over there. The mini-mart."

I looked over at the establishment. It was buzzing with activity. Patrons ambled in and out of the store in a seemingly endless stream, the procession reminiscent of a medieval trading post on market day. I was about to turn back when I noticed two teenage girls with long burnished hair, in crop tops and faded denim, planted under what had to be one of the last working pay phones on the planet. The pair was having what could best be described as an urban picnic. They sat cross-legged on a raggedy purple blanket, a large bag of Doritos and a half-gallon plastic jug of Ocean Spray cranberry juice perched between them. They drank big gulps from their Styrofoam cups, then refilled them from the unwieldy jug. One of them made intermittent entries in a spiral-bound notebook while her companion nodded in approval.

"Yeah, I see it," I said, quite taken with the scene of community.

"Buddy of mine flew back on a red-eye from Vegas. Stopped in there on the way home for a pack of cigarettes.

Before he could even get out of his car, these guys pull up in a pickup, box him in. One of them flashes a pistol, tells him to stay put if he knows what's good for him. The others unload two large floor jacks from the bed of the truck. Next thing he knows, they're going to work on his Camaro with a pair of impact drivers. Stole his wheels clean off the hubs in less than a minute. All professional, like they were a NASCAR pit crew or something. Left him high and dry, sitting on cinder blocks."

"What did he do?" I said, the thought of the man's exposed brake rotors shimmering in the moonlight striking me as highly amusing.

"What could he do? Bought his smokes and called the cops. Before they showed up, which took them almost an hour, he was robbed a second time. Some white-trash girl with orange hair and a big bubble butt stuck a nine-millimeter in his face, made him hand over all the cash in his wallet. Stuffed it between her tits and sashayed off. When the police got there, they didn't do a damn thing, just questioned him, all suspicious like. He told them all he was after was a pack of smokes and anyway, wasn't this America, and didn't he have the god-given right to engage in commerce unmolested, no matter the hour? They laughed in his face. One of them was a real comedian. Told him he should've tried the patch, that if he had, he'd still have wheels to roll home on. Can you believe that?"

No, I couldn't, actually. The story sounded fishy, like maybe the man had traded his cash for an hour of carnal exercise with the bubble-butt girl, then experienced a nasty case of buyer's remorse, maybe even herpes. I suppose it was possible it was a setup, and while the man and his "date" rustled around in the bushes, a team of accomplices went to work on his car. The part about the law-enforcement patch ridicule sounded legitimate though, given what I knew about police attitudes toward avoidable victimhood. When I presented my theories to the driver, he shook his head and emitted a noise approximating the rushing sibilance of a punctured bicycle tire.

I looked out the window again. The picnic had been relocated a few feet westward by a guy in a white muscle shirt and baggy jeans, who was yelling indecipherable obscenities into the receiver of the pay phone. The girls shot him pubescent glares of disdain while they munched their chips, one after the other, their fingertips stained yellow by the Cool Ranch flavoring.

Questions filled my head as I watched the girls. Why weren't they in school? Why this gas station for a midmorning, alfresco get-together? What were they writing in that notebook? One of them saw me staring, smiled coyly, and gave me a reluctant wave of the type designed to ward off impending awkwardness.

The cabdriver noticed the girl waving and became visibly indignant. "Jesus Christ, look at that. They're trying to turn tricks in broad daylight, the little hussies."

Little hussies? Turning tricks? I leaned forward. "How about you shut your mouth. And get a new wardrobe while you're at it." I opened my door, grabbed my luggage, and jumped out. The driver, confused, rolled down the passenger-side window. I threw the cab fare at him, sans tip, and snatched the box of kolaches from the passenger seat. I stared him straight in the eye, daring him to object, but as I expected, he didn't say a word. I turned and walked in the direction of the girls, who were observing the unfolding scene with suspicion. The light turned green, and the cab pulled away while the driver yelled at me for "stealing" his sausages.

I strolled up to the girls, kolache box in hand. I realized I didn't really know what to say. They sat there, frozen, trying to make sense of my sudden presence. The uncomfortable silence was making them nervous. Or was it my mawkish expression? I decided I should say something.

"Oh, hi there. Nice day, isn't it? I saw you guys, and I, well, I thought you might want these for your picnic. I mean for whatever you're doing here. Anyway, here you go."

I opened the box, lowered it into their field of vision, and showed off the contents like they were the Crown jewels. Inside were two soggy kolaches stuck to the grease-stained cardboard. I was relieved they would each get a whole one—that I wouldn't have to ask them to share.

Sadly, my offering didn't impress the girls. The one with the notebook spoke up in a weary voice.

"Hmm, uh, we're vegans, but thanks anyway."

The other girl chimed in with words of agreement, her cranberry teeth on full display. "Yeah, we saw that movie. About the chickens. Oh. My. God. That's some messed-up shit."

I wondered how long ago they'd made this life-altering commitment to consume only plant-based proteins. I wanted to be charitable. Still, I guessed two weeks, three max.

The girl with the notebook spoke up again. "Maybe somebody over there might want them." She motioned to no one in particular, but that seemed to be the point.

Deflated, I wished them long and happy meatless lives and walked off. I shoved the soggy box into an overflowing trash can situated by the door to the store, having to exert a substantial amount of force to get it to stay put.

I was done with cabs for the day. Apparently, long periods in a seated position listening to AM radio attracted extreme personalities bent on imbecility. The airport was only a mile away, a straight shot down Broadway. To get to the passenger drop-off area, I'd have to navigate a ramp that rose sharply above the surrounding neighborhood, but how hard could that be?

The usually mundane airport journey became novel and peculiar from the vantage of a pedestrian. I passed countless low-slung apartment complexes billeted behind ominous wrought-iron fences. Little children watched me with perplexed stares from behind the bars. Several people honked when they passed by. A few were short, friendly beeps, others long, sinister blares. The occupants of a pickup whooped at me as if I were on the last mile of a marathon. When a Metro bus rumbled by, however, the greetings were not as convivial—I counted at least three middle fingers proud behind the tinted glass of the rear window.

I was halfway up the ramp when a car pulled over a few feet in front of me. The driver was a tanned man with a full head of neatly combed silver hair. He rolled down his window and spoke in a concerned, leave-no-man-behind tone, while the woman in the passenger seat stared at me uneasily.

"Hey, son, my goodness, you've worked up a sweat, you need a ride?" He motioned to his companion, and she fished a few tissues out of a square box ensconced in an intricate knit cover.

A member of the greatest generation offering brave assistance! Rude people behind us honked. The man ignored the honking, acting like he didn't hear a thing. Either that or the volume on his elaborate hearing aids was turned all the way down.

I wiped my forehead and thanked the couple but declined the ride. I soldiered on, determined to finish the last few hundred yards of my airport pilgrimage unaided. It wasn't long before my right hand went numb from the vibrations of the plastic wheels of the suitcase rolling over the grooved concrete. To save my shirt from additional sweat damage, I took it off and tied it around my waist.

I summited the ramp, and my destination came into view. The scene was a chaotic amalgam of vehicles, people, and luggage. As I approached the entrance to the terminal, I fended off the high-pressure sales pitches of the eager skycaps idling by the curbside check-in.

I walked into the expansive hall and felt a blast of air wash over me. The air was frigid and biting. I looked down to see goose bumps all over my exposed flesh. Exposed flesh, sweet Jesus! I turned around and saw the spurned porters laughing laughs of sweet revenge. I threw my shirt back on and entered the security line farthest from the scene of my licentious display.

The stain of my exhibitionism followed me through the X-ray machine and onto the concourse. A little girl clutching an enormous stuffed armadillo pointed me out like I was an amorous zoo animal servicing his submissive cage-mate. Her parents glared in my direction and ushered her along. They promised teeth-rotting snacks and other goodies if she kept her little legs moving and averted her gaze from the "bad man."

I sat and waited for my flight to board, my fellow passengers granting me a generous three-seat buffer. I was about to scan my boarding pass when a blond TSA lady walked up. She flashed her badge and asked me if I would like to follow her. I said I wasn't necessarily against it but my preference would be to complete the boarding process because I had pressing legal matters to attend to in the Tampa Bay area. She must have interpreted my response to be evidence of surreptitious intent, because her words became more concise and her tone terser.

"Follow me." She pointed to a narrow opening next to the departure gate across the hall, where a group of animated men wearing giant sombreros and slurring out exaggerations were waiting to board a flight to Cancún.

Chapter Eleven

THE TSA WOMAN ESCORTED ME DOWN a hallway and into a small room with one of those obligatory wire-meshed windows embedded in the door. In the middle of the room sat a metal desk surrounded by four flimsy folding chairs. A Houston Police Department officer occupied one of the chairs. The cop had loose yellow smoker skin and saurian eyes barely visible behind droopy eyelids. His chair flexed under his girth when he turned to take a look at me. A brown paper bag sat at his feet, and he was flipping through a magazine entitled *Ducks Eternal*.

On the wall behind the cop hung a photo of President Barack Obama, and next to the president was one of a government lady with bristly salt-and-pepper hair and a name I remembered sounded like ice cream. I'd have spent the rest of the day trying to guess her ice-cream name had it not been for the helpful inscription:

Janet Napolitano
Secretary
US Department of Homeland Security

The lady motioned to one of the empty chairs. I crossed the room, and Obama stared straight ahead with executive dignity, while Napolitano's dark, hardened gaze fixed on me, meting out intimidation. Napolitano's presence confused me because she didn't even work for the feds anymore. She had resigned and been replaced by a guy whose name was too quotidian to remember, a major terrorist attack on his watch probably the only event that would etch his identity into the American subconscious.

The cop removed a squashed white box from the bag and plunked it down in the middle of the table. He opened it to reveal the contents: two kolaches, one with a sizable chunk missing.

"Recognize these?" said the cop.

"No, I don't think so."

"No? You're going to sit here and tell me no?"

"Like I said, I don't know."

"You're saying that at no time this morning did you have in your possession a box of sausages wrapped in pastry?"

"I didn't say that, but these don't look like mine. I had two whole ones."

The cop picked up the half-eaten kolache. He held it up to the light and studied it in a pointless forensic bluff. If these were indeed the remains of kolache number two, what happened to the other half? Did one of the girls succumb to the irresistible lure of greasy meat, extract it from the trash, and take a healthy bite before being overcome with vegan guilt?

"Let me get this straight. You didn't steal these kolaches from a taxi?"

"Wait, what?"

"We received a 911 call. A white male matching your

description was reported to have stolen a cabdriver's breakfast and stiffed him on his fare."

"Let me guess who called that in. Look, I stiffed him on the tip, not the fare. And he didn't complain until after he drove off. Anyway, I took them for the girls."

"What girls?"

"Two teenage girls in the parking lot of a convenience store."

"You offered stolen property to minors? Do you mind telling me what you were looking for in return?"

I tried to explain my intention to spread goodwill and friendship, but it was pointless, his existence one jaded encounter after another, his soul occluded like a cheap diamond.

"When did you begin fraternizing with underage females?"

"It was an innocent gesture to two of my fellow citizens. What does age have to do with it?"

"Sounds like you're admitting to solicitation of a minor. Two counts."

"Shouldn't you be out there trying to catch real criminals? Rumor has it there's an orange-haired hooker with a healthy rump running a wheel-stealing operation right under your noses, and you're wasting time asking me about sausages?"

"What do you know about that?"

"How many people matching that description can there be, stalking around convenience stores in the middle of the night? A bubble butt isn't uncommon, granted. But coupled with fluorescent hair?"

He became defensive. "We're working on it, all right. Not everything's as cut-and-dry as it sounds."

I nodded in a sarcastic manner, which irritated him

anew. He kept the pressure up by adding another alleged offense to the mix.

"Obstructing the lawful flow of traffic."

"Seriously?"

"A report was made that in the nine thousand block of Broadway, a suspect matching your description jumped in front of a Buick Roadmaster. Sounds like obstructing traffic to me."

"The man pulled over and offered me a ride, voluntarily. I mean, his wife didn't look too thrilled, but she didn't object, at least not verbally. A few people honked, but that doesn't make it a crime."

"You accessed the airport via a vehicular ramp."

"How else was I supposed to walk here?"

"You don't walk to the airport. Nobody walks to the airport."

"Maybe some people should, from the looks of things." I lowered my gaze to the cop's healthy paunch.

"Can you believe this guy?" said the cop to the TSA lady. The woman nodded but didn't seem too interested in my state law crime spree. She leaned back and resumed filing her fancy nails. The one she was working on at present was painted with the head of Toro the bull, the mascot of the Houston Texans football team. Her aggressive filing had taken Toro's proud horns all the way down to his ears, making him look like a depressed heifer.

The cop pulled a device off his belt and pecked at the screen like a European waiter ringing up dinner table-side. After a minute or two of this rather inefficient data entry, a pink piece of paper rumbled out of the top of the machine. He tore it off, handed it to me, and took great pleasure in pointing out my appearance date in municipal court on a misdemeanor charge of obstruction of traffic.

The cop basked in his smug indictment afterglow while he made small talk with the TSA lady. When he stood to leave, the woman touched him on the arm and asked him to hold tight until she returned from the restroom. There was something about the way her fingers lingered on the man's jaundiced forearm that made me think there was more to their relationship, possibly a bit of cross-jurisdictional bridge building that hadn't been approved through the appropriate channels.

I admit, however, my suspicions may have been unfounded. A couple of months ago, Dave Trout had handed out copies of *Ditch the Twitch: How to Harness the Power of Nonverbal Communication* at a sales meeting and urged everyone to read it. He suspected some of us had lost sales on account of facial tics and other careless contortions. The book was informative, but the downside was I now often found myself consumed with the meanings of what were probably nothing more than rote spasms.

The lady walked out, and the cop went back to his magazine. I loitered in the awkward silence. After a couple of minutes, the cop began to spout duck trivia. He rattled off a few statistics about migration patterns and announced there were roughly fifteen hundred eider feathers in an average down pillow. I asked him if he knew the typical top speed of a duck traversing a pond. It wasn't a matter I was really that curious about, but I couldn't think of much else to keep the conversation going. The cop thought for a second before declaring, with a boastful arrogance, that an adult mallard could surely reach an absurdly high speed of fifteen miles per hour atop open water.

I had no ability to refute the cop's claim at that time but found out later that his figure was totally inaccurate when I became privy to the pioneering work of one Maurice H.

Dustman. In his seminal study from 1954, *Locomotion of Ducks and Other Waterfowl*, Dustman reported that he'd clocked the fastest duck chuffing across his local pond at four miles per hour. He noted a duck's actual top speed on a flat-out run under duress would undoubtedly be two to three miles per hour faster, being that waterfowl only cruised on the surface for leisurely pursuits. In a lengthy footnote, he stated he'd applied to the Indiana Conservation Commission for funding for additional speed experiments—something about floating lanes made out of electrified chicken wire and a short-haired pointer of lean build—but had been turned down due to budgetary constraints. I discerned from Dustman's sharp language he believed this reason mere pretense, that the state legislature didn't consider matters of duck velocity sufficiently urgent for fiscal allocations no matter the state's financial position. Regardless, even spotting the cop Dustman's extra three miles per hour, he had still been way off.

The cop's phone rang. He put the magazine down on the table and walked out the door. I examined the cover and noticed two shrunken figures with orange vests on the bank of a reservoir. They had their tiny shotguns trained in the direction of a giant duck, swollen by the magic of perspective. I reached over, opened the magazine, and read the table of contents. Between articles entitled "Shotgunning: The Van Buren Method" and "How to Sex Up Your Decoys for Maximum Allure," there was a recipe for wild goose jalapeño sausage poppers. I was in the middle of reviewing the ingredient list for the poppers when the door opened, and the TSA woman came back in with a sheet of paper in her hands.

After the heavy-handed tactics of the City of Houston, the TSA lady's federal approach was a refreshing reprieve. I asked her about the Napolitano photo, and she apologized for the mix-up. She said they were waiting on photos of the current DHS secretary—some guy with the last name of Johnson—but there had been a shipping mishap and their box of Johnson photos had ended up at an IRS office in Ogden, Utah. The IRS people had promised to forward them on after tax season, but that was over a year ago and there was still no sign of their Johnsons. The higher-ups had decided to keep Napolitano on the wall even though she was now a private citizen rather than leave the commander in chief up there flying solo.

She asked if she could go through my bags, and I immediately consented, every second at that point a precious commodity. She removed my toiletries and half my clothes and ran her gloved hands around the edges of the suitcase. When she was done, she returned my button-downs with the delicate precision of one of those famous sushi chefs who spends all day obsessing over rice.

She admonished, in a motherly fashion, that for my safety, it was highly recommended I take approved modes of transportation to the airport in the future. And I was required to keep my shirt on at all times unless there was a fire in the terminal or the air-conditioning stopped functioning for prolonged, unspecified periods. She escorted me out, told me to have a pleasant flight, and handed me the sheet of paper. It directed me to a website where I could fill out a short questionnaire about my airport experience. The lady made clear that the questionnaire was for the federal part of my experience only. If I had any comments or suggestions of a municipal nature, I would have to take those up with the city directly.

Chapter Twelve

THE GATE CREW WERE AGITATING AROUND their podium like fire ants on a dead insect. I was ushered down the gangway and left to my own devices to find a seat. No surprise, the only one available was in the last row of the plane, next to the toilet.

The overhead bins had suffered comprehensive and negligent violation, so I was forced to shuffle a few items around to make room for my case. I opened the compartment above row thirty-two to reveal an all-too-familiar armadillo. When I attempted to relocate it to a bin a few rows up, an uptight man in a blue gingham shirt and pleated slacks started to ride me. He claimed I was crushing the animal. All I'd done was bend its saffron-yellow snout ninety degrees so I could wedge it into the space I'd made for it between a canvas backpack and a guitar case covered with stickers predicting environmental doom, but the guy acted like I was feeding it through a wood chipper. The elongated snout was the problem. It was an unfaithful approximation, closer to the size of an elephant's trunk considering the scale. If the ungainly creature had been sewn to the proper proportions, it would have fit fine in the new home I'd carved out for it.

"No respect," he said to no one in particular.

"If you're so worried, how about we put it there?" I pointed to the pedant's footwell.

"No. Why would I do that? It isn't mine. Do I look like someone who would own *that*?"

"Then why do you care?"

"It's rude. Treating other people's property like that. Who do you think you are? You board at the last minute and act like you own the place."

The man scowled and fidgeted. He was hemmed in between a giant dressed like an Alaskan lumberjack and a woman inhaling a soggy bun stuffed with unidentifiable meat. I left him to his punishment and crammed the animal into its relocated habitat. I was about to close the compartment door when I heard a plaintive cry.

"Mama, Mama," the weak voice pleaded. "It's that man again. He's hurting Dilly."

Thankfully, at that moment, the intercom came alive, and a flight attendant's voice ordered me to my seat so she and her partner could begin the emergency briefing. I acted like I hadn't heard the girl's cries and hurried to close the bin door. I had to push hard to secure the latch over the resistance put up by Dilly's bulky haunches, another of the animal's inauthentic features.

I was relegated to a middle seat, next to a sulky teenager in athletic shorts and sneakers with no socks. The boy grunted something indecipherable when I motioned to my seat, so I had no choice but to squeeze past him. When I rubbed up against his bony adolescent legs, I pushed hard into him to extract a price for his lazy discourtesy.

The window seat was occupied by a forbidding woman with ossified grayish-brown hair the shade of dirty mushrooms. The bracelet on her left wrist had lots of little gold discs in the shape of human heads dangling from it. There was a name and date inscribed on each tiny head. A bulbous muffin inhabited her tray table, and she was picking out the chocolate chips like they were ticks on the family dog. Every time she freed a chunk, the pygmy heads rattled together in a chorus of annoyance.

The security briefing was a song-and-dance number, the pair of flight attendants now Broadway understudies. The tall, older one sang out cautionary, instructive verse about seat belts and oxygen masks while her younger, heavier male companion danced around beside her. He moved his arms up and down and left and right, in a cheer-leading routine that was supposed to divulge the location of the emergency exits but was too imprecise to impart any confidence we'd be able to disembark with expediency if the plane went down in the oily waters of the gulf.

I had my phone on even though the flight attendant had told us to turn them off, and the bracelet lady was glaring at me, self-righteously, despite the fact her tray table was still down and her seat was reclined an inch or so from full upright. A text from Barb popped up. She had received word from Rusk that the restraining order had been granted. She would overnight the service documents to my hotel. They would arrive early the next morning.

I was about to put my phone into airplane mode when it rang. I answered it, assuming it was Barb. Instead, a man was on the line.

"Sattler."

"I'm sorry, who?"

"Don't play games, Sattler. You've gone too far this time. Charlene's giving me ultimatums. You think I'm just gonna sit around and let you mess with my business?"

111

"I think you've got the wrong number."

"The hell I do. Charlene's ridin' me, wants a new mouse. Says she'll probably need a whole new computer. Not only that, she's making other demands. She's in the break room this very instant with Trickle. They want the entire lot paved with concrete and they're pressing me hard for office parties, some crap about morale. Crawfish every week? I asked them, how am I supposed to do that, they're not even in season right now. You know what Charlene told me? 'Not my problem. You're the damn fat cat, you figure it out.'"

"Look, I'm sorry about all that, but I'm not Sattler. It's Mr. Dugas, right? Can I ask you—"

"Sattler, you don't fool me. What is this, a burner? Well, I didn't call to bellyache. I warned you when you messed with my sign—'BAD Towing,' that's the best you could do? Anyhow, I wasn't going to tell you how I got even, that was gonna be my little secret, but you've pushed me too far this time."

Dugas hung up before I could get another word in. Not ten seconds later, my phone pinged, and a notification popped up with a thumbnail photo attached. I studied the tiny image. A donkey in cowboy boots was jostling up against a Himalayan yak. The yak had on a decorative costume emblazoned with the livery of what I guessed was a remote Nepalese village.

Puzzled, I pushed down on the thumbnail to open the full-size image. It took me no more than a second to take in the unholy horror. The donkey was actually a hairy man with his pants around his ankles. The yak was a linebacker of a lady with bleached-blond hair, her gaudy smock hiked up to reveal a pair of cellulite-cratered thighs. Dugas had described this barbarous affront as "sampling the pleasures of Autumn's buxom delights," an overly wordy yet surprisingly poetic outburst for a man of his obviously depraved character.

The nosy woman next to me must have been looking at my screen, because she took to prodding her call button like she was stuck in an unruly elevator. The flight attendant soon arrived but didn't look as perky as when she was up front, hoping to be discovered.

The lady told the attendant she wanted to move to a different part of the plane. "He's looking at pornography, pure smut." She pointed to my phone. "Bestiality involving large, hideous animals."

I told the flight attendant it wasn't bestiality, at least not in the traditional sense.

"I know it looks like a donkey in boots, but it's actually a hominid by the name of Alton Dugas. He runs a towing outfit that's embroiled in a labor tussle. The hairy yak's a woman named Autumn. I haven't seen a marriage certificate, but I believe Autumn is married to a guy named Sattler. And I think it's fair to say she's not opposed to intimate relations in uncomfortable positions with men other than her husband. But it's not that objectionable, let alone pornographic. Have you watched any prime-time TV lately? It's basically a parade of ass. Less hairy, firmer ass, granted, but ass nonetheless."

The bracelet lady butted in, claiming smut expertise. "I know depraved filth, I can just smell it," she said, butchering the rather arbitrary concurrence of former Supreme Court justice Potter Stewart.

The flight attendant had no interest in either the finer points of constitutional law or finding the objectionable crone a new seat. She told us to behave ourselves, confiscated the woman's muffin, and ordered her to return her seat to the full upright position. Vindicated, I adjusted my air vent for maximum flow and stared straight ahead while the plane reversed from the gate in preparation for its taxi along the airport tarmac.

The rest of the flight was uneventful, and when I say "uneventful," I mean from the perspective of aeronautical stability only. The ease with which the narrow-body jet cut through the atmosphere belied the turbulent conditions on board. The bracelet lady kept wanting to get up from her seat and roam free like a maiden in spring. She gave excuse after excuse for her restlessness, each paired with a corresponding affliction. She had a weak bladder, with the capacity of what sounded like no more than a small party balloon. She had thrombosis in her deep veins. The discs in her back had been removed, and the remnants of her spine had been fused together into what I imagined was a bone post with the torsional rigidity of a flagpole.

Amid excursion number two, I suggested to the lady that the next time she flew, she consider aisle seating and its appurtenant conveniences.

"What do you know, you sicko," she said as she rammed into the unyielding teenager, who flatly refused to move. She tried to push past him, and their bodies interlocked in an awkward congress reminiscent of a rugby scrum.

After I endured the third of these pantomimes, I tried to broker a seat-switching deal between the kid and the lady. My close-quarters Camp David failed because she refused to recognize my role as peacemaker, calling my attempts to find a mutually agreeable solution illegitimate. She also claimed she didn't negotiate with terrorists, which was what she had taken to calling the disagreeable kid. I told her she should be careful throwing that word around. I knew about such matters because I had been detained by the TSA earlier in the day for not much more than thirty seconds of bare-chested exhibitionism in the terminal.

At that point, the woman joined the kid in shutting up. Had I known an allusion to my accidental nakedness would elicit such blessed silence, I'd have painted the picture much earlier in the flight, possibly at the Texas-Louisiana border when the flight attendants began to hand out the stale peanuts, but definitely no later than when the drinks cart came by, which, by my estimate, was around Lafayette.

Chapter Thirteen

THE PLANE LANDED, AND WE DISEMBARKED through
a sea of people crowding the gate like the gangway led
to the last plane out of Saigon. I rode the escalator downstairs to baggage claim and proceeded down the hallway
to the rental car desks. On the wall, a banner announced,
"The Tampa Bay Convention & Visitors Bureau Welcomes
the International Funeral Directors of America." I paused
to admire the presumptuous overreach of the American
morticians. They had taken a page from Major League
Baseball by laying claim to global supremacy for what was
really no more than a regional consortium.

The rental car area was packed. Throngs of people
wearing dour expressions were lined up between belts of
stretched fabric. They talked solemnly, weighing the anticipated wait against the horrors of filthy cabs and public
transportation. I joined the line for my outfit. I'd reserved
a car of the largest size possible. I was in an unfamiliar city
and did not think it wise to scrimp on horsepower. Request
anything less than a two-ton sedan in the premium category
and you're liable to end up with a cardboard box with the
torque of a ride-on lawn mower.

In the next twenty-five minutes, I witnessed more paperwork being signed than it took to close a real estate deal or redirect a postal delivery. I shuffled forward, a foot at a time, at last reaching the front of the line. The sweaty young clerk's tie was loose around his unbuttoned collar, and his sleeves were rolled up to his elbows. He pulled up my reservation and told me the bad news.

"Man, sorry, but all we've got left are economy models." He lowered his voice. "These IFDA people, they've got a special corporate deal. They've stripped us bare."

I told him the morticians' preference for size was probably rooted in the fact they spent most of their time riding around in sturdy vehicles designed to present an air of robust serenity. I added that a more percipient operation would have foreseen the demand and adjusted its inventory accordingly. He shrugged and handed me a laminated card that pictured the range of models available. Thick black X's had been scribbled over all of them except for one in the lower left corner. The bug-eyed contraption looked like something a Japanese delivery driver would be forced to use to traverse the alleyways of Tokyo if bicycles were outlawed.

The clerk tried to sell me on the incredible gas mileage and parking versatility of the speck. He noted how much fun it was to "row your own gears." He jerked his right arm around to simulate the rowing. His erratic wrenching led me to believe he'd never operated a manual transmission before. If he had, the gearbox would have been toast after no more than six blocks. I huffed and puffed a bit to let him know I wasn't buying his pitch. He continued, undeterred.

"It's technically designated as a smoke-free vehicle, but don't worry, light up as much as you want." He leaned in close and told me about the "miracle" cleaning chemicals they sprayed all over the interior fabrics and left overnight to cure. He went on and on about the chemicals like he was trying to sell a rejigged formula of Agent Orange to the Pentagon.

There was more. If the formaldehyde-soaked interior wasn't enough of a deal sweetener, how about a free GPS unit programmed with not only the major points of interest but also a few more obscure but equally interesting attractions? Had I heard of Father Luis Cancer de Barbastro, the great missionary who'd befriended the native peoples of Guatemala before setting his sights on comity with the tribes of La Florida? I admitted I had not. He leaned back as if to say, "Well, let me tell you then," before embarking on a history lesson of excessive length given the line of people behind me, which now snaked all the way around a kiosk in the middle of the atrium. The kiosk was stocked with an array of defensive items: sunscreen, dark sunglasses, wide-brimmed Panama hats, and the like. From the frown on the face of the colorfully dressed man in charge of the operation, he was greatly concerned about the economic effect of the human blockade that had formed around his puny isle of commerce. He shouted at the line, trying to coax it over at a right angle, away from the kiosk, but after a matter of seconds, it straightened back out again, at which point he shouted anew.

The gist of the rental man's tale was that Father Cancer had gotten a big head after his great success with the Guatemalans. His strategy of ditching the Spanish army and its heavy-handed ways and taking the word of the benevolent Lord directly to the Central Americans had borne great fruit. Father Cancer, now thinking himself a great Indian whisperer, decided to stress-test his techniques on the somewhat more obstreperous inhabitants of the Gulf Coast. Against specific instructions to avoid tribes with previous dealings with the vicious Spaniards, his boat landed, in 1549, in what is now Tampa but was then home to the Tocobaga, a proud people who still had a bitter taste in their mouths from a nasty run-in with Hernando de Soto not ten years before.

The guy became more and more animated the deeper he descended into his tale. He grabbed a copy of *Tampa Bay Metro* magazine off the top of a stack sitting on the counter and rolled it up tightly.

"Guess what happened next?" he asked me.

"I honestly have no idea," I said.

"Come on, guess!"

"All right. How about he and his companions were escorted to the chief of the Tocobaga, and after an evening of festive revelry, Father Cancer renounced his vow of celibacy and took the chief's most beautiful daughter as his lifelong partner?"

"Hardly," said the man, making no attempt to disguise his contempt for my sentimental fairy tale of cross-cultural devotion. He lifted the rolled-up magazine high in the air and brought it down hard onto the counter. He repeated the action, beating the counter with more vigor each time. He had to yell to be heard over the counter-pounding.

"HE WAS CLUBBED TO DEATH RIGHT THERE ON THE SAND DUNES. WHAP! WHAP! WHAP! NO MERCY. NO QUARTER. TAKE THAT, YOU OLD FRIAR. WELCOME TO TAMPA!"

The man groaned out the guttural, deranged laugh of a happy walrus as he lashed the laminate surface again and again. He finally stopped clubbing and collapsed on the counter, spent. A handful of the more mannered people in line clapped weakly, as if unsure how to respond to the rigorous effort.

The man regained his composure and told me that the location of the gruesome execution was programmed into the GPS unit. There was a historical marker embedded in the sidewalk, so I could stand on the very spot where the naive monk had met his end. He said I could find the location by typing in "Barbastro clubbing" or "priest beating," but he advised me not to include the word "Cancer," because that would flood the results with the locations of area hospitals.

I thanked him, more for energetically illustrating the consequences of misplaced zeal than for the pitiable rental. I took my paperwork out to the parking garage, where I woke a man napping in a shed. He retrieved the keys to my car from one of the many hooks adorning a piece of particleboard nailed to the back wall. Why this extra shed step was necessary to the operation was not immediately evident, but I deemed it rude to question the man after I had just roused him from what looked to be a peaceful siesta.

Thankfully, it was only a short drive to my hotel. The wind whipped across the bay, and I had to steer into the gusts with frightening amounts of opposite lock to keep the car from veering into the adjacent lanes of the freeway. I was doing fifty-five, and the engine screamed like it was redlined. I put my foot down, but the motor just groaned out resistance.

Not only had the funeral directors monopolized all the acceptable vehicles, but they'd booked up all the decent bay area hotels too. So I was staying at a second-rate joint called the Theodore. It was down by the east end of the Courtney Campbell Causeway, a long, flat bridge that spanned the bay from Tampa to the eastern reaches of Clearwater. The hotel was located in the middle of a large parking lot, which was mostly empty when I pulled up. The rectangular four-story building had rooms on both sides, each with a meager balcony that jutted out over the drab tarmac. The pointless appendages were crammed full of grimy patio furniture, the whole setup a charade of leisure.

The lady at the front desk welcomed me to the Theodore and proceeded with her booking routine. She was finishing up when she recommended I add a pair of binoculars to my room tab. They were well worth the twenty-nine-dollar rental fee, she claimed. This binocular business reeked of desperation, the future of the Theodore likely hanging in the balance, insistent creditors demanding management wring every last cent out of the failing enterprise. But the woman was pleasant enough, so I let her make her pitch. She claimed each pair was equipped with high-quality lenses that would allow me to glimpse views of the water from any room on the bay side of the hotel. Not only that, but the eyepieces were thoroughly disinfected between rentals, so I had no cause to worry about ocular infections: pinkeye, styes, et cetera.

"What side of the hotel am I on?" I asked the lady.

"You're very lucky. Your room has a splendid view."

"Okay, but am I facing east or west?"

"Don't worry. You won't be disappointed, I promise."

"Look, if my room's not facing west, they're pointless."

"Oh, there are things to see on both sides, trust me."

"Like what?"

"Do you like birds?"

"As much as the next guy, I suppose."

"See, there you go," she said with a determined smile, obviously thinking her bird talk had sealed the binocular deal.

Just then, my phone began to ring, a fortuitous development given the pressure I was under. I grabbed my room key, waved goodbye in a vague manner, and headed to the other side of the lobby.

"Hello."

"Guy Hastings?"

"Yes?"

"Fritz Osterfeld here."

"Who?"

"Osterfeld. Of OPS. Osterfeld Process Servers."

"Oh, yeah, hello, thanks for calling, I was going to—"

"You got your paperwork in order? The paperwork's gotta be spotless. I don't serve defective papers."

"Yeah, pretty much. The judge signed the order earlier today. The original documents should be here in the morning."

"That's a bit tight for my liking. Doesn't leave much wiggle room. But as long as everything gets here tomorrow, I guess. We also need to have a little sit-down about our sortie day after next."

"We do?"

"Yessir, we don't want to go in blind."

"I guess not. What did you have in mind?"

"I'll pick you up at twelve hundred hours tomorrow. We'll grab lunch, go over the plan. Don't want to leave anything to chance. That's how you lose a leg, let me tell you."

"You lost a leg?"

"No, and I don't plan to either. You ever heard of a one-legged process server?" He scoffed as if I were advocating the idea, which I proceeded to do for no good reason other than I'm prone by nature to play devil's advocate.

"It might give you an advantage, the element of surprise."

He told me he doubted it. Defendants tended to be sly, shifty delinquents. Especially the "avoiders." He had tested various methods over the years, but nothing was foolproof. The Bumbling Tourist in Need of Directions didn't require much of a transformation—just a thirty-five-millimeter camera and a bit of purposeful disorientation—but results had proved to be inconsistent. He'd been known to rent a Segway to add an additional layer of tourist camouflage, which also came in handy if an avoider made a run for it, but the rental fee ate into his margins, so he only used one on high-dollar assignments. The Plumber There to Fix a Hidden Leak was a pain because he had to haul around a bulky toolbox. And the Delivery Driver with Urgent Package was played out, wily receptionists claiming they'd be more than happy to sign for the item themselves.

"I even used a wig once," said Fritz in a rueful tone, as though he hadn't reconciled the act with his conscience. "Not the best decision, in hindsight."

"Why's that?"

"The avoider was a doctor. Female parts. Lived in a gated community. When he found out he'd been sued, he locked down his clinic, put in a video intercom. My wife Nancy's cancer wig was collecting dust, so it got me thinking. Maybe it would help me get through the front door. Hell, worth a try, right? Sure enough, I'm buzzed right in. Didn't want anyone to get a good look at me, so I hit the deck the moment I crossed the threshold. Began rolling around, yelling in pain. The avoider came running out of the back like the building was on fire. You should've seen it. I pulled the petition out and pinned it on him. Ripped off the wig and said, 'Consider yourself served, Doc.' The look on his goddamn doctor face was priceless! Won Serve of the Month for that one."

"What?"

"FOPPS. Serve of the Month Award. Johnny Escalante

christened it the Damsel in Distress. Scored me a twenty-dollar gift certificate to Dorothy's. It's not the greatest, but the meatloaf's edible if you order extra gravy."

"Sure, yeah. What's FOPPS?"

"FOPPS?" said Fritz as if I'd been living under a rock. "Florida Organization of Professional Process Servers. Ring a bell? Well, anyway, the Damsel is ancient history. Deacon made sure of that when he sicced those drag queens on me."

Unfortunately, according to Fritz, the warm feelings of professional triumph didn't last long. The week after his cancer-wig hijinks hit the FOPPS newsletter, his office was picketed by a group of burly activists from a local drag bar holding signs protesting his damsel tactics.

"I couldn't make heads or tails of it. But when that reporter showed up, I knew the whole damn thing was a setup. The local news had a field day with it, made me out to be some crazy cross-dressing lunatic."

He had no hard proof, but he believed a process server named Deacon was behind the stunt given the man's penchant for unsavory spectacle. Deacon was a former wrestler who had been known as "the Depraved Duke" during his years on the semipro circuit. Deacon saw no reason for a costly rebrand when he changed careers, so the Duke he stayed, his only nod to decorum the dropping of the "Depraved" moniker. He was renowned for a sensational billboard on the outskirts of downtown, which featured him atop a rearing horse, adorned in a floppy, feather-plumed hat, his brawny legs clad in the tight stockings of a seventeenth-century musketeer.

According to Fritz, Deacon had garnered a nasty reputation for his heavy-handed service tactics. There had been numerous complaints lodged against him for his aggressive methods. One avoider claimed the Duke had immobilized him with what was later determined to be a scissored armbar while ramming a child-support petition down the back of the man's slacks. The Duke protested he was acting in self-defense, only resorting to the armbar after the avoider's girlfriend tried to douse him with pepper spray. The whole incident was filmed by a teenager who lived across the street. He posted it online with the description "Dude! OMFG! That did not just happen!"

Fritz was serving on the FOPPS disciplinary committee when the trouser violation came up for adjudication. The committee spent several hours on the case, reviewing the cell phone video and a DVD of the Duke's most "famous" bouts, which he sold on his website under the title *The Duke Does Depravity—Vol 1*. The ensuing debate was heated. Fritz had recommended immediate expulsion. Pepper spray or no pepper spray, the washed-up wrestler needed to be dealt a severe punishment, be made an example to all.

"But a couple of the others caved after we watched that DVD," said Fritz.

"Why?"

"It's all as fake as the Damsel, but they got spooked, although they'd never admit it, damn cowards."

What tipped the scales against expulsion, according to Fritz, was the Duke's signature move, a southern interpretation of the Boston Crab the Duke had christened the "Tallahassee Tangle." One committee member made them rewind the DVD over and over again, pointing out the abject agony on the face of one of the Duke's opponents. The Human Hernia writhed around in spasms of pain while the Duke rode his obese opponent's lower lumbar and torqued the man's fat legs back on themselves, the Hernia's hairy back bent to an inhuman degree. By the end of fifteen minutes of this well-scripted violence, Fritz knew he no longer had the votes for expulsion.

Ultimately, all the Duke got was a slap on the wrist. Twelve months' probation and a public reprimand, which was nothing more than a few words of weak admonition printed, in small type, on page twelve of the monthly FOPPS newsletter. Fritz had warned the rest of the committee their appeasement was a license for further Deacon aggressions.

"None of them had even heard of the Sudetenland, let alone the Munich Agreement," said Fritz, going into great detail about how the committee's milquetoast sanctions were no different from Hitler's many green lights into the heart of Poland.

"How did the Duke find out you voted for expulsion?" I asked Fritz, trying to head off another history lesson.

"Must have been a leak. That committee sings like somebody's got a boot on their scrotums."

I suspected the lady at the front desk had not given up on her rental mission because the binoculars were still unsheathed on the counter in front of her. When I finally got Fritz off the line, I kept my phone pinned to my ear to give myself time to plot evasive maneuvers. The woman picked up the binoculars and put them up to her eyes, making a mockery of her claims of scrupulous hygiene. She played with the focus adjustment for a few seconds, then started to scan the lobby. When she made it over to the corner where I was standing, she stopped and fixed on me like I was the subject of a stakeout. After an uncomfortable twenty seconds or so, she began to scan in the other direction.

I made a mad dash for the elevators, darting by a small boy in big sunglasses with a beach towel draped around his neck. The towel was thick and heavy and weighed the little tyke down. He bore his towel burden wearily, snorting like an overladen mule traversing a steep mountain pass. The boy had appeared out of nowhere, and it was a miracle I avoided knocking him over.

"Hey, mister, sloooowdown," the kid yelled at me. He waved one of his little paws in my direction as if trying to swat a bug from the air. The swat was enough to throw off the boy's balance, and he tumbled, headfirst, into a dense potted bush that sat next to the elevator door.

The impaled kid groaned and kicked his legs around like an Olympic swimmer. "Gemme me outta here, arghh!" he screamed.

"Hold on, don't panic." I grabbed one of his flailing legs and pulled. Just then, I heard woman gasp.

"Lyle, my goodness, what's going on?" said the lady as I let go of Lyle's leg.

"That man knocked me over," said Lyle in an aggrieved tone. He tried to finger me but failed because his head was in the bush, obstructing his sight lines.

The woman shooed me away and went to work on Lyle. Her bush extraction technique was slower and more methodical than my blunt yet more expeditious approach. She gently pulled apart the gnarly branches and extricated Lyle's head, inch by inch, with the firm precision of a doctor delivering an obstinate baby.

"What's wrong with you?" she said, her back to me, her attention still on Lyle. "He's just a little boy. You could have killed him!"

I stood there and took her scolding. Fair enough, I suppose. I couldn't deny Lyle and his towel had been making decent progress until I came along and churned up the waters. But the boy wasn't blameless when it came to his bush predicament, his lousy balance and all. Still, I decided it was imprudent to provoke this she-bear while she was tending to her precious cub.

An elevator finally arrived and I slunk past the woman, through the open doors. "Looks like you've got it under control," I said, and flattened my body into the corner, out of view of the evolving scene. When the elevator started its ascent, I could still hear Lyle groaning while his mother untangled the rest of his head from the grip of the coarse thicket.

Chapter Fourteen

MY ROOM WAS ON THE EAST SIDE of the building, so skipping the binocular rental proved to be a smart move. I pulled back the curtains and surveyed the parking lot. The only bird life of note was a couple of pigeons over by the dumpster, pecking away at a rotten banana. They attacked the mushy pulp with a thirsty brio, and I admit, for a moment, I regretted not shelling out for the binoculars.

My stomach rumbled, which reminded me I hadn't eaten anything all day other than airline peanuts and a couple of mints I'd dug out of the cupholder of the rental car. I went downstairs to check out the hotel restaurant, but the letterboard sign said it didn't open until five thirty. I slipped out a fire exit to avoid the girl at the front desk and pulled out my phone to search for options. There were more choices on the other side of the causeway, so I headed in that direction, strolling down a street lined with mangy palm trees with limp yellow fronds until I hit the main road, a six-lane river of asphalt.

The city planners obviously harbored a deep disdain for the pedestrians of Tampa, because there were no sidewalks and the stoplights never allowed a sufficient break in traffic for safe passage. After a couple of cycles, I realized my only option was to divide the crossing into two parts. So when the eastbound traffic stopped, I sprinted over to the slim center median, where a goateed man in baggy jeans and a white T-shirt was carrying on like the lead in a small-budget stage production. His shirt had "Smokin' Hot? Don't Worry, I Put Out" printed on it, fierce amber flames licking up the sides of the letters. He was attempting to extract donations from any drivers unlucky enough to be caught at the light. An upturned fireman's helmet in hand, he rapped on windows and waved his arms around with an operatic fervor. His routine looked to be paying off, because the helmet brimmed with a mess of notes. If anyone ignored his cheerful chauvinism, he feigned deep hurt.

"What, you don't like firemen?" he yelled at a prim-looking woman in a minivan. "C'mon, doll, how about it?"

I joined him on his island stage, and he glared at me with the petulance of a territorial diva.

"Well, well, look what we have here. Hey, pal, I bet you're not so good with your hose. You'd better leave it to the professionals, y'know what I'm saying?" He turned back to his temporarily captive audience and made a mocking gesture in my direction. I prayed for a red light on the westbound side to save me from further ridicule, but traffic kept streaming by, unimpeded.

"Come on, ante up, cheapskate. Don't worry, I'll give you a receipt. You won't get in trouble with your accountant."

Trapped, I ponied up to the coffers of the belligerent fundraiser. When I dropped a couple of dollars into the helmet, I noticed it was stuffed with wads of play money in a shameless attempt to make his collection efforts appear more fruitful than they actually were. Not only that, but the logo on the helmet was a generic jumble of firefighting implements, the words "Tampa Fire Rescue" suspiciously absent.

He noticed me eyeing his charity bait. "Eyes up, Mr. Big Spender, nothing to see here. And thanks, that'll buy us a lightbulb."

The westbound traffic finally stopped. I made it to the other side of the road and pressed on, trying to brush off the shame of victimhood. I followed a tree-clad road around a bend, past an amalgam of oddly shaped office buildings. Closer to the bay, several restaurants dotted the shore.

The first establishment I came upon was a colorful Caribbean joint called Shucka Mama's Seafood Palace. It looked to be the sort of place that served frozen drinks in hollowed-out pineapples, then had to find a use for all the pineapple innards, so pretty much everything on the menu came with pineapple. The entryway was encased in a giant acrylic lobster. The smiling crustacean towered over the front of the building, its imposing claws affixed to wooden posts on each side of the doorway.

A woman in a blue T-shirt and tan shorts was on a stepladder, polishing the lobster with a microfiber cloth. Her long ponytail swayed from side to side as she buffed the leviathan pincer to a lustrous shine. I wondered what kind of product produced such a high-gloss sheen on the creature's shell. I guessed maybe a wax with a high carnauba content or possibly one of those new German polymer-based liquids. Either way, something we could definitely use at the dealership to replace Trout's substandard pastes.

"Hi, you guys open?" I asked the woman.

She stopped polishing and peered over her shoulder.

"No, sorry, not till six."

"Too bad. Is anything else open around here that's any good?"

"Depends on what you mean by 'good.' I wouldn't bother going there." She nodded in the direction of the place next door, where a muscly guy with knotted hair was emptying case after case of domestic beer into an aluminum horse trough. The trough was positioned next to a tiki bar, and little tiki tables dotted the perimeter of a sandy expanse. In the middle of the tiki milieu was a beach volleyball court with a frayed, sagging net.

"Try the hotel down at the end. They've got a restaurant with a decent bar. I think it serves food all day, but don't hold me to that."

Sure enough, the hotel was right where she said it was. A monolithic six-story structure with sloping sides and a flat roof, the building had the appearance of an ancient pyramid abandoned in the early stages of construction. I walked through the lobby to the restaurant. Inside, a strapping bartender was wiping down a long wooden bar. He made a series of perfunctory orbitals on the resined oak with a white rag. They were apathetic motions, nothing approaching the tight circles of the lobster girl, who had him beat, hands down, on technique.

At the end of the bar, a man and a woman were eyeing each other warily. A few stools down, an olive-skinned guy in a dress shirt and slacks leaned over a draft beer. He was cupping the mug with both hands and studying it with the urgent intensity of a psychic trying to coax the future out of a crystal ball.

In the far corner of the room, four professionally dressed women were seated at a table, sipping pink cocktails out of large martini glasses. The women were living it up, swapping the specifics of their recent vacations. An animated, moon-faced brunette meted out words of delight and approval after every detail offered by her companions. When one of the other three shared a photo of the ocean view from her room at some all-inclusive resort on the Mayan Riviera, the brunette squealed excitedly.

"Y'all, can you believe that? Look at the sea, it's, like, see-through. Oh my god, that's so perfect, I looove it! I'm going to lay down the law and get Alan to take me there next year, I swear."

The pair at the bar had to be on a blind date. It was obvious from the man's body language that he was danger-ously infatuated with his companion, a lean, attractive woman of about thirty with streaky blond hair and thick, dark eyebrows. The same couldn't be said for the woman. Her face revealed a total and utter dissatisfaction with her predicament. Every time the man spoke, her bushy eyebrows arched skyward like a cat stretching in a laundry basket. The guy's outfit couldn't have been helping any. His shirt, tie, pocket square, and cuff links were all shades of pink. The ensemble matched his florid complexion, imbu-ing him with the flamboyant vulgarity of a TV preacher flush with the spoils of mail-in donations.

I grabbed a stool next to the guy in the business casual. The bartender dropped his rag and walked over with a menu. I ordered an IPA and a BLT, no tomatoes or lettuce, bacon extra crispy. Basically a bacon sandwich, which I considered a purer, less fussy use of bacon.

The bartender returned with my beer, then mixed up a fresh batch of pink cocktails for the table of boisterous women, who had moved on to describing their favorite sex toys. The bawdy brunette extolled the innumerable virtues of her pink rabbit over her husband Alan's miserable fumblings. She wiggled the tips of two fingers to imitate the contraption's nubby little ears, and her companions nodded knowingly.

The man next to me looked up from his beer. He introduced himself as Russ Mullen. "Haven't seen you here before," he said.

"First time."

"Yeah? You staying here?"

"No, across the causeway. At a place called the Theodore."

"Really?" he said, as if I'd just informed him my life savings were denominated in Congolese francs.

"So, you're a regular?"

"Yeah. Lately, more than usual," said Mullen. I sensed he wanted me to ask him about the "more than usual" part.

"Why's that?"

"Tony, can I have another?" He drained his mug. "Long story. You don't want to hear about it. Everyone's got their burden to bear, right?"

I wasn't sure about that. Some people were doing just fine shoveling their burdens onto others. Willis Delaney, in particular, came to mind.

Tony walked up with a fresh beer, the mug rimed with a thick layer of frost.

"Thanks, Tone," said Mullen. "Tony's getting sick of me. I've been here every afternoon for at least two months."

Tony shook his head in an ambiguous fashion and returned to his polishing. Mullen took a healthy swig of his beer. He returned it to the bar and wiped a glob of foam off the tip of his nose.

"I used to sell industrial marine valves. Good quality, patented, five-year warranties. Our hydraulic actuation technology was the best in the business. They basically sold themselves. But the patents expired a year ago, and the Chinese immediately flooded the market with generic imitations. Nine months later, the entire company went bust."

Mullen traced the demise of the valve outfit to a lack of investment in R & D. The company should've had new valves ready to go before the patents expired. He didn't blame the owner. The poor man couldn't help that he was suffering from Alzheimer's and had often forgotten what the company produced.

"We might as well've been making steel wool or coat hangers for all the old man knew about his products," said Mullen. "The worst was when he thought he'd been kidnapped and called the cops. I was in the office that day, working on a quote, and ended up spending the entire night down at the station trying to get the whole mess straightened out." Mullen took another swig of his beer. "My wife thought I was screwing around again."

Mullen said the old man's slothful progeny were the real reason for the downfall. After the man's two sons took over, everything went to hell. Instead of putting their heads down and coming up with new valve designs, they bought a party barge with company funds and took to spending most days floating around the bay, an entourage of scantily clad hangers-on in tow. After the Coast Guard fined them for exceeding the maximum capacity of their barge, they bought another and floated them both out, in tandem, people swimming between vessels when the mood struck them, each barge offering a slightly different party vibe.

"The older one played that techno music, tons of heavy bass," explained Mullen. "His brother preferred country and western. But two wasn't enough for them, I guess, because next thing, they've spent the company's cash reserves on two more. Four damn barges in all."

Mullen said the sons soon tired of the drunken commuting between vessels and roped their barge armada together. The new, makeshift craft was a mobile isle of decadence that moved around the bay at the whim of the lazy heirs and the prevailing currents.

"If I wanted to talk business, I had to take a boat out to the barges, which took forever if they'd drifted south and the tide was against us. Last time they summoned me out, they told me the party was over. Good, I thought, now maybe they'll actually do some work. But by 'party,' they meant the business. Bankrupt. I got stuck paying for six months of boat rides."

The company was liquidated several months ago. Since then, Mullen had spent every weekday morning out knocking on doors, looking for a job, with nothing to show for his efforts. He suspected prospective employers were chalking up his seven-figure sales numbers to the protections afforded by the valve patents, Mullen the victim of a cruel side effect of state-sanctioned protectionism.

"What are you doing in Tampa?" he asked me.

"Legal matters," I said. "Trying to track down a client, collect a fee."

Mullen stared at me with envy over what he must have assumed was my high-flying career. I told him not to worry. I wasn't an attorney working some lucrative case. I was nothing more than a law school dropout who sold cars, trying to tie up a loose end on account of my uncle's death. I had contracted for the assistance of a local process server by the name of Fritz Osterfeld. Osterfeld had impeccable professional credentials but employed unorthodox methods at times. I told Mullen about Fritz's supposed run-in with Duke Deacon.

"I don't know the guy," I offered. "He was probably exaggerating."

"No, I've seen that billboard," said Mullen. "The Duke's as real as a heart attack. And he's got style, a real showman. And those pecs. Jesus, the guy's ripped. If I have to sue those deadbeats for my expense money, I'm telling my lawyer to hire Deacon. I hope he scares the hell out of them."

Mullen turned back to his beer, his face rife with gloom. I hardly knew this man—morose to the point of depression over his career problems—yet I felt a mysterious obligation to speak words of comfort, offer up brotherly succor. My marriage no great beacon of success, I told him about Whitney and her demand for a trial separation.

"Hey, Tone, listen to this." Mullen motioned to the bartender. The story of my trial separation had cheered him up, while having the opposite effect on me.

"Yeah?" said Tony.

Mullen looked at me. "Tell him."

I explained to Tony about my unhappy wife, and like any good barkeep, he had words of banal advice standing at the ready.

"That's too bad. But hey, don't sweat it. These things happen. I'm sure it'll all work out." He turned to Mullen. "Have you met Rick Dewey? The chiropractor?"

"Think so. Stocky guy, muscular forearms, right?"

"That's him. Get this. His fiancée ran off with a minor league hockey player a year into their engagement. A Manitoba Moose. The guy was in town for a tryout with the Lightning. The next thing you know, she dumps Dewey cold and moves to Winnipeg with the Moose. Then, the following spring, she turns up on Dewey's doorstep, shell-shocked, begging him to take her back. She looked the same except her skin was white as a sheet on account of the sunless winter. And she was fainting all over the place. Some doctor diagnosed her with dangerously low vitamin D levels. Anyway, she started taking prescription supplements, stopped passing out, and they were married that very summer."

Tony added that the marriage turned out to be solid, surprising everyone. It had produced two kids so far, and the woman had even been able to attend a few of last season's NHL home games without triggering her flight response. Tony recommended I give Whitney space, a bit of room to breathe and figure things out, and if I did, she would come running back just like the Dewey woman.

I nodded, but in truth, I didn't see the analogy. The Moose probably grunted monosyllabic hokum out of a heinous gap where his front teeth used to reside. And Winnipeg? The supposed "Gateway to the West"? No wonder the vitamin-deficient woman dumped the Moose and slunk back from the frozen tundra to reunite with Dewey the chiropractor under the radiant Florida sun.

Our attention was drawn to the other end of the bar. The man was making a desperate move on the woman. It was going badly, about as badly as these things can go. He tried to convince her to join him for dinner at Shucka Mama's. He played up the pineapple angle, but that just made it worse, the woman claiming a near-fatal allergy to the fruit. She stood, her facial features arranged in a contorted grimace, her furry eyebrows now even more animated. She backed away from the bar as if performing a strange jig, all while defending the sanctity of her phone number with the ferocious vigilance of a thirteen-year-old girl guarding her diary confessions.

The man gave up on the digits and tried for an email

address, but the woman stood her ground. "Um, I think maybe we . . . I mean, you're a nice guy but . . . Anyway, look at the time. I really have to get going. I'm really late for . . . I have to run."

The guy beseeched the woman to reconsider, dignity draining from his reservoir of self-respect like coolant from a leaky radiator. The woman turned around and walked out, leaving him hanging midsentence, one arm half-raised in the air. After an uncomfortable ten seconds or so, he gave up and turned back to the bar. He waved to Tony, who prepared him another drink, a concoction called a Rooster Tail, which Tony promptly delivered, on the house.

From then on, the propriety of the evening devolved in direct proportion to the amount of alcohol consumed. In a show of male solidarity, we invited the spurned man to join us. He was grateful for the company and bought several rounds of Rooster Tails. I felt the spicy liquid burning the skin off the roof of my mouth, but when either Mullen or I objected to more of this Mexican firewater, the man pooh-poohed our protests and insisted on another round.

We learned his name was Nelson. After Napoleon's dogged nemesis? No, just Nelson, he said, somewhat disappointed his parents hadn't named him in honor of a great admiral. He sold custom-tailored suits at an outfit called Nicholas Ditton and collected rare coins in his spare time. He'd married the love of his life when he was twenty-five, but she died in a car accident three years ago. He was trying to get back on the horse but wasn't having much luck. A nervous hypochondriac, he admitted to scouring the Internet with dread at the onset of even the most minor of symptoms. At present, his disquiet centered on a large hairy growth on his left shin that he worried might be cancerous. He hiked up a cuffed pant leg to show us the problem area.

"Damn thing itches like hell," he said, and gave his shin a good scratch.

We bent down to examine it. The patch looked like a small puddle of motor oil, a splotch of errant 10W-40. Our amateur consensus was one of sober concern and that he should get it checked out sooner rather than later.

At ten, I decided it was time to take my inflamed mouth back to the other side of the tracks. I left my companions at the bar, heatedly discussing the pros and cons of suspenders, and walked out into the night. The tiki place was alive with loud music and drunken hooting. A guy was crawling around the volleyball court on all fours, barking like a terrier. There was a sloppy game going on around the canine impersonator. The slow-moving obstacle exhorted members of his team to use his back as a launchpad to attain greater elevation for their spikes. The other team protested the use of the human springboard, claiming unfair altitude. An agreement was reached, points were deducted, and the man crawled off and parked himself next to the beer trough.

The traffic had eased on the causeway, and the bellicose solicitor was, thankfully, nowhere to be seen. I made it across the road in one spirited dash, my path more or less a straight line. I was tired and drunk, so I didn't much care that the springs of the hotel mattress dug into my lower back or the pillows smelled like moss. After I'd been in bed for a few minutes, I got back up and fiddled around with the curtains to try to eliminate a twelve-inch crack in the middle that was letting in harsh beams of parking-lot light. After ten minutes of frustrated tugging, six inches still remained. I conceded defeat to the obdurate pulley system, returned to bed, and buried my head in the moss pillow to protect my eyes from the relentless onslaught of stray illumination.

Chapter Fifteen

I WOKE UP WITH A START AT NINE, my gums smarting from the Rooster Tails. I stood in the narrow bathtub, showered under a fitful stream, and dried off with a threadbare towel. The towel was embroidered with a few sparse letters. "Theodore" had been reduced to "T od ," the d on its last legs. For a moment, I regretted not being named Tod. If I were, I'd have taken the Tod towel home with me and pulled it out at intimate gatherings whenever some gloomy skeptic claimed there was no great satisfaction to be found in modest coincidence.

I dressed and went downstairs, hoping it wasn't too late to hit the complimentary breakfast buffet. The buffet was still going, but it had been picked over pretty good by the early risers. I grabbed a plate and squeezed by a lady in a drab uniform and orthopedic sneakers. She was tending to a large bowl of fruit, adding fulsome chunks of melon to what was already an overly melon-heavy mix.

"Would it be possible to get some fresh scrambled eggs?" I asked the lady, whose name tag identified her as "Constance."

Constance paused her melon work and surveyed the

contours of the buffet landscape. "Sorry, not until those are gone." She pointed to a coagulated brownish-yellow lump in the corner of a large aluminum pan.

"Oh, okay," I said, chastened. She nodded and turned her attention back to the fruit, confident she had settled the egg matter.

I placed no responsibility at the feet of Constance. Her hands were probably tied by some unyielding buffet-replenishment policy designed to pad the bottom line. But I wasn't about to give up, so after she disappeared into the kitchen, I scraped the congealed slag allegedly once eggs out of the pan and into the bottom of a basket of powdery rolls. I replaced the rolls and adjusted their positions to ensure maximum camouflage.

Constance emerged from the kitchen with a plate of ham slices rolled up like little carpets. She noticed the empty egg tray and eyed me with suspicion. She placed the ham next to a plate of rubbery-looking Swiss cheese and walked back toward the kitchen.

I had time to kill until my egg ruse bore eggs, so I placed a piece of bread on the conveyor belt of the industrial toaster. I watched with a child's curiosity while it slowly disappeared into the mouth of the machine. I waited and waited, my anticipation building, but no toast emerged from the other end.

Constance came back with fresh eggs, and I spooned two heaping piles onto my plate. I really only wanted one spoonful, but sometimes guilt manifests itself in unexpected ways.

I checked the machine. Still no toast. I bent down and peered into the glowing slot. Nothing! I was about to give up when smoke began to billow from the top of the machine. Constance reappeared next to me wearing thick gloves. She popped the hood of the toaster and rooted around in the guts with a pair of tongs. After much rooting, the tongs emerged with the charred remains of what I guessed was my slice. She dropped the sooty lump onto my plate, and it hit the porcelain and shattered, causing a plume of particulate matter to erupt upward. I watched as cinders settled on the slopes of my egg hillocks, my breakfast now an ash-strewn, postapocalyptic mess.

I had abandoned any hope for untainted nourishment and was stalking around the lobby trying to find a cell signal when the courier delivered the Delaney envelope. Papers in hand, I anticipated the appearance of Osterfeld, which meant lunch wasn't far off. He arrived twenty minutes late. A tall, lean man in his midsixties, he strode in with the purpose of a health inspector tipped off to sanitary violations. He was wearing a green blazer over a yellow polo shirt, pressed khakis, and a blue cap. The USS *Nimitz* was sewn onto the front of the cap. I knew the craft to be the Nimitz because the words "USS Nimitz CVN-68" were embossed, in gold lettering, around the ship, leaving no need to speculate about either the identity of the vessel or its hull classification.

Fritz sized me up through dark aviators. He shook my hand and patted me on the back as though we were old friends.

"I'm a bit early, hope you don't mind." He pointed to his watch without looking at it. "So, you ready for lunch? Hope you like seafood, 'cause we're going to the best place this side of the bay. Scottie's with me today. You'll like him. Good kid, but seven shades of spacey. His mother almost lost him to those damn Scientologists. You know, aliens and volcanoes and all that horseshit. I have to make one quick stop on the way, won't take more than five, ten minutes tops."

We walked out of the Theodore, and Fritz strutted ahead in a pair of fancy running shoes. He motioned to a boxy red two-seat convertible with the top down. A lanky teenager with thick chestnut-brown hair and bloodshot eyes occupied the passenger seat. His most prominent feature was the base of his forehead, which protruded out over his eyes with the imposing ruggedness of a mountainous overhang. I studied the impressive promontory, unable to look away. Fritz thought I was admiring the car.

"You like? 1989 Cadillac Allanté. She's a classic. Don't see many of them on the road these days. Bet you've never even heard of it, young fellow like you."

In actuality, I had. The Allanté was conceived by Detroit for members of the greatest generation who desired top-down motoring but wouldn't think of buying German on account of war grudges. The weak power plant, fiddly roof, and high sticker price doomed it from the beginning, but GM, in a fit of corporate optimism, pumped them out for six years. Dad had taken one in on trade from a local dentist, who'd bought it after his wife ran off with a real doctor. The dentist claimed the wind disturbed his new paramour's hair, so he swapped it for an Eldorado with a fixed roof. The Allanté sat on the lot for a year until a newly widowed woman from Shreveport bought it with some of her insurance money.

The kid waved as we approached.

"That's Scottie," said Fritz. "Scottie, come on, time to put you in the back."

"Yeah, all right, Fritz," said Scottie in a languid tone. He had on shorts and a thick white hoodie, a prudent garment for cruising at highway speeds with the roof down, this outing obviously not Scottie's first rodeo.

The back, so to speak, was nothing more than a small parcel shelf behind the seats. Fritz moved the seats forward as far as they would go and proceeded to contort Scottie into the meager cavity. Once he was wedged in, Fritz adjusted the seats backward, maybe six inches, until Scottie yelped in pain.

It was about as cramped up front. Fritz had his knees up around the steering wheel like a bus driver. I hoped we didn't have a frontal collision. Without an airbag, I'd be doomed for sure. And Fritz, even with one, wouldn't fare much better given the lack of acceptable distance for proper inflation. Scottie was cocooned, an infant in an undersized womb, so he'd make out fine unless we were rear-ended by a fully laden semi.

Fritz shifted into drive and goosed the gas pedal. The Allanté lurched forward and black smoke poured out of the tailpipe. Fritz said he wished, on rare occasion, he'd opted for the '93 model with the more powerful Northstar 32V engine, but it had the reputation of blowing head gaskets, and when he got down to brass tacks, he was too practical a man to trade horsepower for reliability. I asked him about all the smoke, and he said he didn't mind the motor burned oil, claiming it deterred tailgaters.

I checked my mirror. Scottie's chestnut locks were blowing around his frontal bossing. He had a blank, placid look on his face. It was the calm aspect of a family dog, along for the ride, its hirsute head out the window, resigned to the buffeting.

We turned right at the causeway and headed east toward Tampa proper. My shoes were slipping around in the footwell on what felt like bare metal. I peered down and noticed there was no carpet. On closer inspection, I realized somebody had drilled lots of quarter-sized holes through the bottom of the unibody. I watched the road roll by under my feet and became slightly mesmerized by the effect.

"Drainage," said Fritz.

"Huh?"

"Holes for drainage," he repeated. "Water, rain. Any sort of liquid, you name it. Spill a cup of coffee, it runs right out onto the pavement."

Fritz explained. He said his canvas roof was toast. It had been split open by would-be thieves with designs on god knows what. He was not stupid enough to leave valuables in an automobile, especially one with a fabric roof, but these modern criminals were simpletons and didn't think twice about wasting their criminal time defacing property on the basis of pure speculation. Instead of springing for a new top, which would undoubtedly meet the same fate, he'd pulled out all the carpet and drilled holes in the floorboard. Problem solved, he said, except for the occasional rodent looking to nest, which he took care of by taping pellets of rat poison to the kick panels.

"What about the structural implications?" I asked. "The floor's part of the frame."

"You think this is some run-of-the-mill tin box? Hell, son, this car was built by Eye-tally-uns, out of pure aluminum." Fritz explained that the frames had been fabricated in a factory in Turin and shipped back to Michigan on 747s, fifty at a time. This modern-day Silk Road was known as the "Allanté Airbridge," he declared. If that wasn't enough to cement the car's legacy, how about the fact it served as the official pace car for the 1992 Indy 500, with none other than Brickyard legend Bobby Unser leading the field around the world-famous oval? And contrary to popular belief, the name "Allanté" was not borrowed from a rural village in Macedonia. Point in fact, it was selected by a cadre of corporate bigwigs from a list generated by a supercomputer that Fritz claimed was the size of a walk-in freezer. He attached much significance to this supercomputer-naming business—too much, in my opinion, as though the whirring box had spit out an elegant solution to cold fusion or some other unsolvable paradox.

I interrupted the Allanté talk to ask Fritz where we were going.

"To Ybor City, north of downtown, the old Cuban district. Don't worry, it's not far. How you doing back there, Scottie?"

Scottie mumbled something indecipherable over the wind noise, and Fritz pretended he understood the garbled nonsense.

"Good boy. You ready for some action? I bet you are. Young buck like you, wanting to run free, it's natural." He turned to me. "I've gotta serve civil papers on a guy named Santi Fernandez. Intel is he's a little Cuban fellow about five and a half feet tall, thick head of curly black hair."

Fritz said Santi the Cuban and his twin brother, Freddy, had been partners in an outfit called Dos Hermanos Handmade Cigars until a petty dispute over Freddy's cigar-rolling technique drove a wedge between them. At some point in the protracted feud, harsh words were exchanged, and Santi moved Freddy's antique rolling table out to the curb on heavy trash day. Dos Hermanos became Un Hermano, forcing Freddy to lawyer up.

We exited the freeway and soon pulled up in front of a row of brick buildings with Spanish-looking façades. Fritz put two wheels up on the sidewalk and turned on his hazards. An elaborate sign over the door of one establishment declared, "Un Hermano Handmade Cigars." It was obvious from the differing shades of paint that the sign had been recently touched up. While I judged the brotherly words to have been acceptably altered, the attempt to airbrush out Freddy's likeness was less successful, his inky black hair still visible through what looked to be several coats of fresh paint.

"We're going to have to unpack Scottie," said Fritz. "He's in training, aren't you, buddy?"

"Are you sure you need me, Fritz?" said Scottie. "I'm fine out here, really."

"Need you? Son, you need this for yourself. Now, get your mind right."

"But I can't feel my right leg," Scottie whined.

Fritz was having none of it. He scowled at Scottie like he'd just disobeyed a direct order. We freed the kid, and he leaned against the trunk and started to stretch out his stiff limbs.

"Goddammit, Scottie, watch the paint, will you?" Fritz shouted at him. "Come on, outta the way." He popped the trunk. It was surprisingly spacious and packed with a ragtag assortment of items. Next to a box full of files and a nylon briefcase were a couple of rain ponchos, a roll of garbage bags, a pair of bolt cutters, eight quarts of motor oil, and a plasticky yellow gun.

Fritz removed a manila envelope from the box and picked up the plastic gun.

"Here, take this." He handed me the contraption. "If you see anyone make a run for it, act like you're going for their neck. Don't actually pull the trigger or anything, just wave it around. You'd be surprised how compliant avoiders get when they're staring down the barrel of fifty thousand volts."

I politely declined Fritz's offer to threaten strangers with electrocution. He grumbled under his breath and handed the stun gun to Scottie.

"Suit yourself," he said, as though I'd just turned down a big slice of Grandma's apple pie. "But if you see a cop or a meter maid, do me a favor and move the Allanté, will you? Damn parking tickets are killing me." He tossed me his keys. "Come on, Scottie, let's go. Watch that thing. Keep it down by your side, out of sight, unless I give the word."

Fritz went into the store and Scottie trailed behind. The kid held the stun gun out in front of his body, his rigid arms and careful shuffling that of a nervous priest transporting holy water for a sacred ritual.

I went to close the trunk and noticed a comb-bound booklet wedged in the box. The cover featured a medieval wizard in a purple wizard robe holding a thick wand. The wand hovered over the head of a rangy, red-eyed druid who looked to be gasping for air through its wide, fanged mouth. The booklet was titled *Deprogramming with CARE: Beating the Odds with the ODDS*.

I opened the booklet and scanned the table of contents. "ODDS" stood for "Objective Detention and Deprogramming System." "CARE" was nothing more than a generic acronym consisting of the words "communication," "action," "response," and "execution." I flipped through the pages. They were littered with more bullet points than a corporate HR manual, each paragraph loaded with bland aphorisms and suspect advice of the type usually found in books about how to lose weight or break the bonds of consumer debt.

As I was perusing a paragraph entitled "Discredit and Contradict—Making the Most of the Subject's Time in Confinement," a man with a round belly and stubby legs bolted out of the cigar shop and scampered off with the purposeful determination of a well-nourished squirrel traversing an expanse of fresh-cut grass. His thick black hair bounced up and down, the curly pelt reminding me of Diego Maradona, in his prime, darting through a crowd of flummoxed defenders. Seconds later, Fritz appeared, screaming, "Runner! We've got a runner!"

I pointed in the direction of the stumpy doppelgänger, and Fritz ran off after him, loping down the street with surprising speed for his age. An instant later, Scottie stumbled out of the shop, his eyes aflame, his healthy forehead rippling with panic. An irate, heavyset woman in a yellow apron was close on his heels. She yelled at him in Spanish.

"Bastardos sucios, hijos de perras," the woman cursed. She held a thick wad of raw tobacco leaves and began to beat Scottie over the head with them. Scottie raised his hands to protect himself from the blows, and the woman countered by whipping his exposed torso with the ropey crop, leaving brown skid marks all over the back of his white hoodie. Thankfully, the woman's girth was working against her, so it wasn't long before whipping poor Scottie tired her out. Breathing heavily, she bent over and put her hands on her knees to rest. A moment later, she pulled a phone out of her apron and punched away at the screen. I wasn't sure what she was up to, but I wasn't about to stick around to find out. I jumped into the Allanté, fired it up, and yelled at Scottie to get in.

We cruised up and down the adjacent streets searching for Fritz, but neither he nor the little cigar man was anywhere in sight. While we crept along, Scottie picked pieces of tobacco leaf out of his hair and filled me in on what had gone down in the shop.

The tobacco whipper who'd just ruined his favorite hoodie was working the front counter when they walked in. She was friendly at first, but when Fritz asked to speak to Santi Fernandez, she turned nasty and obstinate. She claimed to know no one by that name and demanded they leave immediately. *"No eres bienvenido, largarse,"* she kept screaming, over and over.

I asked Scottie if he knew what that meant.

"Not sure, man," he said. "'No welcome'? 'You're not welcome'?" He said he'd taken Spanish in ninth grade but admitted he spent more time studying Ms. Garza's long, tanned legs than memorizing all the tedious conjugations.

Undeterred, Fritz had flashed his badge at the lady and pushed past her, through a beaded curtain, into the back of the store. Almost immediately, a man shot out of a side door and ducked past them with surprising agility.

"Holy shit, Fritz talks about avoiders, but this is my first one," said Scottie, still racked with adrenaline.

"Are you working for him?"

"Nah, he's my neighbor. My mom told his wife, Nancy, I was mixed up with the Scientologists, you know, over in Clearwater. The Flag building. Looks like a space castle. Nancy convinced my mom that Fritz could help. She said he'd done a few prisoner interrogations when he was in the navy and taken a course in Omaha from some guy named Dale, Dale Card, or something like that."

"Dale Carnegie?"

"Yeah, that might be it. You know him? So my mom's desperate. She's crazy scared I'm going to join up and turn into one of those zombie kids running around downtown Clearwater. Next thing I know, she's arranged for me to spend a day each week with Fritz. All summer! I told her, 'Mom, I'm not even that into Molly Madsen.' Sure, she's cute and I wouldn't mind . . . Well, you know. But I'm not going to run off and sign my life away just to get laid. It's not like I don't have other options."

151

Scottie told me that Molly Madsen was a limber brunette who topped the cheerleader pyramid at pep rallies on account of her diminutive frame and superior sense of balance. Her whole family were die-hard Scientologists, all under billion-year contracts to something called the Sea Org, which sounded like the navy if the navy sold off all its seaworthy vessels and replaced its sailors with gullible rubes content to do pointless menial labor for no pay.

Scottie had gone to a few meetings with Molly, which he claimed had paid off handsomely, each post-indoctrination make-out session allowing his restless hands greater ingress toward Molly's fructuous garden. Sure, he had to sit through hour upon hour of weird Scientology shit, and he was under serious pressure from a guy who claimed to hold the "rank" of ensign to register for something called a "Communication Course," but he thought he would be able to slide into home plate before the coercion got seriously out of hand. But just before he was about to round third base with Molly, his mother, who mistook teen lust for ritual brainwashing, intervened. She called in Fritz, and now this poor hormone-riddled pussy hound had to waste precious days of his adolescent summer riding around in a leaky Cadillac listening to Fritz rattle off dubious truisms from a pamphlet he'd mail-ordered from a guy in Waco, Texas, who'd made a name for himself in the nineties deprogramming Branch Davidians.

"It's fine today, but when it rains, we have to put on those ponchos and cover the dashboard with garbage bags," said Scottie, claiming the only thing that made it tolerable was his pre-Fritz preparation, which consisted of several hits from a large bong he kept hidden in his buddy's garden shed. He said he was, at present, high as a kite and quite hungry, come to think of it. I told him about my lackluster breakfast, and he said he was glad someone else was on the same page with him, hunger-wise.

We turned a corner and I spotted the *Nimitz*. It was beached on the sidewalk next to two overstuffed trash cans, a stray cat batting at its hull with a mangy paw. Scottie jumped out, and the cat arched its back and hissed. He grabbed a half-eaten hot dog from one of the cans. The way he fixed on the wiener made me think he was going to take a bite, but much to my relief, he bent down and used it to lure the combative animal away from the *Nimitz*.

Scottie grabbed the hat and jumped back in, and I made a right at the next light, sure that Fritz couldn't have strayed too far. Scottie spotted him first. He pointed at a slumped figure sprawled out on the sidewalk, nursing his right ankle.

When Fritz saw us pull up in his beloved Allanté, he struggled to his feet and winced in pain. Scottie tossed Fritz the hat, which perked him up a bit. The cat had torn loose a chunk of the *Nimitz*'s flight deck, but Fritz wasn't concerned. He said Nancy and her fancy sewing machine would patch the old girl up better than new.

Fritz told us what had gone down during the chase. He claimed it was an evenly matched contest. While he had a certain advantage due to his long strides and superior fitness, Santi's powerful legs and low center of gravity allowed for greater maneuverability in urban environs. Sure enough, as he was about to slap the papers down onto Fernandez, the wily Cuban made a sharp cut and sprinted down a narrow alley, disappearing off into the distance.

"I planted to make the turn and my foot went straight into a crack in the sidewalk," said Fritz. "That's all she wrote, down I go."

"Scottie didn't fare so well either," I said, pointing at

Scottie's soiled hoodie.

Fritz ignored me. "Damn ankles have never been the same since I fell off that roof," he said, without further explanation of the roof mishap. He put weight on his right leg, grimaced in pain, and collapsed back down onto the sidewalk.

I heard an ominous rumble a block or so away. The noise grew louder and louder, the deep basso of high-displacement combustion approaching rapidly from the south.

"Oh shit," said Scottie as the sound enveloped us.

A bright red Dodge Viper idled noisily up to the curb, the resound of its mammoth pushrod V10 filling my skull with a lumpy resonance. A bulging hulk of a man pervaded the interior, his head a good six inches above the roofline of the open-topped two-seater. His long, frizzy blond hair was held back by a purple bandana, and his elaborately ruffled white shirt was unbuttoned almost all the way down to his skintight trousers, revealing a dense copse of curly chest hair. A good portion of his stubbly face was hidden behind a pair of sleek wraparound sunglasses.

The man spoke in a series of raspy snarls. "Well, well, if it ain't the rat, crawling around in the gutter. What's wrong, Fritz, losing your touch?"

"Don't go there, Deacon," said Fritz. "You're on probation, remember? You so much as shake someone's hand too hard, I'll have the committee yank your membership faster than you can say "roid rage.'"

"You still driving that foreign piece of crap? Why don't you get yourself some real wheels, a nice slab of American iron?" Deacon gestured vigorously in the direction of his long hood.

"My engine's made in Detroit, just like yours, you

dope."

"Now, now, Fritz, be careful, don't step on your meat, sausage man. Be a crying shame if the fine ladies of the Glam Royale decided to relocate their show in front of OPS again. Of course, it'd be their decision, I'd have nothing to do with it."

"You pull that stunt again, Deacon, and it's World War III, you hear?"

The Duke turned his fiery gaze on Scottie and me. "Hey, girls, when you get tired of nursing Grandma here, look me up. I'm always on the hunt for new talent."

He laughed maniacally and made a series of sharp gestures I took to represent a wrestling move, possibly the famed Tallahassee Tangle. He revved his engine, waved one of his oaken arms above his head, and rocketed off down the street.

"Wow, dude, was that really him?" said Scottie, massaging his temples as though he'd just witnessed some rapturous apparition.

"Sonofabitch is stalking me," mumbled Fritz. He was rubbing his swollen ankle again. I suggested we drive to a clinic so he could have it X-rayed, but he shrugged off my suggestion.

"And miss lunch? You kidding me? Let's go, get in." He got up, adjusted the bill of the *Nimitz*, and limped over to the Allanté.

Chapter Sixteen

WE TOOK THE SELMON EXPRESSWAY out of Ybor City, exited onto a four-lane road, and headed west. A muddle of commercial establishments whizzed by as we skipped from stoplight to stoplight. Most of the businesses were the usual fare: banks, gas stations, pet stores, fast-food restaurants, the names instantly recognizable and easily forgotten. I did note that an eatery named the Whole Enchilada Bus had abandoned the vicissitudes of the road for an old Pizza Hut, and Odin's Lightning Fast Auto Repair and Tires supported the troops, or so its signage claimed, the garish façade striking a rather bellicose note among its less demonstrative neighbors.

Scottie was in the back with his hood up, fast asleep. Fritz leaned forward on the steering wheel and squinted at the dashboard, trying to make sense of the digital display, which had become illegible in the midday sunlight. He turned right by some rusty train tracks and followed the road past some concrete-mixing equipment that was churning away next to two large aluminum silos, which may or may not have been part of the concrete operation. The Bay Squall Oyster Shack was at the end of the road, wedged between an industrial marine repair outfit and a natural gas terminal.

Fritz killed the ignition and poked Scottie. He grunted but didn't open his eyes. After a few more vigorous jabs from Fritz, he came to, his heavy brow flexing like a giant caterpillar rousted from a pile of moist tree bark.

The guy working the front of the house led us through the restaurant and out to a wooden deck overlooking the bay. We installed ourselves at a butcher-block table with a napkin dispenser in the middle that resembled a toaster. Fritz told the man he could keep his menus. He leaned back, relishing his command of the Bay Squall's laminated opus. When the waiter arrived, Fritz ordered three catches of the day, the "Keep 'em Coming Platter," and a large "Mountain of Oysters."

Our drinks arrived, and the waiter presented each of us with a lobster-emblazoned plastic bib, a small hammer, a nutcracker, a tiny fork, and an ice pick. I joked that the shrunken tools looked like implements Ken might employ for residential burglaries if he were forced to turn to a life of crime to fund Barbie's high-maintenance lifestyle. Scottie laughed, but Fritz didn't so much as crack a smile. He examined his utensils like a prudent surgeon and opined that they'd definitely come in handy when interrogating diminutive insurgents while attempting to stay within the bounds of the Geneva Conventions. He tied his flimsy bib around his elongated neck and straightened out the wrinkles in his lobster with several firm chest strokes. Satisfied, he reached into his jacket and pulled out a small spiral-bound notebook of the type TV detectives use to jot down license plate numbers. He began to ask me questions about Willis Delaney, some more relevant than others.

"Hair color?"

I opened my file and pulled out the newspaper article. Fritz examined the black-and-white photo.

"Indeterminate," he said, and scribbled "indeterminate" into the notebook. He had to break it into two parts with a hyphen in the middle, the single word filling the entire sheet. He flipped the page and continued.

"Height and weight?"

"Height, I'm not sure about. Weight? He was definitely portly in '94." I tapped on Delaney's newspaper gut.

"Dangerously corpulent," declared Fritz. He began to write and soon ran out of room. He shook his head, flipped to a new page, and wrote, "Lardass." He continued without looking up. "Demeanor?"

I scanned the Delaney quotes in the newspaper article. "Quarrelsome bordering on combative." Fritz glared at me and I remembered the pathetic notebook. "Sorry, let's go with 'hostile.'"

"Occupation?"

"Dispossessed slumlord, presently the owner of an illegally funded fishing operation. I'm not sure I can sum that up succinctly."

Fritz turned his notebook sideways and scrawled, "Pirate."

"Fair enough," I said.

"Marital status?" Fritz asked.

"I'm not sure," I said. "How does that help?"

Fritz ignored me. "Hobbies," he barked.

"Golf," I said. "With balls, possibly Frisbees."

Scottie picked up his hammer and pounded the table with it, attempting in vain to squash a hornet that was feeding on a glob of sugary residue stuck to the surface.

"Goddammit Scottie, cut it out, will you?" Fritz yelled. He went back to the notebook. "Is he known to be armed?"

"I don't think so . . . Hold on. He did threaten a band of would-be criminals with the sharp end of his one-wood, but that was more for general deterrence, I'd guess."

Fritz sighed, obviously hoping for a more binary response.

The waiter arrived with a slew of cohorts in tow. Each one bore a portion of our excess. They soon determined there was no way our table was going to accommodate our gluttonous banquet. One member of the team, possibly destined for heights greater than the Bay Squall, suggested they push a couple of adjacent tables together to create our own personal buffet setup.

Our feast properly positioned, we went to work. Fritz immediately began to slurp down oysters. Scottie popped open mussels with his butter knife and skewered the little orange blobs with his tiny fork. I was overwhelmed by the bounty and succumbed momentarily to the paradox of choice before I regained my bearings and went to work on a crab claw with my nutcracker. It was a ferocious display of consumption from all, our elbows akimbo and pieces of crustacean shell flying through the air at such velocity that Fritz put on his sunglasses to protect his eyes from wayward shrapnel.

As the food disappeared, the small talk picked up. I asked Fritz if he was a native Tampan.

"Native? How about twenty-four years, does that get me something? Hell, most of the so-called natives don't know a damn thing about the area. See there?" He pointed south to a peninsula jutting out into the bay. "That's Port Tampa. Teddy Roosevelt embarked from that very spot to kick some Spanish rear down in Cuba. You think any of *these* people have heard of the Rough Riders?" He gestured in the direction of the four or five other occupied tables in the vicinity. "Rough Riders, any of you people heard of 'em?" he yelled to no one in particular while the other diners scrutinized us with worried confusion.

"And see there." He motioned to a bridge in the distance, its suspension cables forming two gigantic sails that were no more than apparitions in the midday haze. "That's the Sunshine Skyway Bridge. Opened in '87. Some dumb SOB in a tugboat plowed into the old one. Killed thirty-five people. Bet you wish you were lawyering around here when all that went down."

"Where did you live before you moved to Tampa?" I asked Fritz, hoping to skirt a discussion of my stalled career.

Fritz told us he'd grown up in Omaha but abandoned ship on account of the claustrophobia he'd experienced being landlocked on the flat plains for long periods. Sure, he said, there was Lake Manawa, right across the border in Iowa, but that shallow offshoot of the Missouri River wasn't a significant enough body of water to alleviate his distress. So, on his eighteenth birthday, he marched down to the local navy recruitment office and signed up for duty.

The next thing he knew, he was on a destroyer in the South China Sea, witnessing the end of the Vietnam War up close and personal. He spent most days fishing helpless refugees out of the water after their makeshift boats capsized in the rough waves, which he and his fellow sailors took to calling "bobbing for apples." After the end of the war, he moved over to the USS *Nimitz* and embarked on a more conventional military career.

Fritz stayed in the navy until his father died unexpectedly. Gunther Osterfeld was crushed to death when a wall of sausages toppled over onto him while he was conducting an inventory count in preparation for Oktoberfest. The Osterfeld Sausage Haus needed a replacement Osterfeld, and a thirty-six-year-old Fritz applied for an honorable discharge to return home and attend to the sausage business.

"Heard the old saw about not wanting to see sausage being made? There's a reason for that." Fritz told us the first thing he did when he took over was to brick up the big picture window in the managerial suite. He claimed that single act alone increased office productivity by 20 percent.

He ran the sausage operation for five years. Unable to bear even one more week of supervising the filling of animal intestines with ground offal, he put the company up for sale. He accepted the only offer the commercial broker received. It was from a competing operation on the other side of Omaha, a company that produced sausages Gunther had reviled because of their artificial casings and high-bread-crumb content. Not wanting to upset the dead, Fritz contemplated holding out for a more quality-conscious buyer, but by then, his plains angst had returned with a fury, and neither waterskiing on Lake Manawa nor sitting in a cold bath at three in the morning did anything to soothe his anxieties.

"I got out my road atlas and we paged through it. I picked St. Ignace, Michigan, being it's within an hour's drive of three of the five Great Lakes. Nancy picked the Tampa Bay area, said I was too hung up on fresh water and wasn't giving sufficient weight to the climate."

Fritz said he and Nancy decided to flip for it—heads St. Ignace, tails Tampa. He retrieved a silver dollar from his wall safe and gave it a good toss. But when it hit the table, it took a nasty bounce and fell onto the floor, head side up.

"Nancy made me flip again, but it came up heads a second time," said Fritz. "That's when she told me she'd divorce me before she'd move to northern Michigan."

"You think she was serious?" I asked Fritz. Since my banishment, I'd become obsessed with the inner workings of other people's relationships.

"Serious? About divorce? Hell, you're married to a woman the caliber of Nancy, you'd be dumb as a sandhiller to ask a question like that. Scared the damn doodinkus out of me when she got that cancer."

"Is she okay now?"

"Yeah, thank god. Been in remission the better part of five years. You don't realize how . . ."

Fritz's voice trailed off. He turned toward the bay and stared off into the middle distance. I didn't know what to say. Scottie began hammering the table again. This time, Fritz didn't say a word. The three of us sat there in silence, except for the deafening sound of the hammering.

Fritz walked off to use the restroom seconds before the waiter arrived with our check, a multipage handwritten affair. It was all in order except for a side of hush puppies that Scottie and I agreed we couldn't remember eating, although due to the delirium of the last two hours, neither of us was a hundred percent sure. We summoned the waiter. After a lengthy discussion, he agreed to remove the hush puppy charge, which was nothing more than a Pyrrhic victory given the effort it took to save $3.60. By the time we had it straight, fifteen minutes had passed, and there was still no sign of Fritz.

"You think he's okay?" I asked Scottie.

"He's probably hiding in a stall until the check's paid. He pulled that stunt last week too."

"What'd you do?"

"I only had five dollars on me, so I had to wait him out."

"How long did that take?"

"Dude, you don't wanna know. Sucks being broke."

I summoned the waiter and paid the bill. Not a minute after I signed the credit card receipt, Fritz emerged, looking about as happy as I'd seen him all day.

"Ready, boys," he said, and motioned to the door.

By then, it was late afternoon. I asked Fritz to drop me at the unfinished pyramid hotel. Tony and Russ Mullen were there, whiling away the afternoon, but it wasn't quite the same without Nelson and his fragile innocence.

Tony asked me if I'd heard anything from Whitney.

"Not a word," I said. "It's been over a week now. I called her before I left Houston, but her phone went to voicemail. And I tried her office, but the receptionist said she was out for a few days."

"Sounds odd," said Mullen. He shot a cautionary look in Tony's direction, which Tony returned with equal concern.

"Yeah, strange," said Tony. "Have you checked online?"

My only online presence to speak of was a Twitter account I'd opened because Whitney had begged me, over a year ago, to follow Dupont Homes. I pulled out my phone, went to my account, and selected the Dupont Homes page. The latest tweet contained a link to a virtual tour of a three-bedroom house in a drab development north of town, for which complimentary upgrades were apparently available, but only for twenty-four hours, according to the melodramatic message. The days-old post had garnered a mere five likes, the attempt to whip up viral panic for the property in North Mill Oaks obviously not producing the desired result.

One of those likes had been posted by Whitney. I selected her account and scrolled down her timeline, but it contained nothing more than retweets of Dupont Homes postings. I noticed that the account @realdealronnied had also liked the post. I tapped it and up popped a photo of Ronnie Dupont himself.

Mullen leaned over and peered at my phone. "So, anything interesting?"

The only recent tweet in Dupont's feed was from earlier in the day. The sun-drenched photo featured a chunky hand holding a curvy daiquiri glass filled with a frozen, pale red liquid, the rim awash in slices of tropical fruits. The glass was framed by a pair of protuberant trotters splayed out at forty-five-degree angles at the bottom of a chaise lounge. Between the disagreeable feet, an emerald-green expanse of water stretched out to the horizon. The message above the photo read, "In Seaside, livin' the Dupont dream!!!"

I tweaked the screen to zoom in and accidentally hit on Dupont's big ugly toes, which were covered with coarse patches of curly black hair.

"Damn," said Russ Mullen.

Revolted, I zoomed back out. I was about to give up when I noticed something to the left of Dupont's chaise. I zoomed in again and strained to identify the pixelated object. It was a woman's foot, partially buried in the sand, one delicate toe peeking out with the reticence of a hermit crab on the hunt for a new shell. The flawless toenail, mani-cured to feminine perfection, was painted Bama crimson, the official color of Whitney's alma mater and her favorite color. I zoomed in more, hoping to spot a mole, scar, or other deformity that would mark the toe as somebody else's, but alas, nothing.

I studied the lonesome toe and cycled through possi-bilities. Was it hers? Surely not. But what if it was? No, impossible. Not impossible, possible. More than possible, probable. Deciding to run with "almost definitely," I mentally reconstructed her body upward from the ground, trying to imagine what the rest of her looked like at the moment that photo was taken. I added body parts in sequence, starting with her left leg, toned and muscular from her daily runs. Then came a shapely hip, defined abs, and her small but perky chest. After I topped her head with long, shiny auburn hair, I moved on to dressing her. Not a lot to do there, unfortunately. She was probably wearing that orange bikini, the one that routinely failed to contain her right butt cheek, which popped out whenever she took a few steps with any sort of purpose.

This image hit me hard. There she was, standing next to Dupont, her exposed cheek being caressed by the coastal breeze. I bet Dupont had leered at that lovely glute all day long . . . Leer? Who was I kidding? They were frolicking around on a sandy beach, consuming potent fruity cocktails of the type amorous vacationers imbibe to numb their inhibitions. No, there was no way around it—shaggy-toed Ronny Dupont was likely rubbing his werewolf feet all over Whitney and doing god knows what else to her.

I tossed my phone onto the bar in disgust. "I think that might be my wife's toe in that photo," I said, fully aware of the implications of my words but surprised to hear myself say them aloud because I was the type that usually bore suffering in silence.

"Ah, Jesus, man, I'm sorry," said Tony. Mullen offered a few terse words of sympathy, his downcast mutterings those of a neighbor who's just learned about your burglary and is worried his house will be next.

I drank five more beers and inhaled two cheeseburgers, then stumbled back to the Theodore and passed out in my clothes. When I woke up, it was five thirty in the morning, and my mouth felt like I'd eaten a box of chalk. I got up, turned on the TV, and watched a morning anchor in a sleeveless purple dress make traffic predictions for rush hour. It was a vigorous presentation, Chita Romero's trim arms pointing out soon-to-be-clogged arteries and historically troublesome hot spots on the large map projected behind her. The freeways were all pulsing green at present, but Chita promised a sea of red come seven thirty. I turned the volume down on Chita, which detracted little from the segment given her excited gesturing and my unfamiliarity with the local road network.

Chapter Seventeen

AT SEVEN, I WENT DOWNSTAIRS to meet Fritz. He wasn't in the lobby, so I walked outside, where I saw the Allanté parked in the fire lane. A tackle box was wedged into Scottie's quarters, and several fishing rods jutted skyward from behind the seats. The rods flexed in the breeze like the antennae of a mutant insect, making the vehicle resemble a float in a small-town parade.

I went back inside and spotted Fritz at a table near the breakfast buffet. He was attacking a tall stack of syrupy pancakes and drinking a generous glass of grapefruit juice, his cheeks puckering with every considerable gulp. Constance stood next to him, and Fritz was regaling her with details of yesterday's action.

"Slippery little fella, I tell you. Thought he was armed, but it was a bushel of cigars. Those fat ones, look like torpedoes." Fritz spotted me. "Sleeping Beauty. Well, well, counselor, glad you could make it. Damn good spread they've got here, puts the navy to shame."

I wasn't hungry enough to risk another run-in with Constance and her tongs, so I grabbed a banana from the buffet and sat across from Fritz. He'd exchanged the *Nimitz* for a red cap with "Huskers" scrawled on the front in cursive lettering. An assortment of freshwater lures was pinned to the cap.

"So, you're still a Husker fan after all these years?" I asked him.

"Not everything's crap in Nebraska," he replied, without mention of the Cornhuskers' recent mediocrity on the gridiron.

Fritz scarfed down the last of his pancakes, and we walked out to the parking lot. I noticed he was still limping. He said Nancy had made him soak for a couple of hours in a tub full of lavender bath salts, ergo, if he smelled of lavender, that was the reason. He knew the soaking wouldn't do anything, but Nancy was adamant. He complained some more about the indignity of the lavender treatment, throwing around a few military metaphors that were hard to follow. I listened, but all I gleaned was that there were often uncanny similarities between marriage and trench warfare.

Fritz asked me if I was married.

"Yes, although it's complicated," I said.

"Complicated?"

"We're in the middle of a trial separation."

"Trial separation? What in the goddamn hell is that? You're either married or you're not. Whose idea was that?"

"Hers. I told her the same thing, but it didn't do any good. The worst of it is I think she's sleeping with her boss. I believe they're shacked up at a resort in Seaside as we speak."

"Does he wear a uniform?"

"No, I don't believe so. Why?"

"Women like a man in uniform. And not just the armed forces. Plumbers, bus drivers, pest-control men, they're all known to punch above their weight with the ladies."

"What about double-breasted suits?"

"Waste of fabric. Want to dress up like a sailor, join the navy."

"No, as a uniform."

Fritz thought for a moment. "I suppose it's possible certain women might treat it as such, the lapels and all."

I explained about the toe and recited my other evidence: the lint picking, my harsh, premeditated ejection from our marital residence, the unreturned phone calls, and my general sense of foreboding.

Fritz frowned and nodded. "Did you say Seaside? You mean up near Panama City? Hell, what is that? Four hundred miles? Counselor, you can make that drive in six hours, seven tops. I'd make it in five if I had a roof. What I'm saying is that if some playboy were up there with Nancy, trying god knows what, I'd sure as hell wanna know."

"You would?"

"Sure, you can't be living in limbo, it'll drive you outta your mind. Just ask Hal Diggle."

"Who?"

"Long story, but suffice to say, Diggle was eaten up with suspicions. Ruined his life. I'll leave it at that."

"Did Diggle ever find out if his wife was cheating on him?"

Fritz laughed. "Wife? Hell, Diggle was never married."

Last night, before I passed out, I texted Whitney a copy of the Ronnie Dupont "Livin' the Dream" photo. I edited it on my phone beforehand. I drew a red circle around the toe and added a couple of chunky exclamation points. My final drunken touch was the word "BUSTED" scrawled diagonally across the entire sordid scene.

Whitney texted me back this morning: "omg what does this mean whats wrong with you ru losing it?!" I'd scoured this text many times, trying to unearth clues to her state of mind. Was the message an expression of wifely concern about my mental well-being, or were the words those of a wanton adulteress, frustrated at being caught in flagrante? I couldn't make up my mind. I did note, with a sense of unease, she'd skirted the issue of the toe evidence completely.

I concluded Fritz was right. Not knowing one way or the other was going to eat me alive. I told him to head to the marina without me. I'd grab my things and meet him there. After confronting Delaney, I'd head north, directly to Seaside. With any luck, I'd have my answers by the end of the day tomorrow.

I packed my suitcase and checked out of the Theodore. In my absence, careless seagulls had pelted the windshield of my rental car with bird crap, the splotchy droppings baked onto the glass like Teflon by the relentless sun. I rode the Campbell Causeway across the bay, into the heart of Clearwater, my windshield wipers on high and my thumb pegged on the washer button the entire way. I passed the Flag building, where the Scientologists were supposedly holed up by the thousands, polishing latrines and fighting over bunk beds and table scraps. I squinted through the shit-stained windshield at their galactic headquarters. I wasn't sure about Scottie's futuristic description. To me, the building projected the confused tastelessness of a low-rent Vegas casino, one miles away from the Strip, the creation of nervous architects scared to commit to an overriding theme.

I followed the road west and took a second causeway, ultimately reaching a barrier island known as Clearwater Beach. I parked and soon found Delaney's berth, where the *Buzzard of the Brine* was tied up between two other fishing boats. A ropey guy in denim shorts and flip-flops was arranging fishing equipment on the deck. Fritz was in the boat with him, showing off his rods.

"Delaney coming today?" Fritz asked the man, who didn't appear happy to have him at such close quarters.

"Yeah, he'll be here. Not sure about the weather though. The radar's showing a band of low pressure out in the gulf. Either way, it'll be a while before we set sail, so you may be more comfortable on the dock."

Fritz ignored the less-than-subtle instruction to disembark and took to spit-shining some gunky residue off the stern, old habits dying hard. I waved at him to snap him out of his navy trance. He finally got the hint and climbed out of the boat. I told him the court documents were in my backpack. When I judged the time right, I would yell out a secret phrase, his cue to retrieve the papers and serve them on Delaney.

"What's the phrase?" he asked.

"I'm not sure, any ideas?"

"How about 'It's time to deliver the baby'?"

"Shouldn't it be something I can work into conversation?"

Fritz thought for a moment. "Hold on, doesn't matter, does it? We'll be out on the water, so it's not like he can make a run for it. How about you just yell out 'Sic 'em, Fritz'?"

Fritz had a good point, which led us to agree there wasn't any need for a secret phrase. We decided when the time was right, I'd pull the papers out of my backpack and hand them to Fritz in a casual manner, without yelling "Sic 'em."

The guy on the boat motioned in the direction of an old man being helped down the dock by a young guy in a hat with floppy side pieces, the kind of thing British explorers used to wear when crossing African deserts. "There they are," he said, and waved to the men.

The old man shuffling down the dock bore no resemblance to the testy guy in the newspaper photo. Not only were there no physical similarities, but this codger was far too old to be Willis Delaney. Based upon the photo, Delaney would be in his midfifties now, sixty-five tops. This frail coot, who struggled to walk unassisted, had to be at least seventy-five.

The man in the Saharan headgear slunk off to join his crewmate, and the old man extended a withered arm. "Willis Delaney, pleased to meet you." He shook our hands. "You gentlemen ready to drop some lines in the water? Ray's telling me a little weather's supposed to move in. Don't worry, we'll keep an eye on it. Storms usually blow over in a few hours. Worst case, we should be out by lunchtime."

Given I hoped to be in Seaside by the end of the day, I needed to move things along. "Sir, I'm Guy Hastings. I'm here to talk to you about a lawsuit you were involved in, but I'm confused." I handed him the newspaper article with the Delaney photo. He pulled a pair of glasses out of his shirt pocket and scanned the page.

"Oh my, no no, that's not me, that's Alton, my nephew." He shook his head and chuckled. "That was years ago, but I remember it like it was yesterday. We were playing golf and a local news reporter caught us coming off the green at eighteen. Something about golf clubs being stolen. I'd never heard nothin' about that, but it sure fired up Alton."

Delaney said the newsman egged on Dugas to gin up some controversy for his article. "He insulted Alton's manhood. Suggested if a criminal came for Alton's clubs, he looked like the kind of guy who'd gladly hand his bag over, right after he soiled himself. Not only that, but he'd be so scared he'd probably offer to caddy a round for the robber. Woo boy, that got Alton hot as a welded seam. He was dancing around, ranting and raving about how he'd do this and that. That's when the reporter took that photo."

Delaney told us that the reporter had mixed up their details, which resulted in the erroneous photo attribution.

"They issued a correction, but it wasn't nothing more than one line on the back page," said Delaney. "Poor Alton was all tore up he missed his fifteen minutes."

I told him I'd called Alton's towing place, and he had gotten equally fired up about a man named Sattler.

"That sounds like Alton. Good heart but terrible temper. And can't keep it in his pants. But what can I do? He's the only kin I've got left."

The old man's story sounded legitimate, but what about the Dynasty Terrace? He admitted that after his first bypass operation, the maintenance did suffer, but it wasn't all that bad, far from a slum.

"Sure there was crime, but it wasn't out of control. My lawyer, Blow, kept writing all these crazy letters to the city, which riled them up, made things worse, started a war. And he was billing me for every one. Bleeding me dry! I finally had to fire him."

Delaney said Blow was a staunch libertarian who'd made a run for the state senate the year after Delaney cut him loose. Blow had posted the Dynasty Terrace letters on his campaign website—evidence, Blow claimed, of his free-market credentials. But they were so dense with jargon that even potential voters interested in abolishing public libraries and state parks didn't make it past the first paragraph.

"He got less than two percent of the vote," said Delaney, noting he wasn't sure what had done in the hardscrabble campaign. It could have been the entrenched apparatus of

America's two-party system or possibly Blow's pompous air. Maybe even his ill-fitting trousers.

"How can a man seeking higher office have such a bad tailor?" said Delaney. "His britches were at least a foot too long. He looked like he had accordions strapped to his ankles."

I didn't know what to believe by this point, so I revealed my identity and confronted Delaney with the check for $500,000, pointing out the signatures.

"It just showed up one day," said Delaney. "The city sent it to me by mistake." He said he'd called Harry, who told him to sign both their names, deposit it, and write Harry a check for his cut. "So that's what I did. Sent it to his paralegal the next week. But Harry never cashed it. I called, left messages, but didn't hear anything back. It was ages before I was able to get ahold of his girl."

"What was her name?" I asked him. "Was it Reese Walters?"

"Yes, sir, that's it. Claimed she hadn't received it. She seemed preoccupied, like she had better things to do than talk to me."

"She quit right around that time," I said. "I've been trying to sort out the mess at Harry's office but—"

"Damn shame about Harry. He was such a fine man. You know he used to live two doors down from me when he was in middle school?"

"Really? No, I had no idea."

"That was over fifty years ago, I reckon. Anyway, he took good care of me, that's for sure." Delaney added that the settlement money had been a godsend. It was allowing him to spend the time he had left doing the thing he loved most. He was too weak to fish, but that didn't matter, just being out on the water with like-minded folk was enough.

Delaney continued, "I stopped payment on that check and sent a replacement. Another month or two went by, then I heard Harry had died. I sent flowers. Assumed someone from his firm would get ahold of me. And here you are, thank goodness. That money's been a weight, I tell you."

I remembered the punch list, pulled it out of my backpack, and showed it to Delaney.

"You talked to Mrs. Simpkins, did you? Oh my. She's something." Delaney said he believed poor Mrs. Simpkins suffered from a combination of terrible anxiety and undiagnosed paranoia. She had almost backed out of the deal on several occasions, the last being the day before closing. To finalize the sale, once and for all, Delaney had bought her a comprehensive home warranty from a national outfit with a solid reputation.

"I kept pleading with her to call the insurance people," said Delaney. "Sounds like she still hasn't figured it out."

"No, but I did tend to a few repairs while I was up there investigating." I told him I'd tightened the disposal clamp with a butter knife because she didn't have a screwdriver. Delaney said a butter knife sounded like a perfectly good substitute, although he preferred a coin himself. Fritz declared he favored Nancy's metal nail file in a pinch.

After we finished discussing the relative merits of the screwdriver proxies, Delaney suggested we go straight to the bank so he could transfer the funds, there was a branch less than ten minutes away. Fritz offered to give Delaney a ride to the bank in the Allanté, which would allow me time to plan my route to Seaside and secure lodgings for the night.

"Don't worry, the top's toast, but there's rain gear in the trunk." Fritz put an arm around Delaney's sloped shoulders and guided him back up the dock, toward the parking lot.

There was only one hotel in Seaside that I knew would meet Whitney's rather elevated standards, a four-star joint right on the beach called the Pastel Shore Inn. I grimaced at the assault of pastels and the exorbitant rates and reluctantly booked the cheapest room on offer.

Fritz and Delaney returned from the bank. I told Fritz he should stick around and wait out the weather, have Scottie take my place on the *Buzzard*. He agreed and dialed Scottie's number. After several rings, someone picked up.

"Hi, Mrs. LeDuff, it's Fritz . . . Oh he is, is he? Well, wake him up, could you? He'll want to hear what I've got planned for him this afternoon."

It was a good five minutes before Mrs. LeDuff returned to the phone.

"No, no, we're not going back to that Cuban joint. It's fishing. Offshore . . . Yes, ma'am, apologies for that. Did you try the heavy cycle, with bleach? A tablespoon works like a charm for Nancy . . . Okay, yes, ma'am, I'll hold."

Understandably, Scottie was more interested in fishing than revisiting the scene of his tobacco flagellation. He soon got on the line, and Fritz gave him the address of the marina.

"Make sure you gas up before the causeway," Fritz told him. "Under no circumstances do I want you stopping in Clearwater, you hear?"

I thanked Fritz for his help and extended an arm, but he brushed it aside and grabbed me in a tight bear hug.

"Get outta here, counselor," he said. "You've got a lot of blacktop to chew up before the end of the day."

I apologized to Delaney for getting the wrong end of the stick about him and his real estate holdings. I asked him to tell his nephew Dugas it was me, not Sattler, who'd disrupted his towing operation. I guessed the Dugas-Sattler relationship was beyond repair—the brass-necked doggie style and all—but I expressed the sentiment nonetheless.

"Fritz tells me you need to head north," said Delaney. "I hope you get the answers you're looking for."

"You and me both," I said, and shook his hand. I turned and walked back to the parking lot, anticipating the long drive ahead.

Chapter Eighteen

I WOUND MY WAY OUT OF CLEARWATER, then headed north on I-75. Even with the wind at my back, the rental struggled to maintain highway speeds. Air streamed in around the window seals, and I was forced to crank up the radio to drown out the high-pitched howl.

After an hour, I pulled off the interstate to fill up. I paid for the gas and purchased a Phillips-head screwdriver and a roll of duct tape that I'd found on a dusty shelf, between a three-pack of bungee cords and a few tins of shoe polish.

I pulled the rental away from the pump and over to the "Inflation Station," which was nothing more than a greedy coin slot attached to a grimy air compressor. I fed in a couple of quarters, and the machine rumbled to life like a vibrating bed in a cheap motel. I filled the tires to ten PSI over the maximum recommended inflation level to reduce rolling resistance, then went to work on the car, covering the window seams and panel gaps with the dull silver tape.

The gas station was across the street from some joint called Duffy's Down Home Eats. I was taping the windshield seams along the A-pillars when I heard laughing and hooting coming from the restaurant's parking lot. A group of bearish-looking men with droopy mouths stood around two jacked-up pickups. They were observing my actions with a leering skepticism, like I was a lazy stripper not putting enough heart into her table dance.

After I finished taping, I removed both side-view mirrors with the screwdriver and threw them into the passenger footwell. I didn't know how much of a benefit all this improvised streamlining would yield, but I remembered reading somewhere that innovation is often born of great frustration, so I'd be lying if I said I wasn't expecting to see tangible improvements before I reached the panhandle.

The men at Duffy's continued to taunt me from a distance. I kept my cool, not wanting to be coal-rolled all the way to Gainesville. They finally got bored and fired up their trucks. They gunned their big diesel engines and thundered out of the parking lot, enveloping a family lounging in the folksy rocking chairs out front in a thick cloud of soot.

The gas station duct tape was cheap and started to peel off before I'd even made it past Ocala. I was being overtaken by everyone. My only conquest was an old green truck with a wooden bed loaded full of ripe oranges. The driver was losing about five oranges per mile. They bounced out of the bed in the random, unpredictable fashion of hand grenades in a video game. I had to swerve several times to avoid being fragged.

After about ten miles of dodging citrus, I'd had enough. I pulled out and made my move, the rental shaking like a washing machine full of heavy blankets. I crept up alongside the truck and pointed at the bed to alert the driver to his inventory shrinkage, but the man just smiled and tipped his frayed straw hat in my direction, seemingly unconcerned about the attrition of his harvest.

The morning evaporating, I tried another tactic. I

tucked in behind a big rig and pulled up close, until its "How's My Driving?" sign filled my windshield. I took to cruising inches off the truck's bumper. The driver couldn't see me in his mirrors, but I could tell he knew I was there because he kept changing lanes to try to shake me off. While speed wasn't the rental's strong suit, I had him on maneuverability, so I was able to stay planted in his slipstream until he exited the freeway near a town called Irvine. When he pulled off, he waved a balled fist out the window and yelled words lost to the wind.

I settled into the monotony of the drive, and my mind turned to Whitney. We'd met at the end of the summer after I graduated from college, right before I left for law school. I worked for Dad that summer, helping Alphonso change fluids and doing other basic maintenance in the shop. When one of the salesmen quit without notice, Dad told me he needed me to cover the sales desk.

After a week on the sales job, a man showed up looking for a car for his daughter, something reliable that would see her through her last two years in Tuscaloosa. He was a square-jawed fellow with the thick, fussy mustache of a Civil War general, and he spoke in a curt, irritated manner, like someone had just stepped on his foot. He told me, rather gruffly, he was after a sturdy, reasonably priced vehicle with low miles that he wouldn't be underwater on if it ended up totaled.

"Oh, so your daughter's not the greatest driver?" I asked him.

"She's all right, plays her music too loud, like all those college kids. No, I'm more concerned about the other dumbasses, especially over in Louisiana."

He went on to recite a bunch of evidence, all of it anecdotal, to support his theory that if there were a fifty-state ranking of the most head-up-their-ass drivers, Louisiana would come second, after New Jersey. He harbored great loathing for the citizens of the Garden State because they didn't pump their own gas. He went on and on about the gas-pumping business. He claimed it weakened constitutions and fostered dependence. What would the government do for them next, come to their houses and flush their commodes? I pointed out that Mexicans weren't light on fortitude even though the Pemex people hadn't let them near a gas pump for years. When I mentioned the refueling practices of our southern neighbors, he stared me down with cold, contemptuous eyes.

I showed him a handful of domestic sedans, all in pretty good shape. After we test-drove four of them, he picked two and told me he would send his daughter over to make the final choice. Sure enough, Whitney showed up later in the week. I don't know what I was expecting, but suffice to say, I wasn't expecting what showed up. She was stunning. Her close-cut navy shorts showed off her tanned legs, and her pale blue linen shirt was knotted above her navel, leaving a delicious sliver of her toned midsection exposed. Her belly button was taut and shallow, the kind that could go months without snagging a stray piece of lint. It glowed like a little sun as she glided into the sales office with the grace of the Mexican actress Isaura Espinoza, or so Alphonso told me later, while we were draining the brake fluid out of a Kia Sorento with an unfortunate dent in the hood.

I introduced myself and showed her the two cars her dad had picked out for her. She turned up her nose at both of them.

"How about that one." She pointed to a pristine BMW 3 Series parked out front, on full display, its pearlescent-white metallic paint sparkling in the sun. It was at least

$7,500 more than the others, but when I told her the price, she didn't flinch.

"Well, you let me worry about that," she said with a wistful flourish of her wrist, as if holding court in a Jane Austen novel.

We took the BMW for a spin, and she told me she was in love. With the car, that is.

"Oooh, I'm smitten," she purred in a sultry voice. She rolled down the windows, turned up the stereo, and grabbed the steering wheel with two hands. She clasped the wheel in an exaggerated fashion and moved it from side to side in small increments while blowing through red lights and honking at pedestrians like the daughter of a Russian oligarch.

We returned to the dealership, and she confirmed that the BMW was the only acceptable option. I told her we'd clean it up over the weekend, and she could pick it up the next week, assuming she talked her dad into ditching the domestics. I said I wouldn't be around then, but the new salesman, Rod Essex, would take good care of her. I hadn't met Essex, but Dad usually hired salesmen with agreeable demeanors, so I didn't think I was out on a limb there.

"Oh, so where are you going?" she asked while she fiddled with the presets of the satellite radio as though she already owned the car. The way she kept fiddling while she talked made me think she didn't really care about my answer.

I said I was moving to Houston the next Monday. Almost in passing, she asked me what I was going to be doing in Houston. I told her I was starting law school in a few weeks. It was then I sensed a slight shift in her attitude, a small flicker of curiosity.

I can't remember how I summoned the nerve to suggest

we meet up before I left town, and I can't remember what I said either. My mouth began working in "Hastings Overdrive," a dangerous fugue state of quantity over quality, where words flow freely, one after the other, with no logical connection among them. Whatever I said, it couldn't have been too terrible, because we agreed to meet for a drink that very evening at a bar called the Longhorn. She suggested the place because she had sweet-talked the bartender into overlooking the fact she was not yet twenty-one.

The Longhorn was a timber-clad joint with a set of shabby horns mounted over the door. The bartender Whitney had sweet-talked wasn't working that night, so she sweet-talked his replacement. When that guy's shift ended, she sweet-talked his successor, a sweaty woman with a soft rectangular torso that reminded me of a waterlogged bath sponge.

The night shot by in a flash. The conversation flowed easily while we engaged in the timeworn rituals of courtship. We shared our passions and preferences, including our favorite books, movies, and food. She told me her two biggest fears in life were not living up to her great potential, compensation-wise, and getting cancer and having to wear a wig made of donated hair. I said mine was getting locked in the trunk of a car, one manufactured prior to 2002, before the feds mandated those little plastic emergency-release pulls that get in the way when loading bulky cargo. I told her my second was running out of supplemental oxygen on the high faces of the Himalaya. She asked me if I had plans to summit the world's highest peaks. I admitted I didn't at present, that my fear of mountain hypoxia was the product of a restless mind eager to contemplate hypothetical danger. She shot me a confused look, which I chalked up to her unfamiliarity with the depths of male reverie.

The evening went so well we made plans to see each other the next day. Saturday turned into Sunday, and I put off going to Houston for several more weeks. I didn't make it there until the day before classes started. I rolled into my new apartment complex just after the lady in the leasing office shut up shop and was walking out to her car. I caught up to her, and she told me I was lucky she had an accommodating nature—her weak spot, or so she claimed—and was willing to work "after hours." When I pointed out it was only 4:50 p.m. and the office didn't close until 5, she glared and told me I obviously needed a new timepiece. I remember this vividly because she said it as if I actually had a defective pocket watch hidden in one of the many pockets of my cargo shorts.

Whit and I did the long-distance thing for two years. It was a heady time, absence and anticipation fuel on the fire of our burgeoning relationship. We married in an elaborate ceremony the summer before my last year of law school. Then Dad died three weeks after the wedding, and we didn't end up back in Houston for another two years, enough time for all the vague doubts I'd nurtured about my chosen profession to coalesce into terrible certainty.

I should have listened more to Dad. After I'd told him I was considering following in Harry's footsteps, he began to drop admonitions full of less-than-subtle reproof. If I mentioned Harry, he would say things like "He doesn't brag about the ones he loses," or "Every day's not the Super Bowl," or "Ask him why he's taking those high-blood-pressure pills." If I brought up law school, I'd hear about all the top-shelf inventory that could be acquired with the tuition money. I discounted his comments because Dad had never been his brother-in-law's biggest fan. It stemmed from Harry's car-buying habits, something Dad never got over.

"He unloads vehicles like Liz Taylor unloads husbands," he'd said, on countless occasions. And it was true. Once a year, before his tires even needed rotating, Harry would swing by the Mercedes dealer and drive home in a new fully loaded S-Class. Dad viewed this wanton swapping to be material surfeit on par with the House of Saud. Not to mention Harry never once offered to sell Dad his trade-ins.

It wasn't long after I'd started clerking for Harry that the law began to shed her Siren allure. After those first few months, I started to second-guess everything. I'd looked to Harry for reassurance. I asked him how he would describe being a lawyer. What was it really like, day in and day out?

"When things are going your way, you can't beat it. You're a champion bullfighter, prancing around in the ring in front of an adoring crowd, a beloved hero who can do no wrong. On other occasions, the bull chases you down and gores you in the goddamn testicles."

While I was attempting to clarify the number of days of matador glory versus testicle goring, we were interrupted. When I asked him later, he didn't remember anything about bulls or testes. I never did get a straight answer, but that didn't stop me from ultimately piecing it all together. I realized I lacked, among other things, Harry's preternatural ability to bend fact over his knee like a naughty toddler and his Hollywood-level talent for morphing into whatever role was needed in a given instant. One minute, he'd be buttering up a judge like the maître d' at a fancy restaurant, the next exploiting an opponent's weakness with the ruthlessness of a Russian grandmaster. In between, he displayed a legendary capacity for shutting himself in his office with his phone cradled under his ear for hours on end.

I imagine the moment it clicked—what the routine of

the practice of law actually entailed—was like the fateful day of plumbing school when they introduce the trainee plumbers to the concept of raw sewage. But by then, I was engaged to a woman with rapacious consumer appetites running up debt obligations to rival an Eastern European country committed to costly infrastructure renewal, so I decided I had no choice but to stay the course. But two years in, when Dad died, I was presented with a convenient excuse to interrupt the inexorable pull of a career I secretly knew I wasn't cut out for.

I never worked up the resolve to tell Whitney about my reservations. My long sabbatical from law school disappointed her. I knew this because she would tell me straight out, and not only when I brought home a smaller-than-usual commission check from the dealership. Even in the flush months, she'd call me unmotivated and accuse me of lacking drive. Not wanting to upset her further, I obscured my true feelings, claiming I'd go back to law school one day, yet coming up with one excuse after the other when each reenrollment deadline neared. Now, with the distinct possibility that Ronnie Dupont had gate-crashed my marriage like a plundering Hun, I worried my indecision might reveal itself to be a frightful miscalculation.

Thinking about Dupont made me realize I needed to take a leak. I took the next exit and relieved myself at one of those grimy gas stations that make you buy something first. When I pulled back onto the interstate, traffic was moving at a crawl. I endured a good two hours of painful stopping and starting before I reached Gainesville. I stayed on the freeway and skirted the west side of the city, passing the exit for the Devil's Millhopper. The Millhopper was a 120-foot muddy-bottomed sinkhole that the state touted as a sunken rain forest of diverse ecology. The hole used to belong to the University of Florida until Gator administrators got sick of paying for cleaning crews to descend into its depths to fish out broken beer bottles and used condoms. After one particularly rampageous football season, the university unloaded it onto the State of Florida. The legislature set about domesticating its new acquisition. It slapped the pit with a state park designation, erected a gate, and started charging for parking. This all happened back in 1974, so today, as I cruised by the sign, the murky depths of Florida's greatest hole beckoning, the era of unfettered Millhopper access was nothing but a distant memory.

Chapter Nineteen

BY THE TIME I PASSED GAINESVILLE and the Millhopper, I'd grown tired of the interstate. I exited the freeway and headed due west, a more direct and hopefully faster route given the traffic.

I was somewhere between Fort White and Branford when I heard an ominous knock coming from the engine. I scanned the instrument cluster and noticed a dim red glow in the lower left corner. I squinted and realized it was the temperature warning light, barely visible through the scratched plastic. How long had it been on? Minutes? Hours? All that effort trying to make meaningful improvements in the coefficient of drag with contrivances dug up at a gas station and I couldn't even bother to keep an eye on the dash?

I decided to pull over to assess the situation. Thankfully, I spotted a gas station in the distance. I approached the entrance and passed a yellow rental truck parked on the shoulder, about twenty yards short of the station, its hazard lights flashing on and off. A short, stout man with a luxuriant head of white hair stood behind the truck. He had on a pair of thick brown houndstooth trousers, and his oxford shirt was soaked with sweat and ballooned out like a parachute. The man was watching a crew of heavy-booted laborers unload bags of ice from a dolly into the back of the truck. I decided he looked out of place, as though he'd materialized at mile 374 of US 27 as a result of some mysterious glitch in the laws of the universe.

I veered into the station and parked next to one of the unoccupied pumps. I ripped the remaining tape off the car and let the engine cool for a few minutes. I opened the hood and didn't see anything amiss. Deciding I had nothing to lose, I fired up the car again. Immediately, a hellish clang came from the engine bay, followed by a cacophony of metallic grinding noises.

"Oh goodness, that doesn't sound promising." It was the sweaty, dapper man, and he spoke with a proper British accent.

"I think the motor's blown." I knelt down and peered under the car. Oil was seeping out onto the concrete, confirming my worst suspicions.

"Repairable, I trust?"

"No, the engine's toast. At least it's a rental, I guess."

"Mine too." He pointed to the midsized box truck. It was a dated design, the cargo hold mounted to a medium-duty chassis. The rectangular metal grille and round headlights gave the truck a contented, agreeable appearance, the vehicle and the man sharing a similarly sanguine aspect.

"What's going on with yours?" I asked the man.

"Don't know exactly. Doesn't want to go into gear. Stubborn bugger."

"What's with all the ice?"

"The ice, my good man, is a desperate attempt to keep my inventory from overheating."

"What's back there?"

"A sizable quantity of wine. Wine that is cooking in this oppressive heat as we speak, I'm afraid."

Something about his stoic resignation made me want to help him. I offered to take a look at the issue.

"Would you? Oh, thank you. That would be marvelous."

"Guy Hastings," I said, extending a hand.

"Percy Templeton. The pleasure's all mine."

I walked down the shoulder and Percy waddled along next to me like an injured duck. I opened the door to the cab and jumped in. The bench seat was piled high with an assortment of notebooks and papers. A plastic container of tea bags and a six-pack of Mars bars sat on the seat among the paperwork, and a box of wine was wedged into the passenger footwell. I looked down at the shifter. A floppy plastic boot sagged down the long black shaft, and a hiero-glyphic shift pattern was etched into the dimpled surface of the knob.

"They rented you a manual?"

"I told them I would accept nothing less. Never driven anything else. Wouldn't know what to do with an auto-matic."

Fair enough. A man's transmission choice is one of those sacred judgments better left unexamined, like whether Truman should have dropped Fat Man so soon after Little Boy. I turned the key and the truck rumbled to life. I depressed the clutch pedal and tried to shift into first, but the gear lever wouldn't engage properly—as soon as I released the shifter, it popped back out with a metallic ping. Second gear, however, worked fine.

"You've got issues with first gear. Possibly a synchro or the linkage, maybe something more serious. You can use second instead, but you'll have to get the revs up before you let out the clutch."

Percy looked confused, so I said, "Hop in, let's try it."

He latched the cargo bay doors and climbed in. I shifted into second, gunned the throttle, and dropped the clutch. The truck thrashed about with the rambunctious instability of a blindfolded toddler attacking an elusive piñata. It finally settled down and crept forward. Percy yelped with glee as we pulled into the gas station. I shut off the ignition, and we both clambered out.

"A miracle, absolute miracle, I can't thank you enough."

"Where are you heading?"

"California or bust." He gestured in the general direction of west, as if the Golden State were mere miles down the road. He told me that while his ultimate destination was California, his planned course would take him through all the major cities en route to San Diego, with detours here and there for interesting attractions and monuments of historical significance. I asked if he'd visited the Millhopper. He shot me a blank look, so I explained the basics but left out the part about college students humping each other amid piles of trash.

"I must say, your devil pit sounds intriguing," said Percy. "But in my experience, landmarks with hyperbolic sobriquets are invariably a letdown."

"Fair enough. So how did you end up here?"

He said he'd departed Orlando midmorning. After he joined I-75, he hit bad traffic, probably the same mess I'd encountered.

"The traffic snarled up. It was barely moving. Then it ground to a halt, and oh dearie me, I must have fallen asleep."

He didn't know how long he'd been out cold. He said his afternoon "kips" usually lasted twenty, thirty minutes tops, but napping on an American interstate while recovering from jet lag was a whole different matter, so comparisons would, by definition, be unreliable. All he knew was it was long enough for him to have lapsed into a vivid dream.

In the dream, he was at his local pub, eating something called a Scotch egg, when the thatched roof fell in. He was forced to escape by climbing up the chimney. He had just freed himself from the top of the sooty stack when he was awoken by a loud knocking. He opened his eyes and tried to focus. A rail-thin man with tight, pale skin was rapping his knuckles on the driver's-side window of his truck. The guy looked exactly like a character in a movie he'd seen recently—an elfin-featured mountain man who'd danced a jig on the porch of a log cabin in the heart of rural Appalachia.

"Frightening wake-up call, I must say," said Percy, explaining that in the seconds it took him to come to and gain his bearings, his mind became consumed by the fate of the main character in the same movie—a timid accountant from the suburbs of Phoenix who'd ventured into the deep woods to find out what had happened to his son. The son was still missing a full year after he'd set off to hike the Appalachian Trail, and the father suspected the worst.

Percy said the movie was fresh in his mind because he'd watched it a few weeks ago with his good friend Oliver Sutter. After ten minutes of flipping through his on-demand queue, Sutter suggested the film. It was set in the bowels of America's heartland, and wasn't Percy about to set off on his own multistate adventure within mere weeks? Maybe the film would serve up a few useful pearls of custom that would better prepare him for his travels? By then, Percy was so weary of trying to decide, he agreed to Sutter's selection.

The out-of-shape accountant turned out to be woefully

unprepared for his adventure. Not only was he unfit and ill equipped, but his diffident constitution did not bode well for survival on the harsh trail. It wasn't long before he was beset by all manner of misfortune. Wild animals—wolves, bears, and other smaller yet no less dangerous predators—stalked him through the wilderness. And he couldn't even get a campfire going until an hour into the movie.

Percy missed the campfire business because he'd been in the kitchen mixing up a fresh batch of Pimm's. "He's finally figured it out, thank the Almighty," yelled Oliver. But by the time Percy made it back to the living room with the cocktails, a torrential rainstorm had extinguished the pitiable pile of smoldering twigs, which threw the hapless protagonist back into his default state of depressed gloom.

Fifteen minutes later, when a grimy hillbilly emerged from a thicket of tall pines, stole the accountant's remaining possessions, and hacked off all the fingers on his left hand, they turned the film off. Percy said he understood cutting off the man's ring finger because years of torpor had caused it to rise like dough around the man's gold wedding band, meaning it would have taken ages for the hillbilly robber to get the ring off by conventional means.

"But the rest of the fingers?" said Percy. "Three more, and the thumb? No, even Oliver agreed the additional amputations were nothing but gratuitous, bestial excess, so we decided to watch *Chariots of Fire* for the umpteenth time."

After his soporific lapse and the frightful flashback, he'd abandoned the interstate, and here he was.

"Well, good luck and be careful. If I were you, I'd head to Tallahassee or Panama City and get them to set you up with a new truck."

He thanked me again, waddled back to the truck, and

disappeared inside. He emerged moments later with a bottle of red wine. "2010 Templeton Vineyards Dornfelder. Aged to perfection. All yours. Please."

I took the bottle and examined it. The label featured an illustration of a medieval knight in full armor standing in front of a barn. The knight had a sword in one hand and a bunch of plump red grapes in the other.

"2010 was a fantastic vintage, almost broke my back trying to bring that harvest in. Didn't have enough Romanians that year. Had to wear a brace for six months. Couldn't even tie my shoes. Wore slippers all winter."

I heard someone behind us yell, "Damn good stuff." I turned to see a hoary man in a flannel shirt perched atop a ride-on lawn mower. He took swig after swig out of an identical bottle of the prized Dornfelder, and streaks of wine dripped down his stubbly chin with every savage glug. He fired up his mower and rolled out of the parking lot, onto the shoulder, kicking up a cloud of brown dust that lingered in his wake.

As I watched him rumble off, I heard honking coming from the other side of the gas station. The laborers were now packed into the bed of an old dually. One of them was holding a bottle of Dornfelder in a protective manner. He meted out the wine in shot-sized amounts with the meticulous possessiveness of a sommelier supervising a fancy tasting. The men downed their diminutive portions in one gulp, then presented their empty cups to the steward, who grumbled before pouring another tiny round. When the truck departed, the men smiled and waved at Percy, a couple even giving him a big thumbs-up.

I thanked Percy for the gift, shook his hand, and said goodbye. I turned back to my broken shell of a car, trying to figure out how I was going to secure a replacement. I had just fished the rental paperwork out of the glove box when I heard the sound of Percy revving the truck's engine. The revving was followed by a loud juddering noise as the clutch disc chafed against the flywheel. Then a deep thunk and the motor died. Percy tried again, with the same result. After several more bouts of revving and stalling, he got out and walked back over to me.

"Impossible, bloody thing. I'm not sure what I'm doing wrong, but I guess I don't have your touch. I'm worried I'm going to mortally wound the old girl. Tell me again, what is your port of call this evening?"

"It was supposed to be a beach town called Seaside. It's about forty-five minutes past Panama City. But I'm not going to make it there today." I pointed at my rental car, which was now encircled by an ever-expanding puddle of oil. Anyone who wished to gas up was forced to pirouette around the slick. Some accomplished this with more dexterity than others.

"A proposition for you, my good man," said Percy. "Since we both have Panama City on our itinerary, how about we team up? Like during the war when you chaps gave us a bit of a hand with the Jerries. If you can prod that stubborn cow down the road, we can both make it there, hopefully not long after this beastly sun decides to set."

Like Napoleon's great frontier fire sale of 1803, this was an intriguing cross-continental offer at a fortuitous time. I was marooned, and it would be tomorrow at the earliest before I could sort out a new car. Percy was no better off, and the way he was spreading his English moonshine around made me worry for his safety, the prevalence of desperate alcoholics probably greater in this unrecommended stretch of the Sunshine State.

After briefly reflecting on Jefferson's good sense to

jump on Bonaparte's giveaway, I told Percy I would be happy to accept his generous offer.

"Marvelous, old chap!" He slapped me on the back and walked off to clear out the cab. I retrieved my suitcase from the rental and loaded it into the cargo area, which contained about fifty large cardboard boxes. Bags full of ice were strewn among the boxes, and the cardboard was absorbing the moisture beading on the surface of the plastic.

Percy helped me push my rental over to the side of the gas station, and I went inside to inform the clerk about her new oil situation. I noticed a case of Percy's Dornfelder on the floor, next to a crate full of gallon jugs of antifreeze. The woman behind the counter was writing something on a bright orange piece of cardboard that looked like a cartoon explosion. I cleared my throat, but she ignored me and kept writing. The pungent chemical odor of her thick black marker filled the air while she scribbled away. After she finished, she walked around and taped the explosion onto the wine box. "SALE. GENUINE ENGLISH WINE. ONLY $9.97!!!!!!!" it proclaimed with optimistic zeal.

I told the woman about the spill.

"How much oil?" she asked.

I'm not one to sugarcoat problems, which sounds like a fine quality but is quite a handicap when sugarcoating would be the more expedient option.

"It's not the Deepwater Horizon, but it's a sizable amount. The car's a rental, so I'm not sure about the capacity. Unfortunately, whatever was in the engine is now on your cement."

"This much?" She held her arms apart at a distance that approximated the length of a loaf of bread.

"No, much more than that."

She doubled her arm distance. "This much?"

I told her no again. She kept increasing her arm distance, asking the same question, over and over. When it got to the point where her arms were stretched out like a warden attempting to slow disorderly traffic, I stopped her.

"Look, your arms are not long enough for an accurate approximation of what we're dealing with here."

She became annoyed, as though I'd branded her arms inadequate for other, more routine human endeavors.

As a peace offering, I bought three bags of cat litter and sprinkled the contents onto the puddle to make the woman's remediation job easier. After I was done, I tried to catch her eye, hoping for a gesture of recognition for my efforts, but she was busy printing out lottery tickets for a lady with loopy earrings, who was squatting down in front of the counter.

The hoop-eared woman grabbed one of Percy's Dornfelder bottles. She spun it in her hands, trying to make sense of the exotic elixir. After much examination, she shook her head and returned the bottle to the box, paid for her lottery tickets, and walked out the door. She stared down at her numbers as she strode to her car, her mind full of lottery dreams. I yelled out to warn her, but she must not have heard me, because she walked right by pump number two, straight into my gooey, coagulated oil mess.

The woman peered down at her shoes, now decorated with little jewels of oily gravel. She stood there, not moving a muscle, angry and helpless. Resigned to her predicament, she examined her tickets again. Her smile immediately returned, her confidence in the most unlikely of probabilities soothing any disquiet she felt over her befouled sneakers.

Chapter Twenty

ONCE WE GOT GOING, I FIGURED OUT that if I double-clutched the transmission and wiggled the shifter just so, first gear would engage about 70 percent of the time. The other 30, impatient people honked while I fumbled around in vain, and Percy cowered, on edge and tittering, until I was finally able to coax the transmission into gear.

Percy was no less nervous when we picked up speed. He pointed to a car stopped at the next intersection.

"Up there, at that junction. Be careful."

"What?"

"A car!"

"Yeah, I see it."

"Of course you do. You don't need my help. I'm sure you're a fine driver. You hold the wheel properly. Nine and three is a sensible position, although I tend to prefer ten and two myself."

"He'd have to be bent on suicide to pull out in front of this thing," I said.

"I must admit, he didn't look happy. Those were the cold, hard eyes of a cynic."

I told Percy I meant the brakes, not the man's sardonic

appearance. They were atrocious. Pressing on the pedal felt like stepping on a pile of wet sand.

"I thought he was pulling out," said Percy. "I saw his tires move. I admit it was slight, but I swear I observed his treads creep."

"Don't worry about it."

"I'm a horrible backseat driver. My wife banned me from her Vauxhall. From now on, I'm going to sit here and keep quiet, I promise."

Not two minutes later: "Over there, look out!"

I turned and looked. A man was biking up to the highway from a side road. He was eating some sort of fruit and pedaling along in a high gear. Something about his half-hearted pedaling and the sloppy manner in which he was consuming the fruit made me conclude he possessed no other mode of transportation.

"Yeah, I see him. He's ten yards back from the road."

"Ah, sorry. I thought he was on a motorbike. I was sure he was coming right for us."

"Relax, okay, we've got a long drive—"

"Traffic light!" Percy yelled, and grabbed the dashboard. "Stop, for heaven's sake!"

I slammed on the brakes, and the driver behind us laid on his horn.

"What's all that honking about?" asked Percy.

"It was a flashing yellow."

"Was it? I'm sure it was red."

"It was yellow, and yellow doesn't mean stop."

"I suppose if it was yellow, you're probably right."

"Have you been stopping at those?"

"Yes, I guess I must have. They all appear red to me for some reason. These wretched cataracts, they make primary colors bleed together."

"It's not a good idea to stop at yellow lights. You're going to upset people doing that."

"What people?"

"The people behind you. Like the guy that honked at us. This isn't England. These people will fill you full of buckshot sooner than they'll ask you over for tea."

Percy went quiet and gazed out his window. I felt bad for scolding him, so I changed the subject.

"What's with all the wine in the back?"

He perked up and gave me an "I'm so glad you asked" look before launching into a comprehensive and unabridged history of Templeton Vineyards.

Percy told me he'd studied organic chemistry at university. In the years that followed, he and a partner developed a formula for a hair-regeneration tonic. The animal trials went swimmingly. The lab rats regrew thick, wiry fur that made them look like little land-based beavers. He even used it himself, to impressive effect. Once these promising results were announced, a multinational pharmaceutical company snapped up Percy's hair outfit, patents and all.

The human trials conducted by the pharma giant weren't so successful. While most participants did experience some fresh growth, the new hair was meager and wispy. Not only that, but a few of the subjects developed nasty rashes, which left their domes looking like sun-scorched putting greens. Luckily, Percy had sold out by that point, his healthy nest egg unaffected by the lawsuits over the desiccated scalps.

The sale happened back in the eighties, before he'd even hit forty. He was too young to retire, so he and his wife, Hazel, purchased a sheep farm in West Sussex. The farming business turned out to be a big mistake.

"I did my research," said Percy. "The prevailing

literature was all in agreement. Sheep are supposed to be intelligent, loyal animals with sensible dispositions and excellent vision. Well, my bloody sheep were the exact opposite."

Percy explained that his sheep turned out to be silly, nervous creatures and near blind to boot. They rolled around in dirt and got their woolly coats caught on barbed wire. They drowned in shallow watercourses and stood there while opportunistic jackdaws pecked off their ears. They cuddled up to metal fence posts during thunderstorms and lay on their backs during heat waves, their pale pink undercarriages exposed to harsh ultraviolet rays.

After two long years of this ovine travail, Percy and Hazel sold the sheep farm and the unfortunate sheep. A package deal. They did, however, hold on to the farmhouse and a few hectares of adjacent land. The land was planted with rapeseed, a weedy yellow crop used to make cooking oil. I asked Percy twice about the rapeseed, thinking I'd misheard, puzzled how the plant had escaped a marketing rebrand.

So it was back to square one. Percy was bored and Hazel wanted him out of the house. He considered the utility of their remaining smallholding. The cropland had chalky soil and a southerly exposure, which got Percy, an amateur oenophile, thinking. Might it be possible to plant vines? The English wine industry was virtually nonexistent at the time, but so was English hair tonic before he'd worked up his proprietary formula.

Percy uprooted the boring rapeseed and dedicated himself to the challenge. But what grape variety to plant? He needed vines that could endure frosty winters and the occasional summer bereft of sunlight. After an extended trip to the Rheinhessen region in Germany, where he padded around steep vineyards while trying his best to avoid suspicious Germans, he settled on Dornfelder, a dark-skinned, early ripening varietal that produced hearty, rustic table wines.

"The Dornfelder vines took to our soil like unruly houseguests," said Percy. "Fecund beyond belief. In less than five years, we were producing over twenty-five hundred bottles annually."

Percy's phone started to ring. He picked it up, studied the screen, and declined the call. He told me it was his daughter, Lilith. Hazel had died four years ago, and in recent years, Lilith had encouraged him to live a little, go somewhere on vacation. She suggested he start at a domestic seaside town called Bognor Regis, which used to be just Bognor until the opportunistic locals shamelessly capitalized on a brief royal visit. If that went well, Lilith said, he should venture overseas the year after, maybe to a sandy beach resort on the Costa del Sol in Spain. Suffice to say, she was more than a little shocked when he revealed his plan to ship a pallet of Dornfelder to Miami, rent a truck, and set off for San Diego. She tried to talk him out of it. When that failed, she insisted he take her husband, Norman, with him.

Norman was a nice man, said Percy, but a total bore. He'd recently installed an elaborate weather station in his back garden, and all he wanted to talk about was barometric pressures and dew points. When he ran out of weather data to recite, he would drone on about his latest match of lawn bowls, dissecting it roll by excruciating roll. Percy explained he never had any intention of traversing the continent with that tiresome nudnik prattling on next to him the entire way.

"How did you convince Lilith he shouldn't come?" I asked.

"Well, I suppose I didn't, really."

"What happened then?"

"It turned out to be a bit of a mess, I'm afraid."

Percy told me they'd both made the trip to Miami. The flight was pleasant enough, and Percy was having second thoughts about ditching his son-in-law. But with two hours to go, Norman retrieved a stack of papers from his carry-on and spread them out on his tray table. He used the rest of the flight to try to convince Percy that he'd uncovered statistical anomalies in one of the globally accepted climate models. He was still at it when the pilot ordered "cabin doors to manual and cross-check." Percy decided then and there enough was enough.

After they'd made it through customs, Norman asked Percy to watch his bags while he went to the restroom. The instant Norman disappeared around the corner, Percy seized the opportunity. He pulled out a piece of paper and scribbled a note: "Norman, thank you for abetting me in this important mission, but I need to complete it alone and nothing, god willing, will stop me. I will see you soon, across the great blue. I hope you understand. Goodbye, Percy."

Percy left the note on top of Norman's suitcase and made a run for it. By the time Norman returned, Percy was long gone. Norman's luggage must have been turned in to security by some vigilant snoop, because it was gone too. When Norman went to the TSA desk to report the strange series of events, he was brusquely detained and subjected to intense questioning. Norman tried to explain that the note didn't express the last words of a greedy martyr in pursuit of a disproportionate number of the stockpiled virgins, but it didn't help. The TSA people, who Norman suspected were eager to test out their new robot probe, hauled his bags out back, into a secure area, and let the robot go to town.

"Its sharp little arms tore Norman's luggage to ribbons," said Percy with a chuckle. Norman had gone on and on about his new, supposedly indestructible luggage with a lifetime warranty, so Percy had been well amused to hear it had disintegrated like tissue paper after a bit of light prodding from what was probably nothing more than a souped-up Roomba.

Norman was released that evening and reunited with the remnants of his luggage, but it was days before he was able to fly home. In the interim, he spent his time stalking up and down Miami Beach, south of Fifteenth Street. Lilith, who was tracking her husband with an app, went nuts when she uncovered the significance of the demarcation. Percy said he felt partly responsible for the whole tawdry situation.

I told him not to blame himself. "You can't help that. He's a grown man. Anyway, most of them have their tops on. And the ones that don't? Well, good luck. I'm guessing he didn't share a beach towel with a supermodel."

The phone rang again, and Percy declined that call too. After the fifth of these cycles, he gave up and answered. Lilith's voice was shrill and probing. It wasn't long before Percy admitted he'd picked up a stranger at a gas station, which didn't go down well. After a bout of harsh scolding, she demanded he put me on the phone.

"Lilith, hi there," I said. "Nice to meet you. Over the phone, that is."

"Excuse me, why are you traveling with my father?"

"Well, we were both having vehicle trouble, so we decided to team up, like during the war."

"The war? And who might you be?"

Something about her sharp barristerial tone made me

nervous, and I began to blabber. "Guy Hastings. From Houston. I was attending to legal matters in Tampa. I had to track down a client of my uncle's firm. Well, it was his firm. He's dead now. I thought he was a slumlord—the client, not my uncle—but it was all a big misunderstanding. Anyway, my car broke down on the way back. Lubrication issues. I was thinking I'd have to sleep in it, there in the parking lot, until your father—"

"Are you a transient? Daddy has a soft spot for the downtrodden and afflicted, a trait I thankfully did not inherit. You'd better not try any funny business. I know exactly how much money he took with him. If funds are unaccounted for, I'll be holding you responsible."

After an awkward silence, I tried another tack. I compared our partnership to the teamwork of the great explorers of the continent's heartland. In this somewhat bumbling analogy, I was the local guide, skilled in dealing with the natives, and Percy was providing the transportation to see us through hostile territories. The truck was now a primitive barge, and the Dornfelder morphed into bearskins of fine quality.

"Sounds like he was doing okay before he met you, even after abandoning my nitwit of a husband. And the truck's apparently fine, so why does he need your help?"

I explained about the finicky transmission, then lowered my voice and enumerated some of Percy's general vulnerabilities, but that made her even more suspicious. I tried to think of some other information to allay her concerns, but I didn't think my multijurisdictional quest for marital clarity would appear as innocent if reduced to terse sound bites. Luckily, it was dinnertime in England. When a pot of leeks started boiling over on something called an Aga, she had no choice but to hang up and deal with the spillage.

Chapter Twenty-One

WE STOPPED FOR GAS NOT LONG AFTER the Lilith inquisition. Percy had been rubbing his eyes for the last ten miles, and they were red and oozing with moisture. He daubed the seepage with a thick monogrammed handkerchief he'd pulled out of the deep recesses of his houndstooth trousers.

"Do you have any sunglasses?" I asked him.

"What the dickens for?"

"Your eyes look terrible. I think the sun's getting to them."

"Really?"

"Yes, you look like you've just come from a funeral."

"Oh, I do tend to cry at funerals. Can't help myself. Did you know that grief is contagious? As contagious as the common cold."

"The sun is more powerful here. We're closer to the equator."

"Yes, what is our latitude? Do you have the exact coordinates? I'd like to record them for Oliver. He loves maps."

I finally convinced Percy to check inside the gas station for sunglasses. I filled the truck with diesel and went in to pay. Percy had located the sunglass options. He spun the display rack around and around in search of suitable candidates. He tried on a tortoiseshell pair with thick temples and gazed at his reflection in the tiny mirror attached to the rack, tilting his head from side to side like an inquisitive puppy. They were clearly meant for a woman and imparted the butch, self-regarding air of a matronly socialite.

"I don't think those suit the shape of your face," I suggested.

He considered my critique, returned them to the rack, and tried on another pair, a square-framed number with blue lenses. They made him look like an aging pop star trying to stay relevant with a younger audience.

"What do you think?" he asked me.

"Much better. You look like a cross between Elton John and Bono."

"Who?"

"Elton John. You know, Rocket Man."

"Yes, I know who he is. Who's the other chap, this Boner fellow?"

"Bono. Of U2. The Irish band."

"Oh, we used to have all sorts of trouble with the Irish. Damn shame about old Mountbatten."

"You going to buy them? You need any cash?"

"Cash? Good god, man, don't talk to me about your Yankee tender. Bloody silly currency. Dull and green and all the same size. Can't tell it apart to save my life. You'd think a country that helped build the Panama Canal would have clearer denominations."

He told me he'd been having all kinds of problems with his American banknotes. He'd brought $2,000 with him, mostly big bills, but he was already down to $927. He wasn't sure what'd happened to the rest, but he had a sinking feeling he'd been paying for his Mars bars with hundreds instead of ones and walking off before receiving his rightful change. And they weren't even good Mars bars like the British ones. No, they were bitter colonial imposters that were, for reasons unknown, missing the delicious caramel layer that was supposed to sit atop the nougat.

I went to use the bathroom. When I returned, there was a case of Dornfelder on the counter, and Percy and the clerk were engaged in a heated discussion. Several people stood behind Percy in a line that stretched back to the beer cooler. They observed his ebullient presentation with a mixture of curiosity and frustration, like he was Anthony Hopkins trying to overcome the limitations of a bad script.

The clerk held his ground. "Sir, look, I just work here. If you want shelf space, you'll have to go through corporate."

"My dear fellow, I can tell you're a reasonable man," said Percy. "Let's say we skip the foreplay and jump right into the matter at hand."

"Sir, please, people are waiting."

Percy turned around and held up one of the bottles. "Who amongst you hospitable Floridians would find it convenient if this establishment became a purveyor of fine English wine?"

"How much yeh asking?" somebody shouted from the back of the queue. The inquiry came from a rangy man in knee-high rubber boots. He held two twelve-packs of beer, one in each meaty hand. He gripped his beer suitcases by the pop-up cardboard handles and swung them back and forth with the expectant impatience of an eager vacationer, ready to board.

"Sir, your question is well asked, but you'll have to consult this upstanding gentleman." Percy motioned to the clerk. "I will leave the matter of pricing in his capable hands. As you can see, he has a benevolent countenance, and I trust he will not press his advantage given the limited supply."

The boot man guffawed. "Jesse? Upstanding? Benevolent? Shit . . . So how much yeh gonna ask for it, Jesse? They teach you about wine over there at that fancy college you dropped out of?"

"Shut your mouth, Art, you hear?" The clerk turned to Percy. "Sir, I'm begging you, please get this box off the counter so I can get on with my job. I don't need any trouble, understand?"

"A smidgen above wholesale, that's all I ask. The pound may be experiencing a bout of cyclical weakness at present, but that will not stop me from consummating this transaction at a competitive price."

Jesse the Clerk snapped. "Move that damn wine, and get your goddamn foreign ass outta here!"

Upon hearing this outburst, Art heckled Jesse the Clerk mercilessly. He called him a "real people person" and told him he should go back to mopping floors at the Country Porker. He made fun of his Caesar haircut and dared him to fasten the bottom button of his red gas-station vest. Jesse the Clerk countered with something about the towing capacity of Art's truck and his brisket, which Jesse claimed had the tenderness of alligator skin.

Percy tuned out the sparring and internalized the rejection. "Fine, fine, I will be on my way," he said in a wounded voice. "If any of you wish to sample my 2010 vintage, which I must say is of outstanding quality, I'll be outside, over by the purple kangaroos." He pointed out the window to a squat metal cage full of propane tanks. The propane company must have paid some high-priced advertising firm to cook up a new marketing plan, the exuberant kangaroos with orange flames erupting from their furry pouches the result of long sessions of corporate brainstorming.

At the mention of free alcohol, a murmur of interest rose from the line. Jesse the Clerk yelled out a curt objection to Percy's plan, something about how he would be in deep shit if his manager happened to swing by and find ingress to the kangaroo propane impeded by "a bunch of drunk dumbasses."

Unfortunately, the party by the propane was sidelined before it got started. I looked out the window and spotted two guys hefting box after soggy box of Percy's wine into the bed of a beaten-up pickup. I yelled and waved and ran outside. They saw me, jumped into their truck, and sped off with at least fifteen cases of wine bouncing around in the bed.

Percy raised his arms in a gesture of hopelessness and defeat. He slumped down onto the curb, crestfallen. His Dornfelder had been summarily spurned in an arguably hostile manner, and worse, a good portion of his inventory had been brazenly poached by unidentified panhandle bandits. He rubbed his temples while viscous fluid streaked out of his sun-damaged sockets. It ran out the bottom of his new sunglasses and down his rosaceaed cheeks.

A crowd gathered around Percy and waited out what appeared to be mournful sobs in the hope of free wine. They paced around in front of him with the restive anticipation of domestic cats waiting to be fed.

"What a bleeding stupid idea this was," said Percy.

"Look on the bright side," I offered. "At least they didn't steal our luggage."

Percy had no interest in looking on the bright side. "I'm nothing but a daft twit thinking I'd be able to rekindle the Templeton brand with a silly road trip. I was one of the first, you know. Hardly anyone tried to make wine in England before me. Oh, the Romans wanted to, but even with their straight roads and battlefield medicine, they only dared dabble. The Americans, the tourists, they loved it, bought it by the case. I even had a distributor over here. On the phone every month, asking for more. 'We'll take all you can give us, Percy,' that's what they'd say, practically begging. And now it's nothing but sparkling wine this and sparkling wine that. Did you know there was an article in the *Sunday Times* last month calling Sussex the 'new Champagne'? If I hear one more word about bloody champagne, I'll . . ."

Percy told us that his red wine business had been dealt a crushing blow by climate change. Late-to-the-party, deep-pocketed competitors saw great opportunity in the warming weather. They snapped up surrounding farmland and planted fancy champagne varietals. In a few short years, sparkling wine became the literal toast of the island nation, everyone clambering to cash in on the new English bubbly craze.

I listened intently, mulling over this roller coaster ride on the undulating tracks of capitalism. An innocent question had triggered this entrepreneurial case study a hundred miles back. It had kicked off on the edge of the Mallory Swamp as a saga of restless ambition and artisanal dreams. Now, as it sped toward its sad denouement in the thick of the Wakulla State Forest, it revealed itself to be a cautionary counterpoint to the economic theory of first-mover advantage.

The crowd milled about, chatting among themselves, impatience growing. Percy was indifferent, deep in a well of self-pity. He lamented that his once-prized output was now viewed as cheap and uncouth, nothing more than expensive cooking wine. I tried to counter his defeatist hyperbole, but he said he wasn't exaggerating. Last winter, unbeknownst to him, a local supermarket ran a promotion packaging a bottle of his Dornfelder with two pounds of chuck roast and a sack of root vegetables. "Fancy a Hearty Stew? Our Rump's Got Your Rump Covered," declared the end-of-the-aisle display placard, rather embarrassingly, in Percy's estimation, not only for the low-rent bundling but also for the crass rump irony.

The crowd soon took matters into its own hands. A woman with tangled blond hair, who was clad in an absorbent-looking outfit better suited for residential lounging, emerged from the store and passed out paisley-patterned cups she had looted from the gas station's coffee setup. A burly man in starched Wranglers offered up a corkscrew he'd removed from his comprehensively outfitted key chain. Percy was oblivious, checked out on the cement. Head in hands, he'd moved on to revisiting other events he believed had contributed to his present nadir.

I decided I needed to take action. I retrieved a few bottles of Dornfelder from the truck, and the man in the stiff denim pulled the corks with surprising technique. But just as the festivities were about to kick off, a pair of sullen-looking sheriff's deputies pulled into the parking lot in a squad car. The cops parked and unbuckled their seat belts. They lounged and drank coffee and punched away at a screen mounted to the dashboard, occasionally looking up to observe the goings-on in front of them.

I debated reporting the theft. I could describe the pickup and one of the two thieves. Best case, the cops would know immediately who the perpetrators were by my description. We would follow the officers to a ramshackle dwelling, where they would apprehend the culprits in an aggressive fashion. We would retrieve the bulk of the Dornfelder, Percy only out whatever the men and their inbred relatives had put back in the time it took to put the raid together. We would taunt the men while they were perp-walked out of their hovel and hauled off to the county jail. I would shoot them looks of disdain and call them disgusting, vile offenders from behind the thin blue line. Percy would do the same, possibly adding a few British invectives that would further confuse and humiliate them. We'd soon be back on the road with the rescued Dornfelder and a mildly interesting story that would inevitably become more action-packed with each retelling—such is the nature of brushes with the criminal element.

Despite the police presence, the parking lot soon took on the ambiance of an open bar at a shotgun wedding. I observed the hubbub while contemplating the more realistic outcome. I had no idea how long it would take to interest Wakulla County's finest in Percy's misfortune, but based upon all the screen fiddling and coffee drinking I'd witnessed in the last ten minutes, I was not hopeful for a SWAT-style urgency to protect and serve. It would probably take them hours to complete the report, and god forbid they dragged us down to the station.

I asked Percy what he wanted to do, and he said, "Sod it. They can take it all, just take it all." This was a worrying development. Where was the phlegmatic British resolve, the legendary stiff upper lip? What about a spirited defense of your island whatever the attendant sacrifice? Bloody combat on beaches and in fields and other less scenic theaters? I asked him who "they" were. The robbers? The crowd? The police? He didn't answer, so I made the decision for him. We would make a tactical withdrawal, get back on the road, live to fight another day.

Jesse the Clerk apparently subscribed to less forgiving tenets. He was hell-bent on engaging the deputies and ratting out his customers, which made little sense business-wise. It was, however, true to character given his flat refusal to hear Percy out on the wine. He strode over to the patrol car and spoke to the deputies in an agitated tone.

The ample-booted man toting the beer suitcases yelled, "Look out. Jesse's gonna get us locked up. We're all gonna be sleeping in the big house tonight!"

The crowd erupted in raucous laughter, raised their paisley cups in defiance, and yelled a series of truculent taunts at Jesse the Clerk for trying to protect his cup inventory.

All of a sudden, the police radio blared out a serious-sounding string of letters and numbers. A code something-or-other was in progress, and all units in the vicinity should respond immediately, commanded the staticky voice. The cop in the passenger seat flipped on the light bar, and the cruiser shot out of the parking lot with the siren wailing away. The crowd roared with approval at this speedy departure. Jesse the Clerk slunk back into the store while everyone jeered and heckled his histrionics in a way that made me think they were all related.

The blonde in the infomercial outfit handed me a coffee cup and called me "hon." The man in the durable denim poured me a healthy portion of Dornfelder. I took a generous swig and worked the liquid around the inside of my mouth. It went down with a jolt, shocking my taste buds with a blast of bitter fruit. It was a rough and ready yet not altogether unpleasant sensation, similar to biting into the charred rind of an overcooked hamburger patty.

I huddled next to Percy, put my arm around his shoulders, and gestured to the merriment encircling us. "See how much fun people are having? It's all because of you and your wine. People love it. If you'd stayed in England, they'd be home watching daytime TV and drinking malt liquor, poisoning their minds and their livers." I admit, I was laying it on a bit thick, for the most part.

Percy looked at me and nodded, but I could tell he wasn't convinced. He asked me what type of whiskey these country folk preferred. I told him I was referring to a different type of malt beverage. He asked me what kind, and I said I wasn't exactly sure, but it was potent and came in forty-ounce bottles people concealed in brown paper bags. He asked me about the bags and I told him I believed they helped avoid police harassment, but possibly a deep-rooted sense of shame contributed to the bag use too.

Country music began to blare out of the open window of a primered El Camino with a cactus on the dashboard. The blond woman became excited and started to skip around the parking lot. She hopped from one person to the next, locking arms and circling the pumps. She whirled over to Percy, coaxed him to his feet, and two-stepped him around the obstacle course of fuels while the rest of the crowd clapped in rhythm to the sad chronicle of broken dreams and greedy ex-wives.

Chapter Twenty-Two

THE FILLING STATION DEBAUCH WENT ON for a good
hour. Percy donated two cases of Dornfelder to the shindig.
People drank and danced with nary a care in the world
except for when a few aggressively piloted vehicles headed
for the super-unleaded and honked at the revelers imped-
ing their path to the 93-octane.

By the time we were back on the road, the sun had
disappeared behind the tops of the tallest trees. Thankfully,
Percy's mood had done a 180 since he hit rock bottom on the
gas station cement. He was now riding a party high, basking
in the riotous response to his Dornfelder and the accolades
he'd received from the locals for his adept two-stepping.
He shifted about excitedly on the worn vinyl and scanned
out the windshield in an intense fashion. The road was long
and straight and boring, so his scanning didn't yield much.

We tunneled ahead. Layers of lush, thorny forest
encroached on the road from both sides. Every five miles
or so we'd break out of the dense briar and plow through
some drab outcropping before plunging back into an abyss
of green.

As the miles ticked by, I began to notice more and more

roadkill rotting away on the tarmac. It was as if Noah's ark had spilled its comprehensive pairings onto the hot Florida asphalt, and Noah had kept on trucking, oblivious to the carnage abandoned in his wake. Percy noticed the decimation too. He enthusiastically identified the piles of mangled gore as if seeking a game-show jackpot.

"Badger!" He pointed in the direction of a black-and-white lump lying spread-eagled on the shoulder.

"You won't find badgers this far south," I said. "That was a skunk."

Percy wasn't interested in skunks, he wanted to talk badger.

"Fastidious animals. Haul their mossy mattresses out into the sun once a week to air them out. And what insatiable appetites. They can devour a wasps' nest whole in less than an hour. Oh, and strong, are they ever strong, the second-strongest creature in the world, pound for pound."

"What's the strongest?" I asked, genuinely interested.

"Dung beetle. Those little scuttlers can pull a thousand times their body weight. That's six double-decker buses to you and me. I recently observed a fine specimen heft a pebble down the length of my patio and all the way back again. Returned it to the very same spot. No one can convince me he wasn't bloody well exercising, the little brute."

"Loaded or unloaded?" I asked.

"What?"

"The buses. Full or empty?"

"Well, I'm not sure. I believe Attenborough may have neglected to specify. But I bet if we think about it . . ."

We were in the middle of some back-of-the-napkin dung beetle calculations when he noticed something else on the road.

"Stoat!" he screamed.

I looked. A furry brown mass with a tire track that ran the length of its back lay rigored on the hot cement. All I could make out at speed was a pair of fat cheeks and a bushy tail.

"I believe that was a squirrel." I knew a stoat was a slim mustelid in the weasel family but there, unfortunately, my stoat knowledge ended, hence the qualification.

Percy spotted another corpse. "Anteater!"

"No, that was an armadillo."

"What's the difference?"

"Armadillos have a hard shell."

"Yes, well then, I judge the anteater a more sympathetic beast," said Percy. "It takes its chances with vulnerable flesh exposed, a very human quality."

We joined Highway 20 just before the Ochlockonee River and Ed & Bernice's Fish Camp. The definition of the roadkill subsided measurably on the 20, which made Percy's game impossibly difficult. I turned on the headlights to illuminate the hard shoulder, where most of the specimens were located, but it didn't help.

Ten miles on, we passed through a small town that consisted of dueling gas stations and an elementary school. Red plastic cups embedded in the chain-link fence surrounding the school spelled out "Thank You" without further detail, causing us to speculate about the exact nature of the gratitude. I guessed it was a message to our troops fighting in godforsaken deserts. Percy conjectured it was in memory of a popular teacher who had died after a long, painful illness. We rolled on without an answer, unable to decipher the roadside tea leaves.

I was having an even harder time seeing the road, so when we made it to a town called Billerson, I decided to check the headlights.

"Look, oh look, the Country Porker!" exclaimed Percy. "So the gentleman in the long boots did not lie." He suggested we pull in so he could document this "American curiosity of the first order." He was only a tad disappointed when I told him it was one of a chain of regular old grocery stores, none of which were renowned for top-shelf pork.

I took up four spaces at the rear of the optimistically proportioned parking lot, and we climbed out. Sure enough, the headlights weren't working.

"As useless as eyes on a mole," said Percy matter-of-factly. He turned his attention back to the Country Porker and studied the store's sign, mounted high on the brick-work, trying to figure out the best angle for his photo.

"I'll take it," I said. Percy handed me his phone. I centered him between "Country" and "Porker" but realized I'd obscured the cartoon pig head and his tiny cowboy hat, so I backed up to adjust the perspective. I aligned the bottom of the pig head with the top of Percy's thick white hair, which made the little piglet cowboy appear to be float-ing atop a billowy cloud. I took the shot and handed Percy's phone back to him. He examined the photo and smiled at what I'd like to think was my inspired composition.

We went inside to explore our options now that it was almost dark and we were still over an hour and a half from Panama City. I walked up to a uniformed woman working one of the registers. She was umbrellaed under a mass of corrugated brown hair. I considered complimenting the hair but struggled to come up with something that didn't include the word "dense" or "voluminous." Thankfully, flattery wasn't needed. The woman helpfully volunteered that the only motel in town was a place called the Sunbird Inn, roughly a mile down the road. She said we couldn't miss it because two white birds were bolted to the roof. The birds were supposed to be flamingoes, but the interminable Florida sun had long ago bleached all the color out of their cheap plastic bodies. Consequently, she suggested I forget flamingoes and keep my eyes peeled for egrets, herons, or any other pair of white-feathered, long-legged waders I was apt to recognize at a distance of twenty yards.

I reflected on the woman's helpful pragmatism and deep reservoir of bird knowledge as I walked off to locate Percy. I found him in the produce department, talking to a teenager spraying down the leafy greens with a garden hose. When the forceful jet impacted the firm icebergs, stray water bounced off onto the neighboring vegetables, which, from their sad appearance, weren't appreciating the indiscriminate irrigation.

Percy quizzed the boy relentlessly about the store and its offerings.

"Dude, you've never been to a Country Porker before?" the kid asked, incredulous he was a witness to what he rather crudely described as the popping of Percy's "Country Porker cherry."

"No, I have not, young man," said Percy. "What do you recommend, other than your stemmed fruit?"

"Huh?"

"What is your bread and butter, your raison d'être? Cured meats, poultry, mouthwatering pies? Your produce certainly looks well watered. Tell me, my boy, how should I best spend my American dollars inside your Porker?"

The kid thought for a second. He said the Meat Bundle #4 was a pretty good deal because you got forty pounds of pork for a hair under eighty dollars. It was the best price on volume quantities this side of the Truckload Sale, but one of those wouldn't happen again for at least a couple of months.

Percy thanked the kid for the inside information. He was about to embark on a search for this El Dorado of protein when I stopped him.

"Our options are limited, and when I say 'limited,' I mean a motel called the Sunbird is it. We'll be able to find it by looking for the birds on the roof."

"What exactly is a sunbird? Dare I ask, are we hunting mythological creatures? Beasts of legend and fable?"

"No, the birds are flamingoes."

"Flamingoes on the roof at this hour? I didn't realize they were nocturnal."

And so it went. He reluctantly agreed to abandon his meat crusade, but it still took me ten minutes to shepherd him back across the store. We were almost clear of the snack aisle when he spotted a wooden display table piled high with frosted Bundt cakes encased in translucent plastic containers. He picked one up, held it sideways, and stared into the void in the center like it was the event horizon of a black hole. It took two or three vigorous shakes of his left shoulder to break him free of the spell of the high-margin cake. When we made it back to the truck, I had to plead with him not to lug a box of Dornfelder into the Porker to try to cut another one of his now-infamous consignment deals.

We cruised down the main drag of Billerson, passing the Achapotita Forest Ranger Station, the Freedom County courthouse, and the local high school. The school was housed in an abandoned grocery store. Either that or grocery store architects had been hired to empty the contents of their limited imaginations into the design. Down the road, the Dollar Armada looked to have gone to war with the Dollar Squire directly opposite. The Dollar Squire had lost the Billerson campaign, the only evidence of its bargain existence a boarded-up building and blacked-out sign.

It soon became evident that Billerson was a church-heavy outpost. The number of churches even exceeded the sum of the auto parts stores and gas stations. I knew this because Percy kept count.

"There's another, that makes five."

The House of Radioactive Love was housed in a long, thin red-brick building with a faded gray spire welded to a tin roof. The church's rectangular sign was moored in a patch of barren dirt. The sign was topped with a three-dimensional model of an atom, little electrons whizzing around a weighty black core. A silver cylinder of unidentified gases was beached in the grass alongside the building, bolstering the scientific vibe. The service looked to have just ended because a group of earnestly effusive people was out front, congregating around the atom. They shook hands and hugged each other with great vigor, as if trying to live up to the promise of quantum decay.

I asked Percy to keep a lookout for the Sunbird's faded flamingoes. I needn't have bothered. There was no missing the motel's hot pink façade, and the albino birds were all but invisible from the road in the fading daylight.

The Sunbird Inn resembled the prison complex of a sparsely populated Caribbean island. It consisted of a pair of one-story brick buildings positioned in an L-shaped configuration. The shingled roof of each structure extended over the frontage, forming covered walkways that were littered with an impressive diversity of detritus. A three-foot wire fence surrounded the perimeter, and a sign out front promised free basic cable and clean rooms with beds. The type of beds on offer was a mystery because some inconsiderate stump grinder had taped a piece of cardboard that promised "Cheap Stump Grinding" over the sign, obscuring the bed descriptors.

The parking lot was full, so I circled the block. We parked on a side street and walked over to the motel's office. The girl at the front desk looked to be in her early twenties. She had on loose-fitting clothes emblazoned with a pompous surname. Neither attractive nor unattractive, she hovered in that strange purgatory with female relatives and young nuns. Perched Indian style in an office chair, she was leaning forward and staring at something in front of her that was tucked under the counter, out of our view. The motel phone rang away, but she made no attempt to answer it.

The girl didn't notice us when we walked up, so I reached down and waved a hand between her head and the obscured materials. She snapped out of her trance and gazed upward with surprise. I told her we needed two rooms for the night and she flared her nostrils like she'd just inhaled caustic solvents. She opened a green ledger book and flipped through the pages. I was unsure why the Sunbird's limited room inventory wasn't available for immediate recall, but she held our fate in her hands, so I kept quiet and let her flip. After much flipping, she opened another identical green book and undertook some third-world-style cross-checking.

"No, sorry, we don't have any vacancies. The Gordons were supposed to check out today, but their son's bail was delayed by a few hours, so they're staying in room two again tonight."

"Bail?" I asked.

"Yeah, he's in Freedom Correctional. The prison, ten minutes up the road."

"What's he charged with?"

"I think they said armed robbery. Maybe sexual assault? Or was that the Gibson boy in room twelve? It's hard to keep them all straight." She exhaled and motioned to the green volumes, which were full of line upon line of indecipherable scrawl.

"So they're out?" I asked, trying to gauge the extent of the threat posed by the Sunbird's patrons.

"Who?"

"The Gordons' son. The Gibson kid. The armed robber. The rapist."

"Yeah, they both made bail. If they're convicted, they'll probably be locked up again though. People joke that we should change the name of this place to the Jailbird Inn. But innocent until proven guilty, right?"

Percy piped up. "I vote for Jailbird. It has a devil-may-care ring to it, a hint of excitement, possibly even a tinge of danger. And what's a sunbird anyway? Some tribal talisman, a mythical fantasy creature born of primitive superstition?"

The girl thought for a second. "Sunbird, you know, they're old people from up north who come down south for the winter."

"Isn't that a snowbird?" I offered.

"Huh. Could be. Makes sense, the snow and all."

"Do you get many snowbirds here?" I asked, curious about the felon-to-snowbird ratio. Other than the size of the Country Porker parking lot, I had seen no evidence to suggest Billerson filled up with people streaming across the Mason-Dixon Line at the first sign of frost.

"A few, I guess. But it's mostly people coming for the prison."

"So you've got nothing available? We're pretty desperate. Not to the level of your criminal clientele, of course."

"No, sorry . . ." She scanned her green books again. "Oh, actually, wait a second. There's one room that's vacant.

It's being held though. Mr. Broadus was supposed to let me know before he went to dinner if he still needed it. It's for his assistant. I have his number here somewhere, let me try him."

Miraculously, she was able to retrieve the Broadus number from one of the green books with just a few more page flips. She dialed it but nobody answered.

"You know, he only left for dinner about twenty minutes ago. If you can get him to release the room, it's all yours." She swiveled in her chair. "Curtis, hey, Curtis, get out here and take these nice men to the Achapotita and point out Mr. Broadus, will you?"

We politely declined the escort, but the girl was insistent. After a series of threatening exhortations, a beefy kid with a flattop lumbered out of the back room. He was wearing a T-shirt and long shorts that hung down to the tops of his bulbous calves. The T-shirt was adorned with an ironed-on decal featuring a covetous leprechaun. The leprechaun hugged a pot of gold and celebrated his good fortune at the bottom of a faded rainbow. The boy's facial features were concealed by an ample layer of girth, so it was hard to pinpoint his age, but if forced, I would have guessed about nine, give or take. He walked right past us without stopping and waved over his shoulder as he opened the door. Once we were outside, he tried to hurry us along.

"C'mon, let's go, I've got stuff to do."

"Thank you kindly, young Curtis," said Percy. "It's a pleasure to make your acquaintance." He held out his hand, which Curtis summarily ignored.

"You talk fancy, mister, where ya from? You some kinda foreigner?"

"Yes, I suppose I am, young man. England. West Sussex, to be exact. One of the home counties."

"No kidding? Wait till I tell my daddy I met a real live England guy. He says you England people are all dumb limers. We kicked y'all's butts 'cause y'all marched around in circles while we picked you off like dumb ol' turkeys."

"I'm not sure that's exactly how it went down," I chimed in.

"Yes it is. My daddy said so. You think you know more than my daddy?"

What now but to firmly rebut this belligerent jingoism? Percy offered up a polite defense of Cornwallis and the British colonial strategy, something about battlefield decorum and Atlantic supply routes.

Curtis was having none of it. He brought his arms up like he was hefting a musket. He shot Percy with his imaginary weapon, then turned his attention to the cars cruising down the highway. "Pow. Pow. Pow," he yelled as he took down driver after driver, one after the other. While admittedly an energetic reenactment, it was utterly unrealistic because Curtis had forgotten to take into account the time necessary to reload his primitive firearm.

One driver objected to being targeted and laid on the horn. Curtis took umbrage. "Eff you too." His musket transformed into two balled fists with fat middle fingers protruding upward. After a few vigorous up-and-down motions with the chubby sausages, he turned his attention back to Percy.

"You still having trouble with them Nazis? Daddy says you'd all be speaking French if it wasn't for the US Marines."

"I think you mean German," I said.

"No, I mean French. I guess you've never seen that movie where we kicked all that French butt and rescued that Demon guy from the zoo movie."

I gave up. When we got to the restaurant, Curtis walked

in ahead of us like he owned the place. It was a typical diner: a Formica-topped bar with wooden stools bordering an open kitchen. Tables were strewn around the dining area in no discernible pattern. A few people were eating away dutifully.

"There he is," said Curtis. He pointed to a table where ten people were seated, consuming excessive quantities of food and carrying on in a noisy fashion.

"Which one's Broadus?" I asked.

"Duh, I'm pointing at him." Curtis gestured more vigorously, oblivious to the distortions of vector orientation.

"The guy with the napkin tucked in his shirt?" I asked.

"No, the one next to him."

"The sallow guy?"

"Huh, what? Speak English, dummy."

"Sallow. You know, pale yellow, sickly. The pale yellow, sickly guy?"

"No, idiot, not him, the other side." Curtis pointed in the exact same direction again.

We finally figured out he was trying to identify a long-faced man with a well-manicured beard who was alternating between talking and sipping on a straw protruding out of a frosted cup. His calm demeanor and measured tone led me to conclude he was the leader of the ragged discussion.

I thanked Curtis even though I didn't mean it, and he stuck out one of his grimy paws. I wasn't about to tip the surly brute, but Percy seemed to feel some sort of obligation, possibly the result of Stockholm syndrome. He pulled out his wallet and slapped a bill into the kid's bloated palm.

Curtis looked down. "Wow, thanks, mister," he said, a smile now partially visible in the creases of his facial padding. "You England people aren't so bad after all." He pocketed the bill with great haste and made for the door with an improbable alacrity.

"What'd you give him?" I asked Percy.

"A dollar, nothing more, the bumptious knave."

"You sure? He looked pretty excited."

Percy pulled out his wallet again and dug around in it. "Good god, please don't tell me I tipped that little bugger a hundred." He cursed our paper currency anew and wobbled out of the restaurant in pursuit of the newly flush Curtis.

Chapter Twenty-Three

I WALKED UP TO THE TABLE. The man identified as Broadus was talking, so I took a seat between the sallow man and a middle-aged woman who was dressed like she'd just returned from a séance at Stonehenge. The sallow man put down his cheeseburger and handed me two items: a binder with "Florida Bureau of Natural and Cultural Resources" emblazoned on the cover and a spiral-bound pamphlet entitled *RAGE—Residents Against the Government's Annexation of Eden.*

I opened the RAGE booklet and read the first page. I was only mildly surprised to learn that this group of hungry zealots believed God's sacred greenbelt was located a mere mile north on Highway 14. Apparently, Noah's ark had been cobbled together there too, out of some special local wood.

I listened to the discussion going on around me. The beard-heavy Broadus was obviously present on behalf of governmental forces to quell native unrest. He spoke in a steady diplomatic voice and didn't react to the many pointed remarks being yelled at him from all directions.

I opened the government's binder, a comprehensive

study of the panhandle paradise with an appendix full of newspaper clippings and magazine articles that detailed the history of the site and its botanical wonders. Behind the next-to-last tab was an old newspaper interview with the figure who'd put Billerson's Eden on the map, a taxman turned preacher by the name of E. V. Cleveland.

I learned Elbert Vance Cleveland had been born in rural Mississippi in 1889. The footloose young Cleveland enjoyed a pleasant but strict rural upbringing until the local Baptists excommunicated him for grievous sins, something about his "limber hips." After he broke free of the "bigoted igno-ramuses with no appreciation for an energetic carriage," he embarked on what sounded like a lifetime of frustrated striving and middling achievement.

As he approached retirement, an evangelical thirst welled up inside him. In a fit of inspiration, he concocted his own spiritual credo. He ditched the fire and brimstone of his parents for a bohemian mishmash of love, tolerance, and kindness, generously salted with the soul-cleansing forces of self-reliance and free markets. So here we had a less anal version of Richard Nixon, a Nixon in some parallel universe who'd skipped some boring government meetings to attend Woodstock, hooked up with a long-haired hippie girl, and returned to the White House a changed man, at least on matters unrelated to economic policy.

I turned my attention back to Broadus. He was attempt-ing to explain the particulars of a genus of rare ferns that grew close to the bluffs but was being shouted down by the RAGE people, who attacked his religious bona fides.

"You even a Christian? If so, how come you're helping the deep state do this to the Lord's garden?"

"I bet you're one of those people who won't say the entire pledge of allegiance."

"Open your wallet. I want to see if you scratch out 'God' on your money."

The bohemian woman next to me spoke up, in a less abrasive tone than the others. "Mr. Broadus, I'd like to ask you about something you said a couple of minutes ago. Surely you're not implying Elbert never met Dr. Spivey, are you?"

I asked the sallow man about this Dr. Spivey. He put his hand on his forehead and shook his head.

The woman must've heard me, because she proudly presented me with a publication of her own. It was a dog-eared, stapled-together mess of papers containing text printed in an elaborate purple font reminiscent of home-made birthday cards. The title read, "Elbert V. Cleveland and Dr. Greyson Spivey: The Truth Behind the Spirit Realm's Grand Plan to Bestow Peace and Harmony on Humanity." The author was someone named Carol Babinski, whom I knew to be the woman next to me because of the photo Scotch-taped to the front cover.

Not wanting to appear impolite, I delved in. According to Carol Babinski, at age fifty-seven, Cleveland's life took an abrupt turn when he crossed paths with a doctor by the name of Greyson T. Spivey. It was 1946, and America was in a postwar boom when Cleveland purportedly traveled to Spivey's "modest and cozy houseboat," then moored in the shallow waters of Port St. Lucie, Florida, where this doctor of unspecified qualification, by then an old man, had taken to churning out what sounded like dense tomes of impressively diverse, religious-tinged pseudoscience.

What was discussed at that fateful meeting between Cleveland and Spivey had been lost to history. What Carol Babinski claimed we did know was that the very next day, Cleveland, no different than the pint-sized tree climber of the New Testament, abruptly quit his governmental tax job. Not long after that, he split with his wife of thirty years and decamped to the piney woods of Freedom County to await further instructions from the mysterious doctor.

The sallow man watched me read. When I turned in his direction, he made the universal gesture for unhinged lunacy, spinning a forefinger in concentric loops beside one of his waxen ears. I almost laughed out loud at the irony. Babinski was obviously a confused soul, no doubt deluded, childhood traumas spurring her to search for meaning in a morass of chicanery. But the irritable fabulists across the table believed there existed an all-knowing being that'd selected Billerson as the ideal place on the planet to kick-start humanity. So we were dealing with fine distinctions here.

I was curious about the good "doctor" though. What were his divine insights that so enthralled Cleveland? I started to ask Carol Babinski, but she stood the instant she gleaned my intentions.

"Excuse me, excuse me. I've received a question from the floor I'd like to—"

The others shouted her down. Broadus intervened.

"Please, this is an open forum, you have to let her speak."

Carol Babinski said, "Thank you, Mr. Broadus." She shot him a conspiratorial smile. A misplaced gesture, I thought, given Broadus was probably just trying to move things along.

Carol Babinski picked up a book entitled *The Order of Kukulkan and the Thousand Shrines of Ancient Maya.* She flipped to the "About the Author" page and began to read.

"'Dr. Greyson Spivey is the president of the Foundation for Global Sequencing. While a citizen of this great country, he can trace his noble roots back to the Alemanni of Liechtenstein. He has developed sixty-seven systems of numerology yet still found time to outline the framework of the "Federation for Interplanetary Cooperation." He has traveled the world lecturing on the hidden vibratory processes of invisible wavelengths and has experienced firsthand the healing powers of daily applications of first-press olive oil, both internal and—'"

The RAGE people shouted Babinski down again. They disparaged her theories, a competing sect tussling over this remote chaparral like it was the Middle East's great divided city.

"Sheesh, not this new-age bull crap again."

"Nothing but blasphemy, all of it."

"That Spivey's as much of a doctor as my right ass cheek."

"Hey, hey, let her finish, please," said Broadus, looking weary.

"Thank you, Mr. Broadus," said Carol. She took a second to glare at the RAGE people before she continued.

"'A prolific writer, he has authored books with such diverse titles as *Dare to Invest in Rare Bullion* and *Harnessing the Power of Lactic Acids*. No boring workaholic, his hobbies include buffing brass to an irradiant shine and wallpapering interior antechambers. While his restless passions flow in many directions, his supreme talent is for sprightly exuberance. Even at the age of ninety-six, he requires but a mere three hours of sleep a night, and his favored consorts are fellows yet too young to commit to the sacred bonds of matrimony. He has been known to . . .'"

Carol Babinski went on and on, Spivey's bizarro résumé seemingly endless. The RAGE people heckled her over and over again. Broadus intervened when the sniping became too venomous.

I skipped to the end of Babinski's opuscule. Not surprising given his advanced age, Spivey dropped dead mere weeks after Cleveland moved to Billerson. Carol Babinski opined that a man of more fragile resolve would have packed up and gone home. I judged this a stretch given Cleveland's sunk costs: the moving expenses, divorce settlement, legal fees, and whatnot.

At that point, the competing annals converged. Both the RAGE materials and Carol Babinski's rather more outré narrative maintained that by the end of 1949, Cleveland had purchased a sizable parcel of sandy scrubland that bordered the Achapotita River, just northwest of town.

According to the RAGE materials, in the years that followed, Cleveland enjoyed a chaste, modest bachelorhood. He reverently conducted local services and regularly improved his freehold. I guessed this to be posthumously sanitized speculation given what I now knew about his impulsive nature and shifty pelvic area. I pictured him as a new divorcé, single and ready to mingle, drinking heroic quantities of grain alcohol and trying his luck with the fairer sex of Freedom County.

No matter, everything changed in 1955 when Cleveland discovered from an itinerant botanist that his precious land harbored a rare species of conifer almost wiped out in the last ice age. With the blind fervor of a garage-saler who's convinced their most recent Saturday-morning acquisition is a Pollock, Cleveland claimed he'd bought paradise. He asserted his land, like the Bible's Eden, abutted one of only two four-headed river systems on the planet, and his near-extinct pines were actually "gopher-woods," the very trees named in the Book of Genesis as the source of the timbers for Noah's ark.

Not waiting around for a flaming bush or other divine pyrotechnics, the free-market-loving Cleveland quickly adapted his Eden into a tourist attraction. He threw up a set of pearly-looking gates, carved a dirt track through the woods, and erected a big sign. He charged curious passersby $1.40 per person for admittance—about $15 today—an optimistic sum under any model of discretionary spending in the postwar era, but I suppose he was counting on the Almighty's thumb on the scale if attendance didn't live up to expectations.

I looked up. Broadus was under siege by the RAGE people again. They took turns peppering him with sharp questions.

"So once you've taken it over, how do we know you're not gonna seal it off and hand it over to the tree huggers?" said a red-faced man. He leaned back in his chair and massaged his napkin-shrouded stomach.

"Sir, our plans are laid out in the materials I provided. The existing trail is to be preserved. It will be open year-round."

"What about the signs?" piped in a lady wearing a baseball cap. "I hear you want to rip 'em out." She was dipping greasy fried strips of meat into a bowl of unidentifiable sauce and didn't bother to pause this methodical immersion when she asked her question.

"Yes, the signs will be removed."

There was much consternation over this sign news. I leaned over to the sallow man and asked him what signs they were talking about. He flipped to page eight of the RAGE pamphlet.

Cleveland had pinpointed a handful of sacred locations in his Eden. He'd marked these important spots with hand-painted signs that declared things like "Where God made

Adam sit and name the animals," "Where God cleaved open Adam's chest cavity," and "Where Eve sewed Adam's fig-leaf codpiece." The last photo was of a sign that read, "Large gopher tree." It was nailed to a conifer that nobody could deny was of impressive girth.

"What about the statue?" someone said. "The fish fry last month raised two hundred and eighty dollars."

Statue? Were there plans for a life-sized replica of Cleveland, loose carriage and all? Or, if Carol Babinski had her way, a bust of this shady Spivey character? Possibly Adam and his girl Eve, in bas-relief, appropriately leafed and smiling innocently, welcoming all who came to hike the sandy paths? It didn't matter because Broadus said a statue wasn't happening. The most they could hope for was a small wooden plaque.

The statue news didn't go over any better than the sign news. Broadus, now drenched in sweat, excused himself from the burlesque of grievance to use the bathroom. I intercepted him over by the counter. When he found out I wasn't part of the RAGE group, he lightened up and gladly offered us the extra room.

"I told that girl I didn't need it, that my assistant was under the weather and wasn't coming."

I told Broadus I'd seen inside the girl's green books, which I believed to be the source of much confusion over at the Sunbird. He ignored my critique of the front desk operation.

"Taking over that Eden land was the last thing we wanted to do," he said, and wiped his brow.

Broadus told me that the guy who currently owned the largest part of Cleveland's Eden kept felling trees to extend the perimeter of his scrapyard. The scrap merchant had advanced to within fifty yards of the bluff, and rumor had it he'd bought a new, more powerful chain saw to plow all the way through. The guy was bragging around town he was going to change the name of the place to Riverview Salvage. I reckoned Broadus was right to be concerned about the trees. A man with a new power tool idling in his workshop is prone to exhibit a level of restraint no greater than that of a penniless drunk who finds a crisp twenty blowing around the parking lot of a liquor store.

I asked Broadus about the gopher wood, which I pegged to be the load-bearing wall in the bullish fable. He laughed and said it was a translation error—probably the work of a careless scribe with an attention deficit. Definitely nothing to do with God, Genesis, or even gophers, for that matter. He peered back at the RAGE people to make sure they hadn't heard his heresy, but they were occupied with the question of whether Cain was conceived before or after the disgraced pair was ejected from their Florida paradise.

Percy returned, angry and defeated. Curtis had refused to cough up his hundred. He'd enlisted the help of the girl at the front desk, but she was only able to extract a measly ten dollars from the detestable nipper, even after he gave her a bottle of Dornfelder as a bribe.

I tried to assuage his pique by telling him the good news about the room. We grabbed a table and ate immoderate portions of chicken-fried steak with sides of gravy-soaked mash. I soldiered through the experience while Percy enjoyed the novelty of what, to him, was an exotic combination. He declared, with shortsighted bravado, he was going to eat thick patties of salty fried meat for every meal until he cleared Texas. I didn't have the heart to tell him your first chicken-fried steak is your best, every subsequent greasy slab tasting no better than a hunk of vulcanized tire rubber.

Percy was excited to hear about our proximity to Eden, but

he said the news didn't surprise him. "All people consider their soil consecrated ground. The desire for proximity to the divine knows no bounds or nationality." He broke into forceful song:

"And did those feet in ancient time
Walk upon Englands mountains green:
And was the holy Lamb of God,
On Englands pleasant pastures seen!"

At this thunderous mention of God's blessed lamb padding around on foreign soil, the RAGE people turned and stared, sensing blasphemy afoot. Broadus grimaced as though he'd just witnessed somebody mainline a dirty needle full of the Holy Spirit.

Percy and I agreed we'd feel pretty stupid if the Lord Almighty did indeed inhabit some celestial boondocks and on Judgment Day he found out we'd snubbed his precious cultivation to get a head start on traffic. So, as a precautionary measure, we decided we'd drive over there in the morning and check it out.

We finished our heaping bowls of peach cobbler and walked back to the Sunbird. The girl at the front desk handed me the room key. It was an actual metal key, significant because one of the many criminals who had previously occupied our room could have cloned it at the hardware store down the road for less than a dollar. I asked the girl about this. She agreed my concern was warranted but claimed there was nothing she could do.

"You could put in those locks that take plastic cards," I suggested.

"Locks with cards?" She looked perplexed. I tried to explain, to no avail, so I pulled a credit card out of my wallet and moved it to and fro in the air a few times to simulate the unlocking process. She still didn't get it, so Percy pulled out one of his cards, and we both stood there and pumped away until the concept finally took root.

The girl told us we were in room nine, but the number had fallen off the door a long time ago, possibly before she was born, she couldn't be sure. She yelled out for Curtis to escort us. Fearing more hawkish extortion, we thanked her and hustled out of the office.

The numbers had fallen off a lot of the doors, so when we found room six, we took a chance with the room three doors down. The key wasn't halfway into the lock when the door popped open. Inside the room, a senior couple was lying on the bed, fully clothed, shoes and all, eating corn chips out of a large bag and watching a nature show on TV. Ants marched across the screen carting teardrop-shaped leaves in their sharp mouths. The narrator explained these leaf ants were the strongest insects on the planet, size-adjusted, a direct contradiction to Percy's dung beetle information. The couple smiled and waved like they'd been expecting us. After a round of succinct introductions, we all turned our attention back to the ants, which had taken to zigzagging across the forest floor like tiny sailboats tacking in rough waters.

We checked many doors and introduced ourselves to many likely-dangerous felons before locating our room. The scuffed walls were painted a dark shade of taupe, matching the curtains and the carpet, the sea of taupe possibly a tactic to pacify the criminals. Thankfully, there were two double beds. A paper sign, "Kitchenette," was hanging loosely on the wall above a stack of off-brand appliances. A microwave teetered atop a waist-high fridge, and an electric kettle rounded out the precarious tower of conveniences. The AC unit was mounted in the wall instead of the window and shuddered away in a border of thin plywood.

Percy didn't care for what the American nature program had insinuated about his indomitable British beetles. He tried to find the show on the TV so he could point out contradictions and false assertions. The set was one of those antediluvian tube units with a bulbous rear to house the electron gun. The picture was fuzzy, so I went over and played with the cable wire until the static disappeared. But by then, the ants and their leaves had been replaced by a family of burrowing cockroaches. The roaches were hard at their burrowing and didn't look to be interested in hauling anything around, so we decided to turn the TV off.

Percy filled the kettle to make a cup of tea. I lay on my bed and stared up at the popcorn ceiling, both anticipating and dreading what I'd uncover in Seaside tomorrow. The kettle reached a boil, and the exothermic reaction almost brought the entire appliance stack down. I picked up my phone and checked Dupont's feed, expecting more self-aggrandizing beach buffoonery. Instead, the newest post showed Dupont, hurricane in hand, posing by a sign for Bourbon Street. "In NOLA, Partying Nawlins Style," was how Dupont—no Emily Dickinson—had captioned the photo.

I had filled Percy in on my dire marital situation shortly after we'd quit the roadkill game. He'd been supportive but refused to speculate on my dark theories.

"My wife's not in Seaside anymore," I told him. "She's in New Orleans, assuming she's with Dupont, that is."

"This Dupont fellow gets around. Are you sure he's not traveling for business?" I showed Percy the hurricane photo. "Yes, he does seem to be engaged in leisurely pursuits. Do you think he flies or drives to these locales?"

I didn't want to think about it. Dupont and Whit,

canoodling in first class, joining the mile-high club on the diaper table of a tiny airplane toilet. But would it be any better if they drove, taking every opportunity to pull into dingy rest stops and fornicate behind overgrown bushes? I didn't think Whit would be up for that given her aversion to roughing it among the general populace. But who knew about this new Whit, Whit 2.0, the Dupont version, a definite downgrade in every measurable specification?

Percy went into the bathroom and came out wearing an elaborately patterned silk robe and a pair of velvet slippers. He lay on his bed, eyes closed and body prostrate, an emperor of the Orient, ready for a massage. He could have been meditating or merely involved in general reflection, I did not know him well enough to draw conclusions from his equable stare. After several minutes in catatonic repose, he spoke with the firm wisdom of an oracle.

"Forget about the sodding Garden of Eden. We will rise early and drive straight to New Orleans. We will hunt down this Dupont fellow, and you will know once and for all if he is despoiling your betrothed. The truck is a trusty workhorse, and she will transport us there without further incident."

It was true. Other than the finicky transmission, the truck was running fine. New Orleans was only five or six hours away, and we were mere miles from crossing into the central time zone, which would give us an hour back. If all went well, we'd arrive late afternoon.

All of a sudden, the back wall of our room shook. Dull thuds and throaty grunts emanated from the other side of the drywall. A raspy female voice yelled out a series of muffled admonitions, and a man responded in kind. It was hard to make out all the specifics, but there was no doubt what they were up to.

Percy wasn't following. "Good lord, is the rogue being sodomized with a cricket bat?"

I couldn't think of a non-offensive way to say "titty fucking" so I hedged and told Percy the woman had directed the man to caress her breasts.

"And that's causing him to scream like that? What's wrong with the daft bloke?"

"He's not using his hands for the caressing. He's using, uh, you know."

"No, my good man, I do not. Please say what you mean."

"I believe he is engaged in titty fucking."

"Good god almighty, is this titty fucking something you Americans undertake on a regular basis?"

"Hard to say. On occasion, I suppose, assuming you have enough raw material to work with."

Percy looked appalled.

"My wife isn't really set up for it," I added, pleased to think of one place on Whit's body Dupont wouldn't enjoy violating.

"Well, I don't see the point. What a load of nonsense."

"Fair enough," I said, not really that eager to explore the subject further.

Percy banged on the wall with both fists. "Forget the bosoms and get in there, you scoundrel, finish the job, for god's sake."

The man must have been denied conjugal visits during his long stretch behind bars, because thankfully, no more than a minute later, the screams rose to a thundering crescendo, then abruptly ceased.

I turned off the lights and lay down on my bed. Anticipation for tomorrow's journey rose inside me as I tossed and turned and tried to block out the annoying hum of the air conditioner. Percy must not have been bothered by the noise, because the only sounds from his side of the room were a gentle wheeze and the occasional rustle of fine Asian fabric.

Chapter Twenty-Four

AN HOUR PAST SUNRISE, WE WALKED over to the office to turn in the room key. Curtis was working reception, exposed as a truant. He had his feet propped up on the desk like a benumbed monopolist, and he was tearing long strips of sugary pastry from the perimeter of a bear claw the size of a baseball mitt. A half-empty bottle of Dornfelder topped the green motel books, and comics and candy were strewn on the counter, likely the spoils of Percy's accidental largesse.

"Shouldn't you be at school?" I asked him.

Curtis licked a mess of stray sugar from his top lip, which was stained a burgundy shade of red. "No, it's Slatterdee," he slurred. "Nooboo go to schoul on Slatterdee, dooh."

Annoyingly, I had lost track of the days, and the churlish sot had wasted no time taking advantage of my temporal disorientation.

Percy jumped in, eager to correct, obviously still bitter about his hundred. "Not true, young man. Pupils in Afghanistan attend classes six days a week—at least the boys do. Bloody terrible how they treat the poor girls. Oh, and the Bengalis, and I believe Indians of neighboring territories as well."

"Ah, ooh caresh aboush the Injiuns, we wupped their ash too. Enwey, I'm homeshoulsh. Daddy says teaters are all iberal like Nobama. They wanna schpeel our guns and make us eat nothin' but shelery and bruk leeg . . ."

I guessed he was trying to enunciate vegetables he didn't like. Broccoli? Leeks? I wasn't sure, my understanding of his vegetable hatred thwarted by a fat ribbon of bear claw that gagged him like a thick sock.

Broadus appeared and poured himself a cup of coffee from a rusty urn sitting on a card table by the door. I'd decided against the urn coffee, but Broadus didn't seem bothered by the exterior corrosion. He told us he was about to set off for Eden to inventory plant life and wanted to know if we'd like to tag along. I thought this invitation was extended because he judged us outdoorsy people with inquisitive minds until he mentioned the heavy equipment he needed help lugging through the piney woods. When we told him we were heading straight for New Orleans, he looked surprised.

"You haven't seen the news?" He pulled out his phone and poked and swiped at the screen. Once he found what he was searching for, he tilted it in our direction. An array of animated yellow and red splotches circled ominously on top of a blue background.

"Tropical Storm Horace," said Broadus. "Appeared out of nowhere yesterday, same as Humberto in '07. They say there's a possibility it'll be a hurricane by noon today and make landfall early evening, somewhere around the Mississippi-Alabama state line."

I detected a hint of schadenfreude in Broadus's voice, but I thanked him for the news nonetheless. We decided we'd better hit the road if we wanted to beat the storm.

First, Percy insisted on presenting Broadus with a bottle of Dornfelder, which led to a twenty-minute Broadus lecture on native German plant species. The German plants had nothing to do with wine, but I suppose botanists are as prone as any group of highly educated specialists to boring pontification.

We gassed up the truck, threw a few more bags of ice onto the wine for good measure, and headed west on the 20. We approached the Achapotita River, and Percy gazed out at the waterway where the RAGE folk claimed Noah had begun his long journey with the animals. It was a slog from here to the eastern reaches of Turkey. I imagined that while the Bible's great drifter had seen a lot in his six hundred years, he'd still been a tad apprehensive when he pushed off, both nervous and excited, like a recent retiree embarking on their first extended Caribbean cruise. He'd probably been a bit puffed up with pride to boot, the size of the boat and all. I pictured him floating away and doing a bit of showboating, maybe a zigzagging sail-by for his soon-to-be-drowned neighbors.

Traffic was light, and we made good progress even though the road shrank to two lanes after we crossed the river. Percy began to quiz me about hurricanes. I tried to explain the finer points of the Saffir-Simpson scale, but he soon became confused.

"So category one is the type that drives straw through fences and cattle into swimming pools?"

"No, that's a four or five. During a one, the cows stay upright. I don't know about straw. I think that only happens during extremely powerful tornadoes."

I shouldn't have mentioned tornadoes, because then I had to spend the next fifteen miles going through the Fujita Scale. Even after I was done with what I thought was a pretty elegant summary, he continued to ask questions. He wanted to know if we'd be better off sheltering in interior closets or empty bathtubs, and if we should seek out shotguns to fend off greedy looters intent on pilfering the remaining Dornfelder. He said he was a decent shot with his William Evans side-by-side. He'd inherited it from his father and it had occupied a box in his attic until the local crows did a number on his crop one year, after which he took to patrolling his vineyards like a prison guard. When it came down to it, he didn't have the heart to blast the feathered transgressors out of the air, but a few shots in their general direction worked pretty well as long as he didn't take too many days off between patrols.

Percy's phone rang. I hoped it wasn't his ruthless interrogator of a daughter again. Thankfully, when he answered I heard a man's voice. Percy responded in a friendly manner, and they talked for a couple of minutes. After he hung up, he told me it was his pal Oliver Sutter. Something called an international test match was being played in the Indian hinterland, and Sutter, a notorious insomniac, couldn't resist calling Percy to fill him in on the second-day action. Sutter's rundown interested Percy more than Ted Fujita's innovative methodologies. He forgot about tornadoes and started telling me about cricket.

"Surely you've heard of Rami Bhatt? Indian chap? He bowls a terrifying topspinner. Jumps off the pitch like a frightened grasshopper. Our batsmen are having an awful time with it. He's absolutely mopping the floor with us, according to Oliver."

I listened and nodded even though I didn't know much about cricket. During law school, Roman Bean, the editor of the law review and a pompous anglophile, talked me into attending an exhibition game he'd organized between a

247

gaggle of out-of-shape British expats from BP and a group of diplomats from the Australian embassy, low-level but in better shape than the oil workers. It rained the entire week before the event, which turned the pitch—a former cow patch on the outskirts of the city—into a soggy bog. Half the game comprised digging the heavy red ball out of the dense muck and the rest attempting to get the wooden dowels to stay put atop the wobbly sticks. Whitney ruined her suede ankle boots in the mud, and the replacement pair cost me half a paycheck.

More important than cricket, how were we going to track down Dupont once we arrived in New Orleans? Even if he was spending most of his time in the French Quarter, it was a long shot, at best. I handed Percy my phone and asked him to search Dupont's feed for clues. There was plenty of new photographic evidence. Dupont, across from Jackson Square, in the middle of a group of acrobats, flashing hand signals with the menacing pride of a newly inducted gang member. Dupont, posing next to a guy in a pointy hat who was spray-painted silver from head to toe. The Tin Man didn't appear happy about the Dupont incursion, although, admittedly, the solemn scowl could have been part of his statue act.

There were also several photos of Dupont at the Carousel Bar in the Hotel Monteleone on Royal Street, the one that completed a satisfying, albeit pointless, circle every fifteen minutes. From the look of his somnolent, basset-hound expression in the last of the bar photos, he must have gotten in several full rotations before dinner, where in the final photo of the evening, he could be seen, bleary-eyed, double-fisting forks and skewering immense chunks of fleshy meat from the sundered shells of two enormous lobsters.

Contemplating Dupont's sybaritic appetites caused ideas to bounce around in my head like loose change in a dryer. In the fever dream my restive mind concocted, I'd rented the binoculars at the Theodore and pilfered them like a bathrobe. Properly equipped, I'd be able to use them to spot my prey in the drunken milieu of the French Quarter. The Quarter's streets were arranged in a grid, and there'd be plenty of desperate people around I could bribe to hoist me onto their shoulders so I could scan down their lengths. I joked to Percy about the ridiculous plan, but he missed the irony, agreeing that it sounded promising so long as I selected a "sufficiently statured inebriate."

We crossed Ram Hatch Road, and I spotted a couple pawing each other by the diesel pumps at the Marathon station. The man's hands were embedded in the woman's copious ass flesh, fingers spread wide as if palming a pair of basketballs. Something about the woman's orgiastic expression set me off, and I began to complain about Whitney. How could she? And with Dupont, of all people. Had she ever really loved me, deep down?

Percy listened. He began to reply but stopped. After a brief pause, he spoke.

"Look, my good fellow, I don't dare presume even the most rudimentary understanding of the female psyche, let alone your relationship. But please permit me one observation."

"Shoot."

"Man with hole in boat drowns no matter the weather."

I nodded solemnly even though I could think of several exceptions to the rather alarmist proverb.

"The Tao?" I asked.

"What?" said Percy.

"That adage. Lao Tzu?"

"No, no. Fortune cookie. Uncle Lee's Garden. The nephew delivers. Sufferable kung pao chicken in a pinch."

The miles ticked by, the road smooth and straight. In an hour or so, at the town of Bruce, we made a right at the Bruce Cafe, which stood across the road from the Bruce Store. Bruce, with all its Bruce amenities, appeared to be a serviceable hamlet for small-town living unless you happened to be named Bruce. Then, it would be one annoying Bruce confusion after another.

Shortly thereafter, we joined Interstate 10 around Ponce de Leon. We hadn't been on the freeway for more than ten minutes when traffic stalled and the GPS showed solid red for miles ahead. I wasn't sure if the congestion was related to the storm—nervous people scurrying about in flustered panic, having lost all sense of logic and restraint—but I didn't want to find out. We crawled along to the next exit and headed north. My plan was to make a grand arc to our destination. Not Saarinen's great frontier tribute or anything, but impressive for its improvised, curving trajectory nonetheless. We would go up and around Mobile, through the De Soto National Forest south of Hattiesburg, then join Interstate 59 and shoot down into New Orleans from the north.

It was slow going for the next hour. The weather was still sunny and calm, but sharp gusts of wind whipped across the road with increasing regularity, obviously harbingers of the approaching storm. Thankfully, traffic thinned as we progressed. We crossed into Alabama on a poorly maintained county road. Much to Percy's disappointment, there was no friendly billboard to welcome us, just a faded sign that announced, "Alabama State Line." That didn't stop him from getting excited about the border crossing. He did some searching on his phone and informed me that, among other things, the official state reptile of Alabama was the red-bellied cooter, a type of rare turtle. I told Percy it sounded like a fine talisman but was probably a pain to identify outside of captivity.

We kept going, running due west, roughly parallel to the Florida state line, a boundary hardened in 1845 after centuries of colonial wrangling. We stopped for gas in a town named Brewton. The gas station sat across the road from a flat-roofed concrete building that housed a laundromat, a bail-bond outfit, and a pet store called Mans Best Friend. At least I thought it was a pet store until I noticed the assault rifle painted next to "Friend."

Percy was one step ahead of me. He pointed out the missing apostrophe and lined up his shot.

"Why don't we go in?" he said.

"Have you forgotten about Horace?"

"We're making good time. Maybe they sell binoculars?"

"That was a joke."

"Please allow me this one indulgence. Look at this place. A bloody great colonial arsenal!"

Reluctantly, I relented. We left the truck at the gas station and crossed the road. The tinted-glass door of the gun store was peppered with stickers. One declared, "In God We Trust," like on the dollar bill, although the nature of the enterprise arguably contradicted the message of divine sanctuary. Below, a cartoon version of the Statue of Liberty stood at attention, hoisting an AR-15 above her spiky crown.

A large cowbell clanged when we pushed through the door. It was immediately obvious the gun merchants had wasted no space in displaying their manifold ordnance. Glass display cases surrounded the perimeter of the room, and the walls were jigsawed with an assortment of high-caliber firearms. Rifles hung from the ceiling by strands of rope, jutting down like stalactites in a dank cave. Others were jammed, barrel first, into circular wooden racks that looked like umbrella stands.

We joked back and forth. Percy said there was easily enough firepower on display to outfit a band of Somali warlords. I countered his African mercenaries with a horde of disgruntled employees plotting an all-day rampage at their populous workplace. I judged mine to be a more relevant send-up, Percy's Somalis a slightly dated reference.

The store was packed. More hurricane-driven panic or normal Deep South retail therapy, who knew? Excited men in thick, ill-fitting clothes examined the merchandise and fidgeted like trophy wives in a jewelry store. Equally sartorially deficient people were ensconced behind the counters, where they frowned seriously and recited specs in gruff tones.

Percy walked over to a metal display rack and examined the elaborate contraption zip-tied to the bars. "Flamethrower—Make Reasonable Offer and It's Yours," read a sign centered above the socket designed to house the pressurized gas cartridge. Percy wanted to know what a reasonable offer would be for such an infrequently practical device. I told him to ignore the duplicitous pitch. It was nothing more than a tactic of deceit, something the indolent Dean Peas had been known to try if he was short of his quota with the end of the month looming.

Something caught Percy's eye, and he wandered off. I decided to check out the store's binoculars. Worst case, they'd keep Percy occupied scouring the terrain for cooters. I stood in line behind a guy who was inspecting a large-bore rifle. The gun was the sort of thing Teddy Roosevelt might throw into his checked luggage if packing for his great African holocaust today. I stood back to give the man plenty of room. The way he was examining every last detail on the rifle reminded me of tire kickers we get at the dealership, and sure enough, after much pointless fiddling, he handed the gun back to the man behind the counter and walked off.

After the sales guy returned the rifle to the rack, he turned around and asked me what I needed. When I told him binoculars, he became annoyed.

"What does this look like, a sporting goods store? All we got is guns. And stuff for guns."

"What about those?" I pointed to a large display case full of knives. They were of every conceivable size. A few could have been more aptly described as swords.

"They're knives. What do you think they are?"

"They're not guns. Or stuff for guns."

The guy thought for a second. "They're weapons, aren't they? If someone can't pass the background check, you think they want to go home empty-handed?"

There it was, the wall of knives, a sales-driven tactic designed to capitalize on rural disappointment and desperation. I paused to admire the perverse logic.

"Anyway, what do you need binoculars for?" the man asked. "You some sort of bird-watcher?"

"Do I look like one?" I tried to picture the typical outfit donned by men disposed to scouring open marshlands for rare warblers. The best I could come up with was how Broadus had been dressed that morning. He'd had on a middle-class, light-duty hiker pastiche—an ensemble more suited to a trip to the mall with the family in tow than wading through remote, mosquito-infested mires.

The man said, "It doesn't matter what you look like, it's how you carry yourself. See that guy over there? No one's going to mistake him for an animal nut, no matter how he's dressed."

I realized he was gesturing at Percy, who was talking to a guy on the opposite side of the store and pointing a shotgun with two immense barrels upward with great purpose, as if the corvids that menaced his vines were roosting above the water-stained ceiling tiles. The pair were getting on swimmingly, the powerful weaponry bridging the cultural divide like Kofi Annan in his prime.

I turned back to the man, drawing a blank. Finally, I lied and said I needed the binoculars to observe tugboats on the Mississippi. I told him I enjoyed watching sailors go about their daily routines on the mighty river, that it brought me a winsome gratification. In hindsight, using the words "sailor" and "gratification" in the same sentence was a mistake.

"What are you, some kind of pervert?" He eyed me up and down as if deciding where he'd put the first bullet if I were dumb enough to try to steal a rusty tire iron off his front porch. I considered asking him whether an optical sight could be repurposed as a telescope but decided against it because of his hostile essence, which I chalked up to a bad night's sleep or possibly a childhood bereft of love.

I walked off to find Percy. He was now over in the far corner of the shop, standing in front of a coin-operated machine with "The Claw" emblazoned on the cabinet. In the glass compartment, a metal grapple hovered over a pit of gun-store jetsam. In the midst of the Second Amendment potpourri, I discerned a pair of plastic safety glasses, a sachet of multipurpose lubricant, a packet of confrontationally worded stickers, a pocket-sized Constitution, and a snakebite kit.

Percy fiddled with a red joystick, and the claw jolted across the top of the box. He said he was trying to line it up with the stickers, which he planned to affix to his tractor as a warning to thieves. His second choice was the snakebite kit because adders had, on occasion, been spotted slithering around his vineyards. I told him not to get too excited either way, the game was rigged against him.

"The salesman told me I was out of luck with the shotgun," said Percy. "American citizens only, I'm afraid."

He hit a glowing button with an open palm, and the claw dove downward. Seconds later, it rose from the farrago with the snakebite kit. Percy yelped with joy at his minor triumph, which caused everyone in the store to look around for the source of the girlish squeals, cold eyes of judgment fixing on us in the midst of the munitions. We made a hasty, slinking retreat with the Claw spoils, but our surreptitious exit was foiled by the cowbell, which rang out in alarm when we opened the door and stepped out into the unrelenting sun.

Chapter Twenty-Five

IT WAS MIDAFTERNOON BY THE TIME we crossed into Mississippi. The geometrically pleasing route was taking longer than I'd anticipated. Not to mention all the time we were losing because Percy demanded I slow down every time we passed a drainage ditch so he could scan for cooters. After the eighth impromptu cooter safari, I'd had enough.

"Didn't you say they were endangered?" I asked.

"Yes, why?"

"Well, what are the odds?"

"They're red. It shouldn't be that difficult."

"You think they're going to be lying on their shells, wiggling their scaly little legs in the air, waiting for us to drive by? Not to mention you're borderline colorblind. Everything looks red to you."

"I don't believe we know each other well enough for such personal censure, thank you."

"I've seen you in a kimono."

"That was a yukata, totally different fabric."

Traffic was moving with a nervous energy, drivers anxious to get where they were going before the storm arrived. We were passing through the umpteenth small town, another road wart, indiscernible from the others, and I was fiddling with my phone to retrieve an update on Horace. If the storm was still on course, I guessed it would be directly south of us by roughly a hundred miles. My signal was weak, which caused the radar map to load in jagged chunks. Just when the Horace piece was about to appear, Percy spoke up.

"Red light."

Thinking he was crying wolf again, I hesitated, my eyes still fixed on my phone. A second later, he exploded with panic.

"Look out, it's red. Stop, for Pete's sake, stop!" He pointed furiously outward and upward.

I looked up in time to see a flashing red light hanging down over a four-way intersection. I slammed on the brakes. The pads squealed as they abraded the paper-thin rotors. I cursed the paltry friction while the truck hurtled toward the intersection. We were halfway into it before we finally came to a stop, mere feet from a bread truck, its flank emblazoned with a cartoonish image of a coy blond girl munching on a heavily buttered slice.

We had no time to enjoy any sense of fortitude because we were immediately shunted from behind. Luckily, my foot was still firmly planted on the brake pedal. Even so, the impact caused our torsos to strain against our seat belts with considerable force.

"Sorry, my bad," I said.

Percy sniffed the air. "What a divine aroma!"

I registered the sweet smell of fresh loaves while the bread guy got out and told me what he thought of my driving. We watched the epic tantrum through the windshield like dates at a drive-in. Percy waved apologetically, which only angered the bread guy more. I didn't respond,

257

knowing that, soon enough, concern for his undelivered inventory would return, his rage tempered by the pull of Smith's inscrutable hand.

Sure enough, after a couple of minutes, the bread guy quit screaming and climbed back in with his bread. I signaled out the window to the driver of the van that'd hit us to follow me across the intersection. I pulled into a country store about thirty yards down the road and parked to the right of the doors, next to a hopper of chicken feed. I got out and examined the back of the truck. Thankfully, it was fine except for a couple of scuffs on the bumper, nothing a can of spray paint couldn't conceal from a pedantic rental clerk.

The store's parking lot was alive with activity. Two youngish guys in short-sleeved dress shirts and dark slacks were boarding up the windows of the store with sheets of plywood. A man in a cowboy hat stood behind them, his hands in the pockets of his denim overalls. Nearby, a casually dressed woman was fiddling with the elaborate camera perched on her shoulder, and a meticulously groomed guy, around my age, was checking himself out in a pocket mirror. A big gray and white dog with a thick woolly coat was sprawled out by the man's feet and eyed the goings-on with a torpid boredom.

The camerawoman handed the man a microphone and said, "Okay, Celeste is sending it to you in three, two, one, and . . ."

Suddenly, the reporter's expression transformed from preening indifference to grave seriousness. "Thanks, Celeste. This is a KPOX News on-the-Scene Precision Weather Alert from the southern part of our Pine Belt viewing area. I'm coming to you live from Willie-T's Country Store and Feed on Route 98 in Forrest County. This is still the calm before the storm, but residents and area businesses alike are taking no chances with Tropical Storm Horace. In the short time I've been here this afternoon, I've witnessed a torrent of people inundating Willie-T's, filling their tanks with gas and stocking up for what will likely be a long stretch without power. I haven't been able to get firm details on the amount of fuel left, but I assume they're running low. And I was informed a few minutes ago that the store is almost out of bottled water and batteries . . . Indeed, Celeste, you heard me correctly, the shelves are pretty much bare. And not only are provisions almost gone here at Willie-T's, but the owner is taking no chances with his property."

The news guy turned and pivoted to his right. "As you can see behind me, they're currently boarding up the windows with sheets of extremely thick plywood. A labor-intensive job, but with a storm like Horace rolling in, it's no time to gamble. And rightly so given the latest KPOX high-definition radar update that shows Horace strengthening, possibly on the cusp of becoming a hurricane."

I assessed the scene in light of the news guy's tapestry of abject desperation. A lady in an SUV, who appeared in no great hurry, was pulling away from the only occupied gas pump. A man walked out of the store, empty-handed. He was doing his best impression of a factory foreman during the industrial revolution—pacing angrily while mumbling words of callous disgust, something to do with lottery tickets. Another guy ambled to his car carrying three bags of beef jerky and a two-liter of Big Red. He got in and drove off, leaving Percy's rental the only vehicle in front of the store besides the news van.

The reporter walked over to the man in the overalls.

"Sir, do you have a second? We're live on KPOX." The newsman reached out an arm and shepherded the guy into the frame. "I take it you're the owner of this store?"

"Yessir. Owner, plumber, carpenter, electrician. You know how it goes, Mr. . . . I'm sorry, I didn't catch your name, fella."

"Ryaaan French. KPOX weather."

"Mr. Ryan French. Pleased to meet you. Didn't think for the life of me I'd get the real live news out to my li'l ol' store. No sir, wait till I tell my boy, Henry, about this, he won't believe it. He's up in Oxford, goin' to school. Yessir, smart kid. Wish I could say he's a chip off the ol' block, but to tell the truth, he gets it all from his momma." The man beamed at the camera.

"So, you're Willie?"

"Guilty as charged, Mr. French."

"Willie, thanks for joining us on KPOX this afternoon. You've been tracking Horace today, and I see you've determined this is one serious storm, and you need to take severe measures to protect your store?"

"Don't know I've been doing much tracking today. Been busy with other, more pressing business. Trying to get the lottery folk out to fix our machine. It's all jammed up something terrible. People sure do get upset when they can't get their tickets, the jackpot's up to—"

"Tell me about your employees. I see you've got a couple of them out here boarding up the windows. Better safe than sorry?"

"Those boys? No, sir, they ain't employees."

French regrouped. "Celeste, I'm happy to report it appears neighbors in Forrest County are pulling together in this time of need. Willie, you must be proud of your community?"

"No, no, Mr. French, afraid they ain't from around here."

French was not about to abandon the saccharine.

"Celeste, even more remarkable, people are coming from far and wide to lend a hand here at Willie-T's. Stores like these are the heart and soul of our communities, and in dire circumstances, it's our Magnolia State spirit that sees us all through. Willie, can you tell our viewers where these generous volunteers hail from?"

"Not sure. Think Reed said he was from up north some-where." Willie nodded in the direction of the larger of the two apprentices, a muscular, freckle-faced all-American guy who looked like a Kennedy heir. "Believe he said Spokane. Might as well be Canada, eh?" Willie chuckled and jabbed at French with an outstretched elbow. "The other one lives by some lake. Name's Ricky. Nice boy. Sure got lots of energy. They showed up this morning, on their bicycles, and started talking to people in the parking lot. Asked my wife if they could help with anything, so she put them to work. I told her this storm wasn't going to be nothing by the time it made it up here, but you know how ladies like to—"

French cut off Willie, possibly to avoid the impending sexism, more likely for downplaying the severity of Horace. "So Willie-T's is a family business. Is your wife helping out with preparations for Horace?"

"Oh yessir, she's in the back marking up the prices of the items that might run low if folks panic. We're hurting real bad with our lottery machine jammed up and all."

French cut his losses. "Willie, thanks for talking with us live on KPOX. I think that's all the time we have right now—"

Just then, the second member of the plywood duo jumped into the frame, inserting himself between Ryan French and Willie. He wrapped his arms around their shoulders and eyed the camera with a rakish cupidity. He was rail-thin with smooth skin and the slick bouffant hair of a seedy lounge crooner. His trousers were stretched tightly over his pelvic region like plastic wrap on a heaping bowl of leftovers, and his eyes twinkled with mischief.

"*Hola, amigos!*" he wailed, his body pulsing with a lusty, pent-up energy. "Hey, Papi, show everybody those moves we practice earlier. Time to let the big wide world see what Mr. Papi got!"

Willie shot the camera an expression of coquettish embarrassment. "I dunno, Ricky, I'm not—"

"C'mon, Papi, move your hips for me, amigo. *Bailar conmigo!* Dance with me, Papi, don't be no shy!"

Ricky wouldn't take no for an answer. He grabbed Willie's hands and the two of them attempted an awkward samba while Ryan French looked on in nervous bemusement.

"Celeste, as you can see, the people here at Willie-T's are not letting Horace dampen their spirits, that's for sure." French turned in the direction of the shaggy dog, who had perked up and was studying something on the other side of the highway. The reporter bent down, to dog level, but the animal ignored him.

"I think our regular viewers know what time it is. Doppler, can you send it back to Celeste in the studio with a special Doppler—"

Before French could finish, Doppler bolted across the parking lot, onto the road. He narrowly missed being T-boned by a shrimpy Korean import. The car was lucky. Its pygmy subframe would have suffered grievously in a collision with the hefty beast. Doppler ignored the weak bleats of the feeble horn and trudged up to a majestic oak tree. He stared up the trunk and barked rabidly.

French laughed through a wince. "You've got that right, Celeste. Yes, he's fine. I'm sure he senses the storm approaching. Animals have an amazing sixth sense for these things . . . Yes, exactly, like during that tsunami. Indeed, one of the many reasons he's such a valuable member of the KPOX weather team . . . Great . . . We'll be standing by all afternoon to give you the latest updates on preparations for Horace. This is Ryaaan French, KPOX News, signing off for now."

French lowered his microphone. His look of eager comity disappeared, replaced by the scowl of an irascible tot ordered to eat his peas. He strode across the road, in the direction of Doppler, whipping the dog's leash against his thigh. Doppler spotted French approaching and proceeded to run circles around the oak, eluding the newsman's attempts to corral him.

I walked over to the vehicle that'd hit us. The boxy step van was not much different from the bread truck, nothing special except for the paint job. On the side of the van was the most marvelous, unexpected mural. It looked like something Michelangelo might have painted on the ceiling of a rich Italian kid's bedroom if he'd had a falling-out with the papacy and needed to come up with a few lire in short order. It depicted a local fair, but without the paroled carnies and boozehounds vomiting in trash cans. Against a soft-hued backdrop, balloons floated upward, filling the azure sky. Frolicking children ate bushy swirls of cotton candy. A red-cheeked clown laughed in a kind, caring, not-at-all-sinister fashion, and an excited crowd extended outstretched arms in the direction of an elephant adorned with a heavily jeweled crown.

I felt a tap on my right arm. I turned to face a woman probably not much younger than me. Sunglasses held back her flaxen hair, and she had on a white T-shirt and white jeans rolled up above well-proportioned ankles.

Dad always told me to pay attention to the ankles. "Ankles, son, always check out the ankles, they're like crystal balls," he'd admonished one day while we were in line at the bank. I didn't understand why he'd brought it up until I noticed the thick, fleshy hams bulging out of the sneakers of a pushy woman who was trying to bully the teller into accepting a sackful of unrolled nickels.

"You and your friend okay?" said the woman.

"This is yours?" I asked, motioning to the truck, surprised because she didn't possess the utilitarian girth of your average delivery driver.

"Yes and no," she replied.

"Well, sorry about the late braking. Totally my fault. You're not hurt, are you?"

"I'm fine. I was probably following too closely. I'm not used to this thing. It doesn't have a hood. How am I supposed to judge distances without a hood? Where have they hidden the engine?"

"It's in the regular place. Up front. Transversely mounted to save space."

"Good to know. I'm going to spring that one on my dad. He'll think I've been abducted by interplanetary visitors." She smiled, and I laughed.

"Any damage to your van?" I asked.

"Just a dent in the bumper. No big deal."

"What's in it?"

"Impulse buys."

"What?"

"The random stuff on racks by the register. Playing cards, cotton candy, balloons. My dad supplies lots of these little country stores. I'm doing his route for a few weeks while he recovers from knee surgery. This is my final stop. I was hoping to get back to Baton Rouge before the storm hits."

"Nice artwork." I motioned to her van. "Much better than that bread truck. That little girl looked far too desperate for the bread."

"My dad's Christmas present last year. Took my sister an entire week. She's an artist. I paid for the paint and helped a little. We finished up on New Year's Eve, just in time for some neighborhood delinquents to egg it. That's why the sky's so cloudy."

Something about her wry lilt caused me to overshare.

"That's great. The mural, I mean, not the egging. I gave my mother a mug for her birthday once. Made it on a pottery wheel in art class in fifth grade. It had a tiny hole in the bottom, so the first time she used it, coffee leaked all over the carpet. She relegated it to the bathroom and used it to hold her toothbrush."

"I'm sure she appreciated the effort."

"Don't think so. We had to get new carpet in the den. She told me from them on she would only accept retail items and she'd be checking receipts. I didn't realize she was joking until the next Christmas. Everyone in the family had a good laugh at that one, me and all my paperwork."

She asked me what I was up to in the rental truck with Percy, whom she described as "that adorably disheveled British man with the poofy white hair." I turned around to locate my charge. He was talking to Willie, a bottle of Dornfelder in hand. He was in the middle of his sales pitch, but Willie appeared more interested in Ricky's dance lesson than Percy's generous by-the-case discount.

"It's a long story," I said. "How much time do you have?"

"I guess not much, given the storm and all."

"Fair point. Let's say it's been a long journey, and my

life has sort of imploded while I've been gone."

"A modern-day Odysseus."

I laughed. "Something like that, although I'm not sure my wife's a paragon of virtue like Penelope."

"Oh?"

"Come to think of it, I wouldn't mind putting a sharp arrow through Dupont's outsized block."

"What? Who?"

"Sorry, I'm thinking out loud. A bad habit, especially for a lawyer."

"Oh, so you're a lawyer," she said, as if I'd just disclosed a contagious malady.

"No, not at present."

She eyed me suspiciously, as though Percy and I were on the lam, the rental truck a prison vehicle left unattended by indolent guards.

"Another long story," I added.

"Maybe you should write a book."

"I'm Guy Hastings, by the way."

"Liesl Guidry. You know, *The Sound of Music*. My mother's a big fan. I'll never forgive her. My friends call me Lise."

We shook hands, and I helped Lise haul her wares into Willie-T's. I exited the store and spotted Ryan French, who was back on the scene with the dog. Both French and the animal had taken an interest in Percy. French quizzed him and scribbled notes onto a small pad. Meanwhile, Doppler rubbed his fleecy pelt against Percy's houndstooth trousers, coating them with a thick layer of fur and making him look like he had on a pair of leg warmers.

French quit writing and the camerawoman counted down.

"As you can see, Celeste, they're still busy boarding up the windows here at Willie-T's. And I've got a special guest with me who's traveled all the way from Europe. That's right, we have a visitor from the British Isles joining us today on KPOX. One Percy Templeton from . . ." French peered down at his notes. "Sussex . . . No, Celeste, S-U-S-S-E-X . . . Yes, we want to make sure we get that right, wouldn't want our viewers getting the wrong end of the stick. Percy, thanks for talking with us today on KPOX. I bet you don't get storms like Horace over there in merry old England."

"Incorrect, my good fellow. I'll have you know the Great Storm of 1987 was every bit as powerful as one of your cyclones. Flattened the trees of Chanctonbury Ring, had to replant the entire circle—"

"What do you make of all the activity here at Willie-T's? People chipping in, lending a hand. You must be impressed by the Southern resolve you're witnessing here in the heart of Mississippi?"

"Just arrived, my good man. I will concede those two are sweating like a pair of obese sows." Percy motioned to Willie's volunteer labor. Reed was on a ladder, attempting to heft a piece of plywood up to one of the top windows. Ricky was under him, wrestling the sheet upward, straining under the weight of the heavy board and complaining loudly in Spanglish.

"And I understand you're on your way to New Orleans today?"

"Correct. My traveling companion's wife appears to have run off with a man of corrupted quintessence. We are on our way to confront the disreputable lothario and his misguided paramour."

Ryan French cast his eyes downward and fidgeted with the collar of his jacket. "Okay, well there you have it, Celeste—"

The instant French turned his attention back to the camera, Percy grabbed his microphone and wrestled it away. "One moment, my dear fellow. I'd like to mention I'm close to securing an agreement to stock my wine at this superior establishment. Willie and I are in the final stages of our negotiations. If your viewers are a tad tired of hiding their malt ales in brown bags and wish to sample a more cultured libation, I suggest—"

French seized the microphone by its stem and pried it from Percy's hands with a constipated grimace. He wrapped up his segment by trying to coax a performative sign-off out of Doppler, but the dog was lounging by Percy's feet and refused to cooperate.

I walked over to Percy, who was trying to cheer up French by offering him a bottle of Dornfelder, gratis.

"I don't know why they make me haul him around," said French. "He'll only perform when he's in the studio." He looked down at the stubborn animal, who eyed him back as though he knew he was being talked about.

French complained that his role at the station had devolved into an incongruous hybrid—one part weekend weatherman/field reporter, the other part circus performer, the dog a misguided attempt by the station's manager to hike the ratings. French expounded on his act with the disdain of a telemarketer explaining their call script. He told us that during the Saturday evening forecast, he was required to whistle to Doppler, who would plod out from behind the stage for what was dubbed the "Pooch Predictions" segment of the weather. If Doppler barked three times and rolled over, it meant rain. If he got up on his hind legs in a begging position, it meant sunshine. French said he'd been ordered to work out routines for other conditions, such as strong winds and dense fog, but Doppler couldn't grasp the extra cues no matter how many liver biscuits he shoveled at the ornery animal.

The dejection in French's voice was so palpable that both Percy and I felt the need to pat him on the back. I concentrated on the intensity of my strokes, trying to convey a stolid commiseration free of condescension. Percy thwacked away like French had something stuck in his windpipe.

In Lise's absence, a passel of scraggly children had assembled in the parking lot. They'd materialized with eerie stealth, like a horde of demon-possessed orphans who resided in the dense tangle of an overgrown cornfield. The pack crowded around Lise's van, restless and agitated. When she walked out of the store with an armful of empty boxes, they swarmed her.

"Hey, lady, we want ice cream, give us ice cream," demanded the leader of the pack, a coal-eyed girl of about seven. She poked Lise in the ribs with a bony finger.

"Oh, I'm sorry, this isn't an ice-cream truck. But I bet there's some inside the store."

"Ice cream! Ice cream!" the girl chanted. The others immediately began to parrot the baleful discordance.

"Ouch, ooh, I'm sorry. . . I don't . . ."

The kids kept up the ritual chants, filling the air with their unreasonable demands, a little union, insisting on impossible terms.

"What do we want? Ice cream! When do we want it? Now!"

Lise laughed nervously. "You guys are a persistent bunch. I'll tell you what, wait here a second."

She walked to the back of her van and unloaded a box. The pack followed her, impatient with anticipation. She cut it open and handed out bags of cotton candy to the sinister rascals. They immediately began to gorge themselves on the fluffy pink glucose, tearing at it like famished dingoes devouring a kangaroo carcass.

Just then, I noticed a yellowy-green puddle of fluorescent liquid surrounding the left front tire of Lise's van. I bent down to locate the source.

"I hate to tell you, but your radiator's leaking." I motioned to the puddle. "Must be punctured. Probably happened when you ran into us."

"That doesn't sound like great news, but you're going to tell me it's not a big deal, right?"

"Wish I could. You might make it twenty miles, but at some point before you hit Louisiana, the engine's going to overheat."

"Twenty miles? What am I supposed to do then?"

I looked down at the puddle again. "Make that ten," I said, and took a step back to avoid the advancing fluid.

Chapter Twenty-Six

BEFORE LISE COULD RESPOND, DESPERATE SCREAMS rose from the other side of the parking lot. I turned in the direction of the distraught caterwauling, half expecting to see one of the sugar-drunk urchins gnawing on somebody's exposed calf. Instead, the tortured wails came from Samba Ricky. He was writhing around on the ground, blood spurting with hydrant velocity out of a giant gash that ran the length of his lean, hairless forearm.

Reed looked down at his compadre with the exasperation of an overworked roughneck. He showed no interest in trying to cap Ricky's blood gusher. We yelled out suggestions, exhorting him to do something, anything. Lise suggested he use his shirt as a bandage. Reed demurred with an annoyed glare. An inspired suggestion that meant no personal sacrifice on their part, the assembled onlookers enthusiastically got behind the shirt-bandage idea. Percy even yelled, "What's the harm? Aren't you wearing the magic pajamas underneath?" Realizing feed store sentiment was now squarely against him, Reed begrudgingly stripped off his button-down and tied it around Ricky's cleaved forearm.

Ricky stared down at his cosseted appendage. He moaned and yelled, first in Spanish, then in English. *"Oh, mi brazo está jodido,* my arm, my arm. Forbush, what the fuck? You dropped the wood on my arm, *pendejo."*

"Ricky, it was an accident," said Reed. "Calm down, take a deep breath, and relax." He bowed his head and prayed in a showy fashion. "Dear God, benevolent Lord, please be with Brother Peña in his time of need. If it is your will, in your infinite wisdom, please stop the bleeding and please . . ."

By the end of Forbush's ponderous intercession, the shirt bandage was soaked through, and Ricky Peña's blood was cascading down his denuded arm, onto the concrete, where it pooled around his right hand, a crimson lake of concerning depth.

Percy and I looked at each other with helpless horror. Willie stood straight as a two-by-four and mumbled something about the deserts of Kuwait. Suddenly, Lise sprang into action. She ran to the circus van, climbed in, and soon emerged with a family pack of party balloons. When she reached Peña, she ripped open the bag and extracted a couple of cylindrical ones of the type birthday-party clowns use for dachshund torsos. She brushed Forbush aside and tied the balloons around Peña's arm, directly above the gaping wound. Thankfully, the makeshift tourniquet worked—the geyser of blood soon subsided into nothing more than a weak trickle.

The balloon-wrapped Ricky Peña lay there in woozy stupefaction, groaning like a recently shot-up heroin addict awash in a pained bliss. We huddled next to him and talked in low, hushed tones, trying to figure out what to do next. Before we could decide, Ryan French moved in. He went live and expounded on Peña's dire condition for the local viewers. He described the mutilated volunteer as the "first victim of Horace." He was so happy to have some real action to narrate, he didn't notice when Doppler lumbered into the frame with one of the derelict children on his back. The grimy kid was holding on to the dog by his collar and riding him like a trail pony. Doppler plodded over to the accident scene, nuzzled up to Peña, and proceeded to lick generous helpings of his blood off the dirty concrete.

The camerawoman tried to get French's attention. She waved frantically with her free hand, but he was too engrossed in his chronicle of fortuitous carnage to notice the woman's furious motions. Somebody in the studio must have caught sight of the carnivorous display, because all of a sudden, French stopped talking and looked over his shoulder. When he turned back to the camera, his face was rife with aggrieved disbelief.

"Celeste, well, I . . . Okay, oh goodness. Yes, he's definitely going to town. Must be thirsty, poor guy. I'll think I'll send it back to you while we get him cleaned up. This is Ryaaan French, KPOX News."

Percy ambled up and elbowed me.

"Attempted murder," he said in a hushed voice.

"What?"

He nodded in the direction of Forbush and Ricky Peña. "Those two."

"Huh? The Mormons?"

Percy chuckled at my naïveté. "Mormons they may be. All I know is the Irishman tried to kill the Spaniard. I saw him look down with anger before he dropped the pressboard. It would have decapitated the dainty fellow if he hadn't moved at the last second."

"Why would he want to kill him?"

"A mystery we will get to the bottom of in due course,

my good man."

"Are you sure? Murder? I'm pretty certain that's a recipe for eternal damnation in almost every religion."

"They're mortals, flesh and blood, no different from us. Dare I remind you about what happened at Mountain Meadows on that fateful day in 1857?"

I knew nothing I said was going to stop him from telling me about it. Sure enough, I soon learned a surfeit of grisly details about how a band of bloodthirsty Latter-day Saints dressed up like Indians and butchered a convoy of innocents seeking safe passage through the rugged canyons of what is now southern Utah. This information was accompanied by a crude reenactment in which Percy danced in front of the rental as though it were an overturned wagon full of soon-to-be-scalped pioneers.

After Percy quit the feverish nonsense chanting and tomahawk chopping, I asked him how he knew so much about Mormons and their history. He told me that back when he and Hazel were sheep farming, they'd been visited regularly by a couple of missionaries who were only too happy to tend to his moronic flock in exchange for non-caffeinated beverages and extended conversations about the contents of the ancient Egyptian plates Joseph Smith claimed to have dug out of a muddy berm thirty miles southeast of Rochester, in upstate New York. He still exchanged Christmas cards with one of them—a devout, gentle giant of a man from American Samoa named Koa Tupuola.

Peña had stopped bleeding, but it was obvious he needed medical attention. I estimated it would take at least twenty stitches to close up his arm, and he was in no shape to pedal himself to Hattiesburg. Lise's van was out of commission due to my careless stupidity. There was no choice. No different from Noah himself, I'd have to load up the entire motley assembly and embark on my own Old Testament–style journey through the doubtlessly inhospitable landscape.

I walked over to Lise, who was tending to Peña like a battlefield nurse. I explained my Noah proposal, except without mentioning Noah, figuring it would brand me a narcissist, the grave importance of the old man's mission and all. She was worried about the prospect of having to abandon her dad's van amid the coven of creepy foundlings.

"In hindsight, the cotton candy wasn't the best idea," she said.

I looked in the direction of the Lilliputian mob, which had taken to running sharp circles around Percy like he was an about-to-be-immolated heretic.

"Don't worry, I'll arrange a wrecker for your dad's van," I told her. "And I'll make sure you get to Baton Rouge tomorrow."

I eyed the pack again. One of the boys pointed at Percy's fur-coated trousers and cackled. He got down on all fours, craned his head skyward, and barked at an invisible moon. The impish wails excited Doppler, and the dog began to howl, the duo filling the parking lot with their feral chorus.

I introduced myself to Forbush and offered to ferry Ricky Peña to the hospital. He mumbled out a terse thank-you. I tried to read him for homicidal tells—a sociopathic revulsion for unsavory exhibitionism or some sort of repressed psychosexual depravity—but the only thing that registered was a pungent musk emanating from the general direction of his magic undershirt.

The Mormons spread the good news on expensive electric mountain bikes with fat knobby tires. I loaded them into the rental truck, next to their bulky satchels. We carried Peña into the back and laid him down on top of the wine boxes. He sank into the soggy cardboard, and it molded around his diminutive frame like a pillow-top mattress. Peña had latched on to Lise with hysterical enthusiasm, so she agreed to ride with him in the back. Forbush tried to climb in with Peña and Lise, but Percy intervened.

"No, no, my good man, there's plenty of room up front, hop in." He turned to me and rubbed the palms of his hands together with the anticipatory relish of a craps player on a hot streak.

We set off. Every time I was forced to drop the clutch, we heard Peña's muffled screams through the thin fiber-glass shell as the truck shuddered forward. It wasn't long before Percy spoke up.

"Reed, I'm well versed in your sacred tenets. A Samoan used to tend to my sheep on occasion."

"He did?"

"Koa Tupuola. Mountain of a man. One afternoon, on a stroll, we spotted a couple of ewes beached on a knoll in a flooded pasture. Lord knows how the silly buggers ended up there. Tupu didn't hesitate. He waded in after them, came back with one under each arm."

"Goodness."

"We dried off his hulking frame, which, I'll tell you, took the better part of ten minutes and four towels. It was a cold July afternoon, and a raging fire was burning in the open hearth. We huddled together with piping hot mugs of Bovril and polished off an entire box of Jaffa Cakes."

"Sounds cozy. What's a Jaffa Cake?"

"Reed, may I address you as a brother even though we are not consecrated as such?"

"I guess."

"Brother Forbush, Tupu explained many things to us that chilly summer day. We learned about the angel Moroni, the Lamanites, eternal marriage, and proxy baptism."

Forbush sat up. His expression was how I imagined Dean Peas had looked when he stumbled on my Massey deal after I'd done all the heavy lifting.

"Mr. Templeton?"

"Please, my boy, call me Brother Percy."

"Okay. Brother Percy, have you ever considered dedicating your life to the Lord? Undergoing the sacred rite of baptism?"

"Unfortunately, Tupu's visits were many years ago. I've become a little rusty on the finer points of your doctrines. Would it be possible for you to give me a rundown on the three kingdoms of glory? Where, exactly, would a man who commits premeditated murder fit into your heavenly schema? Please, help me understand, if you would be so kind."

Percy's attempt to rattle Forbush would no doubt plunge us deep into an ecclesiastical abyss. I had no interest in the specifics of one Mormon kingdom of glory, let alone three, so I said, "Before we get into all that, I have a few questions of a more practical nature."

Percy glared at me from across the cab.

"Oh?" said Forbush. "Could it wait a few minutes?" He tapped his foot with a salesman's impatience, obviously annoyed I'd butted in while he was trying to close Percy.

"I just need a quick Mormon perspective on someone I know."

"Actually, we don't use that term. We prefer 'Latter-day Saints.'"

"Yeah, okay, whatever. So anyway, I know this guy . . ." I told Forbush about Ronnie Dupont and his life of seamy intemperance.

"The Lord will forgive any sin, no matter how grave, so

long as the sinner is sincere in his atonement," said Forbush.

"How convenient," mumbled Percy.

"Okay," I said, "assume he doesn't repent of his sordid iniquity. He keeps on riding raw. What's his eternal lot then?"

"Riding raw?"

"The stuff I mentioned. Bottle service, coke, fornicating with other people's wives, et cetera. What's he got coming to him then?"

Forbush frowned and said, "Hmm. Let me think . . ."

Percy looked at me as if to say, "Wrap it up, it's my turn."

Finally, Forbush said, "There are those that will not be gathered with the saints. Doctrine and Covenants 76:103: liars, and sorcerers, and adulterers, and whoremongers . . ."

Forbush rattled off the relevant passage like the star pupil at a madrasa. We parsed the ignoble list. There was some debate on the question of whether Dupont was an adulterer, given he wasn't married. But whoremonger? Percy and I agreed it sounded promising. After a bit of light prodding, I got Forbush to acknowledge that while Whitney hadn't been prancing down an inner-city back alley in fishnets when she met Dupont, the crux of the whoremongering was the licentious coupling, not the subsequent remuneration for services rendered.

That settled, Forbush said Dupont's whoremongering punishment would begin with a thousand years in a "spirit prison." Percy and I nodded a tentative approval. Forbush continued, explaining that after Dupont served this initial sentence, he would be paroled, get his distasteful body back, and be free to go about his business here on earth, which Forbush was now referring to, for reasons unexplained, as the "telestial kingdom."

"Hold on a second," I said. "He's not stuck down there forever? That's it, a measly millennium, then he's walking around as though nothing happened? Does anybody go to your Mormon hell on a permanent basis?"

Forbush looked unsure for the first time. Percy jumped in, outraged.

"Where's Hitler? For Pete's sake, he's getting out too? Stalin? Pol Pot? Idi Amin? Even genocidal madmen aren't subjected to everlasting torment?"

Forbush muttered something about the mysterious workings of the Almighty, but even he didn't seem convinced by what he was saying. The whole thing sounded absurd. No eternal perdition? No Dantean hopelessness? No concentric torture? How could anyone belong to a religion where there's nothing at stake? It sounded about as pointless as spending a lifetime in Vegas playing Hold'em for buffet coupons.

Percy started back on the murder business but ditched the opaque innuendo. "You tried to kill him, didn't you?"

"What? Who? No!"

I slid into the role of good cop. "I'm sure you had your reasons. Everyone has their breaking point. I saw his shameless pandering to the camera. That must have gotten on your nerves. Come clean and we'll do our best to go to bat for you."

Forbush denied it. Percy turned up the pressure.

"How about we call that news fellow? What's his name?"

"Ryan French," I said.

"French, that's it. You know what he'd do for a scoop like this, a poor menial stuck performing with that obstreperous canine all day?"

We tightened the vise on Forbush. Finally, when Percy

yelled, "The truth, Forbush, nothing less than the murderous truth!" while banging on the dashboard with a closed fist, Forbush cracked.

"Okay, okay. I wasn't trying to kill him, I swear. I just thought . . ."

"Spit it out!" bellowed Percy.

". . . if he was hurt they'd have to replace him. You don't know what it's like. He tells everyone we meet he grew up in La Paz, near Lake Titicaca."

"Ah, Lake Titicaca!" said Percy. "Highest navigable body of water in the world!"

"So, what's wrong with that?" I asked Forbush.

"It's what he does when he says it. He acts all suggestive and creepy. If a lady answers the door, he'll run up to her and start grinding away."

Forbush slid down the bench seat and leaned into Percy. Before Percy could react, Forbush began shaking his arms and legs about in a fit of Pentecostal quivering. "*Hola, señorita*, I'm Ree-keey from Lake Teeh-teeh-caah-caah."

Percy scowled and elbowed Forbush out of his personal space. I laughed. Forbush looked more like an angry Muppet than a rhythmic Bolivian. His silly gyrations utterly failed to capture the louche gambol of a South American caught up in the *fiebre loca* of a pulsating *discoteca*.

Forbush wouldn't shut up. He recited a litany of Peña grievances. The Bolivian took the Lord's name in vain with regularity, in two languages, no less. He drank at least two cases of Mountain Dew a week. He thought the King Follet Discourse—the treasured last oratory of Joseph Smith—was a rap album. He ignored the clean-living admonitions of the Word of Wisdom like they were assembly instructions for Swedish furniture. He even dared to own a cell phone, on which he religiously watched *America's Got Talent* and tried to arrange trysts with middle-aged women on a dating app called On the Prowl.

I'd had enough of Forbush and his vainglorious piety. "That doesn't mean you're allowed to maim him. You want to be stuck down here in the shitty-whatever kingdom with us? Seriously, get your head in the game, Forbush. You signed up for this. You'd better hope he's okay, because if I find out he's been sent back to La Paz, you're going to be in serious trouble."

The rest of the journey was completed in disapproving silence. Forbush stared straight ahead, wallowing in the loneliness of his guilty exile. I followed the GPS to the hospital, which resembled an extended-stay motel hastily erected next to a regional airport. We pulled in and parked under a flimsy ramada, behind an ambulance from which a trio of medics were extracting a decrepit old man with no discernible ailments, age imposing its cruel decay from inside out. A couple of bored orderlies, smoking menthol cigarettes and tipping their ash directly onto the concrete, were leaning against a wall and observing the painstaking exercise.

Peña's clothes had absorbed significant moisture from the makeshift mattress. He groaned out bilingual accusations at Forbush while we carried his soggy body into the waiting room. We deposited him lengthwise on a row of hard fiberglass seats, and I went up to the check-in desk to summon help. The receptionist pushed a stack of forms across the counter. She asked me pointed questions about Ricky Peña's insurance and financial solvency, and when I told her I didn't know, she frowned and pushed across a second, thicker stack.

I fanned the hefty reams with my thumb and walked back, defeated by heartless bureaucracy.

"We're screwed," I said, and threw the paperwork on a vacant chair.

Lise was daubing Peña's forehead with a tissue. We exchanged worried looks. Then a puckish smile spread across her face.

"I have an idea," she said. "How about we get creative?"

"Sure," I said, open to any plan to unload the wounded Bolivian, no matter how unorthodox.

"We're all going to have to play our parts," said Lise. She told us what she had in mind, and we batted ideas around until the plot coalesced.

Lise bent down and whispered in Peña's ear. He looked puzzled, so she repeated herself in impressively fluent Spanish. I don't know if Peña was acting or not, but he immediately began to scream and flail about like a member of his country's soccer squad. After about twenty seconds of imitating the consequences of a light jostle in the penalty box, he went limp and closed his eyes.

Lise screamed, and I yelled, "We're losing him!" Forbush had been taking a leak while we cooked up the script, so I nudged him and told him to start back up with a bout of the same Peña-impersonating arm-waving he'd done in the truck. Percy stood there looking confused, so I jumped in.

"Quick, quick, that disease-ridden cooter's done a real number on him. The blood, it's everywhere. He's gone into anaphylactic shock. Somebody save him, for god's sake!" I was pleased with my improvisational range, especially pulling "anaphylactic" out of thin air.

Finally, Percy turned in the receptionist's direction and projected forth. "Madam, this man needs immediate attention. He's been exposed to a rare bacterium. If he doesn't get immediate assistance, I'm afraid he's going to expire on your seats."

We all looked at each other, wondering who was going to speak next. I broke the silence.

"Who are you, sir?" I said, in an attempt to coax Percy into character.

"Dr. Percy Templeton," he boomed. "World-renowned infectious disease expert. Man of many talents and irrepressible appetites."

"Thank you, Dr. Templeton. Tell us more about this poor man's condition. I understand—"

"I enjoy my martinis at room temperature. I have a foolproof system to win at backgammon. I've been known to take freelance assignments for MI5. I own many fine properties around the world but spend most of my time in a cozy mews in St. John's Wood, canoodling with my young lover. I have surfed treacherous waves and dived to perilous depths. I can—"

"That's great, Dr. Templeton, but can you get back to the matter at hand? This man is dying before our eyes, remember?"

"What? Oh, right . . . of course, of course . . ."

Percy returned to the script. He delivered a moving performance, at one point leaning over Peña and reciting a requiem of such emotional import that when Percy kissed him on the forehead, the Bolivian wept.

The woman at reception observed our absurdist tragedy with the studied skepticism usually reserved for high-end hairpieces, ones that are trimmed in situ after being glued on yet, for all the effort, are still ersatz embarrassments. Despite her obvious doubts, she picked up her phone. Moments later, the orderlies who'd been smoking out front arrived and hoisted Peña onto a gurney. They rushed him through a set of double doors, into the belly of the building. Forbush stood there, indifferent, until I reminded him about our heart-to-heart in the truck, at which point he ran after Peña, looking concerned.

We unloaded the missionary paraphernalia from the back of the truck. I wheeled the bikes into the waiting room and leaned them against the wall, under the TV, which was tuned to KPOX. The anchorwoman—evidently Celeste—was going on about "technical difficulties" with their feed from Willie-T's, which probably meant French had lost control of the dog again.

I heard someone shout, "Hey, you can't leave those there." I turned to see the receptionist glaring at me.

"Why not?"

"This is a hospital."

"They belong to those guys, the ones that just went through those doors."

"You'll have to put them outside."

"But I'm with Dr. Templeton."

"Who?"

"Him." I pointed at Percy. I was hoping for another forceful Dr. Templeton pronouncement, but being no Daniel Day-Lewis, he'd already broken character, so all I got was a meek smile and a pallid wave.

"Sorry, rules are rules."

"They'll get stolen."

"Not my problem."

I walked over to the lady's desk and sized her up across the counter.

"Come on, they're nice kids, more or less. Ricky Peña came all the way from Bolivia to swim in your creeks. He left the shores of . . ." Annoyingly, the name of the great Bolivian lake escaped me. "Titi something. Titi . . ."

The lady scowled and crossed her arms in front of her chest. "You heard me. Move the bikes. They can't stay there. Regulations."

I asked the woman for something to write on. She slid a pad across the counter and observed me with suspicion.

I wrote, "Dear Reed Forbush and Ricky Peña, your bikes are outside. Or that's where I left them. I wanted to leave them in the waiting room, under the TV, but I was ordered by"—I read the woman's name tag—"Dawn to leave them outside. So if they're gone, it's Dawn's fault. The hospital probably has insurance for this sort of thing. I advise you to hire a lawyer to write a threatening letter. Maybe your church has a firm on retainer? From what I hear, it has ample resources. Anyway, keep this note as evidence. Good luck. I hope you work out your personal differences. Best, Guy Hastings."

I signed my name to the bottom of the note, folded it up, and pushed it across the counter.

"Please give this to one of them," I said.

Dawn grabbed the note and unfolded it.

"Don't open that, it's personal."

Dawn ignored me. After she read the message, she crumpled it into a ball and threw it in the trash. "Now move those bikes or I'll call security."

I shook my head in an exaggerated fashion and walked off.

"We can't leave their bicycles outside!" exclaimed Percy.

"What's wrong with that lady?" said Lise.

"We're not putting them outside," I said, and explained my plan. We all agreed it was the only sensible course of action in light of Dawn's inflexible hubris.

While Percy and Lise proceeded casually to the exit, I

approached the bikes and unwrapped a chain lock coiled around one of the seat posts. I looked back at Dawn. She was occupied with the parents of a kid who looked to have had a nasty run-in with some unyielding object, a blood-soaked bandage wrapped around the boy's head, a look of dizzy pride on his face. I wheeled the bikes toward the exit. When I neared a row of vacant seats, I stopped and snaked the chain through the bike frames and around a metal support member bolted to the floor. After scrambling the combination lock, I turned and sprinted for the doors.

We piled into the cab of the truck, and I fumbled around with the key before finally getting it into the ignition. I fired up the engine and laid on the horn. Dawn looked up, realized she'd been outmaneuvered, and took to hopping around and yelling into the receiver of her phone. Percy and Lise waved like supercilious monarchs as I revved the engine and dropped the clutch. The old barge shuddered violently forward. We rumbled out from under the awning, laughing and carrying on like we'd just pulled off an elaborate heist, on the way to enjoying a lifetime of leisure, rich beyond our wildest dreams.

Chapter Twenty-Seven

IT BEGAN TO RAIN. SHEETS OF WATER cascaded down on us, making the road near invisible. The windshield wipers were no help, useless squeegees that did nothing but smear muck around the glass. Percy and Lise didn't seem concerned about our visibility problems. They carried on like a duo in a vaudeville production, slinging high-spirited verse around with great amusement. When Percy went hoarse, they began to regale each other with anecdotes from their favorite movies.

"And then she takes Carl into her bosom and tells him he's a day late," said Percy, reciting the denouement of *The Harvest of Regret*, one of the few recent flicks that'd garnered a thumbs-up from both Percy and Sutter.

Percy couldn't contain himself. He shared every last detail of the movie. The plot revolved around a half-dead curmudgeon named Carl and the contents of a mysterious letter. The very day Carl receives the single-page, handwritten missive, he hot-wires a combine harvester belonging to a local farmer and hits the road for purposes then unknown to the audience.

En route from his bucolic hermit lair, Carl encounters

much travail. Ironic, lighthearted action ensues. The police try to corral him, but he eludes them by trundling across a patchwork of fields, firing up the sharp blades and cutting a broad swath through seas of dense wheat. As he progresses north, he morphs from creepy recluse into irascible folk hero. People line village streets, holding up signs of support and cheering him on. Schoolchildren play hooky and run alongside the harvester like eager fans at the Tour de France. He soon becomes a media sensation, his weathered sourpuss mug plastered on the front page of every major tabloid in Britain.

I thought it sounded like a pretty decent comedy until Percy started on about a forbidden love child, a convent of callous nuns, and a reunion thwarted by the cruel hand of fate.

"I've seen that movie," said Lise. "Some tearjerker. Did you know Ian Dyer wanted to play Carl so badly he agreed to work for scale? And the cinematography is fantastic."

Lise continued to expound on the film. She delved into technical minutiae that went way over my head. I asked her how she knew so much about the nuts and bolts of movie-making.

"Sorry, I turn into a colossal bore when I talk about movies. In my defense, I'm in the middle of an MFA in cinema at USC."

Percy and Lise continued to chat away. He told her about his Dornfelder with the pride of a new father. He retrieved his phone, pulled something up, and handed it to her.

"Oh wow, I love the retro vibe," said Lise. "Have you seen this?" She tilted the screen in my direction.

The barebones web page looked ancient, like a fossil from the burgeoning eight-bit era of the Internet. The navy blue background was littered with neon-yellow knights atop silhouetted horses, lances tipped for battle. The Templeton name was scrawled across the top of the page in medieval script. Below, an animated wine bottle with vines for arms and legs danced slowly across the screen from left to right and then back again. The bottle had fat white Hamburger Helper hands, and its spindly legs disappeared into bulbous sneakers with purple laces. Its grape eyes winked rhythmically while the bottle shimmied across the page, and its mouth—an engorged banana floating below its nose—gave it the exuberant, slightly intoxicated appearance of a dazed Looney Tunes villain.

"My grandson, Wills, put it together for me. Brilliant boy, not to be trifled with either."

Percy told us that several weeks before his trip, Lilith had dumped the boy on him for a few hours while she displayed her hydrangeas at the village flower show.

"I had a hankering for sausages. Not the cheap, fatty ones from the supermarket. No, I drove over to Fittleworth to pick up a pound from the farm shop. Figured I'd serve them to Wills for lunch and eat the rest for supper the next day. Anyway, I cooked them up for us with some new potatoes and runner beans. When we sat down to eat, I told the little tyke, 'Wills, my boy, I made a special trip to Fittleworth to buy these sausages for you, I hope you enjoy them.' Do you know what the little rascal told me? 'Oh, Grandpa, that's poppycock.' Oh my! Poppycock! I nearly fell out of my chair. Cheeky little monkey!"

We pressed on, and I drove faster and faster, a frantic race against the advancing darkness. Thankfully, we made it to New Orleans a hair before nine. It wasn't even raining when we arrived at the hotel that Lise had booked for us on some app—a quaint Spanish-style courtyard number on Chartres, in the lower reaches of the Quarter. I turned off the street, into the cobbled drive, and spotted a valet. He was standing next to a chipped podium with the bored, distracted vigilance of a weary soldier guarding a remote outpost, waiting for rumored barbarians.

I cut the engine and hopped out, and the valet began to fulminate in front of me with the outraged disbelief of a scientist with an unreasonable boss demanding he bend the laws of physics on his lunch break.

"No, come on. What? This? No way, man, you can't be serious. Forget it!"

I tried to reason with the guy. I told him we were guests of the hotel, weary from a hard day on the road, lucky to escape the wrath of Horace. When that didn't work, I tried a more abstract approach.

"I want you to imagine a fireman. Somebody drops an unwanted newborn into the abandoned-baby hopper in front of the firehouse. The fireman can't refuse it. He has obligations. Legal, sure, but, dare I suggest, moral too. The bottom line is he's got no choice. He has to take it in, look after it. Not forever, but at least overnight, or until he can unload it on social services."

The guy stood there confused, which forced me to have to explain, the elegant simplicity of my metaphor ruined.

"You're the fireman and *that* is the baby." I pointed at the truck.

The valet mumbled "fireman" and nodded, proud a stranger judged him capable of fighting unruly blazes. But then his face soured.

"*That* ain't no baby, man," he declared with a dismissive wave. "That is a giant headache."

I employed additional analogies, delivered in a louder, more forceful register. Percy tried to bribe him with a bottle of Dornfelder and a couple of melted Mars bars. Nothing worked. Lise hung back and watched our serial failures with droll amusement.

We were saved when a trio of couples stumbled out of the hotel's restaurant. The men were portly, balding, and loafered, the women well-preserved and baubled to the hilt. They were loud and lit, and none appeared sober enough to drive. That didn't stop them from dumping three claim tickets onto the valet in the abrupt, whimsical manner of members of the House of Bourbon addressing a low-ranking servant. While the valet was examining the tickets, I stalked up and slipped the truck's key into his jacket pocket.

"Here you go," I shouted as we hurried toward the entrance. "First gear's shot. Use second and give it plenty of revs."

We checked in, and I volunteered to run out and grab us some food. The mood in the lower Quarter was festive but restrained, nothing approaching the drunken revelry undoubtedly taking place a few blocks west. When I returned with the grub, we went out onto the balcony of Percy's room and people-watched while we ate shrimp po'boys, which we washed down with ice-cold bottles of frothy Abita ale.

We checked on Horace. Before the storm hit land, it ran into cooler air, which prevented it from strengthening into a hurricane. Contrary to Ryan French's dire predictions, the extent of the damage was a bit of localized flooding. We all agreed this fortuitous turn of events would likely relegate French to dog duty for the foreseeable future.

Percy's insisted I tell Lise about Whitney and Dupont, so I explained the basics and showed her the kompromat.

"Tell me what I'm looking for again?" She zoomed in

and grimaced, the stock reaction to Dupont's grotesque feet.

I pointed to the toe buried in the sand.

"It's so tiny," she said. "How can you be sure?"

"I'm not. Not a hundred percent anyway. I guess that's why I'm here."

"So what are you going to do if you find them?"

I had cooked up all manner of damning retorts for that very moment. I shared a few with the group.

"Two peas in a pod, or should I say, two lovebirds floating in the putrid waters of an E. coli–infested pond.

"Your spirit prison awaits, Dupont, hopefully in this life but definitely in the next.

"I hope you enjoy wearing woolly socks to bed every night, Whit. You're going to need them to keep those Brillo pads he calls toes from ruining your pedicure."

Lise didn't get the bacterial reference, so I explained about Lago Imperial and Dupont's plumbing shortcut. Percy told her about Forbush's thousand-year purgatory. After a brief deliberation, we all agreed that "Brillo pads" contained the right balance of cutting irony and practical reproach.

I told Lise I'd get up early the next morning and rent her a car so she could drive back to Baton Rouge, but she was more interested in the prospect of joining us on our search.

"An urban safari!" she exclaimed.

Her metaphor was an apt approximation, our hunt undoubtedly as futile as tracking down a reclusive gibbon in the dense jungles of a tropical river basin. Percy and Lise huddled around my phone while I checked Dupont's feed for more hedonistic bread crumbs, but he hadn't posted anything since the lobster plunder of the previous evening.

Chapter Twenty-Eight

THE NEXT MORNING, WE HEADED OVER TO the French Market and ordered scalding-hot café au laits and heaping plates of beignets from a bow-tied waitress at Café du Monde. Despite my warnings, Percy took a plentiful swig of steaming coffee and burned his tongue. He panicked and shoved an entire beignet into his mouth, coating himself with powdered sugar in the process.

After we dusted him off, we walked across Decatur and spotted the spray-painted Tin Man. He was atop a wooden box in the middle of St. Ann Street, glinting in the morning sun. I shoved the photo of him with Dupont in front of his frozen face in an abrupt fashion. He ignored me, his gaze fixed afield. Percy pulled out a five-dollar bill and flashed it in front of the man's metallic mien, but it failed to coax him out of his catatonic act. Percy pulled out another five, doubling his bribe. The man still didn't react, standing firm, committed to his art. Percy began to wave the bills in front of the human statue, first slowly, then faster and faster, like a rhythmic gymnast desperate for a medal. A crowd assembled and clapped in unison with Percy's gyrations, thinking he was part of the show. When generous revelers began to shove tokens of appreciation into the waistband of Percy's trousers, we deemed it time to extract him from the exuberant rabble.

I suggested we take a carriage through the Quarter. It would allow us to cover more ground from a superior vantage. And Percy's money dance had inflamed his arthritic knees, so there was that too. We arrived at Jackson Square, and Percy doddered down the line of carriages, stroking manes and slapping haunches. Mules whinnied and snorted their objections. He stopped next to one with handsome pointy ears in a position of high alert. The mule sniffed Percy, then made a sudden lunge for his collar. Percy fought off the beast valiantly but not before a good portion of his spread-point had disappeared into the animal's circumnavigating chops.

"Bloody cheek!" said Percy while the mule chewed up vast swaths of his pale blue chambray, making him look like a disheveled vicar in need of a tailor. I suggested we tighten the selection criteria, possibly limit the slapping of hindquarters, but Percy viewed the collar munching as proof of the mule's irrepressible spirit, so after a brief negotiation with the driver, we clambered into the fire-engine-red carriage and set off.

The mule trotted us around the Quarter, dodging sunburned, fanny-packed tourists and bachelor parties still drunk from the night before. I jumped out on occasion to flash Dupont's photo to passersby but was summarily dismissed with head shakes and curt waves.

"You're scaring them," said Lise.

"How?"

"You're acting like a backwoods sheriff."

"Really? I was trying to channel Lew Griffin."

"Who?"

"The private investigator in *The Long-Legged Fly*. His office was above a bakery on St. Charles."

"'Dirtbag cokehead'? And what was that stuff about drowning him in the Mississippi?"

"Blame James Sallis, he created him."

Lise frowned. "Stop threatening to kill him. Be nice. Make something up, like he's gone missing. People respond better to emergencies, it brings out their empathy."

I wasn't sure about that. Churchill didn't have much luck getting FDR to sign on the dotted line until the Japanese went all rock-star-in-a-hotel-room in the Pacific theater. And what about the years of fence-sitting over the Balkans? By the time I'd remembered the public's abject lack of interest in Rwanda, I was almost hoping for the fateful day when the forces of the cosmos would pull the corpus of humanity apart like Laffy Taffy in the hands of a curious three-year-old.

Lise mistook my troubled contemplations for lack of inspiration.

"You guys need to loosen up, let your creativity percolate." She closed her eyes, pinched the air, and performed a few meditative salutations. While low-toned sounds vibrated out of her lips, I took the opportunity to try to locate the source of her understated allure. After a quick survey, I decided it had something to do with the geometric symmetry of her cheekbones.

"Come on, we're a team," she exhorted while I studied her bone structure.

We finished humming like devout lamas and opened our eyes to find ourselves in front of Lafitte's Blacksmith Shop, alleged to be the oldest structure in America operating as a bar. The mule became agitated, which I attributed to coincidence considering the place hadn't housed an anvil in at least two centuries.

"I'll be right back," said Lise. She jumped out, ran inside, and soon returned with three gargantuan plastic cups. "Voodoo daiquiris. These should do the trick."

I looked down at my cupful of icy purple slurry, sadly now inexorably intertwined with the legacy of the rakish swashbuckler and his daring high-seas larcenies. Here was a depressing allegory if ever one existed. Jean Lafitte, a brave privateer who helped trounce the British at the Battle of New Orleans, memorialized by nothing more than sugary grog flogged to thirsty libertines. Oh, and a park, some swampy, unincorporated marsh thirty miles south of town. That too, for what it's worth. Then what hope for us today, men neutered by the loss of frontier, options narrowed, ambitions thwarted, all surely to be swallowed up and forgotten by history?

I discussed the demeaning association with Percy, without mentioning the British ass-drubbing. We both admitted it was just a beverage, yet some distant allegiance caused us to pause. Lise was having none of it. She noticed our hesitation and projected forth like a salty sea captain.

"Drink up, boys, these things are surprisingly tasty."

Percy took her admonition to heart. His mouth sought out the thick straw, a look of dutiful commitment on his face. He slurped his down in less than a minute. I followed, albeit with slightly less industry.

"Refreshing," said Percy. "But I'd recommend they add a dash of alcohol."

I pointed out it was basically nothing but alcohol.

"Bloody impossible, can't taste a drop," he said with the blank incomprehension of a medieval serf witnessing alchemy. Before we could object, he disappeared into the precarious wooden building to buy another round.

Once we were back under way, Lise went into director mode.

"I want you to try again, and forget about accuracy. All we care about is finding him, right? So embrace the method."

She grabbed me by the arm and yanked me out of the carriage, into the path of two grizzled battle-axes in colorful tank tops, their enormous hairdos topped with sparkly tiaras. Countless strands of plastic beads hung around their wrinkled necks, a burden to rival Coleridge's murdered albatross.

The women stared at me with anticipation. Paralyzed by stage fright, I stood there, mute. I am not someone who is well practiced in purposeful deception. I rarely make up grave emergencies when pulled over for speeding, and I'm more than happy to leave Halloween to the trick-or-treaters, so suffice to say, I was not well suited to sidewalk improvisation. Finally, after a bout of strained concentration, a dull spark ignited an idea, a reprise of Percy's performance at the hospital yesterday.

"Hello, ladies, permit me to introduce myself. I am Dr. Ralph Hyde, a specialist in psychiatric traumas. This man, a Mr. Ronald Dupont, was committed to my care for perverted, violent displays." I flashed them the photo of Dupont on Bourbon Street. "I was treating him with strong tranquilizers when he escaped from my clinic. He was spotted in the Quarter recently. Would you be so kind as to tell me if you've seen him?"

They studied me with an aggressive incredulity. I scrolled to the photo of Dupont assaulting the lobsters. They examined it and talked between themselves about how plump and appetizing the buttery crustaceans appeared in the soft candlelight, although in slightly less poetic terms.

"I could murder one of those right now," said the taller of the pair.

"Damn straight, girl," said the other one.

"No, ladies," I implored. "The man, the hair, the jowls, the smug grin. Focus, please." I spoke in a serious, haughty tone, trying to imbue Dr. Ralph Hyde with the requisite gravitas.

"That chump?" said the tall one. "Haven't seen him."

Her companion scanned around. "Come on, what is this? Where are the cameras?"

"Huh?"

"This has to be a setup. You, a doctor? Please. How gullible do you think we are?"

"Plenty gullible, I reckon," said the tall one.

"Did we win anything?" added the other.

"We should definitely get something out of this," said the tall one with a leer.

The other woman cackled. She eyed me up and down and moved her chest into my personal space.

The next thing I knew, I had wizened cleavage coming at me from all angles. I did my best to avert my eyes from the fleshy crevasses, but it was useless due to the size of the chasms and their intimate proximity. The women drove a hard bargain, and I was forced to agree to a quick flash. Dignity compartmentalized, I pulled up my shirt to expose my chest. The women whooped in a depraved fashion and threw a few strands of beads at my feet. A group of frat guys across the street heckled the definition of my abs.

I lowered my shirt. "Everybody done?" I shouted.

Percy stood in the carriage and clapped. "Bravo! Bravo!" he yelled while I bent over to pick up my hard-earned spoils.

After Lise stopped laughing, she critiqued my performance. "What in the world was all that? Tranquilizers? Escaped? The weird voice?"

Next up was Percy. Lise said I'd set the bar low with my Dr. Hyde, so he had nothing to lose. He jumped up, eager for the spotlight. He told us he planned to inhabit the persona of a recently released convict whose daughter had been murdered while he was serving hard time. The poor girl had gotten mixed up with Dupont, a craven drug dealer with ties to Mexican cartels. Percy had robbed a bank to obtain the funds to travel from the industrial wastelands of northern England to New Orleans, and he wasn't going to leave until he found out what'd happened to his beloved Poppy. In the meantime, he planned to torture Dupont to within an inch of his life, mostly for information but partly for sadistic pleasure. He began to search around for suitable subjects to spring his bleak noir on.

"How about them?" He pointed to a family of tourists standing on the sidewalk. The fussy father was snapping photo after photo of one of the historic Miltenberger houses while his humorless wife attempted to interest a couple of bored teenagers in the building's fancy iron railings.

"I don't think that's such a good idea," said Lise, shooting me a worried glance.

"Look at the time, the day's getting away from us," I said, somewhat reluctantly, part of me secretly wanting to see Percy channel his inner Terence Stamp on the family of innocents.

On the way back to Jackson Square, we stopped a few times to accost random strangers. Lise was fearless, approaching people left and right, shoving my phone in front of them, imploring them to search their booze-tainted memories. One guy from Houston recognized Dupont from a billboard.

"Welcome home, dude," he yelled, and held his thick, stubby arms out in a wide arc. His three kids followed his lead, and they all stood there, miming away, a family of sea lions performing for herring.

"Yeah, okay, but have you seen him this weekend?" I asked.

"No, man, can't say that I have." He turned and waddled off down Dauphine Street, his ragged brood in tow.

Back at Jackson Square, we clambered out of the carriage and said our goodbyes to the mule from a safe distance. We crossed Decatur to watch a pair of street acrobats perform their daring finale even though they weren't the crew in the Dupont photo. A ripped, shirtless guy in shiny silver jogging pants was lining up a row of tourists for his skinnier yet equally shirtless partner to vault over. He addressed the crowd.

"We got eight. That enough? What? I can't hear you! More? Nine? Nah, man, c'mon, that'd be a world record!"

The crowd chanted, "One more, one more, one more . . ."

"All right, all right, one more. Who we got? They better be small. Don't give me no fat man."

The guy turned and spotted Percy.

"What's your name, mister?"

Percy looked from left to right. "Who, me?"

"Yeah, you. Who'd you think I was talking to, him?" The guy gestured to a building of a man who looked as though he could start at nose tackle for the Saints. The crowd laughed. The giant kept walking, oblivious.

"Percy?" said Percy in a furtive voice.

"Percy, my man, you short but your hair ain't." The guy laughed. His wide-eyed partner nodded and pointed to Percy's hair with both hands like he was warning inexperienced Boy Scouts about a patch of poison ivy.

"You think you can clear that hair?" the man said to his sinewy partner.

"Dunno, man, that's some fluffy business he got going there."

"Who wanna see him clear Percy and his shag pile?"

The crowd roared its approval. The men went through a whole comedy routine before the bigger of the two ordered Percy and the rest of the participants to bend over. He walked down the line of volunteers and pushed them into position. The stringy guy walked halfway down Decatur for his showy run-up. On the count of three, he bolted toward the haphazard pack. He leaped over them, barely clearing Percy. The crowd erupted in ribald appreciation.

Percy walked back over to us, a ball of excitement and relief. Some sort of static reaction had taken place between the man's pants and Percy's scalp. His hair stood bolt upright and strained skyward as if under some great magnetic force.

"You look like a less seamy version of Don King," I told him.

"The talk-show bloke? Is he still on the air?"

"Never mind."

After we dealt with Percy's unruly coif, we headed to the location of a confirmed Dupont sighting. Every seat at the Carousel Bar was taken, so we huddled off to one side and watched people slowly rotate by until a group of four idlers sucked down the dregs of their cocktails, paid, and walked out into the afternoon. We climbed onto the ornate bar stools, and I showed the bartender a photo of Dupont.

"Yeah, he was in here a couple of nights ago," said the man. "Arrived at the end of my shift. Part of a big group.

Half of them were at the bar, the other half were over there by the window. The guys were yelling across the room to each other. Real comedians. I had to tell them to quiet down."

I showed him a photo of Whitney.

"I don't know. Maybe. There was about a dozen of them, and like I said, it was the end of my shift."

We stayed at the bar until the novelty wore off, which I can report was somewhere between two and a half and three rotations. As we walked out of the hotel, Lise declared that Percy was not leaving the Big Easy without experiencing Creole food at its finest. She made a couple of calls, pulled a few strings, and reserved us a table at the legendary Commander's Palace.

Lise left us to buy something to wear to dinner. She strolled off with purpose down Royal Street, and I couldn't help but admire her good posture and confident stride. She was in front of a dingy drugstore when she stopped abruptly. I watched as she knelt down next to a blanketed homeless lady sleeping under the window. They talked for a few moments, then Lise dug into her purse, pulled out a few crinkled bills, and placed them gently into the lady's tarnished coffee can.

"Did you see that?" I asked Percy, but he'd walked off and was busy exchanging stories of rheumatoid tribulation with the creaky doorman who was trying to hail us a taxi.

A cab finally pulled up. I tipped the doorman after Percy released the man's palm from a two-handed death grip. We climbed in, and the driver rocketed off down the pedestrian-heavy street like he was planning to bed in a fresh set of brake pads. When we arrived at our hotel, I realized I hadn't looked for either Dupont or Whitney once the entire terrifying ride across the Quarter.

Chapter Twenty-Nine

I ALMOST DIDN'T RECOGNIZE LISE when she walked into the hotel lobby that evening. If inhabiting a skintight cocktail dress were a professional sport, she would have been flagged for unsportsmanlike displays. We walked out to the cobbled courtyard, and the still-bitter valet hailed us a cab after demanding a sizable tip. We piled into the ancient sedan and bounced out of the Quarter, onto the freeway. After rattling along for a few miles, it plunged down into the western reaches of the historic Garden District.

We ate delicious, indulgent food in an atmosphere of plush decadence. Bottle upon bottle of fine wine was downed with gusto, the sommelier making expensive suggestions that we went along with, no questions asked. We toasted new friends and better days ahead while we swilled Bordeaux from various vintages and both banks of the lizard-tongued estuary, a metaphor the sommelier sprang on us while she decanted our third bottle over a rapidly melting candle.

Lise asked me what I'd been doing down in Tampa, so I recapped the story of Willis Delaney and its attendant confusions. She became extremely interested in Fritz and his nemesis, the Depraved Duke.

"So you're telling me there's a blood feud going on in Tampa? Process servers? A cross-dressing sausage maker and a former pro wrestler who dresses like a conquistador in yoga pants are at each other's throats? Am I getting this right?"

"Pretty much, except Fritz would argue the cross-dressing business to his dying breath."

"They'd make amazing subjects for a short. I have to meet this Fritz character." Lise explained that she'd been searching for the perfect premise for one of her graduate projects. She scribbled on a napkin as if writing the script then and there.

"Make sure you book a hotel with a complimentary breakfast buffet," I said. "And if you end up going to lunch, tell him the bathrooms are out of service."

The wine was delectable and disappeared from my glass like there was a hole in it. I'd been drinking since ten in the morning, virtually nonstop, and all the alcohol was not fostering clearheadedness. Lise's presence made me uneasy, as though daring to enjoy the company of this interesting woman would invite misfortune, another accident, perpetrated by her polar opposite, some dumb, hairy primitive with Scottie's forehead and fat ankles the size of lampposts.

No, don't think like that, I admonished myself. Appreciate this evening for what it is. Revel in the high spirits of your companions, absorb the hospitable mirth of their fine words. Here was the type of man suspension bridges were named after. The type of woman ancient city-states warred for decades to reclaim. The type of—

"Cheers to the open road," roared Percy, interrupting my rambling ode.

"Cheers to fiddling with your phone while driving," declared Lise. She looked at me and laughed and pursed her lips in a pouty way as if to say, "I'm kidding."

I felt lightheaded, befuddled, overwhelmed. I tried to concentrate, fixing on a bored woman on the other side of the room who was staring down at her phone, but she kept coming in and out of focus, her sequined dress an explosion of conjoined starbursts.

My unruly mind obsessed about Whitney once more. Was it over? Was she really with Dupont? Why did I feel terrible one moment and slightly relieved the next, like I was about to part with a much-loved yet high-strung exotic before it needed an engine-out belt service? Had I really poured five years of my life into a futile relationship and false start of a career? How did I not see any of it coming? What was wrong with me? I needed help, wise counsel, but Dad was gone, and Harry was asleep for eternity in Rogelio's deep hole. I absorbed the fact I was alone, no better off than a child-king promoted to the throne of a crumbling empire at the very moment barbarous neighbors were plotting a murderous invasion.

"You know, if it hadn't been for Guy here, I don't know what would've become of me," announced Percy.

"To Guy, our hero!" proclaimed Lise. She raised her glass and Percy followed suit. I issued a rigid smile and sat in agitated, brittle silence.

Lise summoned our waiter and ordered us bananas Foster for dessert. When the guy said it would be flambéed table-side, Percy cheered. The sequined lady got up and sauntered past our table, almost blinding me in the process. Sweat seeped from my pores. I drained a glass of water, half of the liquid dribbling down my chin. My pulse was racing, and a worrying tightness invaded my chest. I couldn't think

305

or focus clearly. I needed air, lots of air, and fast. I abruptly excused myself, used each table I encountered on my way to the door as a crutch, and stumbled out into the night.

The street was empty except for a couple of taxis waiting to ferry sated diners off into the night. I walked across Washington and peered through the enameled iron gates of Lafayette Cemetery No. 1, the weathered stone crypts weary in the darkness. Maybe restless spirits were nearby, eager to impart important revelations, glimpses of eternal verities through unseen vectors? Yelling petitions into the darkness, I put the ethereal forces on the clock. After about thirty seconds, I'd sensed no great stirring, so I headed north.

When I reached St. Charles, I stopped and leaned against a gnarled oak tree. Traffic streamed by while I tried to clear my head. The unmistakable metallic rumble of a streetcar rose above the drone of rubber on cement. The noise grew louder and louder until a carriage appeared from the east, bisecting the boulevard, brightly illuminated from within.

Inside, I spotted a kindly-looking old couple. The woman's head was resting gently on the man's shoulder, and their bodies melted into each other, interlocked like splines on a driveshaft. They appeared amiably content, happy to see the back of a busy day well lived. Or maybe they took on a tranquil appearance when fatigued, I wasn't sure. Almost involuntarily, I waved to them, as if my gesture might allow me to tap into their well of serenity. They stared straight ahead, neither evincing even the slightest indication of recognition. I realized then that I was invisible, a specter hidden in the shadows, the streetcar's light-filled interior causing the window to function as a two-way mirror, rudely interrupting my attempt to commune with my fellow man.

After I finished romanticizing the lives of these strangers, I turned and walked back down the street toward the restaurant. I'd covered the better part of a block and was approaching Prytania when I spotted a group hovering near an obscenely long limousine that was parked outside the restaurant, roughly a hundred yards away. Eight—no, ten people stood beside the vehicle. They were carrying on in a boisterous, convivial fashion. The dark-suited driver opened a door, and they piled into the limo, one by one, until there were only two of them left on the sidewalk.

I studied the bulky man and his slim companion while they stood there, silhouetted by the dim light emanating from a row of gas lanterns mounted high on the striped awning of the restaurant. The man moved behind the woman and began to massage her shoulders. He bent down and looked to whisper something in her ear. All of a sudden, he spun her around and enveloped her lithe frame in his thick arms. As he leaned his head forward to meet hers, a small canker of suspicion flared into a seething lesion of actuality.

I broke into a full-on sprint, driven by primal outrage. I was about to cross Prytania when the light turned and I had to stop to let traffic proceed. A big SUV with tinted windows and chrome rims approached the intersection, its body panels vibrating in concert with the deep rumble of hidden woofers.

"Come on, come on, hurry up," I muttered as I shifted about on the sidewalk. The vehicle slowed, now moving at walking pace, and the right rear window began to disappear downward. Moments later, a cylinder of silver metal flashed forth from the void. Before I could react, I heard an alien noise and felt a sharp sting erupt in the middle of my chest. Instinctually, my right hand sought out the location of the pain. I dared to look down. Viscous red blood was everywhere. I pressed my hand to my chest and hunted around for the entrance wound. Finding nothing, I stood there, fazed, for what seemed like an eternity but was probably no more than a second or two, my brain trying to make sense of the madness. But then, as abruptly as the sensation had arisen, it dissipated.

I heard a chorus of laughter ring out. I looked up to see a teenage kid in a striped polo shirt hanging out of the SUV, yelling, "Booyah, sucka!" while blowing imaginary smoke from the tip of the barrel of a paintball gun.

I felt adrenaline ebb as the acrid tang of my impending mortality dissolved into irritated relief. I wish I could report that this welcome resurrection was the pivotal moment when I said farewell to the weight of the past and embraced the possibilities of the future. Alas, instead of pausing to reflect on my life-affirming reprieve, I bolted across the street, running in the direction of the limo with a new, more purposeful force.

The woman had already climbed in and the big man bent down to follow her. I yelled and screamed and ran harder still, closing in on the limo just as the door slammed shut. The back bumper was a mere ten feet in front of my outstretched arms when the driver hit the gas. The vehicle labored away from the curb, exhaust fumes lingering in the dense air. Hands on knees, I watched the limo head south until it was finally eaten up by the darkness.

"Hey, man, you okay?"

I turned to see a thin, neatly dressed guy in a tweed flatcap. He was smoking a cigarette and leaning against the fender of his cab with the confident insouciance of a man who had played the game of life on his own terms, someone who'd won and lost in equal measure, his dues paid, his ledger balanced. Or maybe he was just your average cabdriver, my soused mind in turbid disarray, the state of his accounts and such having nothing to do with his loose posture.

"I think that was my wife." I pointed down the now-deserted street, resigned anew to the ramifications.

"In that limo? Where were you?"

"On St. Charles. I needed some air."

"Give her a call, I'm sure they'll swing back around for you."

"I wish it were that simple." I explained the basics of my marital predicament. The man listened with an expression I took to indicate grave consideration, although, I admit, it could have just as easily been boredom, my heart not really in this latest rendition.

"What's with all the paint?" he asked.

"I was shot. Some kid with a paintball gun. Thought for a second it was a bullet."

"Maybe you should call it a night. You need a ride somewhere?"

Just then, the door to the restaurant opened and Lise emerged, a concerned look on her face.

"Hey, you okay?" she asked, obviously confused by my newly disheveled appearance. "They're about to set the bananas on fire."

"Yeah, I'm fine," I said. "Sorry, I'll be right there."

Lise nodded and disappeared back into the restaurant. The cabdriver eyed me as if I'd just engineered some great cover-up.

"That thing I said about calling it a night, I take it back," he said, eyebrows raised.

"It's not what it looks like. She's a friend."

"Ah, a friend, got it. I've had me a few of those over the years." He smirked, walked to the back of his cab, and popped the trunk.

I suspected this man knew things I didn't, important wisdom gleaned from a life of weighing opportunities and consequences on the patchy tarmac of the Crescent City. What harm then to park myself next to him and get his opinion on my quandary, especially given the dearth of valuable insights volunteered to date? All Fritz had offered was instruction rooted in the unhealthy paranoia of Hal Diggle. And was there really a lesson to be learned from the romantic travails of Rick Dewey, the long-suffering chiropractor? I was about to speak up, ask for the man's opinion, but then, some strange sensation, a peculiar energy, washed over me, directing my thoughts back to Percy and Lise, the only people I'd encountered in the last week who hadn't proffered vague, suspect counsel (except for that business about the leaky boat).

"You'd better get in there if you want to see those bananas," said the man. He retrieved a rag from the trunk and tossed it to me. I thanked him and wiped my paint-stained hands on the frayed cloth.

The man dropped his cigarette on the sidewalk and put it out with a few sharp pivots of a tasseled loafer. "Tell me one thing. What were you asking for over there?" He pointed across the street to the cemetery, and I realized he must have been watching me the entire time.

"Nothing specific, really. Some sort of sign, I guess."

"What kind of sign?"

"I'm not sure."

The man reached inside his jacket and pulled out a pack of cigarettes. "Some people wait around for a sign their whole lives. That's a lot of wasted time if you don't know what you're looking for."

I stood there and let the man's words sink in. Wasted time. Yes, an unspeakable indulgence, precious years evaporating in a miasma of doubt and indecision. No more of that then, I promised myself as I told the man goodnight. I turned and walked back under the awning, through the glass-paned doors, into the restaurant.

Epilogue

PERCY PERSEVERED ONWARD, MAKING IT TO San Diego ten days later. Unfortunately, the Dornfelder didn't. It went missing, along with the rental truck, stolen from a vacant lot on the north side of Rampart Street, or so the hotel claimed. The manager tried to wash his hands of the whole mess, which forced me to have to detail his establishment's myriad failings under the time-honored principles of bailment. I may have been speaking out of turn given my unfamiliarity with Louisiana's revised statutes, but after haranguing the guy for a good fifteen minutes, he agreed to comp our rooms and rent us a replacement vehicle. The three of us hit the road later that morning in a late-model Ford Mustang, the only car the rental company had in stock with a manual, Percy still refusing to drive anything equipped with a slush box.

Percy and I said goodbye to Lise in Baton Rouge.

"Well, it's been a swell forty-eight hours, boys," she said, and gave us each a hug.

I watched her walk up her parents' driveway, past the circus van. Forty-eight hours? Had it really only been forty-eight hours?

"I'll text you," Lise called out to me. "I have to meet those characters. I'll even consider giving you a producer credit if it all works out." She unlocked the front door, turned and waved, and disappeared inside.

When we reached the AmeniLuxe, Percy and I said our goodbyes in the manner of soldiers about to embark for home after a long campaign in foreign lands. I waved while he pulled away. He overdid it with the throttle and careened out of the driveway onto the street, a cloud of tire smoke erupting in his wake. As I walked to the keycarded entrance gate, I noticed Liz Pendergrass eyeing me with disapproval from within the confines of the management office.

I only ever spoke to Whitney once after that. It was one of those heated, accusatory conversations that does nothing but make a bad situation worse. She refused to admit she'd been with Dupont that week, treating me like some kind of paranoid delusional for even entertaining the idea. Despite her outraged denials, I was not surprised when, a mere two weeks later, a dozy guy in a mustard-stained rugby shirt and baggy camouflage shorts approached me while I was gassing up the Alfa.

"Do you mind holding this for a second?" He handed me an official-looking envelope and walked off. His sloppy attire and slack manner identified him as a part-timer, a dilettante, lacking even a modicum of Fritz's martial rectitude or the Duke's extravagant theater.

I tossed the envelope through the window of the Alfa, onto the passenger seat. "You're no Fritz Osterfeld," I yelled after him.

"Who?"

"Fritz Osterfeld. OPS. A true gentleman and a professional, unlike yourself. Duke Deacon would eat your lunch."

"Screw you, buddy," he said as he climbed into his truck. "I hope she takes you to the cleaners."

It wasn't long before I heard rumors that Whitney had moved in with Dupont, followed by near-daily reports of the two of them, out on the town, attending fancy society fundraisers, holding hands at professional sporting events, canoodling in dimly lit booths in the back of pricey restaurants. Not a month after our divorce was finalized, their swanky engagement party hit the society pages, Whitney's delicately tapered ring finger almost invisible in the photos under an obscene lump of solid-state carbon. The photos were accompanied by a paragraph of sickening drivel. I was working at Harry's desk, reviewing a list of the remaining files, when Barb walked in with the magazine.

"You know what this is?" she asked. Before I could answer, she took on the affected voice of a game-show announcer and began to read.

"'Sorry, ladies, but real estate mogul Ronnie Dupont has finally bagged his beautiful princess, or should we say *belle princesse*, given Ronnie's storied lineage. And what a stunning bride lovely Whitney Eastland will make next March when the two wed in the luxurious confines of the Dupont family's Hill Country estate. These two—'"

"That's enough, please," I protested.

"'—up-and-comers were swept up in a hurricane of passion while working in close quarters on a project for Dupont Homes, the uber-successful developer of luxurious enclaves throughout the Houston area. Not only will Whitney be taking the legendary Dupont name, but she'll also be stepping into her new role as chief design officer for the privately held company. We'll be watching these two closely while they conquer the landscapes of our great city.

Here's hoping the stunning couple will invite us to their grand union next year so we can provide our dear readers with the inside scoop. Stay tuned, this party's only just getting started.'"

Barb lowered the magazine in a formal, parliamentary fashion. "See, that wasn't so bad, you survived."

Janice walked in with a stack of bills in her hand. Barb handed her the magazine. "Current events, girlfriend, bone up."

Janice scanned the page. "That's your wife, isn't it?" she said, almost apologetically. "I guess a lot happened while I was in Branson."

I spent less time at the dealership and more time at Harry's office, my goal to wrap everything up by the beginning of November. I found a new lawyer for poor Irv Timms and his devoted wife. And, in mid-October, Shane Burt fell out of his bass boat and drowned in the shallows of Lake Sam Rayburn, a sad turn of events for Burt and his family but of slightly less tragic import to the firm considering his location at the bottom of the shit pile. Shortly thereafter, Janice retired for good. And Barb went to work for Monty Short, the itinerant opportunist Reese Walters having moved on to even greener pastures.

I told Imogen that as much as I respected Harry and his legacy, the law wasn't in the cards for me.

"Don't you fret about that," she told me. "I know Harry would've wanted you to have this, regardless." She handed me a dog-eared copy of *The Man Called Noon*, the L'Amour classic about a confused amnesiac trying to recover his identity on the hard scratch of the plains. Tucked inside was an overly generous check.

The Delaney money a healthy cushion, I gave my notice at the dealership. Dave Trout said he was sorry to see me go, but that was probably more to do with the fear he'd end up with another Dean Peas than any deep professional affinity.

I drove to Beaumont for Thanksgiving, a straight shot ninety miles east. Our family gathering was an intimate one. It was just Mom and me, a half-dozen assorted relatives, and a fifteen-pound turkey I deep-fried in a large aluminum pot out on the porch. The bird sizzled and spit and bronzed to the color of a ballpark hot dog in less than an hour, one of the great culinary miracles of the South.

The Saturday following, I went over to the car lot to check on things. The previous tenant had gone out of business and disappeared a few months ago, leaving oil stains all over the weed-infested asphalt and stiffing Mom on the rent. I called Steve Anderson, a buddy of mine since grade school, and he helped me haul Dad's tools from Mom's garage over to the maintenance shop at the back of the lot.

The next day, I drove the Alfa over to the shop and pulled it into the service bay. I changed the fluids and swapped the plugs and made a few other adjustments, but the engine was still vibrating at high revs. Next, I removed the hood and unbolted components. Out came the battery, the alternator, and the exhaust manifold. After I dropped the transmission and disconnected the electrics, I lifted the engine out with a grease-stained hoist.

It had been a good decade and a half since the engine had been apart. I was only fourteen when I helped Dad with the last rebuild. I guessed it only needed lower-end work this time, hopefully just the bearings and related resurfacing. It turned out to need a lot more than that. Toiling through the winter, into the new year, I was thankful for the mild Texas weather. The work was painstaking. Being no great expert, I took my time. But all in all, the process was cathartic, as if I were committed to some great monastic duty. By the first week of January, the engine was back together, and the car was running great.

Meanwhile, I used Dad's dealer license and a portion of my Delaney money to buy a few cars at auction. I called up Alphonso and asked him if he was interested in doing a bit of work with me, on the side. We fixed up the cars and parked them out front, by the road, the prices smeared on the windshields in white shoe polish. To my surprise, all three sold within a matter of days. I bought a new batch, we fixed them up, and they sold just as quickly. We repeated the process, week after week, to equal success.

By the middle of February, things were going so well that I asked Alphonso if he wanted to resurrect the Straight Arrow Auto Emporium, as equal partners, fifty-fifty. I told him we could even rechristen it, call it something catchier, possibly add a bit of Latin flair.

"What's the Spanish for 'straight arrow'?" I asked him.

He told me it was *"flecha recta,"* which we both agreed didn't possess the ring of plain dealing probity we were shooting for, so in our first official corporate act, we voted, unanimously, to stick with Straight Arrow.

The billboards sprang up in early April. When Steve called me, I thought he was joking.

"Dude, head east down I-10, you can't miss her."

Sure enough, there was Whitney, twelve feet tall, towering over the freeway, Ronnie by her side, taking up more than his fair share of the horizontal real estate. Bifurcating their billboard waistlines appeared a platitudinous pitch: "The Lochs of Laguna. Welcome Home, Golden Triangle."

I couldn't believe it. The Golden Triangle? In what felt like a targeted dose of effrontery, the shameless pair was staking a claim on the outskirts of the awkward isosceles anchored by Beaumont, Port Arthur, and Orange. There were to be countless substandard Dupont shoeboxes positioned around two swampy lagoons a mere hundred yards off the interstate, not five miles from the Straight Arrow.

In short order, several more identical billboards popped up in strategic locations around town. I was soon hemmed in, besieged by promotional blight of a highly personal nature. In what quickly rose to the level of superstition, I took to avoiding the freeways completely, driving around in circuitous loops, pointlessly idling at traffic lights, stewing away. The only bright spot was when Steve told me that a flock of birds had unloaded all over one of the billboard Duponts and his self-satisfied smirk, coating him liberally, making him look like a fat-faced Dalmatian.

While this turn of events was troubling, I am glad to report that the age-old adage about how time is a miracle cure is no false bromide. Not a month later, on the way to the parts store, tired of the tortuous detouring, I impulsively jumped onto the highway. I'd expected this journey to trigger much perturbance, but when I cruised under my amazon-sized ex-wife and her dopey new husband that sunny morning, I registered nothing more serious than momentary distaste.

Lise and I kept in touch. Still trying to make sense of my failed marriage, I tried not to read too much into her erudite, witty messages. But then, an invitation: was I interested in meeting her in Tampa next month? We booked our plane tickets last week. Fritz can't wait. He's already asked Delaney to put us down for a day on the *Buzzard*.

I called Percy yesterday. He's been so busy lately he's hardly had any time to babysit his burgeoning Bill Gates of a grandson. Some thick-bearded wine blogger stumbled on his hardy vines and now, almost every weekend, there's a parade of hipsters beating on the thick oak door of his farm-house, wanting to sit across the table from him and break bread with the "grandfather of English wine." Needless to say, Dornfelder sales have gone through the roof.

He became excited when I told him about my trip.

"The emergency exit row? Bloody good place to spend an afternoon. Your knees will thank you."

"What about Lise?"

"Well, she wouldn't be jetting off with you on some fanciful adventure without intentions in mind, now, would she?"

"She wouldn't?"

"Well, I suppose it's possible I'm misreading the situation."

"Oh?"

"You can never be sure. Women! Strange, unknowable creatures, motivated by hidden, incalculable impulses, the whole lot of them."

"They are?"

"Of course. Men too. Everyone's barmy, more or less."

I absorbed the import of Percy's blanket wisdom. Suffi-ciently daunted, my thoughts returned to Lise. Our trip is next month, and I'm looking forward to the extra legroom.

About the Author

Matthew J. White was born in England and lived there until he was rather abruptly transported to Southeast Texas at the age of eleven. After a childhood rife with cultural confusions and painful sunburns, he moved to Houston, where he practiced law until moving back to the UK in 2017. He likes to race cars and drink wine but generally not at the same time. *A Feral Chorus* is his first novel.

For more information, visit www.aferalchorus.com.

Made in the USA
Monee, IL
21 June 2023

eda99e91-76b0-48c2-a6c5-92b8096988caR01